Son of
Holmes

—— & ——

Rasputin's
Revenge

SON OF HOLMES

&

RASPUTIN'S REVENGE

THE EARLY WORKS OF

John T. Lescroart

DONALD I. FINE, INC.
New York

SON OF
HOLMES

For Lisa

PREFACE

All the events in this book are true, despite the disclaimer
which you have just read if you read a book from cover to
cover. A certain concession has been made so that living
persons involved may not be subjected to inconvenience,
scrutiny, or unwanted harassment. Nevertheless, no names
have been changed, no places altered. The concession has
been the disclaimer, which will convince most of the public
that even this preface is fiction, though this is not the case.

PROLOGUE

THE MARTHA HUDSON dinner had been set for the sixth of January. To followers of the Master, Sherlock Holmes, this date is as important a day as the year offers, for on January 6, Holmes's birthday, his followers from all corners of the globe gather to celebrate his genius. On this date in 1983, I was invited to the Hudson dinner in Arlington, Massachusetts.

At the time, I was living in rather cramped quarters in Cambridge, and a free dinner meant much more to me than intellectual stimulation. I hadn't read many detective stories and knew little about them. However, I'd naturally heard about Holmes and thought the night might prove interesting.

It was bitter cold and snowing—the wet, slushy snow of

the city—when I left my apartment wrapped in an old army coat. The suit I had borrowed for the affair was ill-fitting, and I waited in great discomfort for the bus out of Harvard Square. The ride to Arlington took nearly forty-five minutes, and I kept asking myself as I shivered if all this was worth a free meal.

For the past several months, I had been trying and failing to make my living as a songwriter in the Boston area. I had finally taken a clerical job to pay the bills, but after less than a month had given that up. I turned to giving piano lessons and within a few weeks had several pupils, their combined fees totaling about sixty dollars per week.

I met Mr. Kevin James in November during one of my pupil's recitals. He'd been dragged along by the child's mother, together with a host of other poor souls, and had stood silently near the back door. As soon as the recital began, he slipped out, and I joined him.

"Enjoying yourself?" I asked.

He leaned languidly against the doorpost. "You go to these affairs often?"

"Naturally. I'm the instructor."

"How do you stand it?"

I shrugged. "Comes with the job. Normally they serve punch later." I tapped the pocket of my well-worn coat. "Punch with a punch."

He grinned. "Don't mind if I do."

We became friends, and he had me to his house for dinner two or three times. One night we'd been speaking of detective stories, and he asked me to join him at the Martha Hudson dinner. I was happy to accept.

The dinner was held at a rambling structure in Arlington Heights known, for some obscure reason, as "The Ranch." The crowd was not exactly what I had expected, consisting mostly of people my own age. They all appeared rather more well-to-do than I, however, which was not surprising.

As drinks were served, we all congregated in the large drawing room, the principal furnishings of which were the bookshelves that lined three of the walls, the huge oil portrait of, I later learned, the Master, and a long table upon which had been set bound copies of some reference works, a violin, a pipe, and a cap. Our host, Mr. Hugo Arrowroot, proposed a toast to Martha Hudson, then to Holmes, after which things assumed a more informal air. We ate a fine dinner of which coq au vin was the main course and, over brandy, fell into a heated discussion concerning the actual existence of fictional characters.

"It all began, I imagine," said Kevin, "with Dante, when he included in his fictional *Divine Comedy* portraits of his enemies. I would suppose it's even an older practice than that."

"Much older," offered another of the guests, an hirsute Harvard student. "All the Greek playwrights did it in their comedies. Aristophanes got in a lot of trouble because of it."

"Not surprising," Kevin continued, "and we're all familiar with historical works that are, finally, more fictitious than the most imaginative novel." Several students chuckled.

Kevin was smoking a briar, sitting on the edge of the table, fingering the open pages of one of the reference works. "But consider this angle. Suppose there was a man whose life was as interesting as could be hoped, and he had a companion who was given to writing. Could that companion refrain from biography? A Boswell to Johnson relationship? I doubt it. But again, suppose that the principal involved eschewed this kind of aggrandizing publicity, for any number of reasons, and forbade his companion to publish. What could they do? One solution would be to publish the biography as a fictional account, using fictional names but actual events.

"I contend that in this theory lies the root of truth in our more celebrated detective heroes." He paused and relit his pipe.

"You're not saying that you think Holmes actually existed?" I said.

"Precisely, John, precisely."

Arrowroot spoke up. "It's not a new theory at all. As far back as 1900, readers were proposing it. Holmes was still alive at that time, remember."

"But a man of his supposed stature?" I protested. "I should think that, even fictionalized, he'd be immediately recognizable to the public."

"James Bond isn't," Kevin said.

"James Bond! Come on."

They shrugged at one another. "It's been established that he's alive and working right now. Of course, though it hurts to admit it, Fleming was better at peripherals than Conan Doyle."

"Peripherals?" I asked.

"You know, names of minor characters, addresses, that sort of thing. Fleming never used real names or addresses, at least so far as we know. And while, of course, Holmes was not named Holmes and didn't live at 221B Baker Street—actually we think he lived in Bond Street near Selfridges—Conan Doyle couldn't help but leave a few characters untouched. He was probably leaving us clues. He had such a fine sense of play. But Hugo, here, is really the expert." He turned to Arrowroot. "Perhaps you'd like to take it from here."

"All right," he said, "but I'm sure we'd all be more comfortable sitting down."

We went out to the hall and brought in more chairs. The novices among us, of whom there were about five including myself, joked about this preposterous theory. When we'd gotten arranged and the brandy had been passed again, Arrowroot, from a large chair near the fireplace, began:

"The characters that Conan Doyle—or should I say Watson?—left intact for us were Martha Hudson and Irene Adler. You're all familiar with Martha Hudson; at least you should be after this evening. She worked for the man who was Holmes until he died in Sussex Downs, after which she came back to London and worked for Lord Peter Thatcher, of the Bank of London, until 1938. She never divulged Holmes's true identity, except of course to Thatcher as a reference. In all probability, Thatcher himself knew long before. In any event, when Thatcher died in the bombings of London, the secret of Holmes's identity was lost forever, since Mrs. Hudson died shortly after she began her retirement, and certainly Conan Doyle never told.

"There was also, as I've said, Irene Adler, 'the only woman,' according to Holmes. She was, indeed, a famous continental singer in the late 1800s, who disappeared between the years 1892 and 1894. And mark this: those are the very years that Holmes disappeared after following Moriarty to the Reichenbach Falls." He paused for a moment.

"I've read somewhere," ventured another guest, "that letters addressed to 221B Baker Street get answered, though."

Kevin snickered. "Poppycock. A bank clerk answers those letters. They're not even worth considering."

"Kevin's right," Arrowroot continued. "Those 'public' incidentals mean nothing. The man who was Holmes would have never allowed use of so blatant a giveaway. He might just as well have let Conan Doyle use his proper name as his proper address. No, he saw Conan Doyle's clues, and obviously enjoyed them, as he tolerated them. So the path to the truth follows these clues, not the obvious fictions of names and addresses. And there are a few others. Mycroft, for example."

We all looked questioningly at him.

"Mycroft Holmes, Sherlock's brother, the most brilliant man in England. His last name was not Holmes, of course, but we believe his first name was actually Mycroft. He ran the British Government single-handedly, especially during World War I. As head of the Secret Service, among other things, he was known as 'M,' a title which I'm sure is familiar to all of you. His initial became the title for the head of British Intelligence. That, by the way, is perhaps Fleming's only slip in the matter of peripherals.

"We also believe that Holmes's code name during World War I was actually Altamont, that he raised bees, injected himself with cocaine, smoked a pipe, and played the violin. What we don't believe is that he actually wrote down a few of his own adventures—that again was Conan Doyle with his sense of play. In all, you see," he spread his hands out before him, "there is quite a good case."

"But nothing really conclusive," I said.

"Ever the cynic." Kevin smiled. "Well, no, nothing *really*, finally conclusive. No sworn affadavit. But there is one other major bit of evidence that Hugo has overlooked." He looked to Arrowroot. "The articles?"

Our host chuckled. "Oh, yes, of course." He looked at his guests. "If you read the Holmes stories, you will note from time to time that Watson talks of articles—'little monographs,' he calls them—that Holmes has written about any number of subjects, ranging from beekeeping to medicine to musical criticism. Probably the most famous is his treatise on tobaccos and their ashes. All of these articles appeared in periodicals of the times, and all anonymously. So...nothing conclusive, but it is an interesting array of facts, isn't it?" He stood up. "I invite you all to look through the reference books I have here, and please, help yourselves to the brandy."

Everyone stood up and gravitated toward the center table. General murmur once again filled the room. After a few moments, I found myself again with Kevin.

"Very interesting theory," I said.

"You seemed a bit skeptical," he answered lightly, "but it does sound strange on the first hearing, especially if, as you've said, you've never read Conan Doyle."

"Is Holmes really that good?"

He smiled. "He is the Master—of deduction, of disguise, of detection."

I thought for a moment. "Presumably, such a man—a man skilled in the art of detection—would have no trouble escaping detection himself."

"Quite so," Kevin said, "which is why those who have sought to authenticate the Holmes legend have had such a time of it."

I finished my drink and looked at my watch. Quarter past eleven, and I had students in the morning. I asked Kevin if he were going home by way of Cambridge, and would he mind giving a skeptical friend a lift. We said our goodbyes and thanked Arrowroot, then stepped out into the bitter, Boston night.

I didn't have occasion to think again of that night until nearly five months later.

On January 8, 1983, I received the happy news that four of my songs had been accepted for a television premiere and, with the arrival of a royalty advance, I found myself, at least by my earlier standards, a rich man.

Accordingly, I bid a hasty farewell to my students and to the Boston winter and booked passage on a steamer to Morocco, where I passed the winter and early spring. By mid-April I was anxious to get back to writing, yet in no particular hurry to return to the U.S. One of my songs was having some popular success, and my agent had written several times, asking me to send him a tape as soon as possible. During the three months in Morocco, I had had a fine time but hadn't written a note, so I decided to settle somewhere for the summer and to devote the time to work.

On April 19, I flew from Casablanca to Lyons, France, where a woman I knew had been spending the winter. After looking for several days, we came across an ad in the International Herald Tribune that looked ideal: a summer home, surrounded by oaks and vineyards, with a brook and arbor, near Valence, which is about halfway between Lyon and Marseilles.

I took the train the next day and walked out to the address, a little more than a mile from town. It was an old, white adobe house, not too large, and extremely well kept. The owner was a Madame Giraud-Neuilly, a woman nearing seventy whose family, she said, had lived in the house for nearly a century. We spent the afternoon talking and drinking beer. I found her delightful.

Every one of my friends had warned me to beware of the French—that they were a haughty lot, supercilious, and unfriendly. But if Madame Giraud-Neuilly were any example, my friends had been wrong. I spoke French passably well, and that certainly didn't hurt our relationship. At about 5:00, her husband Jacques Neuilly came home, and they invited me to stay for dinner. He showed me the wine cellar, which they hadn't used since *le père* had died in the '30s, saying I was welcome to use it for storage if I cared to clean it up. We worked out the details after dinner, and by the time I returned to Lyon the next day, I had a house. Ten days later I moved in.

Since the house was furnished, getting settled took no time at all. I spent the first month working the kinks out of my piano playing and writing daily. I took the five songs with which I'd been happiest, taped them, and sent them to New York; then decided to take a few days off to celebrate and explore. I started with the cellar, hoping to find some old wine.

The cellar hadn't been used for fifty years, and it looked it. Boxes were lying everywhere, covered with cobwebs. The casks lining the right wall were thick with dust. I turned one of the spigots, and it broke off. I was about to go back upstairs when I noticed something in the far corner reflecting the light from my lantern. I picked my way back and found that I'd been lucky—it was a half-case of unopened wine. In the other half of the case lay a sheaf of papers, yellow and brittle, bound by twine. I lifted the whole box and brought it upstairs.

The wine was unlabeled, and I assumed that it was home-made. The sediment was thick on the bottom, and I hadn't been careful enough in moving it. Since I had to let the wine sit for some time before decanting it, I picked up the sheaf of papers, got myself a beer, and went out to the arbor, thinking only to pass the time until the wine settled.

The papers were written in a thick, continental hand, in French, of course. After I got used to the style, I became engrossed. I read on, forgetting about the wine, until it got dark, then moved inside and finished the manuscript sitting at the kitchen table. At first I thought it a rather poor attempt at a novel, but as I read on, it appeared to be more and more genuine—a personal account of Madame Giraud-Neuilly's father during World War I. But something else was even more interesting to me: if this were a genuine manuscript, it was proof of Arrowroot's theory, for the Auguste Lupa of the manuscript could be none other than Holmes's son.

The next day, I wrote to Madame Giraud-Neuilly, asking her if she could tell me anything about her father's exploits during the war, specifically any undercover operations he might have been involved in. I then set myself to the arduous task of translating.

Within two weeks, I had my landlady's reply. Yes, her father had been active in the war as some kind of agent. She didn't know too much about it, though, and suggested that I question her half-brother, Jean Chessal, who was living in Valence. He was a retired soldier, pushing eighty, and very reluctant to discuss anything with a nosy American. Finally, though, I persuaded him to take the manuscript. A few days later, I went to pick it up.

"Have you read it?" I asked.

"I said I would."

"Well?"

"Well what?"

"What do you think? Is it true?"

He squinted at me through his thick glasses and scratched at his head, as if trying to understand the question.

"How would I know? I wasn't there."

"But your mother..."

"My mother was Tania Chessal before she married Jules. What does that prove?"

But of course it proved quite a lot.

I returned home to find a letter from Kevin James. I had written to him asking him to send any information he had regarding Holmes's progeny. The letter was mostly tongue-in-cheek, but it did present several facts about Holmes's relationships, none of which were inconsistent with anything in the manuscript. I'd been slightly bothered by the initials S. H. on Lupa's watch, but Kevin assured me that individuals who used aliases often kept their own initials.

I became angry with myself. After some weeks of translating, I'd become convinced of the manuscript's authenticity, with no more proof than its evident age and its conformance to Hugo Arrowroot's pet theory. There was only one thing to do to finally satisfy myself. Accordingly, I spent most of the next few months tracking down and interviewing anyone who might have known or worked with the man who had been Auguste Lupa for the year he lived and worked in Valence during World War I. Those interviews laid to rest my every doubt.

In translating, I have tried to use contemporary Americanisms wherever possible, though in places where the meaning is clear from context, I have retained the French.

Finally, I apologize for the prose style in this prologue. I am not a prose writer by trade and, if I had not come to believe in the importance of this manuscript, I would certainly have left it where I found it, gathering dust in a wine cellar.

1

It was embarrassing, but with a war going on, embarrassment was a luxury I couldn't permit myself.

The deep gray and cold dawn were burning off into a pleasant morning as I walked along the Rue St. Philip in Valence, trying to piece together all I'd heard about the man I was to meet and solicit, Auguste Lupa.

We hadn't made an appointment, but I knew where he would be, since every morning he followed a strict routine: up at eight A.M., a walk through the town garden, then a corner table at La Couronne from nine-thirty until noon, drinking beer and reading newspapers, nearly always alone. During the afternoons, he would disappear for five hours— no one seemed to know where. He'd then reappear just before six, prepared to work as chef at La Couronne, where he was reputed to be a genius even in this land of chefs *sans pareille*. What was embarrassing was that we needed him, and I was chosen to meet him because of a weakness we shared for beer. We needed him, a chef not yet turned twenty-five, because he was the best spy in Europe.

May 18, 1915. The Huns were having a heyday, plumbing the depths to which humanity could sink. They'd already shown their disregard for treaty and commitment by marching across neutral Belgium last August, but the events of this month surprised even those of us who were supposedly inured to their perfidy. Two weeks ago, they'd torpedoed the ship *Lusitania,* killing hundreds of civilians, and on the battlefield at Ypres, they'd just introduced a new element into warfare, the heretofore outlawed poison gas.

The streets of Valence were filled with red-eyed women whose sons, fathers, and brothers had left for the front, determined to repulse the German invaders.

At ten o'clock this Tuesday morning, I arrived at La Couronne and sat opposite Lupa, whom I'd never before seen. There are some men who can sit on a corner or in a room and simply disappear, blending into their surroundings. If such men make good assassins, this Lupa could never be one. He didn't blend in at all. In fact, he very nearly commanded the entire street, sitting at his table, quietly drinking his beer.

Of course it was he—the high forehead and dark brown hair, combed straight back; the eyes not quite open and yet missing nothing; the heavy lips puckering after every swallow. I, too, had a paper, and settled back to watch him. He was a big man and looked immensely strong, even dressed in an ill-fitting brown suit. His yellow shirt, which would have been garish, or—worse—memorable, on an assassin, was tight across his middle, but didn't bulge at the waist.

The *garçon* came out to his table with two more beers, removed the two empty glasses, and was returning when I stopped him for two of my own. Lupa had set the paper down and was leaning back with a beer. He let the foam settle slightly, then took a deep swallow, draining the contents of the glass in a single gulp. As he lowered the glass to the table, his eyes narrowed slightly, and the corners of his mouth turned suddenly downward.

The *garçon* came with my beer. It was still a bit early, and Lupa and I were the only people there. He looked at me briefly when my beer arrived, and I nodded, the informal recognition of two people sharing the same type of moment. His head inclined a mere centimeter, then turned back to the newspaper.

I reached for the beer and took a small drink, making an elaborate face of disgust. Crossing my legs, I sat back and picked up the paper, stopping every two or three minutes to continue my little charade with the beer: a sip, a look of distaste, meant of course only for myself but obvious to anyone, especially to Lupa. I set the first glass down when I'd finished, and with a little flourish pushed the empty glass as far from me as the table allowed. I then stared down the street, glaring.

Lupa finished his third glass and leaned back with his eyes closed, drumming his fingers methodically on the edge of the table. After a few seconds his fingers came to an abrupt halt, and he glanced over at me.

"*Mal,*" I said with a weak smile.

"*Insupportable!*" He took the other glass and poured it slowly to the ground. The corners of his mouth turned slightly upward, and he watched me. "*J'en ai marée.* I've had enough."

I took a gamble and decided to make a scene.

"*Garçon!*"

When he arrived, I spoke too loudly. "This beer is horrible. It is possibly the worst beer in France, and at any rate it's the worst I've had. This gentleman," I nodded in Lupa's direction, "has just poured his to the sidewalk, where it belongs, and I only refrain because I deplore waste, especially during wartime. Take this glass, remove it, and give its contents to the plants or the pigs, then bring me a glass of wine." I looked at Lupa. "Sir, would you join me in a glass?"

He nodded. "Thank you, I would. And Charles," he said to the waiter, "don't pour it on the plants or use it in the mustard. Perhaps it wouldn't completely destroy the pork."

He crossed to my table and bowed, more an inclination of the head than a bow.

"Auguste Lupa," he said.

"Jules Giraud." I motioned to the empty chair.

We sat, and he began to talk.

"I, too, sir, deplore waste, though I could argue that there was no waste involved in pouring that beer to the ground. That beer was waste when it arrived, and what pains me is that I've been putting up with it for months now. I am indebted to you, M. Giraud. Sometimes I need a nudge to act, though I generally decide instantly on matters of taste; but I have an inordinate fondness for beer, and since good beer cannot be purchased here, I've allowed my integrity an unforgivable laxity." He closed his eyes and sighed, and there was, indeed, a burden of sadness around him. "It will be hard without beer, but my taste applauds yours, sir."

The wine arrived, and he raised his glass, after first sniffing it and looking through the dark, red liquid. "*Sante,*" he said, "and damn this war."

We both drained our glasses. He signaled for another, and I began to smile.

"You're amused?" he asked.

"It seems strange," I said, raising the second glass, "to find myself agreeing with a man whose major concern in the midst of European destruction is the lack of quality beer."

"But you do agree."

"Of course, damn it." I smiled again. "The living must

continue to live. But you are wrong about something," I said.

"And that is...?"

"The dearth of good beer. There is a great quantity of excellent beer not four kilometers from where we sit. But it is not for sale."

He looked at me patiently and warily. "M. Giraud, I don't know you, but you don't seem given to idle jesting. I have been cooking here in Valence for the winter and have searched tirelessly for a supply of good beer, and to no avail. I have some talent at discovering things that people try to keep hidden, and there is no beer."

"There is, and it is hidden, and privately brewed by a man who values his privacy. No more than six men know of it."

"They are very discreet men," he said.

"Very," I continued. "They have to be, but that's no matter. Even knowing that the beer exists, you would never find it, for you're not likely to see me again and you don't know the other five." I drained my glass and got up to go. "It's been a pleasant morning, sir," I said. "Good luck."

I hadn't gone ten paces when he spoke.

"M. Giraud."

I turned. "Yes?"

"Would your chef mind terribly if you missed a meal?"

"He goes nearly mad," I said, "but occasionally..." I stopped abruptly. "How did you know I had a chef?"

He nodded, his eyes narrowing somewhat, perhaps with humor. "You've just confirmed it."

"Yes, but..."

"Monsieur Giraud," he said. "There was nothing sinister, I assure you, in the question. It was mere conjecture."

"But how...?"

"Simplicity itself. It's clear that you are a man of taste regarding your palate. Your clothing further bespeaks a cer-

tain degree of wealth, and your accent—indeed, even the
way you hold a wineglass—betrays good breeding. Finally,
your coloring is pale."

"Yes?"

"Surely that is enough."

I laughed in spite of myself. "I'm afraid I don't follow
you."

He ticked off the steps of his deduction with the fingers of
his right hand. "First, you can afford a chef. Second, you
would demand fine meals, especially at home. Third, if you
yourself spent the required amount of time behind a hot
stove, your complexion would be ruddy like my own. It is
not. Ergo, you have a chef."

"You're very astute," I said.

He waved it off. "It's nothing. Child's play. Literally, in
my case. My father was something of a stickler for such
matters. I've kept it up as a hobby, more or less. Just now I
made an educated guess, and your reaction confirmed it. True
deduction is a closed system—it confirms itself."

"Still, I'm impressed."

"Well, then perhaps you'll permit me to impress you with
my small skills as a chef. Would you care to lunch?" The eyes
were sharp now, though the face was relaxed and friendly.

"It's rather early," I said, hesitating a moment.

He continued. "Egg of pigeon poached in red wine, escargots, *rognons aux fines herbes,* all accompanied by the finest
wine on the Côte du Rhone, served at the chef's table."

"It is a great temptation," I said. "You, of course, though
you haven't said it, would greatly appreciate an introduction
to a certain local brewer I mentioned."

He smiled. "Your deduction, though obvious, is flawless."

"And your discretion?"

"Unimpeachable."

I walked back to him.

"At what time shall we eat?" I asked. Later I would recognize that slight turn of the lips as a beaming smile.

"We can begin immediately, if you'd like to come down
to the kitchen."

"Gladly."

We crossed through the tables to a door that didn't leave
much room to spare for us and opened it. A short stairway
led to the kitchen. He stopped at the bottom.

"And the introduction?"

"Pardon?"

"To the brewer?"

"Ah yes. You've already met him."

He raised his eyebrows. "Indeed?"

I nodded. *"A vôtre service."*

And so it was arranged that Auguste Lupa come to my
house the next morning at ten for beer and a light lunch.

2

Espionage, like any other profession, has its ups and downs. Lately, though, it had taken a monotonous turn to the latter.

I'd been one of the few operatives who'd dared before August to suggest that the German thrust would be through Belgium. This was viewed as so outrageous that those of us who believed it were "transferred." Even after the event came to pass, we were still regarded as second class and relegated to desks or to the country. I should have been upset with the demotion, but in fact I'd been happy. I'd begun to feel constrained under the inflexibility of Joffre's[1] yoke.

Consequently, I had spent the past autumn behind a desk, doing nothing worthwhile, and had finally, much to my re-

[1]Commander in chief of French army.

lief, been called back to my hometown for this case. It was to be a break in my routine, a kind of forced vacation. No sooner had I returned to the little white house, nestled snugly amid grapevines and a small grove of oaks, however, than my contact had suddenly been taken dead—officially, an accidental drowning.

The next month I'd busied myself with the beer and light gardening, spending much time with my new chef, a young Swiss with extraordinary promise named Fritz Benet. It had been a pleasant enough time, or would have been without the specter of murder hanging over the house. Normally, living in an atmosphere where people tend to die unexpectedly didn't overly disturb my peace of mind, but somehow, at home, I found it quite annoying.

There were, of course, my friends. Marcel Routier, my closest friend and fellow agent (though we rarely worked together) was now in Valence. My other friends, to whom we were traveling salesmen, included Henri Pulis, a Greek shopowner in town; Paul Anser, an American poet of some small repute; and Georges Lavoie, an Alsatian salesman who dealt in hospital supplies. Including Fritz, then, these were the other five men who knew about the beer.

There was also Tania. I had told Lupa that only five other men in town knew about the beer, and Tania—tall and slim, with long black hair and deep, deep eyes and voice—was as far from being a man as any creature on earth.

Marcel had been sent down after my original contact had "drowned" and had told me the problem. It was believed that the man behind most of the assassinations in the past two years—including Francis Ferdinand's in Sarajevo—was now living and working out of Valence. How intelligence had come to believe that, I had no idea, since there wasn't a shred of evidence that pointed to the involvement of a mastermind assassin. Yes, last spring an agent in Valence had been found with a bullet in his head two days after wiring that he was onto something big. But "something big" could mean just about anything these days, what with half the nations of Europe at war.

There was, in fact, only one event of importance, of real significance, attached to this locale, and that was the arrival, early the previous fall, of Auguste Lupa.

Obviously, that wasn't his real name, but no one had any idea of what it really was, so it didn't matter. In Belgrade, he'd been Julius Adler. At Sarajevo, he was Cesar Mycroft. In Milan, . . . but the list is immaterial, though impressive. Always a reference to one of the Caesars in one of the names— perhaps some family connection. We'd followed him when he broke out of jail in Belgrade a year ago June, lost him briefly, found him again in Geneva, trailing him to Valence. When he actually took a job here, I'd been sent.

Lupa was the unparalleled genius among the agents of Europe and he seemed to work for himself, for no government acknowledged him. As far as we knew, he'd been approached before, by us as well as the British and Russians, and to all he'd feigned an absolute innocence of any knowledge of espionage or even of the affairs of politics. His loves, he said, included only food and beer. In spite of his protestations of naiveté, he'd been jailed for espionage in three countries and had turned over quantities of information, always by leaving a bag loaded with papers in a locker somewhere. The material was always typed, never on the same machine, never with the same paper, almost never in the same language, and always frighteningly exact. He was the best, and he'd been trying to discover the brains behind Europe's assassinations for two years. He obviously wanted us here, or he wouldn't have let himself be followed, and yet he'd made no overtures of any sort and had forced me to contact him. It was barely possible that he didn't suspect my associations, but it was probable that even as I sat down across from him, he was cataloguing everything he knew about me, deciding the time was right, and letting me set the tone of our relationship.

During lunch, I had asked him if he'd mind if a friend of mine were present at the next day's meeting, and he'd said no. Accordingly, I invited Marcel Routier, and he arrived early the next morning, a little past nine o'clock. We sat outside in the sun for our coffee.

"He, of course, knows us," he said.

I shrugged. "It's nearly certain, but he may have been so attuned to his own inquiries that they haven't crossed ours yet. In any case, we'll see before long."

He sipped at his coffee, taking a bite of Fritz's blueberry muffin, and looked out over the grounds. His hair was the color of straw, which made it look as though there was less of it than there was. It was a bit too long for my taste, just touching the tops of his ears, which he said was to make up for the lack on top. This morning he was wearing white pants and shoes, and a high-collared blue shirt, and, except possibly for his face, he looked much more the dandy than the spy. A lot of women had found him attractive, but I couldn't understand why. Tania had said he had classic features, but too many of them. His forehead and nose commanded his face except when he smiled, at which time his teeth commanded everything. He was smiling now.

"Damn," he said, "I wish I'd thought of getting Lupa with beer. Occasionally you show real genius, Jules."

"Perception and devotion, hardly genius. When Fritz told me of the food at La Couronne, it started me thinking. A man who could cook as well as he did, who smuggled in spices for the integrity of his dishes, and yet who spent every morning drinking swill on the sidewalk . . . no, it didn't make sense. That man's taste buds were too refined for that beer, but he loves beer. Simple, actually."

"Like Columbus's egg," he said.

*   *   *

At first, even at Lupa's insistence, Fritz would not come to table with us, but finally he overcame his prejudice against the chef dining with his patron when Lupa got him engrossed in a recipe for pheasant.

"The problem," he said, "is that too often that delicate bird is overwhelmed by tarragon and sage, when it should be coaxed into accepting their favors, as a woman might accept other favors, with a little wine. Set the spices in the wine first, several hours before, and leave it chilled. Then..."

"Gentlemen," I said, "I don't mean to interrupt, but couldn't we continue this discussion at the table?"

So the four of us sat to savor Fritz's delicious sole and honey, followed by a subtle tournedos Béarnaise. The two chefs were very close to the same age, and they seemed to get along exceptionally well, which made the lunch even smoother than it would have been with the fine food. There was no hint of recognition between them when I introduced Marcel and Lupa, though once during the meal they glanced at one another after a remark Fritz had made about the state of cuisine in the Balkans.

"And now," I said, as we were finishing our coffee, "shall we go to the cellar? Fritz, will you prepare the arbor?"

"He is a sensitive chef," Lupa said when Fritz had gone. "Has he been with you long?"

"Actually, no. Less than a year."

"Do you know where he was trained?"

A look of annoyance crossed Marcel's countenance. Lupa must have seen it too, for he held up his hand and continued quickly. "I only ask about his training because it is so evidently superlative. The man is nearly a *maître,* and at his age that is very rare, indicative of great native skill and rigorous apprenticeship. As a chef myself, I would be interested to know where he studied."

"To tell you the truth, I'm not at all certain. He arrived

here on the recommendation of a mutual friend, and his cooking has never given me cause to question his background. My friend was living in Strasbourg before the hostilities began, so I gather he trained in one of the establishments there."

"In Germany, then?"

Finally Marcel got in a word. "That point is most arguable, isn't it?"

"Strasbourg is a German city," Lupa asserted.

"Strasbourg is French! It will always be French, regardless of who its rulers might be."

"Gentlemen, please!" I felt I had to step in or tempers, specifically Marcel's, would flare.

For an instant Lupa seemed inclined to glare and continue the debate, but as I watched him, he swiftly conquered his rising emotions. He spoke contritely. "You're right, of course, Monsieur Routier. I apologize. Strasbourg must once again fly the tricolor. I only meant to comment favorably upon Fritz's cuisine, and I'm afraid my youth carried me into irrelevancies. He is a fine, fine chef—and you, Monsieur Giraud, are a lucky man to have him."

There was an awkward moment as Marcel brought himself back under control, but I could see that Lupa's obvious sincerity had made its mark.

"Well," I said, clapping my hands, "should we begin the tour?"

We all rose from the table and I led the two down to my cellar, the left half of which was reserved for wines and the other for the beer apparatus. There were five stone crocks lined against the right wall, and the smell of yeast and ripening beer lent an aroma to the room that I found pleasant, but that I knew might prove too strong to a novice, even a beer-loving novice.

"As long as the wine isn't opened down here," I said, explaining, "it is ideal."

As we walked along, I went over some of the steps in the

brewing, and seeing the two of them smile patiently, I suggested we proceed to the tasting.

Off to the side of the house, I was blessed with a small arbor of trees, through which ran a clear stream where Fritz stored butter and beer. It was perfectly chilled, and I'd built a table of thick oak, where my friends and I came to sit and relax, out of the glare. We walked out to that table now and silently sat while Fritz brought the beer, left the bottles with us, and departed.

Lupa drank his whole glass at one swill, just as he had the day before at La Couronne, and yet conveyed the impression that he was savoring every drop. Marcel and I drank more slowly but with no less enjoyment. Lupa put down his glass and looked at me.

"Remarkable."

"It pleases you?"

"There are certain advantages to being raised a rich man, eh?" said Marcel. "Certain opportunities to develop talents which otherwise would be buried under the mundane cares of survival." He looked at Lupa, smiling. "He constantly makes me envious. Such beer, such a house, such a chef..."

"Such beer," Lupa repeated, leaning back with his eyes closed.

I poured him another glass. For the next quarter of an hour we sat quietly enjoying the day, the beer, and... was it the company or the suspense? It seemed to me that we were all waiting for another to be the first to speak. Finally, I ventured cautiously.

"Monsieur Lupa, what brings you here to Valence? Could you not accomplish your goals elsewhere, in a larger city?"

He looked at me quizzically, the touch of a smile lifting the corners of his mouth.

"What goals are those?" he asked.

"Oh, the usual for a young chef. Apprenticeship in a large hotel, assistantship to a master..."

But he cut me off. "A man who follows the usual routes obtains the usual results. Like so many other endeavors, cuisine is both an art and a skill. Of course, the French scoff at such an idea—meaning no offense to you, sir. Too often the path to excellence at a skill is a limiting experience, until the mind, finally, is trained to abhor innovation. And, beyond a certain mastery of skills, innovation is what lets a chef stand alone."

When he finished his little speech, he had none of the habits one would expect from one so young, neither the slight embarrassment nor the brash defiance that often punctuates the speech of the insecure. Rather, he reached for his beer and drank.

"It's clear," said Marcel, "that you wish to stand alone."

"Only a dullard would not."

There was a moment of uncomfortable silence.

Finally, Marcel spoke. "But surely you don't mean that."

Lupa nodded. "If I hadn't meant it, I wouldn't have said it."

"What of our men at the front, then? They don't stand alone. In fact, all our hope resides in their fighting together, in the assumption that there are goals that must take precedence over individuality. Are all our soldiers dullards?"

"Probably most. It's always rather meaningless to generalize. Joffre certainly is."

"Then you wouldn't fight?" Marcel was getting angry.

Lupa took a breath. "Fortunately, I'm a citizen of the United States, and we are presently neutral. I'm afforded the luxury of not fighting."

"But would you?"

"I wouldn't like to be mere cannon fodder."

"Because you wish to stand alone."

"Exactly." He drank some beer. "But I see you're getting upset with me. I don't mean to say that I don't believe in causes, or that everyone should have individuality. I applaud our troops at the front. I only refer to men of adequate intelligence, and they are not so commonplace as is generally believed, who attain eminence in a field and then prove themselves incompetent because they lack imagination, individuality, call it what you will. Joffre can execute all the textbook moves. What he cannot do is adapt. Luckily for France, the Germans are even more stupid, or they would have taken Paris months ago." He paused and drank again.

"The key then..." said Marcel.

"... is innovation," Lupa continued. "I don't mean to slur those who follow others' examples, or those who learn a trade and become proficient at a skill. No. We need them. I simply bemoan the lack of creative leadership by people who are, nominally, our leaders."

"I quite agree," I put in.

"Perhaps I misunderstood," said Marcel. "Then you are here as a head chef to learn to innovate?"

Lupa smiled. "One doesn't learn how to innovate. One simply acts, and learns from his actions. But yes, I am here to become a chef. I am already a cook."

It seemed that Marcel was on the verge of questioning him directly about his real work. He leaned toward the younger man with a gleam in his eyes. A slight breeze came into the arbor, though, and Lupa, rubbing his hands together, stood.

"Gentlemen," he said, "I have very much enjoyed the day, but I must now attend to other matters. I'm becoming more and more a creature of habit, and my habits won't brook much flexibility. I'm afraid I must go."

"Well, if you must, you must," I said, "but would you consider coming back this evening? Once a week, I host a gathering of the men I had earlier mentioned to you, and I'm always happy to find another discerning beer lover."

He bowed slightly. "I'd be delighted, though it would have to be after the dinner hour."

"Around ten, then."

We remained seated and watched him until he entered the house. He walked very lightly for a man of his size.

"Well?" asked my friend.

I shrugged. "What do you think of him?"

"He's very polite."

We laughed, and I rose to get some more beer. When I had come back and sat down, Marcel was still smiling.

"He doesn't seem to be in as much a hurry to enlist our aid as we are to enlist his, does he?"

"Hardly. And I must admit that after all this time, I'm starting to wonder if I've been put out to pasture, that there's nothing happening in Valence, and I've been sent here to sit out the war with my cook and my beer. Have you heard of anything at all?"

"I heard from Paris late last week; it must have been after last Wednesday's gathering, and they told us to sit tight, that whatever would happen here obviously was in the planning stage, and the longer the wait, the greater the odds that it's really something big." He took a long drink of beer. "The damn thing is, there's no one worth assassinating here, and no one scheduled to come, and not a clue of planning in progress..." He trailed off. "Nothing."

"Is it possible," I asked, "that this time it won't be an assassination? Suppose, for example, it's sabotage, or kidnapping, or..."

"No, I doubt it," he said. "Our man directs killers, and if we could just think of... my God!" He'd put down the glass and was staring so intently into the trees behind us that I turned around.

"What is it?"

"He is here to assassinate."

"Impossible," I said. "There's not a man in this region of any strategic importance, and no one will be..."

"There's one," he said, his eyes shining.

"Who's that?"

"Auguste Lupa."

We sat for a moment or two in silence, while I thought of objections to what he'd said. In the first place, Lupa had arrived on the trail of our man, but that of course could be a way to have Lupa where he wanted him. Come to Valence so that Lupa would come here, so that he could kill him here? That was far-fetched, and I said so. Why Valence?

"Possibly because Lupa has an embarrassing connection here, and killing him in sordid surroundings would not only be good propaganda but would rid Germany of the agent they most feared." Marcel was warming now to his own suggestion.

"But there would be no propaganda, since the public has never heard of Lupa, since Lupa wasn't even his name a few months ago. Finally, Marcel, he would never have waited so long to move. If he had known who Lupa was and where he would find him, he would have acted and cleared out months ago."

"You're probably right," he conceded, "but he's here for something, and we don't have any idea of who he is, what he wants, or why he's here. We must ask Lupa what he has on him, and tonight."

"It will be difficult at the gathering," I said.

"Then later."

"We'll see, but I can't shake the feeling that the man is here for sabotage."

"To sabotage what? There's nothing here in Valence."

"No, not in Valence itself. But there is the arms factory in St. Etienne, surely close enough to warrant investigation. You know as well as I that all our major defense research is going on there. Our man would also know. Otherwise, why would Lupa be here? It's got to be something damned important. If that factory is blown . . . well, it'll set us back over a year."

He looked down at the ground and picked up his beer.

"It's guarded, of course."

"It's impregnable."

"Well, there you are."

"No. What bothers me is its seeming invulnerability. There are enough troops guarding the place, all right, but in a sense that is really not the point. It can't be directly assaulted, which is of course why they'd have to send a man here—to break it, to find a way in."

"How is security?"

"I tell you, Marcel, that's what puzzles me so much about it. Everything is as it should be. It is completely impossible. It can't be entered by anyone who hasn't been thoroughly checked out. Everyone who works inside has been cleared and cleared again. There are troops all over St. Etienne with 75s ready to shoot down any aeroplanes..."

"Aeroplanes?"

"Probably not, I agree, but one can't be too careful."

"Well, then, it seems as if it's all covered."

"It is, and that's what bothers me. The level of security may have created a degree of complacency. I'm growing more and more certain that we should direct our attentions there. It would also explain why our man has stayed around so long without acting. He couldn't very well break their security in too short a time."

"If at all."

I looked across at my friend. Years of service still hadn't forced him to develop an imagination. He was steady and loyal, always ready for action, and totally without fear, but he could never foresee an event before its occurrence. The times I had worked with him before, he'd been invaluable, but as an active force, rather more like another weapon. And so I'd developed a protective attitude toward him. Not that he needed protection from any known danger—once it was identified, he was in his element. Too often, however, he suspected nothing and would have walked into traps totally unprepared. I don't know how he was with other agents. Perhaps we had been friends for so long that he didn't feel with me that he had to be so much the professional, that our personal relations overlapped. I didn't share his feeling, but he was my closest friend. Now, as I discussed possibilities with him, I couldn't get rid of the feeling that perhaps it was approaching the time for him to get out of espionage. He would perhaps be more valuable as a strategist, directing troops from a defensible position against a visible enemy.

"Time will tell," I answered him.

"Yes."

We got up and started to cross over to the house. A breeze was blowing steadily now, and it felt as if rain was in the air. I put my arm around my friend's shoulder.

"Let's find something," I said, "I'm getting very bored."

He laughed. "Better to be bored than dead. There's a lot of that going around these days."

"Yes," I said, keeping my thoughts to myself. Overhead, the sky had begun to darken.

3

It had rained before the first of the guests arrived, and now the clouds hung low over the land, spent and yet threatening. Occasionally there was a low roar of thunder—the first thunderstorm of the season—but the clouds were low and obscured the lightning.

Georges Lavoie and Henri Pulis arrived first, a little after eight o'clock, and we sat by the front window looking out over the field that lay between my home and the road, some seventy-five meters away. Through some fluke the oaks that surrounded the house did not mar the view out of this window, though with the wind and the swirling branches the scene was neatly translated from the pastoral to the Gothic. From time to time one of the lower branches would sweep across the window like a hand. Twice the wind was strong enough to throw a hail of acorns into the glass, sounding for all the world like the tapping knuckles of that passing hand.

It was, I suppose, a rather strange collection of guests that came every week to my house and shared my beer. We were not confreres by occupation or age; indeed, we had almost nothing in common except a love of beer and companionship. I was by far the eldest, except for Marcel, and the only one of us with any wealth. Usually, we would drink and talk, often playing cards, until midnight. Sometimes Paul Anser would read something he'd just written, horribly translated. He was a great joker and kept the nights far from being dull. Now, with the war, we never ran out of news to discuss, though some nights we still would just sit and read, as in an English men's club, with of course the notable exception of Tania.

Henri Pulis looked like what he was—one of the hard-working bourgeoisie. Some fifteen years younger than I, his hair was nevertheless starting to streak with gray, and his face was set in creases punctuated by a large, drooping black mustache. He always sat slumped over, and this made him look even shorter than he was. Now he sat, nervously yet methodically wiping the foam from his mustache with his left hand, holding the beer in his right.

He'd come to Valence as a young man, perhaps ten years ago, after working for a time as a ship's mate. It was even rumored that he'd deserted from the Greek navy when his ship had docked at Marseilles, and he had moved north, laying low for some months until he decided it was safe to appear. After two or three years, he'd saved enough to open his own shop. We had met because he sold the supplies I needed for the beer, and though he was not as witty as the others, he was no less popular. He often seemed uncomfortable until he'd had a few beers, then he would relax and entertain us with crude jokes that we were all secretly ashamed of enjoying. He had originally come when I'd asked him, he said, to get away from his wife and six children, and though by now we were all friends, I was still not completely convinced that he so much treasured our company as that he considered it a respite from his family's.

Georges Lavoie normally came with Henri. They were friends who often dined together during the weeks when both were free. Georges was thirty-five or thereabouts, a traveling salesman who was often on the road but who made a point of returning by Wednesday, when we all gathered. He was kept from the service by a severe limp—his right leg was shorter than his left. But this didn't hamper him from somehow seeming the most urbane member of our fellowship. His father had been a banker in Brussels, in Lille, even in Coblentz, before he finally settled in Metz, and undoubtedly the company of bankers had inured in him a certain conservatism of dress and deference in mannerism. Nevertheless, he had a ready tongue and a stock of stories which were the more amusing for their incongruity. He, along with Tania and myself, never drank to excess, while the other three often left the house a bit affected. When the war broke out, he had left his native Alsace-Lorraine and fled south. He worked now out of Valence, selling and delivering his wares to factories, hospitals, and arsenals in the towns along the Rhone. He was the latest of our number, except for Lupa.

Henri shuddered, crossing one leg over the other and reaching for his bottle. "Good night to get drunk," he said.

"It's a good night for something," Georges agreed philosophically.

I raised my glass. "To something," I said, and we drank the toast.

Fritz brought in three more beers and left the room, shaking his head sadly. He did not like beer at all.

By now it had gotten dark. The lamps were lit, and the fire stoked, and we had moved to more comfortable seats.

We always remained in the big sitting room for these evenings. With its large front window reflecting the lights back in on us, the warm rug, and the variety of furniture, it was ideal for a small gathering of friends. Last spring, before I was sent north, we'd met in the arbor several times, but somehow, after dark, this room was much more comfortable.

Georges and Henri sat on either side of the large fireplace, which commanded one corner of the room, next to the entrance to the dining area and, behind that, the kitchen. I sat on the divan under the window, looking out for the others' arrival. In the far corner, away from me, were two other stuffed chairs, with a coffee table in front, then the door leading in from the foyer. Just to my left was a china closet and, to my right, bookshelves that lined the wall from the corner to the fireplace. Two other tables held our beer and some magazines, one directly in front of me, the other between Henri and Georges.

The house was really too large for me, but this room was ideal. For a time I'd busied myself with improvements, moving the water closet indoors, installing a shower; but then I'd given up and left the other rooms vacant until Fritz had moved in the year before. I slept in the one upstairs room, directly overhead.

From outside came the sound of a carriage drawing up, and laughter, and in a moment Marcel entered with Paul and Tania.

"Don't bother getting up," said Paul, "just bring a beer for the hero. Fritz!" he yelled, "Fritz!"

Tania crossed over to me and kissed me after she'd sat down. "He really was terrific! The horse bolted and was starting to run as we met Paul down the road, and he jumped on its back like a Red Indian and calmed it."

"It was nothing—really, I assure you—that any American couldn't do. Riding on the plains for days at a time with only stale bread and..."

Marcel was laughing. "Sure, Paul, sure. Fritz, bring him his beer before he tells us about fighting the Indians."

The beer arrived and the newcomers drank.

Paul Anser stood grinning in the middle of the room. He wore his "flyer's jacket," as he called it, a leather affair with a woolen collar; heavy boots; pants that looked to be made out of canvas.

"What a night," he said, "and hello everyone. Your beer is getting no worse, Jules. Are we late? Is there time to catch up with Henri?"

Henri smiled. "Only my second," he lied.

"Ah. Fritz—how are you, Fritz?—two more beers, please. Mustn't let Henri get the jump on me."

Marcel took Paul's jacket, and they both sat—Marcel on the divan with Tania and me, and Paul next to the entrance to the kitchen.

"There must be something in the air," I said. "Henri just said it was a fine night to get drunk."

"Well, by God, let's get to it." Paul poured his second beer.

"Here, here," said Tania, surprisingly, "and then Paul can read for us."

"Alcohol can't hurt my accent. When I slur I sound more French."

"Hardly more French," said Georges, "possibly less American." And we all laughed.

I leaned back with my arm around Tania and listened to the banter, trying to find a good moment to tell them we would have a new guest. We were so relaxed now together that I almost regretted having invited Lupa, but I'd had the same doubts about Georges, and they'd proven groundless. I was finding it difficult to divorce business from my day-to-day life when living at home. The people I met socially had always been friends, and though I liked Lupa, my motive for inviting him was certainly not friendship.

Tania sat easily next to me, sipping her beer and joining

in with the others. Twenty-one years ago she'd married Jean Chessal, one of my neighbors, and over the years had borne him four children, all boys. Jean had been in the service his entire life, and it was natural for the boys to follow him, especially with the war looming. Her husband had been killed in the first weeks of the war, and now the boys were at the front, all miraculously unhurt—so far. She was brave, cheerful without any visible effort, witty, and very beautiful. We had been lovers, now, for six years.

She was not a native of Valence, or even of this region, and even after so many years, her accent betrayed a certain foreignness which I found becoming. When Chessal had returned to Valence with his new bride, there had been rumors of royal ancestry, of some distinctly romantic past. I had no trouble accepting her with this touch of mystery. When we first met, I had been fascinated, but now her antecedents meant no more to me than her accent.

The others had gone on for a time with Paul and finally persuaded him to begin reading a new poem. He wanted more beer, but I'd given Fritz a sign to hold off until everyone had arrived.

After token comments relating to the paucity of his host's refreshments, Paul went to the center of the room and began. He read in English, which only two or three of us understood, and it was quite modern, but he read well—the cadences were rhythmic and pleasing. This was, after all, his only live audience of any size.

When he'd finished, I told him I found the thing incomprehensible, but he didn't seem to mind. He just shrugged and grinned and said something about comic relief, though while he was reading, he did not seem to take it lightly. Suddenly, he turned and cried out:

"I must, must, simply must have more beer!"

Henri, who had sat looking utterly perplexed while Paul read, concurred with a shy belch.

Georges stood and raised his empty glass. "I'd propose a toast to the poet if there were something to drink."

Tania turned to me. "Why are you holding the beer, Jules? Is there some surprise for us?"

The damned woman knew me too well.

"What makes you think I'm holding back the beer?" I asked.

Paul spoke. "You'll never understand women, Jules. Our most secret thoughts are the common currency of their lives. Maybe they don't read the thought but they sense the secret; and although maybe they know less, they understand more."

"Bah!" Georges interjected. "I may be only a simple observer, but I know when a gaffe has been committed. For a man to pretend to understand women is bad manners."

"And for him to really understand them is bad morals," Tania added.

"All right. *Assez, assez.* I've been holding back the beer, I admit it. I'm guilty, but there's a reason."

"One would hope so," said Tania.

"Such a serious matter," added Georges.

"It's not such a great matter," I said, smiling. "We're going to have another guest." I looked around for reactions, but there was nothing special. Henri looked a bit put out for a moment, but I had expected that. As one who cherished his nonintellectuality and tried as much as possible to keep the conversation off-color, he was not disposed to welcome a new guest who might tip the balance of the evening away from purely sensual enjoyment.

"Who is this person, Jules?" Georges asked. "We know almost everyone in Valence. Is he a neighbor?"

"Jules hasn't said our guest is a he, Georges. Perhaps he has invited another woman." Marcel looked at Tania and winked.

"Enough." It was time to end the mystery. "Our guest is Auguste Lupa. I met him quite casually the other day at La

Couronne. He is a connoisseur of good beer, and a very pleasant fellow. Nothing more. He's arrived here only recently, and I thought he would enjoy a taste—shall I say of society? I think he'll fit in very nicely with our group." The door sounded. "Ah, that would be him."

Fritz brought Lupa into the room and announced him grandly.

The big man stood for a moment framed in the doorway, looking at the assemblage. There was a moment of silence, and then I jumped up and performed the introductions. Only Henri seemed ill at ease, while the others nodded cautiously and Fritz went to get another round of beers. Lupa sat by the door and, after another moment, spoke.

"Please disregard my attendance here for a time. Since you are obviously all attuned to one another, you'll want to continue as before. Don't make allowances for me. After a time the novelty will be gone, and I'll join in as one of you, but for now, let me drink quietly and not disturb you."

It was a strange prologue and served more to reinforce the silence than to dispel it.

"Nonsense," said I. "Why don't you tell the group about yourself? It isn't every day we welcome a new member."

"Member?"

"Well, not really a member of anything. Sometimes we do refer to ourselves as a group of sorts, but nothing so rigid as to demand membership."

"Do tell us about yourself," said Tania.

I saw Marcel smile at me. I didn't expect Lupa to drop any information, but having him talk for a while wouldn't hurt.

"Yeah, like where are you from?" That was Paul.

Lupa looked at him. "You're American," he said, then continued almost as though talking to himself. "Northwest, I should say. No, not so far west, perhaps Wyoming or Montana."

"You got it, Mister. Missoula, Montana, U. S. of A. How 'bout you?"

"Born."

"Pardon?"

"Born in America, not bred. My mother traveled quite a lot with her career and fortuitously timed my birth so that I became an American citizen at the time of my first breath."

"You don't talk like an American," said Henri, "more like a Greek, or..."

"Or a Serbian?" ventured Georges.

Lupa smiled. "Exactly. I've never lived in America, though I would like to go there. I was raised by several of my relatives—in England primarily but in other parts of Europe as well."

I was surprised to find him so conversational. He sat straight in his chair, genial and relaxed. Henri and Marcel took out their pipes and lit them, Henri with a bit of ember from the fire.

Lupa raised his head slightly and sniffed at the air. "Ah, the smell of pipes. I love them. They bring back memory of my childhood, of my father. You, Monsieur Routier, you're having a Cavendish latakia mixture, are you not? And Monsieur Pulis—a Virginia tobacco, perhaps even a chewing plug if I'm not mistaken?"

The two men looked at each other, impressed. "Exactly," Marcel said.

"Not to chew, but to smoke," Henri said, his face showing a certain sullenness.

I interjected. "You know your tobaccos, Monsieur."

He nodded. "It was a special interest of my father. Once we were together in Paris, and..."

"Oh, then you're not new to France?" asked Tania, interrupting. "I'd somehow thought you were."

"No, I spent most of my summers here as a youth." He

stopped and looked at Tania and me. "I should say when I was more of a youth."

"What do you do in Valence?" Henri asked suddenly and, I thought, rather belligerently.

Lupa looked carefully at him. "You bear me animus, sir?"

I stepped in. "You'll have to excuse Monsieur Pulis. He isn't happy about having a new member, no matter who it might be. I'm sure it's nothing personal. Isn't that right, Henri?"

"If you'd prefer that I leave..."

"No, no, don't be silly. It's I who should leave," said Henri. "I'm sorry. Sometimes I forget myself. I act like the ass."

"Sometimes we all do," Lupa replied with a pleasant smile. "Such is the effect that troubles sometimes have on us."

Henri nodded, taking another huge drink from his bottle. Then, in a kind of double take, he put down his glass and stared at Lupa.

Georges, however, was the first to speak. "What do you know of Henri's troubles?" The others all nodded in shared suspicion.

Lupa, aware of his faux pas, was nearly successful in smiling. Then he spoke in a self-deprecating tone. "You mustn't mind me, please. Sometimes I get carried away by assumptions I can't help making, and they lead me to conclusions that are often ridiculous. I saw Monsieur Pulis sitting slightly slumped over, and the thought entered my head that he seemed unnaturally subdued, given the spirit of the occasion. Additionally, I noticed that the second button on his shirt is missing and that he wears a wedding ring. He is, therefore, married, but on bad terms with his wife just now, or she wouldn't have let him go out with his shirt unmended. Finally, he appears to be drinking much more than the rest of us, often a sign of someone trying to forget a particularly depressing or difficult situation."

Henri's hand had gone to the missing button. His face clouded over, then he grinned sheepishly. "I've got to be more careful," he said, somewhat enigmatically.

I had earlier marveled at Lupa's perspicacity, so I was prepared to some extent for his displays. The others, I noticed, were beginning to look as though they felt slightly apprehensive, as though they were all unwittingly under some unseen magnifying glass. Before anyone else could comment, however, Fritz entered with the beer, walked to the various seats, and deposited the new bottles, setting a glass before Lupa. He might have simply brought the tray into the room, but the pride he took in his work demanded that certain rituals be performed.

We looked to Tania, who by tradition delivered the first toast after the whole company had assembled. We had not all opened the bottles yet, which Fritz refused to do because, he said, of the danger. Once a bottle had exploded as he was about to open it, a common enough occurrence with home-brewed beer, and since then he'd refused to participate in any opening.

Tania looked at Lupa and then at the rest of us. Georges was still fiddling with his bottle, but she began.

"To our new guest, M. Lupa, and..."

Before she could say "and to France," there was a loud pop, and Georges was grabbing his right hand with his left, swearing. We all leapt up and crossed over to him, and Fritz entered silently with a cloth.

"Damn the bottles," said Georges, and there was general agreement as Tania took the cloth and wiped the blood away. "Have you any gauze?" she asked, and I told her there was some in the bathroom.

Georges said he'd get it himself, that he was all right, and he walked out to clean up. Lupa sat in the chair Georges had vacated, where he'd gone to inspect the bottle, while the rest

of us reassembled ourselves. Marcel said something concili-
atory to Henri, and they retired to what had been the American corner. Tania and I went back to the divan, and Paul
stood joking with Fritz about his wisdom.

When Fritz had finished cleaning up the spilled beer, he
went to get another, and Paul turned and sat with us. "So
much for that toast," he said.

Foregoing the next one, we all reached for our beers and
drank. Henri and Lupa drained their glasses, and Henri had
just yelled in through the kitchen for Fritz to bring more than
one more, when Marcel stood up straight, grabbing his throat.
He croaked out, "I feel..." but before he could finish, reeled
forward over the small table onto his face. Lupa was to him
in a flash, rolling him over and lifting his eyelids. Georges
came back to the door in time to hear him say "He's dead."

The events of the next moments were confused and rapid,
though they seemed to me to follow one another with ag-
onizing slowness. Tania, sitting next to me, put down her
glass and stared, then covering her face with her hands cried
"Oh God, no!" and leaned back. I was aware of Georges
stopping in the doorway, gauze over his recent cut, turning
pale and being the second one to reach Marcel's side. Lupa
had turned him over onto his back and undone his collar, but
it was too late. Georges slapped the corpse several times,
saying "Marcel!" over and over in a scolding tone, then looked
over to me as Lupa finally stopped him.

"What happened?" he asked.

Fritz came to the door as I stood to cross the room, and I
told him to take the car to town and get the police. Paul and
Henri stood where they had been sitting and watched in
stunned silence. I walked to where Marcel lay and felt for his
pulse. There was none.

"Get back! Get away!" I yelled at Lupa and Georges. Paul

had gone out to the hall for his coat, and he returned, placing it over Marcel's head. Georges limped back and forth across the room, hands thrust deep in his pockets. Tania had stopped crying and stood by the settee. Everything began moving at normal speed again, and everyone began talking at once. I went back to Tania and sat next to her, watching the others. Finally Lupa, who had been sitting, stood again and bellowed out "Silence!" and we obeyed. "Let us sit," he said, "and wait for the police."

"Who are you to tell us what to do?" demanded Henri, who seemed quite shaken. Georges, standing next to him, put his arm around his shoulder. Paul sat alone by the fire, looking at the flames.

4

I had supposed that Jacques Magiot, an old acquaintance of mine and the chief of police, would have come out for the investigation, but he sent a young inspector and two gendarmes, who made it clear that their chief's appearance was by no means necessary for the gathering of evidence. The *flics* stationed themselves by the door while the inspector walked around inspecting. He leaned down and sniffed the rug where the beer had spilled.

"Prussic acid," he said.

"Some form of cyanide, at any rate," I answered.

He nodded. "Are you familiar with poisons?"

"Oh come. The almond smell is distinctive."

He noted something in his book.

The others stood about nervously. The inspector spent a

bit of time looking at a spiderweblike impression on the coffee table and after a series of "ahem's" said that he'd like to question each of us separately.

"But before I do, I will say that while you are all free to move about in town, no one is to leave Valence for any period of time without checking with the authorities."

"But I don't live in Valence," said Paul. "I'm from St. Etienne."

"In that case, monsieur, we will escort you to your home by way of the St. Etienne constabulatory, and you will report to them."

While we waited to be called to the kitchen for questioning, Tania and I sat without a word on the divan, her arm linked into mine. She seemed too calm, almost to the point of breaking, as though she were under some unbearable pressure. Undoubtedly this local tragedy had turned her thoughts to her sons at the front.

The inspector first called Lupa, then Georges, Paul, Henri, Tania, and Fritz. The first four were led to the back door and excused, while Tania and Fritz waited in the kitchen after their questioning. The inspector interrogated me in the front room.

"M. Magiot sends his compliments."

I nodded.

"I've made no arrests. Have you any suspicions?"

"No."

"I'm inclined to think of suicide. He was your close friend, was he not? Had he been unduly depressed?"

It went on in that vein for several minutes. I had no information for him, and he had formed no suspicions himself. He thought it odd that so few of my guests had been French, and asked me about it.

I shrugged. "They are my friends."

Finally, a little after midnight, they left. Tania and Fritz came back to join me, and we sat drinking brandy for a time, pensive. The undertaker had come earlier, and my thoughts went back to Marcel's body being removed. I closed my eyes and tried to imagine how he had been only that morning, but I could not. Perhaps it was better that way. I couldn't think of him as a dead man yet. He was the friend of my childhood, and he was gone.

Tania and I went up to bed, leaving the room empty save for Fritz, who sat at the edge of one of the coffee tables, fists clenched and eyes glassy.

I awoke while it was still dark and silently got up. The house was oppressive. I needed to get away for a time.

Two days before, the Rue St. Philip had been warming to a new day as I had walked down it to meet Lupa for the first time. Now, at four-thirty in the morning, with a light rain falling—still falling, I should say—it gave no hint that it could ever be a pleasant street. The cobblestones were slick and too widely spaced, and twice I nearly fell. It wasn't cold, but the wet darkness kept me shivering.

I'd taken the bottle of cognac and headed for La Couronne, planning to see Lupa in the morning, resolving to enlist his aid. It was not professional. It was not even...

That didn't matter. I had to do something about my friend's death. At that moment, I wasn't a professional, and I didn't care.

The tables at La Couronne were chained in place, but the chairs had been moved inside for the night, so I pulled up an empty fruit crate and sat by the restaurant's front door, leaning back against the building. With my coat, I performed the futile gesture of wiping the beaded drops from the table, though it was still raining. There was a small gas light from within, and its slight glare fell across the table. The rain was so fine that it seemed to hang in the air. There was no wind.

I hadn't been seated more than a minute when the door behind me opened and I found myself facing Lupa.

"M. Giraud, would you care to come inside where it's dry?"

I noticed that I was, indeed, very wet, and got up and followed him into the bar. He sat on a stool and looked at me without a word until I spoke.

"I'm surprised to find you awake," I said.

"I was thinking about your friend."

"Yes. I wanted to speak to you about it."

"I don't understand," he said, standing and going around the bar. He poured himself a beer.

"I think you do."

He took a long draught. "Come downstairs," he said finally. He opened the door to the kitchen, and we descended.

"May I take your coat?" he asked. "I'm sorry, sir, but I neglect my manners. I am on edge. Come, let me take your coat. Do sit down."

We'd entered another room behind the kitchen. It was warmly lit and pleasant. Three of the walls were covered with tapestries of a cheap variety, and there were several bookshelves and assorted stuffed chairs. I took one of them.

"I live here," he explained. "You are now my guest. Would you care for some heated milk? Coffee?"

I looked carefully at this man who had been changed so completely by the act of my coming into his living quarters. He went into some other rooms to deposit the coat, then back to the kitchen, evidently to prepare the milk. For nearly a quarter of an hour I sat while he moved back and forth, bringing first the milk, then a pair of pyjamas that he insisted I change into, though they were much too large, then a warm housecoat in which I wrapped myself. He stoked the fire, and before long we were sitting comfortably in silence.

"Now," he said after a time, "what is it that you think I understand?"

I smiled. "I am not a fool, M. Lupa. I am older than you, and perhaps not as naturally gifted, but I have been in my business—perhaps I should say 'our' business—for over twenty years, and I have learned a few things. My efforts have been checked and checked again since coming to Valence, and I feel that yours have been likewise. I think we should work together."

"Indeed," he said. "I didn't know you'd worked as a chef." Suddenly he chuckled. "Of course, I jest. I thought it would be necessary that we work together, but I wanted to be sure of you, and certain of your superiors were less than rapturous in their recommendations."

I bridled somewhat and spoke in clipped tones. "You may be sure of me."

"I know that. I have been satisfied. But have you? Can you be sure of me?"

My head was swimming with cognac and fatigue, and yet I immediately perceived the import of the question. Here, indeed, was a Rubicon of sorts, and I must either cast my die with this man or count him as an enemy. There was, there could be, no middle ground.

And what, in fact, did I know of him beyond the briefs, the heresay, the professional reports that—and no one knew this as well as I—often hid as much as they revealed?

He was an agent. Of that there was no doubt. I was reasonably sure that he didn't work for the Germans, but could I be as certain that he was committed, as I was, to the interests of France? Before hostilities had erupted, Europe had been a checkerboard of conflicting states, and even now, with the combatants clearly defined, only a fool would suppose that the goals of England, for example, everywhere coincided with those of France. Where did Lupa stand?

I felt his eyes boring into my own as his question hung in the room, and yet he didn't seem inclined to press. Could I be sure of him?

The answer, of course, had to be no. We were both agents at war, trained to trust no one. Hadn't Lupa been sitting in

Marcel's seat just before he'd been poisoned? But then another thought occurred to me: it really wasn't my decision to make. I'd been ordered to find and work with Lupa. I didn't have to trust or respect my superiors, but as a soldier I had to obey them.

And there was another point: I had already revealed myself to the younger man. If he was not to be trusted, then my usefulness here in Valence was at an end. Now my own vulnerability, here in Lupa's quarters, could become my own best test of his credibility. Simply put, if I were alive in the morning, he would have proven himself worthy of my confidence. It may not have been the most professional of solutions, but in my wearied state it made a great deal of sense.

One final consideration, even more unprofessional, forced itself into my consciousness. With Marcel dead, perhaps I simply needed to trust someone to fill the hole he had left. With more instinct than reason, I felt Lupa to be the man for that role.

"I have to believe in you," I said at last. "I have no choice."

He sipped at his beer and stared into the fire. Quite some time passed. "I suspect everyone," he said finally.

A wave of regret over the loss of my friend passed over me. "Please," I said. "I need your help." He started to blur before me as fatigue set in. I put my hand over my eyes and felt his come to rest on my shoulder.

"Come," he said, "we'll talk in the morning."

He took me back to his quarters, down a hall that seemed to be a dead end. He put down a mattress on the floor and brought a thick blanket for it.

"Let us be careful," he said almost gently. We were by now speaking in the familiar. "We're going to be needing each other." I lay down and blew out the candle beside me. He retreated a few steps, then stopped. "Do you mind if I call you Jules?"

"No."

"Satisfactory." Another pause. "I am very sorry."

I slept for seven hours. When I woke up, my clothes had been sent out and already returned, so I dressed and walked back out to the kitchen. No one was there. I went outside and found Lupa on the sidewalk finishing his beer. It was still drizzling, but the awning had been pulled.

"Did you sleep well?" he asked.

I felt miserable, so I merely grunted. He ordered me a *petite calva;* and I drank it off quickly.

"Have you been awake long?" I asked.

"Since eight o'clock." I must have looked at him in disbelief, for he continued, "A schedule that may be whimsically broken is no schedule at all. In the end the logical order one tries to impose on one's life is sacrificed to quotidian cares. Even this beer," he said, motioning to the brew, "though it doesn't compare to yours, helps in its way to re-establish the order that last night destroyed."

I thought he was being peevish, so I said nothing. He looked at me and smiled, emptying his glass. "Come with me, Jules. I have an appointment."

We went back down to his quarters, which seemed smaller than they had been in the early morning, or even a half hour before. The hall I'd slept in was off to the left of the sitting room, but we crossed over to a door at the right and into a rather large office. The right-hand wall was covered with pots and pans, costly copper and cast iron, while the left sported a picture of Dreyfus and, somewhat incongruously, a bull's ear. Behind the desk was another of the cheap tapestries that he used to cover the bare rock wall. His entire quarters seemed to be a type of bunker—certainly nothing like the typical cellar one finds around here.

He walked to the corner nearest the bull's ear—a memento

from Spain, I later learned—and lifted away the tapestry, showing a large hole opening into blackness, into which he stepped, motioning for me to follow. He lit a tallow and we moved through a narrow, high cave for several hundred meters. So this was where he disappeared to in the afternoons. I wondered where the cave would come out.

"Handy having all the limestone around here," he said. "It took comparatively little work to finish this passage after I arrived here."

I found that difficult to believe, though I knew that some of the natural caves in the region extended for incredible distances. In the end, the cave proved to be nearly a kilometer in length, and I was totally unprepared for where it abutted. Lupa pulled aside another bit of rug and stepped into a cellar of amazing fragrance.

"Where are we?" I asked. The smell alone had nearly driven away my headache.

He seemed almost playful as he leaned back against a waist-high bench. He held the candle out behind him, and I could make out rows and rows of flowers. He breathed deeply.

"Marvelous," he said. "It always affects me."

Then quickly he straightened up again and moved to a door, which led to a stairway, which in turn opened into a well-lighted planting room. There was a partition in front of the door, and we waited behind it while Lupa peeked out to see who was in the shop. When he was satisfied, we walked out. A woman, about thirty, with dark hair and features, stood talking with a man whose back was toward us as we approached. Lupa went up to the woman, kissed her on the cheek, and said something to her in a language I didn't understand—and I speak five languages. She disappeared to where we'd been.

"Watkins."

"Hello."

The two men embraced and began speaking in English.

"Where have you sent Anna?" asked the stranger.

"She forgot to turn on the cellar lights again. The plants will surely die. I'm glad you're here. We've had problems."

"I've heard already. Routier's been killed. No clues. You were there. Who did it?"

The man was in his twenties and would have looked perfectly nondescript except for the great swelling in his left cheek. His hair was short and brown, his suit common, and he wore no tie. Occasionally he chewed at his cheek.

"I haven't much of an idea," said Lupa. "It could have been any of us. Oh, excuse me, this is Jules Giraud. Joseph Watkins."

We shook hands as the woman returned.

"Look at his cheek, will you?" she said. "Those damned olives again."

Watkins grinned crookedly. "Addicted," he said. "Can't get enough of the blasted things."

"He's been horrible all morning," said the woman. "Eating so many of them he can't talk, spitting the pits wherever he happens to be. I should have tossed him out long ago. If he wasn't so..." she smiled and touched his arm. He moved aside. "Hello," she said, crossing to me, "my name is Anna Dubrov. I've seen you before in town."

I nodded. "Jules Giraud."

Lupa suggested we go to the back of the shop. On the way, Watkins leaned over one of the potted plants and straightened up again without the swelling in his cheek. He was grinning broadly.

"Anyone care for an olive?" he asked, taking ten or fifteen from his coat pocket. When no one responded, he deposited the entire handful into his mouth.

Lupa stood with an arm around Anna, waiting for this frivolous Englishman to finish chewing. When the pits had been stuffed into his cheek, Lupa began.

"Any news?"

"Yes, and specific." Once he started talking, he was entirely businesslike. Perhaps he wasn't as frivolous as he seemed.

"Continue."

"Well, naturally you're here on your own affairs, something about assassinations and so forth, but I thought..."

"You can drop that," said Lupa. "M. Giraud, as you know, is an agent of the French, and he is now in our confidence." He turned to me, continuing, "I am a free operative working for the English government. I know all this has been denied time and again in your inquiries about me. You know how that is. My uncle is a nonambulatory genius whom I detest, but he is probably the most important man in England, and we share some views during wartime."

"So you work for England?"

"For the time being, yes, but I direct my own inquiries."

"By the way," said Watkins, "Altamont says..."

"That will do," Lupa said abruptly. "Let us get on with your information."

"Yes, well, um..." He fumbled a moment, then leaned over and spit out the pits. "We've got information that he is not here for assassination. You're aware of the arms and munitions factory at St. Etienne?"

Lupa's gaze was withering.

Watkins pressed on. "It's going to be blown."

I found myself smiling. "How do you know?"

"One of the boys flushed a Kraut spy and persuaded him to drop a few tidbits, and this was one of them. Unfortunately, our man brought some friends. They all got a bit carried away during the interrogation, and the Kraut died before he could be of much more use."

Lupa looked at me. "And they say that we are fighting the barbarians." To Watkins: "Did you get any descriptions, anything definite?"

"Not of your man, no. But there was something."

"What was that?"

"It's to be an inside job."

I laughed, and the man looked at me angrily.

"What's funny, mate?"

"I'm sorry," I said, "but it would have to be. Have you seen the place? It's guarded rather completely."

Lupa was absently running his fingers through some dirt in a pot next to him. He seemed lethargically calm until he spoke, at which time he fired his questions at the other man.

"Where was he caught?"

"Marseilles. Usual narcotics stuff. He was delivering to their man in St. Etienne."

"Why didn't the fools let him deliver?"

"I think you've answered your own question. The fool—that is, our man—wanted to make sure he didn't escape. They knew something big was going on in this area. He wanted to get a piece of it."

"And lose the pie in the bargain." Lupa was annoyed, and I could see why.

"One other thing bothers me," Watkins said.

"What's that?"

"I think he *is* here to assassinate. That is patently a part of it. Remember, we have had—what is it now?—three deaths of operatives in the past year. It's just a hypothesis, but it is corroborated by the lack of any other overt activity until he moves. That's all. Of course, no clues. But the man must sooner or later make a mistake. He must."

He shrugged and reached into his pocket for some more olives. Someone walked into the store and Anna went to the front. Lupa pulled up a stool and sat down. He seemed completely engrossed in the plant beside him. Suddenly he looked up and spoke.

"I hope you're right. Because if he is only here to blow the factory, then when the job is done, he'll disappear. Whereas if he is here for a dual purpose, one job may give us the clue to the other."

66 *JOHN T. LESCROART*

"You think he's the man who killed Routier?" asked Watkins.

"Do you think he isn't?"

"Then he must have been..."

"Precisely," Lupa said, "he must have been among our gathering last night."

I started to object. After all, everyone who had been there was a friend. But even as I began my defense, I realized that there was no other conclusion.

"That's good," Watkins said. "It narrows the field considerably."

"Yes," Lupa agreed. "Yes, it does."

He got up and beckoned me to follow him. He paused at the screen to the back door. "Joseph, you'll have to go to St. Etienne."

Anna turned around to wave goodbye, and we proceeded back through the cellar, which was now brightly lit and stunning in color as well as fragrance. Another walk through the tunnel, and we reappeared in Lupa's rooms.

I sat across from him. The weight of my friend's death had begun to settle on me again. I must have looked tired.

"What are your ideas?" Lupa had gone to an oversize, overstuffed chair. "I'd like a beer," he said, but he didn't get up.

"I'd like some sleep," I said. We spoke in English.

"I'd say you need it. But first, what do you think of St. Etienne and our list of suspects?"

"That's been bothering me," I said. "I mean the fact that it looks like the man we're after is a friend of mine. Going on that assumption, everyone has a plausible opportunity, but..." I stopped.

He grunted. "It begins to look that way."

"More than you know," I said.

I got up, walked out to the kitchen and up the stairs, ordered two beers at the bar, and returned. He nodded graciously when I handed him a bottle, and took a long drink.

"I detest drinking beer from a bottle, but what can one do?" He drank again. "More than I know?"

"List our suspects," I said. "Paul Anser lives in St. Etienne. Georges Lavoie delivers there, as does Henri Pulis—I would assume even to the arsenal itself. Georges with his first-aid supplies and Henri, of course, with his food. It's one of those new-fangled buildings where the workers have their own cafeteria and medical facility. I've heard Tania talk about it."

"Tania?"

"That's the worst part."

He finished his beer and waited.

"One of Tania's oldest acquaintances, through her husband, who was a French officer... Anyway, one of their friends was Maurice Ponty, who happens to be the director of the St. Etienne arms factory. She still sees him about once a month."

Lupa leaned back in his chair and sighed deeply. "That's everyone."

"Except Fritz."

"No, not except Fritz."

"You have something on him," I asked, "some connection?"

Lupa shook his head. "I was loathe to consider him because of his cooking. He is so *sympathetique*. Still, that is a flaw in my own method."

"But you just said you have nothing on him."

"Nothing definite, Jules, but certainly something. It stretches the bounds of coincidence that every one of your guests has some foreign connection. Until I have satisfied myself with Fritz's references in Germany before the war began, I have to include him among the suspects. I have a man working on it now."

"But what possible... ?" I began.

"Jules, please. I must suspect everyone."

"Even me?"

He was young. A look of ineffable sadness crossed his countenance. "I'm afraid, my new friend, even you."

I stood up. "The beer is terrible, but it isn't that. I must be getting on home. Would you like me to have Fritz send up a case of my beer, if it wouldn't spook you?"

"That would be excellent," he said, lifting the corners of his mouth in what perhaps he thought was a broad smile.

"Meanwhile, I'll get some sleep and then try and contact everyone and see what I can find."

Lupa seemed to consider something, then stopped me from leaving by raising his hand. "Jules," he said, "a small point, but in English the word 'contact' should never be used as a verb."

"*Au revoir,*" I replied with dignity, then turned on my heels, left him, and began walking home through the gray and dismal afternoon.

Stones crunched noisily under my feet as I trudged homeward; the sound a somber coda to the theme playing over and over in my mind. Lupa had said, "I must suspect everyone," and he was right. I walked slowly, hands deep in my pockets, head down.

Everyone...

I thought of the word as a sledgehammer pounding into the wall of reluctance I had built against suspicion of my friends. And they had been my friends, every one of them. Now, until this was all over, they would not be friends, and they might never be again.

I remembered how it had all begun, with Paul Anser. It had been in Paris around 1911. What had he been doing there? Ah yes, publishing something. He did actually publish poetry. I had two or three of his bound collections and even an autographed manuscript at the house. There had been a party, I recall, with lots of young men from London taking the

Grand Tour, as well as several charming young women. I had the feeling that I'd been asked to chaperone, but that suited me. The crowd was lively and intelligent, a far cry from the stultifying soirees held by the wives of military men to further their husbands' careers.

Paul had been the entertainment, or part of it, and he was well received. Afterward, though, when most of the younger set had paired off, I had seen him standing alone, looking rather at sea, and I took pity on him. His command of French then was not so good as it has become, and we spoke English, discovering to our mutual delight that we were neighbors. When he had returned to Valence several weeks later, he had called on me while Marcel had been visiting, and we'd had such a good time drinking beer and—significantly?—talking politics that we all decided to make a regular event of it.

So it had been Paul, Marcel, and me from the start. Seen from a certain perspective, and one that I had truthfully never considered until this moment, it had been, or could have been, a most fertile field for espionage. Back in the beginning, we'd all shared the common confidences of new-found friends. Had it all been masterful grilling on Paul's part?

I thought back. I had aired my disagreements over policy rather freely. Marcel had done the same. To the extent that Paul had been fascinated, hanging on our words, we had felt flattered, viewing him with friendly condescension. Those naive, neutral, isolationist Americans, we had thought. Now I bitterly recast the litany in my mind: we naive, romantic, gullible French!

Dark rain clouds scudded against the overcast sky. I had been wandering, lost in contemplation. Though Valence wasn't a particularly large city, I found myself in an unknown neighborhood as a light drizzle began to fall. Ancient houses leaned threateningly over narrow stone streets. I considered turning around, trying to retrace my route, but since I'd been paying no attention whatever, I realized that I was truly lost.

Turning back wouldn't help. There was nothing to do but continue walking, hoping I would stumble upon some familiar landmark.

Everyone...

Henri had been the next. It had come about naturally enough, since I bought my beer-making supplies from his shop. I remember the first time we'd gotten into a discussion of technique. He had a particularly dependable supplier of excellent German hops. German hops! His interest was so genuine, his personality so forthright, that I had spontaneously decided to ask him around.

And he became the most regular of the guests. His attendance was never in doubt, which, now that I thought of it, was provocative. With a wife and a large family as well as a prospering business, he might have been expected to have the most demands on his time. Instead, our weekly gatherings were obviously a matter of great priority to him.

Why, just the past night he'd left his wife in the middle of a disagreement, as Lupa had pointed out. Were our beer meetings more important to him than his domestic harmony? And if they were, why?

Again I reflected on his bluff exterior—a happy, life-loving Greek. And the more I thought on it, the more incongruous were his business successes and his easy camaraderie with our varied and rather highbrow group.

A dead-end street brought me up short. I was just as content to be lost—the physical disorientation matched my mental turmoil. I was losing faith in the world I lived in—a world where my friends were not as they seemed, where love and trust might be bargaining chips, and duplicity the coin of the realm.

Everyone...

I could not have met Georges more innocuously. Late last summer, just after I'd come down here, I was returning from a bit of business in St. Etienne in my motor car when I came upon a well-dressed limping figure hitchhiking on the roadway. New to the area, Georges had miscalculated the distances between a few of his sales calls in St. Etienne and so had missed his train back to Valence. During the drive, we struck up a fascinating discussion on the question of reincarnation, and I sensed that he would fit in perfectly among my beer guests. And so it had proved.

And yet there were coincidences that a mind more suspicious than my own might not have overlooked. That first Wednesday meeting with Georges in attendance was also Marcel's first day back in the area. In other words, it was within two weeks of our first operative's death. And that of course meant that Georges's arrival in Valence occurred within days of that "accident." Further, of all of our number, he had the least history. I had known of, or had references to account for, each of my other friends, each of the other suspects.

Finally, and more subjectively, I have had a great deal of experience with members of my profession, and if there can be said to be a "type" of mind in the field, Georges's most neatly fit that category—heavily reliant on facts, possessed of enough originality to deduce from those facts (Marcel's glaring flaw and Lupa's forte), plus a certain glibness, a way of getting by on the surface of events while chaos reigns on the operative level.

The psychological babble was fine in its place, and yet the fact remained that Georges had not even been in the same room when Marcel had taken his last draught. And no service in the world would hire a man with Georges's limp—it was simply unheard of.

A recognizable square loomed ahead of me in the drizzle, and I found myself suddenly almost too dispirited to keep moving toward it. What was the point of going home? What, indeed, was home? Another hollow concept such as loyalty, duty, honor—all fine words to fight and die over, but nothing to take too seriously.

But the old discipline directed my footsteps just as my training led my thoughts back to the issue. The stakes here were nothing less than survival, and sentiment must be viewed only as a dangerous luxury, an enemy as deadly as any I would ever face.

Everyone...

How could Fritz have lived in my house for a year without causing me a moment of suspicion? And yet who was more ideally suited to keep tabs on my movements and report on them? No one had had a better opportunity to place poison in Marcel's bottle, except of course Lupa, who had been sitting in that seat. But my trust in Lupa had proven itself well grounded. Or had it? Perhaps he'd kept me alive last night for another, future purpose. Perhaps in some other game, I was a bishop and Marcel a quickly expendable pawn— perhaps and maybe and again perhaps. My mind was beginning to reel with uncertainties, with possibilities.

Everyone...

And even Tania...

No! Not Tania! Not the only woman I had ever loved. It was unthinkable. Even if it killed me, I would not suspect her. I shook my head, trying as best I could to purge the poisonous thought...

...and looked up to find myself in the middle of the square, still confused and lonelier than I had ever felt before.

The rain became fierce, and again I found myself soaked. In no mood to continue an already disagreeable walk, I hired a carriage back to my home. Fritz greeted me at the door with undisguised concern, tempered with reproval.

"Are you well, sir?"

"Damn it, Fritz, no. No, I'm not well. I'm drenched, my clothes are ruined for the second time, I'm tired, and my oldest friend has been murdered in my house. No, I'm not well at all."

He stood back and silently took my clothes.

"I'm sorry to snap," I said, "but it has been a trying time."

"Monsieur Lupa came by this morning and told me you were in good hands. Madame Chessal went home after breakfast. Would you like some tea or brandy?"

He handed me my robe, and I went into the front room to sit before the fire, where I brooded for a while about my age until Fritz came back with tea laced with brandy. After one cup I fell off to sleep.

Fritz woke me again when it was already dark, served me a small meal of coddled eggs with sherry and black butter, and suggested I retire, which I did.

5

Ironically, but predictably, the sun blazed forth on Friday morning for Marcel's funeral, and found me well rested. Fritz always rose at dawn and, when the weather permitted, breakfasted by himself in the arbor. Since I was rarely awake by then, he justly considered this his time, and I was loathe to disturb him, so I poured myself a cup of espresso before walking out. I was ashamed of myself for the way I'd acted the day before. These days at home had weakened me. I resolved to shake myself out of this softness.

I walked to the arbor in my robe and bare feet, enjoying the feel of the wet grass. Fritz sat on a cushion that he'd brought out for the stone bench, eating a brioche with some ripe brie and drinking his coffee. Already, at seven o'clock, the chill had gone from the air. The house and arbor had a striking, newly washed quality. A slight mist rose from the shingles of the roof.

"Good morning, Fritz. Don't get up. No muffins for me. I'll just be having coffee in the mornings for a while."

We sat for a while without speaking. The stream murmured peacefully. At such a time it was hard to imagine the trenches, the carnage, a Europe—perhaps soon a world—at war. Yet it would be fatal to be lulled, to allow oneself to forget.

Fritz pulled me from my reverie after he'd drained his cup. "You're going to the funeral?"

"Yes, of course."

"Madame Chessal, then, asks if you'll pick her up on the way."

In a half-hour, I had dressed and gone to the old servants' quarters where I kept my automobile, a Ford from America that I'd been allowed to keep after mobilization, though there'd been a substantial and very local "tax" for the privilege. The car started without any problem, and within minutes I pulled up to Tania's house. She sat out on the front patio of the long, light blue structure, nibbling halfheartedly at her croissant.

"Good morning," I said.

She stood quickly and came over to embrace me. She looked tired.

"But you," she said, "where did you go that M. Lupa wound up taking care of you? Are you all right?"

I patted her shoulder. "I'm fine. I think I just needed to forget, or perhaps to remember. At any rate, to lay Marcel to rest. I'm perfectly well now. Come, are you ready? You don't look as though you've had such a wonderful night yourself."

She took my arm, leaning a fragrant head for a moment against my shoulder. She sighed. "Sometimes we're so alike it's frightening. I couldn't stop thinking about poor Marcel.

Last night I'm afraid I drank rather too much wine. Danielle had to put me to bed."

"Fritz did the same for me."

We got into the car and drove to the cemetery. The service wasn't due to begin until ten o'clock, so we had nearly two hours to walk through the surrounding countryside and compose ourselves. I decided that my suspicions about Tania on the day before had been ridiculous, but resolved not to say anything unnecessary to anyone until this mess had been cleared up.

When we finally walked down to the cemetery proper, Georges and Paul had arrived. Paul looked especially out of place in a dark suit. In the time that I'd known him, I couldn't ever recall having seen him dressed even semiformally before. We joined them by the gate.

Gradually, some other of Marcel's friends and relatives began to appear, and the four of us who had been in the room that night found ourselves effectively ostracized. Henri and his wife arrived among a small group who left them immediately after they'd passed the gate. Madame Pulis, whom I'd never met, was weeping, and Tania walked over to comfort her. Henri joined the rest of us.

After a few moments of uncomfortable small talk, we walked over to the grave. Marcel's parents had died long ago, and he hadn't been married. I had probably been his closest friend, and yet the others around the grave treated all of us as though we'd been his enemies. We stood in a knot while the usual forms were followed and, when the body had been lowered, were the first to turn and go. Madame Pulis had been constantly crying throughout.

Georges walked crookedly next to me. "Rather ugly, wasn't it?"

"Yes," I said, "but I don't suppose you can blame them."

Gathered around my car, we stopped to talk. Tania packed

Madame Pulis into their carriage and walked pensively back.

"I can't understand those people," she said. "Henri, your wife..." She stopped.

"I know, I know. I suppose I shouldn't've brought her along. She's so emotional. She was fine until we met that other group. They asked if I'd been there Wednesday and acted as if... well, you know. And she's very sensitive to that sort of thing. You'd think one of us killed him, the way they were acting."

Paul was seated on the running board, his tie now off, his coat across his legs. "It appears," he said, "that one of us did."

"Well, I didn't," stormed Henri. "I goddamn well didn't!"

"I didn't say you did, Henri. Calm down. But it isn't unreasonable to assume that one of us planted that poison now, is it? You might as easily assume that I did it."

I looked sharply at him.

Georges spoke up. "Have the police mentioned to any of you their suspicions? Motives, hints, clues?"

Everyone said no.

"The point is, they mentioned to me... well, we shouldn't go around picking each other to pieces. They mentioned that it seemed to them to be at least as good a bet that it was suicide."

"That's absurd," I said. "I'd been with him most of the day. He hadn't been depressed. In fact, he'd been looking forward to the summer."

"Well, the alternative, of course," said Paul, standing up, "is that one of us did it."

"Again, not necessarily," said Georges.

"What do you mean?"

"Not necessarily one of us. One of 'us' isn't here."

"Lupa!" said Henri.

"It does seem strange he didn't come," said Tania, "though some people simply cannot abide funerals."

Paul laughed. "No one likes funerals."

"My wife does." Henri shook his head, and we all laughed as the tension broke. "Speaking of..." he smiled at all of us and began to walk to the carriage. Tania called after him and asked if she might go with him, since I'd told her that I had business in St. Etienne.

The three of us remaining watched them move off slowly, and I asked Paul if he needed a lift. Georges said he had some deliveries to make at St. Etienne and would I mind if he accompanied us? Since he had to pick up his supplies, we all agreed to meet later in the afternoon, and I drove off alone toward La Couronne. On the way, I remembered the beer I'd promised Lupa and detoured back by way of my home.

Chez moi, I changed into something more comfortable and asked Fritz if he'd mind arranging the delivery of several cases of the beer to Lupa. Since it was lunchtime, Fritz insisted I stay and have something to eat, and he quickly prepared a small plate of ham croquettes, fresh bread, and a delicious paté made, he said, from the liver of a wild hare. Since he didn't hunt, I had reason to doubt him, though one of the neighborhood boys might have come around with his catch. Still, wild hare or not, it was excellent. I had one of my own beers to overcome my lurking fear about them, and during the first few sips, Fritz looked at me with real anxiety. I smiled.

"They don't produce cyanide of themselves," I said.

He didn't think that at all funny and crossed back into the house, where he could eat in his cool and shaded kitchen, washing everything down with his daily *demi-boteille* of uncomplicated wine.

I decided it would be a waste of time to see Lupa before I'd been to St. Etienne, and so found myself for the second time that day with some spare time on my hands. I walked slowly up the stairs to my room and reached into the false bottom of my lower left-hand drawer, taking out my pistol.

It was an older but nevertheless effective weapon, excellent for close quarters and concealment. I don't know why I'd stopped wearing it when I'd returned home this last time. That had been foolish. It was a Derringer; its tiny butt over-laid with carved ivory. For all its beauty, it was a terribly powerful weapon—the same gun, though of course an earlier model, had been used to assassinate the American President Lincoln. I carried it in a special holster that I wore under my shirt. Up in my room, I began to clean and oil its few moving parts, so that by the time I left the house, I felt finally prepared for the work I might have to do.

It was still early for our rendezvous—I was meeting my friends at the town fountain at one-thirty—so I stopped by Tania's house to see if she'd come back yet. I found her inside, fuming. Sitting down next to her, I kissed her on the cheek.

"Is something wrong?"

"That man is such a..." She was so angry her voice was shaking. "And I thought you were to be in St. Etienne."

I explained the delay, though her eyes still flashed in anger. "It's not really you, it's him. He's so infuriating, I..."

"Now, now," I continued, "Henri's under a lot of pressure, and..."

"Not Henri. That other man, the one you asked to join us the other night. Lupa!" She stood up and stalked around the room.

"What's he done?"

She stopped and glared across at me. Then suddenly her face softened, and she walked back and kissed me.

"I'm sorry. I'm just very upset. Let's go outside and talk, shall we?"

So we walked out to where she'd eaten earlier that morn-ing. She asked Danielle to bring us some tea, then sat down.

"Now," I said, "what's wrong? What's Lupa done?"

"He's done nothing. He's just so arrogant! He omits doing things, and so superciliously... well, no. I'm being hysterical." She leaned forward and clasped her hands together on the table.

"We were coming back, and as you know, Madame Pulis was very upset by the whole thing, and I was thinking of the callousness of our fellow townspeople. We happened to pass La Couronne on our way, and we saw your M. Lupa sitting under the awning, reading a newspaper and drinking beer. I wanted to scold him—all right, I know I'm too much a mother sometimes—but I did want to. I asked Henri to stop.

"Now," she continued, stopping me before I could interrupt, "don't think I was going to snap at him for missing the funeral. After all, I realized that he hardly knew Marcel. I was just angry. I really don't know why I stopped. Perhaps I was being too whimsical. But nevertheless, I did it. Henri let me out and I walked over and asked if he'd mind if I joined him for a moment. Do you know what he said?"

I smiled. "I'd guess he said something like, 'To be frank with you, yes, I would mind.'"

"Well, of course, he wasn't that rude, but I certainly wasn't made to feel very welcome. After I'd sat down, he carefully ignored me while he finished the column he was reading, drank off his beer, called for the waiter, and ordered two more. Finally, he looked straight at me, and in the sweetest voice asked if I'd like some refreshment.

"I asked for a *café au lait,* and he appeared to shudder slightly as he ordered. I asked him if something was wrong, if he'd rather I left.

"'No,' he said, 'I simply have a prejudice against milk and coffee together in the same cup. Two tolerable beverages by themselves, but together,' and here he turned his mouth up the smallest degree, 'together rather like a man and a woman who individually are pleasant but who fail as a couple.' So we sat in silence until the waiter returned."

Danielle came back with the tea, and we poured.

"I still fail to see, my dear," I said, "what he's done to so upset you. I grant you that he's arrogant and outspoken, but not without a certain charm."

"Well, he's not learned to polish his charms, so they appear cheap."

"All right, now, what else?"

She sipped at her tea. "As soon as the waiter had gone he looked at me in all politeness. 'And now, Madame, what can I do for you? You look at bit tired.'

"'I am a bit tired,' I said. 'One of my dearest friends was buried this morning.'

"'Yes?' he answered, as if to say, 'well, so what?'

"By this time I was so rattled that I'm afraid I rather blurted. 'We were wondering why you hadn't bothered to attend the funeral.'

"'We?'

"'Yes, we. Those of us who'd been at Jules's. We were all there, as was proper. Except, of course, for you.'

"He picked up his beer and drank as though completely dismissing me. I tell you, Jules, I was sorely tempted to slap him. Finally, he put his glass down, told me I was upset, and asked me if I would care to lunch with him. Then he proceeded to speak of his upcoming lunch as though it were all that mattered in the world. I'll try to give you some of the flavor of it."

As she spoke, Tania tried to imitate Lupa's deep baritone: "'Sausages. I was in Spain a few years ago and one day I was standing outside a *tapas* bar, and the smell of fresh sausage pulled me inside. A large, smiling woman, Señora Beran, was grilling ten or more sausages behind the bar, and so I sat down and began talking with her. She said the sausages were prepared by her son, Jerome, and the recipe was his special secret, but I was welcome to try them. As soon as I'd tasted them, I knew them to be superb, and the flavor remained with me until, indeed, I could think of nothing else. Daily,

I went to this same bar and, I'm afraid, badgered that poor woman to distraction. I had to have that recipe. Finally, though, I had to leave and, since that time, have tried unsuccessfully to duplicate that flavor. I've written to Jerome Beran personally, through his mother, but he's been elusive. So now once each month I try again. Not more often because the frustration of failure is bitter indeed. And I dare to call myself a chef. Ha!'"

She looked down into her tea. The forenoon breeze whipped her shining dark hair intermittently into her eyes. She reached out her hand across the table for me to take it. "Can you imagine, Jules? He sat and talked about that sausage as though there were no war, no deaths..." She paused for a moment to control her voice. "Then, when the sausage arrived, he took a bite and immediately removed from his pocket a small notebook and wrote something. 'It's not right,' he said simply. 'I must use less brandy and more fowl.' Thereupon he proceeded to eat every last bit of sausage, pausing at regular intervals to shake his head.

"It was not until he had finished that he addressed himself to me again. 'Now, as to your question, Madame. By the way, are you enjoying the sausage? Excellent wine, even though it's Spanish, don't you think?' Food, food, food. All right, the man's a chef, but really, Jules..."

I patted her hand.

"'Why didn't I attend the funeral?' he finally began. 'There are two reasons. Both, I'm afraid, quite selfish. One, I dislike funerals. A man is a man until his death, after which he becomes mere mineral matter. If one is of a cathartic cast, there may be benefit in public interment, but, even then, the catharsis is misdirected. Death is not tragedy but pathos. Two, lately I've been becoming much too flexible in my schedule, and I decided to end that flexibility.' He looked at me as though he'd explained everything."

"He is rather intractable," I offered.

"I was so upset by this time, I didn't know what to do. He sat looking at me from across that small table, seemingly quite pleased with himself. I wanted to leave, but I wanted to, well, to make him mad, so I stood up and said, 'If I were you I'd be a little more careful. More than one of us believes you killed Marcel,' and I turned to go. He spoke my name then, so abruptly that everyone looked up, and I came back to the table.

"'Let's not be ridiculous,' he said. 'I am an acquaintance of M. Giraud. In fact, I've spoken to him at some length. For now, you are upset, and I suggest you go home and get some rest.'

"With that, he called for a carriage and sent me on my way. What should I think of him, Jules? Is he a friend of yours?"

Of course, Lupa had told her nothing about our real relationship, leaving it to me to make that decision. I'd tried to be honest with Tania as much as possible, though I hadn't told her what I really was. There had been no need. And now, I was reluctant to tell her because I was afraid of her. Afraid that she might not understand or, on the other hand, would understand too well. So I temporized.

"I wouldn't worry about M. Lupa, dear," I said. "I spent the night at his place on Wednesday after my walking took me downtown. He'd come to the gathering only to try my beer, and was genuinely upset at the way things turned out. He'd only met Marcel that afternoon and they had had no disagreements. They seemed to get on quite well. Certainly, he had no reason to kill him."

"But which of us did?" she asked.

I shrugged. "I really don't know. I don't know." I slumped and stared down at the well-kept gravel of her terrace. "I can't believe he killed himself."

"Maybe Henri is right," she said, "with his rumors."

"What are those?"

"He said that he's heard for the past several months that Marcel had something to do with espionage, with the war."

A chill passed through me. "Henri said that? Where did he hear that?"

"I don't know."

"Well, that's absurd. I've known Marcel all my life, and..."

"But what if he was? What if he was, and another of us is, and we don't know, and he was killed by one of his friends to keep... Oh, Jules," she said, "I'm afraid."

I stood up and she rose to embrace me.

"I'm sorry," she said. "I shouldn't be such a baby. It's just with all of this, and the boys away at the front... I just don't know what to make of things."

I kissed her, and suddenly she stiffened against me.

"What's that?" she demanded, putting her hand under my arm where I kept my gun.

I had to tell her. "A pistol, just to be safe."

Her lip quivered. She was going to cry. "Jules, please, don't you get mixed up in this. Please."

"Now, now," I said. "I'm not 'mixed up' in anything. I merely felt a little nervous and decided at least to be in a position to protect myself should any of my friends..." I trailed off.

She buried her face in my shoulder and cried softly. "... any of your friends. Why won't they leave us alone? Oh, poor Marcel." Her voice broke again. She looked up at me pleadingly. "Jules, really, you're not involved? You're not a spy?"

"No," I said, "no, I'm not a spy. I'm a middle-aged man who's getting old and ready to retire with his lover. I don't want anything to threaten that so I carry a gun, but only until we find what happened to Marcel. All I want to do is brew beer and tend my vineyards." I picked up her chin, "and love you."

She smiled bravely.

I kissed her again and stepped back. "I have to go. Georges and Paul will be waiting. I'll pick you up on the way back. We'll stay together tonight."

I watched her walk off into the house, then turned and headed down the stairs to the Ford. The damn thing was, all I really did want to do was brew beer and tend my vineyards and live with Tania. But, then, what if Tania were a spy? No, I wouldn't let myself think that.

It was hot in the car as I turned into the road. I'd have to see Lupa after I'd been to St. Etienne, and I found myself hoping that Fritz would deliver the beer before long. I was as bad as Lupa with his sausages. My rituals were beginning to keep me from the pain of Marcel's death, as a kind of insulation.

But my friend was dead, and when the rituals were over, that would remain, so I drove slowly, thinking of my own best sausage recipe and watching out for potholes.

6

The war was everywhere. If normal life can be said to continue in a town stripped of its young men, then normal life went on. But of course the war touched everyone you knew or met and colored the mood of the entire countryside. Even as the sun shone brightly down on our fountain, where Paul sat with his pants rolled up cooling his feet, the streets were cleared for a convoy of trucks and carriages carrying supplies to the front.

I pulled over and parked across the square, watching the vehicles roll past, then walked over to join my friends. Paul was smoking a cigarette and talking animatedly to Georges. They stopped as I drew nearer, and Paul pulled his feet from the water and rolled down his trousers.

"Ready?"

"Yes."

"Let's go, then."

We helped Georges with his packages. There seemed to be enough gauze for the entire army, but he explained that there was to be a huge shipment to the front with the St. Etienne factory as the central warehousing point. It took several trips but finally we loaded all the bags, and after a *demi* at one of the cafes bordering the square, we left. Paul took particular delight in sitting atop the bundles of gauze. I'd removed the top to the car, and as we drove along he sang off-key but with great enthusiasm. He wanted to forget the funeral as soon as possible.

Finally, when the wind kept blowing his tobacco away before he could roll it, he joined us in the front seat.

"Never had that problem on a horse."

We rode along, then, quickly for a while. The trees passed quickly by on either side of the road. Paul smoked in what he called the "French manner," blowing the smoke out of his mouth and up into his nose. Georges sat against the other door, looking reflectively at the passing scenery.

"Has it occurred to anyone," he asked, finally, "how incredibly inept the police have been about this whole thing? You'd think that it wasn't a possible murder they were investigating but something more in the line of a petty theft."

"Oh, I don't know," said Paul. "I have to register every day at St. Etienne to make sure I don't try to leave the country."

"That's because you're not French. Here I go off on business for the next four or five days, and they've asked me to prepare an itinerary of my stops, but no check-in the towns themselves. If I had killed Marcel, I could be beyond Algeria if I decided to leave. It makes no sense."

"It's the war," I said. "Even forgetting that the heart of the force is gone to fight at the front, for the rest, all of their routines are upset, and without their routines..."

"Well, they might as well be at the front for all the good they do here."

"Now, Georges," said Paul, "I suppose they're doing something, and we just don't know about it. Besides, if you decided to go to Africa, that would be punishment enough for any crime I can think of. What heat!"

We were approaching St. Etienne, and Paul asked to be let out at a crossroads on the outskirts of town.

"I just live about a mile down the road. I mean two kilometers. And I feel like walking. I'll see you all—when?"

"Wednesday?" I ventured. "It would be good to get back to normal." Actually, it would be good to be able to predict where everyone would be at a certain time.

"I don't know if I want to be in that room for a time, though," Paul said. "Why don't we make it somewhere else next week?"

"Fine. I'll get back to you. Is that all right with you, Georges?"

He nodded.

"Okay, then," said Paul, "see you later. *Ciao.*"

With that he turned and started up the road. Georges and I decided to light up cigarettes, and so had not yet driven off when Paul stopped two hundred meters away. A man stepped out from behind one of the trees lining the road and spoke to him. At that distance, I could see nothing descriptive. Since Georges was facing me, he saw nothing; and so without saying anything I engaged the gears and began to move. When I glanced back, both men had gone.

We continued on to St. Etienne, content to remain silent. I was wondering about Paul; in fact, by this time, I was wondering about everyone.

"Do you have time for a drink?" I asked Georges.

"Always."

We stopped at a small, dark bar, and each of us ordered a cognac. We sat near the door, watching over the car and its load.

"What's your business here?" asked Georges.

"Oh, I'm supposed to see some people about a vine graft. In fact, with all this mess about Marcel, I'm afraid I don't feel like doing any kind of business. I was wondering if I could help you in your deliveries. Tania has told me a lot about the factory, or asenal, here. Whatever it is. Her friend Maurice Ponty is the director, and I'd like to see it. Keep my mind from . . . from other things."

"Delighted, Jules! I could use the company. Maybe Ponty could show us around. Normally I only deliver to the gates."

"Oh, you've never been inside?" Somehow I was both relieved and disappointed.

"No. Tight security and all that. Normally Henri and I come down together and leave everything with the attendants."

"Hmm . . ." I said, rather pointlessly.

We finished our drinks and returned to the car. After a few more minutes of driving, we reached our destination.

The St. Etienne Arsenal and Munitions Factory was indeed a large and modern affair. It covered several hundred square meters of land on the eastern edge of the city, bounded by what must have been a tributary of the Rhone that carried away much of the waste. When the day was clear, and the wind from the right direction, you could see the smoke from the stacks as far away as Valence; a thick, sulfurous cloud usually hung over the structure. Brick chimneys to a height of nearly thirty meters had been built to lift the smoke so that it wouldn't settle on the nearby houses. The entire structure was surrounded by a fence of barbed wire and guarded every twenty-five meters or so by troops. The building itself was made of a kind of adobe, which was originally white, but even in the short time since its opening had turned a sickly, dirty yellow.

We went first to the delivery area, where Georges presented his papers and unloaded his supplies. Then we drove to the main gate, parked, and approached the sentry box.

"Yes, what do you want?" said the guard.

"We'd like to visit, if we may," Georges replied.

The guard laughed heartily. "Impossible."

Georges and I looked helplessly at one another, and he began again. "But I've been delivering here since you've opened. We'd just like to look around inside."

The guard stopped laughing and blew on his whistle. Within seconds, four other guards had run up, weapons at the ready. I decided to speak.

"I'd like to see Monsieur Ponty."

At the mention of the director's name, the guards looked at one another indecisively. Finally one of them went into the building. After about ten minutes, which seemed much longer because of the heat and the circumstances, the guard returned with a short, round, cheerful-looking man.

"You asked for me? I am Monsieur Ponty."

"Yes. I am a friend of Tania Chessal. She's spoken so much to me about your operation here. I'd hoped to be privileged with a look for myself. Jules Giraud is my name."

There was a hint of recognition in his eyes, and he nodded to the guards, who started back to their posts.

"And this man?" he asked, indicating Georges.

"Georges Lavoie, monsieur. He has been delivering your medical supplies for some time, and is a personal friend."

He stared for another moment. "Come with me."

We crossed the wide yard of gravel, and I couldn't help noticing the scrutiny with which we were observed from every direction. There were sentries posted at the gates, along the fence, at selected bunkers in the yard, and on the roof. Ponty seemed to notice my interest, and smiled.

He led us through the large glass doors and down a long corridor to his office, the second room on the right. I was surprised to find it so well furnished. There was a bright rug covering the floor, and several prints on the walls, including Van Gogh's "The Field at Arles" which I thought a very strange choice for the director of an arsenal. To the right, behind his desk, were filing cabinets of a light, drab wood; and, to the left, an elegant bar. His desk itself was a flat and large slab of oak which rested on unfinished timbers, although the joints were perfectly matched. It was an efficient office, though not without personality.

We were seated.

"So, you are Jules Giraud. Tania speaks of you often."

I inclined my head slightly. "She's quite impressed with you and this place, you know? Have you known her long?"

"Oh, quite some time. I knew her husband before they were married. A fine man. You knew Jean?"

"Yes, he was my neighbor."

"Ah, yes, yes. Of course."

I didn't wish to speak of Jean Chessal, especially to a friend of his. My conscience was not completely clear regarding him.

"And how is Tania?" he asked.

"Quite well," I said, not entirely truthfully. "She sends her best."

He smiled. "Do ask her to come by soon. She is a welcome guest any time. She doesn't visit nearly enough."

"I will ask her, though I somehow didn't think you solicited visitors here. The guards..."

We all laughed. Then, in a brusque but friendly way, he clapped his hands together and sat up straight.

"Now, what can I do for you?"

"Well, frankly, we decided to come to see you mostly out of curiosity. Monsieur Lavoie, here, had some deliveries to make, and I had other business in town, which I chose to put off. Tania had told me so much about this building, and about yourself, that I thought I'd come by to meet you and to see some of your innovations."

"You did, did you?" There was more than a bit of flint in the mildly humorous gaze.

I raised a hand. "Please stop me if I'm out of line."

"Be assured that I would, monsieur. It is no small matter that you have been allowed to come this far. You're aware of that, of course." It wasn't a question, and he continued. "But then we've carried on this farce long enough. It isn't every day that one meets such a serious rival face to face, is it?"

"I'm afraid I don't completely understand," I said.

"Come, come, Monsieur Giraud. Surely you don't think just anyone can enter this compound. And I do think I'm justified in calling it precisely that. Probably there isn't another man, or men"—here he motioned to Georges—"in France that I would have allowed within these walls without an official reason. 'Just wanted to look over your innovations!' Indeed!" He chuckled at my ludicrous suggestion. "I admit that bringing a visitor along with you, and one with actual business here, is a charming touch that shows real imagination, and I begin to see what Tania is talking about. But let's admit the facts, that you came by here for the same reason that I let you in—plain curiosity, all right—and not about our innovations."

Georges picked up the tenuous threads. "He's found you out, Jules, No doubt of it."

"All right," I said, forcing a grin. I had no choice but to press on, hoping that Ponty would drop some further clue as to what he was talking about. "I'll admit it—I simply had to discover what it was all about."

The director looked suitably downcast. "It's about love."

"Yes," I answered, "it is about love."

"She told you, then, about my proposal?"

"Of course," I said, my stomach sinking since in fact she'd told me no such thing. "Just the other day."

"Yes, I expected she would have. I must admit I never entertained much hope, but I had to try."

Again Georges came to my rescue. "She is a remarkable woman," he said. "Who could blame you?"

Ponty sighed deeply. Then, again clapping his hands softly in what I took to be a characteristic gesture, he regained his businesslike composure. "Well, I am glad to meet you after all. If I have to lose her, it is some comfort to meet the man and realize that he is a gentleman."

I accepted the compliment with a nod, nearly overcome with relief that Tania had turned him down, then distressed anew by the secrets she kept from me. But this was no time to reflect on that. "I'm sorry if my curiosity seems callous," I said. "I had no intention..."

"Please," he said, waving me off, "put the thought from your mind. What could be more natural? But to satisfy your curiosity about me completely, I suppose I should show you our operations here after all, eh? How does the saying go— 'judge a man by his creation'? The St. Etienne arsenal is my 'creation,' Monsieur Giraud. It is the thing of which I am most proud."

At that moment a guard passed in the hall and looked in, prompting Georges to speak up. "Frankly, I'm very impressed with your security."

"Yes," Ponty replied. "I doubt rather strongly that anything save a massive assault could cause us much inconvenience. I might add, we don't envision an assault of that kind around here. Still, considering the kind of work we're doing, we can't be too careful. Come."

We rose and went back out to the corridor. He turned to Georges.

"What is it that you deliver?"

"Medical supplies. Gauze, bandages, no real medicine."

"Ah, yes. Fortunately, we haven't had many accidents. I hope we can keep your deliveries small. Now, then," he stopped in front of the first door we'd passed coming in, "as you know, we make most kinds of arms and munitions supplies here, so really our security amounts to national security. Open that door, Monsieur Giraud."

I stepped up to the heavy door and found it locked.

Ponty squatted down and slid a card under the door, then knocked four times. The door swung open from within onto a small, closetlike enclosure. On either side of the space sat an armed guard. The room was devoid of decoration and contained only a door against the opposite wall. Ponty walked across the tiny area to that door and tried it, but it too was locked. Then he turned and walked back to us, closing the first door behind him.

"The explosives room," he explained. "We change the guards every three hours because the anteroom is so . . . you saw it. With every shift, we change the card-and-knock sequence. I don't mind telling you this because the guards are under orders to shoot to kill anyone who gets them to open the doors by deception. Only myself, my immediate assistant, or the guards' replacements may be admitted into that room. Anyone else will be shot."

I asked soberly. "But you had me try the door."

Ponty laughed. "A perfect way to eliminate my arch-rival, yes? But you see, you were in no danger. Only if you had had my card, knocked four times, and been admitted would you have been shot. I'm sorry if I scared you."

I held up a hand, laughing hollowly. "I don't scare that easily."

He waited for a moment at the door to the explosives room. A janitor pushing a wide broom shuffled his way past us, not so much as lifting his head to acknowledge us. Ponty seemed to be observing him carefully. Clearly the presence of visitors would not be viewed as an excuse to slack off on duties.

"Friendly chap," I ventured.

Ponty shrugged. "Nervous, I guess. Some of 'em are, here." He sighed. "I guess it isn't the easiest thing in the world, working inside what amounts to the biggest bomb in France."

Georges cleared his throat, and Ponty took that as a signal to continue our tour. The next door down the hallway opened into an enormous cacophonous inferno, but Ponty had no hesitancy about gesturing us in. Four huge boilers hissed and steamed against one wall to our right, while two shovel-wielding stevedores fed coal to the burners under them. The room's temperature was staggering.

Like a proud homeowner, Ponty walked us around. The boilers were of heavily reinforced steel, loaded with gauges that screamed under their internal pressures. Lining the back wall of the room was a small mountain of coal being slowly chipped away by the workers. Dozens of arteries—insulated piping—emanated from the heart of the arsenal's power plant.

"What goes on here?" Georges yelled over the din.

Ponty motioned us back outside into the relative cool of the hall. He was beaming. "Impressive, isn't it?"

"Is every room here frightening?" Georges asked.

"That frightened you?"

"It's a vision of hell."

Ponty chuckled. "Well, put like that, I suppose one might say it is, after all."

"It did seem awesomely powerful."

He nodded. "It has to be. We've got power needs here that I can't discuss, but they rival those of many small towns. In effect, we've got our own generator. We've got to be able to control our power, keep it regular, allow no surges. Am I getting too technical?"

"Not at all," Georges said.

"It's rather fascinating," I agreed.

We turned a corner and entered another long and narrow hall. Ponty's words echoed off the bare walls, mingling with the memory of the other room's straining engines. I was beginning to feel the building more as a living thing, and could understand Ponty's nearly paternal pride in its structure as well as his fear for its safety.

"You see," he said, "although much of the work we do here is production line stuff—making ammunition and so on—there is also a great deal of stress-related research and testing. To say nothing of the power needed to keep a place like this heated and lit over three shifts seven days a week. Those boilers never shut down."

Georges seemed to be pondering something. "But compared to the ammunition room, they seemed poorly guarded."

The point seemed to come home to Ponty. "You know, they may be, now that you mention it. But there is so much here that must be guarded full time—explosives are one example, the research rooms are another—and we only do have so many men. I guess we have to draw the line somewhere."

"It seems somehow..." Georges paused, looking for the right word, "less thorough, I suppose."

Ponty stopped before a pair of double doors, which, we would soon discover, led to the development rooms for armored vehicles. But before we entered, he wanted to close the book on this discussion. It probably seemed to him as though we were calling his procedures into question, and he wanted to set the record straight.

"Monsieur Lavoie," he said, "you forget that you are taking this tour with me, the director. The men shoveling coal in that room are soldiers, as are nearly all members of the staff. Perhaps you didn't notice the weapons on their belts?"

Georges shook his head.

"Ah, just so. Anyone entering any room here without authorization does so at tremendous risk to his own life, I assure you."

"And there are always soldiers there?"

"We can never let our power go down. I will tell you frankly, though I can't be too specific, that certain researches we are undertaking, certain chemicals and so on, are held in an extremely precarious balance by electrical currents and constant temperatures among other things. Slight fluctuations can be fatal. No, we take extreme care."

"I'm sure Georges didn't mean to imply any negligence." I tried to calm our host.

"Certainly not," he replied. "I was merely curious."

But Ponty had one more nail to hammer home. "All our rooms are manned at all times. Even my own office, now sitting empty, is guarded. We don't let up our vigilance, ever!"

I was glad I was with Georges, with his cosmopolitan air. He smiled suavely, including us all into his fraternity. "And we are most grateful for that vigilance, sir. The whole country is grateful."

Ponty took obvious satisfaction in the compliment. His eyes darted quickly to me and I nodded, hoping my unspoken affirmation would lessen the sense of rivalry.

Georges continued. "The whole thing is just so amazing to me. I've come here so often to deliver, and I've seen your men loading for large deliveries. The logistics are just too awesome to comprehend. It seems as though every man in France is out there helping load munitions for the front."

Ponty's eyes twinkled. He was obviously somewhat taken with Georges. Often in my career and in my life, I'd noticed that once a person has tapped one emotion in another, a door may be opened to other emotions. Georges had angered Ponty, and the director's response had compromised his natural reserve and professional manner. Once Georges had cooled his anger, the door was open to friendship. We were all, suddenly, members of the same club—men of similar natures caught up in the most serious of endeavors, unable to trust or love or find release from the unbearable tensions of the times.

Ponty smiled warmly now. "I'll let you both in on something, then, since you've been so astute. When we have heavy shipments, everyone helps, even myself. For fifteen, perhaps twenty minutes, we are all pack mules. Except, of course, for the guards at the explosives rooms. They never, ever leave their posts."

Georges returned Ponty's smile. "Your secret is safe with us, eh, Jules?"

"To our graves," I responded.

"And now," Ponty said, opening the double doors, "let me show you..."

Our tour continued for the next hour or so. None of the other rooms, it turned out, were as closely guarded as the explosives room, though security everywhere was tight.

The factory made everything from bullets and bombs to rifles and cannons. The next cavernous room was dedicated to working out the rough edges of a motorized armored car with mounted cannons, which Ponty thought would become a powerful new battlefield weapon. The preliminary sketches and models we saw were impressive, but it seemed to me that they still had a long way to go. Ponty hoped to complete a working model within six months, though, and Georges, after careful consideration, pronounced himself in agreement with that verdict. There were many other research rooms which Ponty could not show us. He apologized for this, and we both assured him we understood completely and had very much enjoyed the look around. Finally Maurice—he was "Maurice" by then—showed us to the door and bade us adieu.

"We don't have visitors very often," he said, "and, as you said, we don't want them, but it's been a pleasure showing you both around." Maurice turned to me. "Jules, I'm glad that you decided to satisfy your curiosity." With that, we shook hands and he disappeared back into the building.

Walking back to the car, Georges and I were thoughtful. It was now dusk. The factories would be closing within the hour, and I wanted to get back home.

"Life is sure full of surprises," Georges remarked, elbowing me slightly.

I said nothing but thought instead of the questions I would have for Tania.

"Very impressive place," Georges said, diplomatically changing the subject. "I wouldn't be too worried about a breach of security if I were Maurice. That anteroom scared me to death, to say nothing of the boilers."

"Yes," I said. "Unless the Germans take St. Etienne—in which case we'll have lost the war anyway—I'd say that factory is safe. Awfully modern building, isn't it?"

"I loved it. I could have stayed all day."

Something was bothering me, so I thought I'd better say it. "Yes, I noticed how acute your interest was. I thought you'd be bored in there, though I was glad you accompanied me."

"Bored? Not at all. Fascinated, truly fascinated. Perhaps I've never mentioned it, Jules, but my initial love was architecture. I studied it for years in school, and only my father's passionate belief that all art was somewhat effete—backed by his promise to withhold any financial aid to myself—persuaded me to enter the dynamic and exciting world of business." He seemed genuinely bitter, the sarcasm heavy.

"I didn't mean..." I began, sorry that I had touched a nerve.

"No. That's all right. People, in the end, do what they truly want to do, I suppose."

We talked on for a few more minutes before I dropped him off at a hotel. As usual, in spite of the large delivery today, he had calls to make for the remainder of the week, the weekend notwithstanding.

"Unfortunately, the need for my products keeps increasing. It may be good for business, but I find it difficult to rejoice in the fact."

"Will you be able to make it by next Wednesday?" I asked.

"I assume so. I'll leave a message if I'm delayed."

"Fine. Until then."

The drive home was long and uneventful. I usually don't like to drive at night, and by the time I had reached the road to Valence, it was completely dark. My headlights flushed a few animals along the way, but otherwise I saw nothing and heard only the sound of engine, which drowned out my soft humming of the "Marseillaise."

7

After dinner—a simple coq au vin and a bottle of beaujolais—Tania and I sat in the kitchen with brandy. The living room still made us nervous, and Fritz said he didn't mind the intrusion. So we sat on wooden chairs across the table from one another. It was a quiet night. The large, stone fireplace crackled from time to time, and Fritz, cleaning up, moved easily about. When he'd finished, he turned down the lamps and left us alone. The room was a montage of pale yellow light and black shadows. Something, probably a mouse, scampered across the floor.

Tania was wearing a light blouse with a tan wraparound skirt that came to a few inches above her ankles. She was beautiful enough to get away with that kind of dress, though it would properly be considered fairly risqué. Her long hair

103

fell across her face, and looking across at her I found it very hard to believe that she was beginning her fifth decade. I got up, came around the table, and kissed her.

"Are you feeling better?" I asked.

"Yes."

"I went to see your friend Ponty today."

Her shoulders stiffened a little. "What were you doing at the arms factory?"

"Georges had to deliver there, and I decided it would be a nice break to put off my appointment today and see this place you've talked about so much. It is a very impressive sight, though I wish they could do something about the smoke."

"I know," she said. "Isn't the smell terrible?"

"Horrible. But I suppose when one works with sulfur, that's impossible to avoid."

We heard Fritz moving about behind us in his room. He usually did exercises and then read a bit before going to bed.

"How did you find Maurice?" she asked.

I described our tour, including the little episode at the door to the explosives room. Tania smiled and said that sounded just like Maurice. We sipped at our brandy, and the silence came back to surround us. There would never be a better time.

"Tania," I began, then stopped, terrified. To me she was the most attractive woman in the world, and to press on now ran the risk of losing her. But I really had no choice—if I couldn't ask, I had already lost her. "Why didn't you tell me about Ponty's proposal?"

Her shoulders sagged slightly as she put her snifter down. "Oh," she said, "he told you about that?"

"It quite hurt me," I said truthfully.

"Oh, Jules, I'm sorry." She reached out across the table and covered my hand. "Maurice and I are only friends."

"Obviously Maurice doesn't feel the same way."

"I know. I was very surprised."

"I don't understand why you wouldn't have told me."

She shrugged, squeezing my hand. "It didn't matter. It had no effect on us. Why did you need to know?"

"Are we operating on a 'need to know' basis now?"

"What does that mean? Of course not. I just didn't think it was so important, or appropriate. And really, Jules, it isn't."

"A marriage proposal isn't important?"

"Not unless I'd have said yes, which I did not."

I covered her hand with my own and stared into her guileless and beautiful face. "I'm afraid I'm uncomfortable with these secrets between us."

She lowered her gaze and her voice. Her words seemed to have been wrung from her against her will, as though the necessity of having to admit it belied its own truth. "There are no secrets between us."

Before I could respond, there was a crashing sound against the front door. I bolted up and ran to see what it had been. Outside, the night was inky black, and I could barely make out even the shadows of trees. Faintly, though, I heard what I took to be several pairs of retreating feet and some high-pitched giggling.

Tania had brought up a lantern and stood behind me. On the ground I could make out a large rock, which I bent over to pick up. There was a paper tied to it, and on the paper a crude drawing of a skull. I turned around and found Tania crying.

"Now, now," I said, "it was simply a group of kids. You know they do this kind of thing often enough. And especially after word spread about Marcel's murder in this house. If you listen you can still hear them giggling. Listen."

And over the quiet fields did come the sound of young voices, muffled and diminishing but still audible.

We moved back inside and stood in the foyer. In spite of my words to Tania, I was shaken. This sort of thing did happen, I suppose, on occasion, but with suspicions already so high, it did my nerves no good. I walked back to the kitchen for another brandy, which I drank much too quickly. Coming back through the dark sitting room, I turned into the stairway and stood transfixed by what I saw.

Tania stood silhouetted against the top of the stairs, holding the lantern in her left hand. Her recent tears still glistened on her face, her hair hung to her shoulders, and she had undone her blouse, which now hung open before her. Very quietly she spoke: "Jules, come to bed. I'm afraid."

Later, I could not sleep. Overcome by the events of the day, ashamed that I had doubted Tania, unnerved by the children's prank, I got up and looked out the window. The only sound was the gurgle of the brook as it flowed through the arbor. A crescent moon had just risen, and it was somehow reassuring. In my mind I went over the details of the St. Etienne arsenal so that I could report the next morning to Lupa. At my desk, I lit the lamp and sketched from memory the general floor plan. That took my mind off my general worries, and by the time I finished, I felt sleepy. I remembered, though, to write Fritz a note to have him wake me early, then I came back to the bed where Tania lay and crawled in beside her.

But just before I dozed off, I thought I heard the sound of a car engine starting, accompanied by indistinguishable voices drifting over the fields, finally fading into the noise of the engine as it roared toward St. Etienne.

8

Tania did not stir when Fritz knocked once discreetly. I rose immediately, tapping once on my bedstead to let him know I was awake. After a fast cup of coffee and several minutes of Fritz's remonstrance over my sagging appetite, I was on my way to Lupa's.

La Couronne hadn't yet opened, but Charles stood behind the bar, dusting, and let me in after only a short wait. Lupa had given instructions that no one was to come to the kitchen without his approval, so I sat at the bar and had another coffee while Charles went to announce me.

He returned and I followed him down the narrow staircase to the kitchen. Lupa sat majestically at the table, clad in a brown silk robe with a yellow monogram, cleaning up the remainder of what had been his breakfast.

"One of the problems with being one's own cook," he began immediately, motioning me to be seated, "is deciding an order of courses that provides variety yet leaves oneself free to enjoy each course without having to tend to the next. These muffins, Jules, have become too cold while waiting for the eggs to set."

I noticed he was having no trouble, however, in finishing off the cooled muffins. The eggs had, by the looks of the plate, long since disappeared. I mentioned this to him.

"Yes, but it's not as enjoyable as it should be, as every meal should be. Every man's life is divided up into eating, sleeping, and miscellaneous. *Omnia vita in tres partes divisa est,* if I might borrow from Caesar. Of their conscious moments, only in their enjoyment of food are all men brothers."

I could think of several other conscious moments that might qualify as universally pleasing, but he was enjoying himself, so I let him expound.

"And here I am, presuming to call myself a cook, a chef. Ha! Jules, I nearly let the coffee boil!"

I shook my head sadly in commiseration. In spite of his petulance, which Tania had found so objectionable, I found him entertaining. He knew as well as anyone, possibly better than anyone, the gravity of our situation, but he wouldn't let himself be bogged down in depression. He was a tonic to my flagging spirits.

"Did you get the beer?" I asked.

"Ah, yes. Thank you. Consistently excellent. Fritz brought it around yesterday."

He pushed back his chair and settled himself more comfortably. After offering me breakfast or coffee, which I declined, he picked up his cup and sipped.

"Madame Chessal came by to see me yesterday."

"Yes, I know. She told me about it."

"She seemed rather upset by my lack of interest in the, ahem, proprieties. I tried to explain to her that worry merely

clouds the intellect, that I meant no slight to Monsieur Routier, that I had been enthusiastic about sausage because I was
talking about sausage, and that enthusiasm is a state of mind
I try to cultivate about many subjects. I'm afraid my explanation fell on deaf ears. She left in rather a huff."

"She was upset about Marcel," I said. "They'd known each
other a long time."

"I understand that. But you understand I didn't want to
discuss Marcel's death with her until I was certain she was
not involved."

"Are you?" I asked hopefully.

"Unfortunately, no."

"You're serious, aren't you?"

"Perfectly, Jules, perfectly."

How could I allay his suspicions when only yesterday I
had harbored them myself? Still, I forced a response. "At the
risk of usurping your methods, do you have anything specific, or is it just a feeling?"

Lupa sipped again at his coffee, smacked his lips with pleasure, then looked levelly at me across his desk. "The questions
I have regarding Madame Chessal's involvement in our inquiries fall into both categories. First, I must confess to a
certain feeling that in a general way she is not being completely forthright, that she is hiding something. It may be
nothing. It may be that she cultivates an aura of mystery.
Many women do, you know, believing that it makes them
interesting. In fact, it creates an impression of a fascinating
personality that is all the more disappointing when the aura
itself is revealed to be a sham." He continued before I could
remonstrate. "I don't say that is the case here. I merely comment on my feeling.

"Specifically, there are several points. My operatives have
stumbled on Madame Chessal many times in and around St.
Etienne. She certainly has ready access to the arsenal there.
As you yourself have pointed out, she has a relationship of

some sort with the director. Secondly, poison is a classic woman's weapon for murder. Additionally, I find it worthy of note that she is the only woman in what would otherwise be a vigorously masculine grouping."

"How is that noteworthy?" I had to cut in. His suspicions of Tania seemed to me to be no more than a general indictment of female human beings, and I told him so.

"It's true. I do have a prejudice there, probably inherited from my father. But I have verified it on my own many times."

"But we're talking specifically here about Tania."

"I understand that. Don't become upset, Jules. I would expect you to defend her, to be blind to the striking singularity of one woman fitting in so easily with five or six different men. It is certainly odd enough to be labeled a hard fact and to warrant some explanation."

"She has always..."

"Not true! I understand that she only began attending regularly within the past year or two."

"With her husband in the area, how could she?"

He smiled, his point won, and finished his coffee in a gulp. "I merely state that it is worthy of investigation, and I intend to look into it. There are other issues that I would prefer for the time being to keep to myself, but I assure you that I view them as significant, or potentially significant. But come. This is a small avenue of pursuit, and we have much more to discuss. Shall we table Madame Chessal for the moment?"

Reluctantly, but seeing the wisdom of the suggestion, I agreed and told him I had the plans for the arsenal with me. He asked me to wait until he'd dressed and then I could report at length. Excusing himself, he went into his quarters.

Almost immediately I heard two voices coming from his rooms. One his, the other female. The woman sounded angry and became more so as they talked. Finally, after several minutes of increasing volume, came the sound of a hand slapping down violently on a table or desk, and Lupa's voice, not loud, but devastatingly authoritative: "Enough! Leave! We'll discuss this later." Then he appeared back in the kitchen.

"Bah," he said, sitting down, "I'm sorry about that, but that woman nags me much too often. Do all women insist on scheduling time for their men?"

"Not to my knowledge," I said.

"Well, I won't have it." He leaned back and closed his eyes for a moment, his face clearing almost instantly. He had excellent control. "Now, then, those plans."

I took the crumpled and hastily drawn sketch from my pocket, and together we looked at it. I explained some of my impressions of the place, pointing out that the arsenal was impossible to enter forcibly. In my years as an agent, I've learned to recall almost completely events, conversations, and impressions, which was lucky, since he asked me to recount everything that had happened the day before since I'd met Tania for the funeral. He leaned back with his eyes nearly closed, and didn't move at all as I talked.

He interrupted me three times. Once to ask if I could identify the man I'd seen meet Paul. Once to ask me to repeat everything I could remember Ponty saying from the time we met him until we were shown the explosives anteroom, and again to ask if I was certain that the rock-throwing incident had been a prank, to which I answered no, I wasn't certain of anything.

When I'd finished, he said, "Pulis?"

"As far as I know, he spent the day consoling his wife."

"He also spent the better part of the afternoon reading a newspaper at the train station," he said. "Can you think of why he might have done that?"

I shook my head no.

"You should call on him, I suppose. You haven't aroused suspicion with any of them, have you?"

"No. I've decided to have another beer gathering next

Wednesday, though I'm not sure where it ought to be. That will give everyone a chance to get back together, restore our confidence in one another, lay some suspicion to rest. Most of them seem to want to believe it was suicide."

"Rubbish!"

"I know, but let them think that for a time. It won't make them wary of me when I ask questions, or at least less wary than if they thought I suspected one of them had killed him."

"Satisfactory," was all he said. I asked him if he'd had any trouble with the police.

"No."

"They haven't been around?" I asked.

"I didn't say that. I merely said I haven't had any trouble with them. I wouldn't speak with them. Charles told them I had gone shopping and I would call them back at my convenience. Then they wanted to search my quarters, which of course would have been intolerable, so Charles said he didn't know where I lived, and they believed him. One thing I don't need at a time like this is the police. I assume they're content to believe it was suicide also?"

I shrugged, since I really didn't know.

"All right," he said. "I'll try to avoid being bothered by them, though when they find out I live here, they'll be around snooping for cyanide and whatnot."

"They haven't been much of a bother to me," I said. I found the police no more competent than he did, but I saw no reason to antagonize them gratuitously.

"You are a rich man, Jules. You have standing in this area. You are, in short, more or less above suspicion. I am poor, a foreigner, unknown—in short, a perfect scapegoat. Of course I could demonstrate my innocence if given enough time, or I could save that time by delivering the murderer. And time is short."

So saying, he took a large silver watch from his vest pocket. All the times I had seen him, he'd been wearing suits of drab brown. He never looked seedy, but neither would well-dressed be an adequate description. Today was no exception, though he had slipped a vest over the pale yellow shirt. He wore no coat while indoors, and when he cooked he wore no tie. Glancing at his watch, he started.

"Nearly nine o'clock! I must be up on the street." He was peeved, I supposed at me for coming down and causing him to vary his schedule. When we'd gotten settled outside, I commented on the watch, which I hadn't seen before.

"Yes, it is lovely," he said, removing it again. "A gift from my parents, one of my few real treasures. Would you like to see it?"

He handed it across to me. It was rather larger than was the fashion and seemed to be made of very pure silver, judging from the weight. Turning it over in my hands, I noticed the inscription on the back, or rather the pair of initials, "S. H. & I. A." and the date, "1897." I was curious, but said nothing and gave it back to him.

"One of my fondest dreams is to someday own a house where I can keep things," he began. "Traveling has so long uprooted me that I think someday I would like a home where I could keep the things I love. I could easily envision myself almost totally sedentary. But now this watch is the only symbol I have of all I would like to have." He sighed.

"I'm surprised to find you so materialistic."

"Not at all. I want nothing more than the simplest shopkeeper has: a house, a sense of place, a few loved possessions. So often a man's surroundings become a man's background. A man who runs with thieves becomes like a thief. Of course," he went on, stopping to order the first of his day's beers, "it's not absolute, but I'd like a house made for my ideals, so that I might grow into it."

He paused while the beer—my beer!—arrived. Charles had thoughtfully brought out two bottles, and we each had a glass.

"Take yourself, Jules. You are an aristocrat. No, no, don't object, that's not so bad. You own land, a house, your interests are your own, not dictated by the exigencies of survival. And it shows. The other night, even drunk, you paused to wipe off a table before setting anything on it, even when it was a patently futile gesture. No, the way you live reinforces the way you act; the way you act finally becomes the way you are."

By this time, I was anxious to be off to visit Henri. I had probably been much like Lupa when I'd been younger. He was so enthusiastic about ideas, about ideals. I couldn't remember ever having known anyone so opinionated, but he wasn't so much objectionable or obnoxious as time-consuming, and as he'd said, time was short. I finished my beer and rose to leave as Charles brought out another one for Lupa, along with a clutch of newspapers. He looked up briefly.

"Will I see you?"

I had barely nodded when he looked back down, engrossed in his reading.

Henri lived in a large apartment overlooking his shop. It was a good distance from La Couronne, so I decided to take a hansom and enjoy the warm morning. I remember not being overly concerned with whether taking a hansom was a particularly aristocratic thing to do or not. It was a pleasant ride over the cobbled streets, and in a quarter of an hour I found myself in front of Henri's door. His eldest son was minding the shop, which was not surprising. I was a regular customer because of my beer supplies, and the sons knew me slightly. Some flaw in my character keeps me from remembering the names of children, and this boy was no exception. So I entered the small and cluttered store and approached the gangling youth with a warm smile of recognition.

"Bonjour, M. Giraud."

Likewise, it seems to me that all children remember my name and glory in greeting me this way.

We shook hands.

"Good morning. Is your father here?"

"He's above."

"Thank you."

Smiling to myself, I walked over to the door that opened onto the staircase and knocked. The boy had followed me over and he turned the knob for me.

"That's all right. Go on up."

Henri sat at the kitchen table, leaning back in his blue work pants and apron. None of the other children were about, though noises behind me suggested their presence somewhere in the flat. Madame Pulis was cutting onions and putting them in a large skillet over the fire. I stood in the archway for a moment looking at the scene before knocking on the doorjamb.

They both turned at once. Madame Pulis's eyes were filled with tears, I assumed from the onions. Henri, seeing me, immediately jumped up and put out his hand in greeting. He seemed even more nervous than usual.

As we sat at the table, we watched his wife finish cutting the onions, and then he ordered her from the room. My Greek friend, now slumping slightly over the table, hands clasped tightly in front of him, was a study in anxiety. His hair was disheveled, as though it had been combed earlier but something, perhaps nervous hands, had disturbed it. There was an unfamiliar tic over his right eye which further enhanced his harried mien. He looked a wreck.

When his wife had gone, he looked at me heavily.

"What's wrong, Henri? You look terrible."

He got up abruptly and paced back and forth slowly across the kitchen, pulling—jerking, really—all the while at his mustache. "It all started yesterday with Renee. You remember? At the funeral? She was crying a lot? Well, it really got to her, all the folks there were treating us as if we were guilty of something, and so she was crying. She cries easily." He stopped walking and looked at me imploringly.

"All that was fine. If you know Renee, you'd know crying is no special event. But some plainclothes *flic* at the funeral thought it was strange that one of the 'suspect's' wives should even bother coming, much less be in tears, so he thought we might know something and followed us home." He sat down again. "You know me, Jules. I get nervous easily and, when he came around, I got rattled. And with Renee crying all over, I just walked out. I know, I know, a mistake. I snuck out, really. I'm a fool.

"So then he started in on Renee. 'What were my feelings about Marcel? How well had she known him?' You know how insinuating they can be, and he was, but she'd only met Marcel maybe twice, so what could she say? Finally, he asks if he can look around the house, and she says we have nothing to hide, so he goes poking into everything and finds the supplies for Robert—you know my second son? Anyway, he finds Robert's supplies for taking photographs, which is his hobby, and right there in a drawer is plenty of cyanide to kill Marcel and a hundred other people, so he says 'Uh huh, interesting,' and leaves. So when I got home at about six o'clock, there's no dinner and the house is dark, and she's left a note that says she's gone to stay with her mother and taken the kids, and I can come get her later.

"Not wanting to wait for her to come back, I decided to go over there and find out what happened, and who do I run into on the street but this same *flic*, come to ask Renee some more questions. He looks at me for a minute and then says, 'You're not a French citizen, are you?'"

He paused for a moment. "I'd like a drink." He rose and got two glasses, filling one nearly to the top with pastis. In the other glass, he put a standard shot and added water. He grinned nervously, handing me the second glass. "Straight, it's just like ouzo. Makes me feel at home." He pulled again and again at his mustache, taking slow little sips of the drink. Every few seconds, he scratched at his head. *"Merde!* Where was I?"

"Are you a French citizen?"

"That's right, French citizen. Well, I told him that my papers were in order, that he could see for himself if he came back to the house, but he just started asking more questions about everybody. You, Georges, Paul, even Tania. Wanted to know if I knew where that fellow Lupa lived. I told him I didn't know anything, I didn't know Lupa, I hardly had known Marcel. Then he started going on again about how well had Renee and Marcel known each other, and it got fairly heated. He said he was going to check all the other houses—Tania's, yours, Paul's—and then get back to me, so I'd better find my wife and be available."

"What did you do after that?"

He was loosening up, as he always did when he drank. "Well, I went to get Renee. Then we all came home and tried to sleep. Goddamn it, Jules, can't a woman even cry at a funeral?"

He put his hand down, looking on the verge of tears. I put my hand lightly on his shoulder.

"Take it easy, Henri. It's just the way of investigators. They bother you, they try to find breaks in stories. Don't worry."

But I was worried. Cyanide was not so common a poison that anyone else would likely have it.

"Where did you go yesterday afternoon," I asked, "when you went wandering around?"

"Oh, I don't know. Just around. You know, when I'm upset, I walk." As if to prove his point, he got up and started pacing again. I didn't want to press it, so I changed the subject.

"I'd like to have everybody meet again next Wednesday. That's the real reason I had for coming up. Do you think you can make it?"

"I don't know," he said simply. Then, "At your house?"

"Probably not. I'll send you a note. I thought it would be good for us all to try and...well, you know."

He nodded. "Will Lupa be there?"

"Yes. Do you suspect him?"

"I'd be lying if I said I didn't. How well did he know Marcel?"

I laughed. "You thinking of joining the police force?"

He smiled weakly. "You're right," he said. "I'm sorry, but it's just that you get to suspecting everyone. But how well do you know him?"

"Fairly well."

"All right. Renee!" he yelled suddenly, "the onions are burning."

His wife came back into the room, apologetic. It was the first time I'd seen her without tears in her eyes. She was attractive in a tough sort of way—the kind of woman I'd expect Henri to be with—short, dark, buxom, subservient. She stood silently by the stove, stirring with a practiced rhythm.

"It might do you good to go down to the store," I suggested. "Take your mind off things."

I hadn't touched my drink. I offered it to him. He drank it off in a gulp.

"Let's go," he said.

On the staircase, we stopped again.

"If it's any consolation," I said, "no one came by to see either Tania or myself last night. Maybe you'll have no more trouble with him."

That seemed to make him nervous all over again. "He said he'd be back here this morning."

"Well, morning's nearly gone," I said. "What time did you run into him last night?"

"Early. Seven or half past."

"What time did you get back with your wife?"

"A few hours after that," he said. "I walked around for a while, just thinking."

We entered the shop and he called out immediately to his son. "Henri, get those crates in line! And hang that new garlic!" He turned quickly to me. "Goodbye, Jules, and thank you. I'll let you know about next week." Then another customer entered, and Henri brushed his hands against his apron and greeted him, as though he didn't have a worry in the world.

Outside, it was bright and warm. Henri lived off the main route, so I had to walk a while to get to a thoroughfare where I could catch a hansom back to my house. I'd found his place stuffy with the smell of grease and onions, and the walking made me decide to stop for a beer. A boy went by with some late editions of the newspaper, and waiting for my beer to arrive, I idly read the news from the front. I leaned back and relaxed, reminding myself that Henri's eldest son shared his name, and wondering if Henri would be persuaded to come next Wednesday. But where, it seemed, was a problem. Maybe Lupa would have a suggestion.

I turned the pages of the *journal*, coming eventually to local news. Then I froze, my beer halfway to my mouth. I put the beer down and looked at the small heading at the bottom of the page. The article read:

INVESTIGATOR KILLED

Police this morning discovered the body of special investigator J. Chatelet, 46, near the outskirts of Valence. The body lay just off the road, partially concealed in a clump of bushes. Chatelet had been with the police for ten years, the past five as an undercover (plainclothes) investigator. He appeared to have been strangled last night after having been attacked from behind. The body was still armed. He had been investigating the recent murder of Marcel Routier, a Valence salesman. He is survived by his wife, Paulette, and their three children.

I put down the paper and stared across the street, which shimmered in the heat. Folding the newspaper carefully, I put it under my arm, left some coins on the table and, standing up, flagged a carriage.

9

"Of course I've read it," Lupa said. "I saw it only a few minutes after you left. Naturally it's interesting that he'd just been to see Pulis, but it proves nothing."

I'd gone back to Lupa's after I'd collected my thoughts. He was not at his table on the street, so I passed down under Charles's gaze to the kitchen and on back. He was not in his apartments either, so I walked into the office, took a candle, and entered the tunnel. At the other end, the lights were on and especially brilliant after the darkness.

Lupa was leaning over, staring intently at some blooming flowers, seemingly lost to any intrigue that might be encircling him. We greeted each other, and then he said something about the peace of working with flora. I had no reply. Rather, I asked him if he'd read about Chatelet's death.

121

"One thing it proves is that Tania is out of it," I said.

He stopped fooling with the plants and straightened up, sighing. "My dear Jules, I realize how much of a burden this must be for you to bear, but it proves nothing of the sort. Didn't you tell me you got home long after dark last night?"

"Yes."

"It became dark some time after seven last night. The sun set at six fifty-two. The ride from St. Etienne takes over an hour, and it was dark when you left, meaning that it must have been after eight when you got to Madame Chessal's home. Chatelet left Pulis at around seven. Unfortunately, that left ample time for Madame Chessal to go do nearly any mischief she had to. I admit it isn't the most likely explanation, but it is possible."

"But the man was strangled."

"Yes, that's the official explanation, pending an autopsy. Even so, one shouldn't underestimate the strength of women. It's true that they often appear helpless and weak, but that's often our perception either because that's what we expect to see, or because that's what they allow us to see. I read recently where a mother lifted a carriage that had driven over the legs of her son, a carriage I'm sure neither you nor I could have lifted. Nor at any other time might she have been able to lift it, for that matter. Stress does strange things to people, as it's doing now to you. Sit down, would you."

I complied.

"You're overwrought. Collect yourself or you'll be worthless to both of us. Now, look around you. Breathe deeply. There is always beauty and it is always a comfort."

He was right. In a few moments, I felt calm and competent to think again. In the meantime, he didn't bother me but kept busy with the plants. Finally, he walked back to me.

"Well," he asked, "is it Pulis?"

I told him what I thought—that I wasn't sure, that my biggest problem was motive. Henri couldn't very well have been a spy for several years, since he'd been here in Valence with his growing family and business. Lupa seemed to agree, though he said nothing. When I finished reporting, he suggested I walk through the plant room with him before returning through the tunnel.

"You know that cyanide is also used to smelt gold or silver from ore. It's such a convenient poison because it's so easily attainable legally. Any photographer would have it, as would any geologist." He shrugged. "No, come to think of it, I don't believe I'll go in to see Anna today. I'll let her stew a bit over this morning's display. Come, there's work to do."

We went together back to the tunnel. I noticed him reach up just inside the door of the plant room and throw a switch.

"We can go back through now. I've turned off the alarm." I hadn't noticed that switch in my earlier passages—another indication of my decreasing powers.

Back in his office, he sat behind his desk after getting out three bottles of beer, two for himself and one for me.

After a great gulp of beer, he spoke. "I've decided it might be wise to have everyone meet here next Wednesday. Naturally, they'll be brooding about recent events, and they may resent me, but I think we can come up with something to make this place acceptable. What do you say?"

"I'm not sure," I answered truthfully. "Some of them may not come."

"If we can think of some way to get them all here, what would you say?"

"I wouldn't have any objections, I suppose. Why here, though?"

"Staging. If I can get them all in one place and question them, I think we may get somewhere. It may be easier to heighten the atmosphere of distrust here than elsewhere, and animosity is a much better catalyst than cooperation."

I drank my beer. "All right. I'll think about a way to arrange it."

"One other thing," he said.

"What's that?"

"I'd be curious to see a photograph of Madame Chessal's family. Could you get your hands on one?"

"Are you serious?"

"Perfectly."

"But why?"

"Because, Jules, I would like to lay to rest, once and for all, my suspicion of her, and I have an idea."

"You have an idea..." I said skeptically.

"Please," he said, "if it's a difficult request, I retract it." He seemed genuinely concerned for me. "I don't want to upset you."

"That's all right," I said, "I'm being peevish. I'll see what I can do."

"Thank you," he said simply. "It might be important."

That night I was alone at my house. Saturday was Fritz's night off, and Tania had left, I imagine, sometime during the day. I was somewhat surprised by Fritz's absence—normally he stayed at the house even on Saturdays—but of course he was perfectly free to go out. Perhaps he'd met a girl while shopping, though he was very shy with women and seemed not to like them particularly. It had taken him some months to be natural with Tania, who was the mildest of creatures.

Beset with a certain heaviness, I wandered about the large and empty house. I felt I should know more, that enough had happened to form some conclusions, but the problem was that—much as I hated to admit it—the actions of everyone involved invited suspicion. I lit a cigarette and sat on the darkened stairs. The house itself had an eeriness clinging to it. Something was making me nervous, possibly a sagging belief in my own competence. I felt I should file a report to Paris, but somehow, even with Marcel's death, there seemed nothing to report. It all seemed so parochial now, a personal matter having nothing to do with the war or with France. I felt out of touch with any national effort, and trapped in a tightening circle of local intrigue.

After a small supper of reheated stuffed bell peppers, endive salad, and several glasses of beaujolais, I tried to read, but found I couldn't shake this feeling of unease. I checked the doors to see that they were locked and then, turning off all the lights save one, went upstairs to my room for the first time since I'd left it that morning.

I had nearly finished undressing before I noticed something on my desk. I crossed over to it, sat down, lit another cigarette. It was a familiar bit of folded paper, probably left for Fritz earlier in the day with instructions to deliver it to me. Opening it, I saw several columns listing farm produce with asking prices in various locations. Wearily, I pulled the tattered code book from where I had it taped under my desk. Smoke from my cigarette burned in my eyes, and I stubbed out the butt on the desk top, impatiently brushing the ashes to the floor. In a few minutes I had the message entirely decoded.

Paris had taken the initiative. They were transferring me to Bordeaux, again for what I interpreted to be desk work, since there was no active theater there. I went downstairs and poured myself a cognac. I'd been moved many times in my career, but I'd never been dismissed from a case before it had been solved. Apparently Paris had decided that I was useless here, or that my usefulness in general was at an end. I paced.

Finally I sat down and pulled my pad in front of me, beginning the even more complicated process of composing a detailed response in code. I would not go to Bordeaux, even if it meant resigning. With that thought, I sat bolt upright and crossed out what I had begun to write. Sometimes a course of action seems impossible until it is defined; once defined, it becomes inevitable. I leaned back in my chair and heaved a huge sigh of relief.

The carefully worded response was completed just as I heard the lock turn in the front door. I came to the head of the stairs and saw Fritz enter. He took off his coat and hung it neatly on a peg in the hall. I called out his name.

He looked up. "Sir?"

"Pleasant evening?"

"Yes."

"Would you care for a cognac?"

"I believe I would, thank you."

I came down and we went into the sitting room. He naturally refilled my glass, then poured his own drink. I handed him the note I'd written and asked him to mail it for me the next day.

"Certainly." He paused, sipping at his drink. "Madame Chessal took me to dinner this evening. Perhaps it's none of my affair, sir, but she seemed quite worried about you. She said to remind you that you were picnicking tomorrow. I've already planned a lunch," he added.

"Yes. I remember. What did she say?"

"Only that she was afraid you were in some special danger. I assume relating to Monsieur Routier's death. I confess that I've been concerned about your appetite recently. Did you read that one of the men investigating his death was killed last night?"

"Yes."

"Well, Madame seems to think there is a kind of plot, and that you're somehow deeply involved."

I shook my head slowly. "Well, you know women, Fritz. They worry about little things. I'm not sure that Marcel's death was not suicide, and that investigator may simply have been robbed. I assure you I'm in no plot. Marcel's death did upset me, and business has been weighing me down—unnecessarily I think—for several weeks. In fact, that note you are holding is a letter of resignation. I've decided to stay here in Valence and live out my days in what peace I can hold on to. God knows I don't need the money, and I do need a rest."

He nodded. "I think that's a good idea, sir."

"Well, fine," I said. "I think I'll be going to bed now. Would you again wake me early?" I raised my glass. "To victory, France, and peace."

We drank the toast and retired.

10

The next morning, I picked up Tania at nine o'clock, and we took her carriage into town for Mass. It was a grand morning, and when I told Tania of my plans to stay in Valence, she threw her arms around me and laughed like a schoolgirl.

"Jules, that's wonderful!"

We sat happily through the service, and I resolved to forget my business for at least a day. Though I had resigned, I had no intention of giving up the investigation of Marcel's death. It was a matter both of pride and survival, for I entertained no doubts that all of us were indeed in some special danger.

I wondered whether Paris would respect my reply or whether they would be difficult. I had worked for them for over thirty years and undeniably knew many secrets, codes, and strategies. The situation might become very sticky. They could be most persuasive if they had to be. I put the thought out of my mind. I would have to deal with that later. For the time being, Lupa might not have been convinced of Tania's innocence, but I was. It was a good feeling.

We returned to my home and picked up the basket lunch Fritz had prepared: a cold roast chicken, hard-boiled eggs, several bottles of beer, and some dried fruits. He'd even managed to find a bit of brick chocolate for dessert.

We left the house and followed the brook across the road and down into the meadow beyond, where a few field horses grazed peacefully. I carried the small folding table and chairs, and Tania the basket. About two kilometers downstream, the brook widens into a placid pond, dotted here and there with fowl and surrounded by a rather dense woods. We picked our way into one of the several clearings and set up the table, which Tania covered with the plain white cloth Fritz had given us. Then she took off her bonnet and shoes and went to wade in the pond. I sat and watched her, absentmindedly shelling an egg.

I called to her, and she came back to the table. We drank beer and ate slowly, talking of food and books. She had just finished *War and Peace* (in Russian!) and contended that it was the greatest book ever written.

"It says everything about everything," she gushed. And then, "I only wish this war would end with a spirit of rejuvenation."

"I'm sure it will," I said, taking her hand. "We're not so old, you know."

"That's easy for you to say. A woman at forty, especially if she has grown children, can't expect much rejuvenation. She gets older, that's all."

I laughed heartily. "And a man in his mid-fifties? What about him?"

"Men are different," she replied.

"*Et vive la . . .*"

Her eyes twinkled. She was half teasing. "Have you read Darwin?"

"A little."

"Do you know he says that humans are the only species whose females live beyond the age of childbearing? Why do you suppose that is?"

"To keep old males happy." I patted her hand. "Come, dear, you're beautiful, and spring is a time for rejuvenation. Pass me another bit of chicken, will you?"

She was about to answer, when I saw a movement in the woods at the other side of the pond. "Shh," I whispered, "what's that?"

She turned to look. "*Merde.* People."

We'd almost finished eating, and Tania quickly gathered what food remained into the basket. She told me to grab the table and chairs and follow her a bit back into the woods.

"Come, come. *Vite! Vite! Vite!*"

She spread the cloth under a large oak tree. "I'm sorry, but I don't want to be bothered. Not today."

I didn't really mind, but I was curious about the other party. I sat with my back against the tree, positioned so that I could look across the pond to where the others were moving, still well back into the trees on their side. Tania opened me another beer and lay with her head in my lap.

"There," she sighed.

The others came down to a clearing on their side, and I saw with some surprise that it was Lupa, Anna, and Watkins. Somehow I had never associated them with a picnic in the woods, but of course they were young and really much more likely than I to be enjoying a Sunday outdoors. They came into the clearing and set up chairs and a small table, and the two men sat down while Anna walked to the pond with a few bottles. She dropped them for chilling into the water.

"You know what I found interesting?"

I looked down at Tania. "What's that?"

"I found myself forgetting I was French. I despised the French, even though at the time I suppose I would have been as patriotic as I am now."

For some reason, this statement made absolutely no sense to me. Lupa and Watkins had set themselves up at their table—it looked as though they were about to play some board game—while Anna busied herself clearing a spot near the water. I took a sip of my beer and frowned.

"When?" I asked.

"The Napoleonic Wars. You couldn't help but want the Russians to win. It made me slightly uncomfortable while I was reading."

"Ah, *War and Peace.*"

The two men across the pond were becoming engrossed in their game and rarely looked up, while Anna was busy making a small fire. Once Lupa called out to her loud enough so that we could hear his voice. At that, Anna got up and fetched the men some bottles from the pond, then went back to her work.

"I suppose we were wrong then."

"I don't believe we'd have thought so at the time," I said. "But of course there are always reasons to start a war, just as there are more often than not no real reasons to end one. Everyone believes themselves right, which is probably understandable, but rather simple."

"You don't think we were right?"

"That depends. At that time I would have thought it, I'm sure. If your sons had been off fighting in Russia, you would never have given a thought to whether or not we were right. We would have *had* to have been right."

"Yes. I suppose so." She closed her eyes and breathed deeply. I thought she was going off to sleep. Anna had started to cook something over the fire, while the two men continued their game. The sun came down in patches there under the tree. It was beginning to get warm. Tania stirred and opened her eyes.

"But what about now?" she asked.

"What do you mean?"

"Are we right, now? Or will some German Tolstoy come along in fifty years and make us all appear to be beasts?"

"Whatever we may appear in fifty years," I said, "for the present time we're at least justified. France has to survive, and now it has to fight to survive." I leaned back and lit a cigarette. "Novelists make us think war is terrible because they tend to make a personal story out of it. Nationally, war is either desirable or necessary, never right or wrong. It's not a personal thing, any more than a storm is personal. If a bolt of lightning strikes down a man, no one says that there's any reason behind it. Some writers try to, saying it's an act of God or whatever, but that doesn't wash. It just happens, like war happens."

"But the people..."

"People don't matter in wars. Countries matter. Nations matter, issues matter. The last thing anyone should think about is people."

She closed her eyes again. "I think about my sons," she said, then added quietly, "all the time. And we both think of Marcel."

"But we don't know Marcel had anything to do with the war."

She looked up at me. "Don't we?"

I wondered how much she did know.

"And if he did have to do with the war, then he wouldn't matter, because people don't matter. Oh, Jules, you don't really believe that?"

I thought of the night before, and the reasons I had decided to stay on in Valence. I had let it become personal, which was absurd. France was what mattered. But finally I didn't believe that, and some sense of that realization had made me resign. I supposed I was, indeed, getting old. I touched Tania's face gently.

"No," I said, "I don't really believe that."

We were silent.

Across the pond nothing changed. I watched for several minutes, after which Watkins, evidently beaten in the game— I heard his "Damn!" clearly—abruptly stood up and stalked over to the fire.

"You know who that is over there?"

Tania sat up. "Who?"

"Your friend Lupa."

"*Your* friend Lupa," she said, frowning. "I'm surprised he had the energy to get all the way out here."

"It's not that he lacks energy, he just chooses a bit carefully how he wants to expend it."

"Well, let's not expend any of ours by calling him."

"I had no intention of doing that, my dear." I leaned over and kissed her.

She stood up. "Would you excuse me for a minute?" she asked.

She walked back a ways into the woods while I sat propped against the tree, watching the scene across the pond. Anna was removing something from the fire, while Lupa was putting up the game pieces and clearing the table. Anna went back to the pond for more bottles.

I took a drink of my beer, long and refreshing, closing my eyes and letting the cold liquid run down my throat. Suddenly there was a loud report. Opening my eyes, I saw Lupa and Watkins drop to the ground, while Anna screamed as she fell, rolling over and over. Behind me, I heard Tania call out my name, and I turned to see her running toward me. There were two more shots.

"You're all right?" I yelled, and she said she was. The shots I'd heard had been the loud ringing noises of a rifle rather than the soft pops of a pistol, so the range could have been great.

I took out my pistol. Tania came up to me. "You're not going—" she began.

I cut her off. "Go see to Anna. I think she's been hit."

"But Jules, you're not..."

I was already moving back toward the road, where the shots had originated. Retired or not, I was a trained operative of the French government and knew how to act around hostile elements. Perhaps I was curt to Tania, but such times call for action, not sensitivity.

No more than a minute had passed since the third shot. As I ran, out of the corner of my eye I saw another figure moving through the woods to my left. It was Lupa, outpacing me as we sprinted.

We broke from the woods at about the same time, all the while moving rapidly toward the road, where we could see a figure retreating into the trees on the other side toward my house. Lupa fell momentarily from my vision, but, seconds later, he appeared at my side astride one of the dray horses.

"Get up!"

His hand grabbed me like a vice as I bounded up behind him. "Over there," I yelled, pointing to a break in the copse just beyond the road. Lupa, holding the horse's mane, leaned into the untrained beast and miraculously was obeyed.

I still held my pistol in my hand, dismally aware of its inadequacy. We were closing on the roadway and within another minute might expect to come upon our assailant, fleeing on foot. It was not to be, however, as over the sound of the horse's hooves we heard a motor turning over and saw, not fifty meters away, an automobile kicking up dust as it spun from its hiding place into the road.

I fired one ineffectual shot—from that range, the gesture was about the equivalent of shouting "Stop!"—but Lupa didn't hesitate. He spurred the horse back a bit to our right, directly toward my house.

"Your car!" he yelled over his shoulder.

"*Tout droit!* Straight ahead." I pointed to the barn.

The car we'd seen had been covered, so we had no opportunity to see the driver or even whether there had been more than one occupant. Still, I would recognize the automobile itself—made of a corrugated iron just becoming popular here and painted a dull green.

We came to the barn and dismounted roughly. I stumbled and fell dismounting, but Lupa did not slow up at all. As I picked myself up, he was pulling back the building's door, grunting with the exertion. I ran past him and threw myself behind the wheel.

It pays to keep one's machinery in top condition, as I had done. Immediately, the motor caught, I slammed the gearshift into position and nearly ran over Lupa as the car lurched forward. He caught the windshield and leapt onto the running board, barely clearing the doorway.

I pressed the hand throttle to its limit, and before we had left my property, we were closing on fifty kilometers per hour. On the unpaved and potted drive, the ride shook my very bones. I hoped the automobile would handle the shocks better.

"Anna?" I began.

"Not now!" Lupa bellowed.

As soon as we hit the road, however, it became smoother. Skidding slightly as we turned left, I nearly lost control of the wheel, but Lupa grabbed it and righted me as we continued our acceleration.

We hadn't gone a kilometer, though, when the ride very nearly ended. What I thought at first was a backfire, or perhaps a blowout, made me lean forward against the steering wheel. That move may have saved my life. Lupa, without the worry of watching the road, spun and evidently made out a glint of metal in another stand of trees by the road. It had been another shot.

"Keep driving," he yelled as I began to slow down. "Let Watkins get him."

"Are you sure?" I asked.

"Our man's in the car." he said. "Drive!"

Lupa pulled a weapon from under his coat. The pistol, an M-1911 Colt American military issue .45 automatic, boomed like a cannon as he fired off four rounds with what seemed to be impossible rapidity, the smoking brass jackets flying out the side of the weapon and onto the road. The fire was returned as we heard one more report from behind us.

"Damn!" Lupa spun around, grabbing his cheek. A sliver of red appeared and he wiped at it with his hand.

"You all right?"

"Scratched. Nothing more."

No more than three minutes had elapsed between the enemy's car breaking from the cover of the trees and our turning into the road in pursuit. With the speed of my Model T, if the chase lasted more than fifteen kilometers, I thought we had a chance of overtaking our prey. I kept the accelerator jammed to the floor while Lupa dabbed at the cut on his face with a handkerchief. Just as I turned to look his way and question him again about the initial shooting and how badly Anna had been hurt, we crested a small hill and I was forced to skid again, braking hard, as we came upon a horse-drawn produce cart from the other direction. We barely missed it as we screeched to a stop.

The driver had leapt off the cart to the roadside and lay sprawled in the shallow grass. "Has there been another car?" I asked.

Clearly furious, swearing violently, he seemed inclined to rush us. Lupa pointed his gun at the man's head and quieted him. "Has there been another car?"

"*Oui.*"

"How many passengers?"

The man shrugged. "I didn't notice," he said. "I was getting out of the way." In spite of Lupa's weapon, his anger spewed over again. "You bastards don't own the road, you know. I'm reporting this, I..."

We couldn't stay to discuss the niceties of *priorité á droit,* but pressed onward. If we were having trouble making headway, perhaps we were not alone.

The top was still off on the Model T, and the wind brought tears to my eyes, slightly impairing my vision. I didn't mind it, pushing the car to nearly 120 Ks. Very few other machines could match that speed. The road's surface, relatively smooth, nevertheless provided its share of bumps and necessitated my full attention.

Lupa stemmed the flow of his blood, then removed the clip from his weapon and refilled it. To my inquiring look, he answered, "We could have hurt him. The range is close to fifty meters."

"Who do you think it might have been?" I asked.

"I don't know." He dabbed again at his cheek reflectively. "I just don't know. Perhaps Watkins will come up with something."

I finally got the question out. "Anna was all right?"

He shook his head wonderingly. "Again, just a scratch. We've been uncommonly lucky."

I thought of Marcel. Our luck had its limits.

Within moments, we were on the outskirts of Valence. Cart traffic and a few military vehicles slowed our progress as we stopped and started, honking, through the narrow streets. The town was a maze of alleys, any one of which could hide the man we sought. But we had no choice other than to pursue his logical path—toward St. Etienne.

The frustrating ride through the city streets, where we were stopped time and again by carriages, children, geese, dogs, and pedestrians, continued and continued. Our only hope was that the car we followed was experiencing similar delays.

Finally, just as we broke from the confines of the cobbled streets and onto the smoother, wider thoroughfare that led to St. Etienne, Lupa grabbed my arm and cried out.

"There it is!"

I didn't know how he could be sure. The car was a mere speck on the roadway, and he'd only glimpsed it before it rounded a curve and disappeared again. Still, it was not a time to quibble, and I pushed the Ford to its limit.

We were gaining. As we took the same curve, we'd picked up perhaps fifty meters. Now, clearly, even to my blurred vision, it looked like the same car.

"Keep low," Lupa cautioned, "they might shoot."

I followed his instructions, and we closed rapidly. In another minute, we were within range of Lupa's weapon, but he held his fire. It would not be wise to shoot until we had seen the occupants.

By the time we reached the first aqueduct crossing the Rhone, we had nearly come upon them, and it was becoming obvious to me that something had gone wrong. They were not pulling away, not shooting. In fact, they paid us no attention whatsoever.

As we pulled alongside, we glanced over at them—two elderly men in officer's uniforms. They looked back at us with mild curiosity, nothing more. At the first opportunity, I turned into a side road, drove on for several hundred meters, then pulled over.

"What now?" I asked.

The breeze blew over us gently. Overhead, a flock of birds chided us with their song.

11

"We're fools," Lupa said.

"What else could we have done?"

"Yes. I'm trying to determine that now."

"There must be a dozen lookalike cars on the road."

"Jules," he explained, "I know the answers as well as you do. We must be asking the wrong questions."

We continued in frustrating and desultory conversation until, in the end, he asked if I would drop him off at La Couronne on my way back home.

"Aren't you curious about Anna?" I asked.

"I am many things in relation to her," he answered, "but almost never am I curious. No, I am sure she has gone back to be ministered to by Madame Chessal. She was fine, Jules, as fine as I am now. I did make sure before I joined with you."

The drive continued in silence. Occasionally I would glance over at my companion. He sat, motionless, eyes closed, pursing his lips in and out. Finally, he spoke:

"Where was Madame Chessal when you heard the shots?"

"With me. Well, she'd gone off into the bushes for a moment."

"So she was not with you."

"Auguste, don't be absurd. She didn't even know we'd be here. She was nowhere near where the shots came from."

He looked at me in exasperation. "There is such a thing as a paid assassin. She wouldn't have to be where the shots came from."

I thought he was stretching the point beyond credibility and told him so.

"Jules," he said, "there are two kinds of women: simple women, accounting for ninety percent of the race, and dangerous women."

If he was brooding, I'd let him brood. I was convinced that his line of reasoning led nowhere, and nothing he said was going to shake that conviction. He seemed to come to the same conclusion, for suddenly he sat up straight in his seat.

"I apologize about the way I spoke of Madame Chessal. I still can't help but feel a great deal of mistrust, but with no evidence, I'm a fool to speak rashly. Forgive me." He sighed, back to business. "I've decided something rather crucial."

"What's that?"

"What did you see, exactly, when you heard the shots today?"

"Actually, I saw nothing. Just at the moment I heard the shots, I was tipping my head back to drink some beer. I saw nothing at all. Just before that, I saw Anna crossing back to the table and you and Watkins—no, just you—seated, pre-sumably waiting for her."

"Correct. Does that lead you to note any similarity between this latest incident and the successful attempt on Routier?"

I couldn't see what he was getting at.

"Let me describe to you what happened today. Exactly. Anna had been at the fire getting our food and had turned back to the table. Watkins stood on the far side of the table, having just returned also from the fire. When the shot came, we were all precisely in a line from the direction of the report. Anna was grazed while leaning over to place the food on the table, and the same bullet passed through the bottom of Watkins's coat. I heard the whistle of the thing as it passed my ear. There! What does that tell you?"

"Nothing," I said truthfully. "Except perhaps that they're both very lucky."

"How about if they were both extremely unlucky? What if the bullet hadn't been meant for either of them?"

I smiled. "What if you are getting upset and nervous and losing your judgment?"

Ignoring that response, he continued. "The most salient point of these two attempts, last week's and today's, is that both attempts were on my own life. Of course, there is a possibility that this was not the case last Wednesday but only the barest possibility. You see—and I don't know whether you noticed this at the time—Routier, after the incident with Lavoie's bottle exploding, went back to the seat I'd been occupying and drank from my already poured glass. The poison had obviously been put there for me; only the chance realignment of our positions saved me and resulted in your friend's death.

"Again today," he went on, "today we were all in a line, and the shot chanced to miss me. You heard the other two? After the first we all dropped immediately to the ground.

The second shot landed somewhere far off, but the last hit the ground not one meter from where I lay, which was far from the other two. No, whoever the killer may be, the intended victim is beyond dispute. It is myself. And whatever else the killer may be, we may be certain that he's getting desperate."

"All right," I said, after a moment, "it might be true. And if it is, what are you going to do?" I negotiated back onto the cobblestones. In contrast to our earlier passage *en ville*, no one seemed to be about.

"I'd like you to go and find out where Pulis was today. Then go to the police station, find where Lavoie is supposed to be, and wire him. As I said, it's possible that there's a hired assassin involved, even though further reflection renders that rather dubious. A hired assassin wouldn't have missed me, and if our man was so concerned about covering up, he certainly wouldn't have done anything at your house the other night. No, I believe he's acting alone on this. I believe he's scared, and a scared man makes mistakes."

"What about Paul?"

"Anser? You're going to see him tomorrow, are you not?"

"Yes."

"Well... question him. Find out what you can. Watkins, remember, will be working in St. Etienne."

"All right, but you?"

"I'm going back to La Couronne. I don't intend to leave my rooms until this is cleared up. A scared man, as I said, makes mistakes. I can't be wondering about my own safety if I'm to be effective. My cooking, too, is suffering. As you see, I should be there now. Charles is no chef, but he's taking over when he can. I try to show him a style, but how do you teach a flair, eh? Monsieur Vernet, La Couronne's owner, is very patient. We are, in fact, distantly related. He is a good man, but he is also a businessman, a restauranteur. He needs a quality chef to survive. Much as I need a quality operative."

He glanced sideways at me. "Would you object to filling that role?"

I could not. It was flattering—but more, necessary. If Lupa was right, then he, not I, was in danger.

"Jules, stop the car!" he said suddenly.

We were passing the fountain in the center of town, from which side streets spread like spokes from a wheel. I pulled over to the curbside and brought the car to a halt.

"What is it?"

"Come with me."

Lupa was already out of the car, his hand inside his coat near his pistol. He disappeared down one of the alleys. Moving as quickly as I could, I followed. The run through the woods, the horse ride, my stumbling, the excitement of the chase—all of that was catching up with me. In the leisurely pace of the drive back to Valence, I had stiffened up considerably. But I was not about to let myself forget that I'd kept up with a man not yet half my age. I thought confidently that Lupa could pick a worse operative than myself.

Rounding the corner, I saw what had drawn Lupa's attention. A green automobile of corrugated iron was pulled up under an overhanging gutter. The driver's window was open, and Lupa had already entered the car by the time I arrived.

"Anything?"

He straightened up in the seat, smiling crookedly. Opening his hand, he displayed one spent rifle shell. "Nothing important," he said. "Perhaps you ought to file a report on a stolen car. I'm sure the owner of this machine is wondering where it might be."

He got out of the car. "I might as well walk from here, Jules. Thank you for your help." He nodded and began down the alley. Then he stopped, turning. "I suppose for form's sake I should ask Watkins to question the residents of this block. They may have seen..."

Then, abruptly, his shoulders slumped. "This is terrible.

My mind isn't functioning. The police will not be able to discover who stole this car. No one will have seen it arrive here... Our function is not pedestrian police work. We cannot depend on that, for if we do we shall fail. Mark my words, we shall fail!"

I tried to calm him, to restore some of his lost self-esteem. It did little good. Finally, I assured him that I would check in on Anna, though he didn't even seem to think that would be necessary. He said I could do as I wished.

As I trudged back to my car, I wondered if even now our assailant was watching me from one of the narrow windows, gloating over his escape. Whoever he was, it was likely that he knew me well and thought me a bumbling adversary, a foolish dilettante, an aging clown.

12

All the shops had been closed on Sunday, and Henri had bickered with his wife and gone fishing alone. No one had seen him. He'd caught no fish, though when he returned, his boots had been wet. Tuesday, tomorrow, he would be making a delivery of condiments to St. Etienne. When I saw him Monday morning, I learned all this. He was nervous as usual, but sober, and I only stayed a moment on the pretext of having forgotten something.

I then sent a telegram to Avignon, where, according to the list he'd left with the police, Georges should have been staying. I expected no reply until evening at the earliest.

It was a cool and overcast day. The changes in weather had been abrupt, but one expected that in the spring. Perhaps the clouds would burn off by the afternoon.

I walked from the telegraph office to Lupa's with my hands thrust deep into the pockets of my overcoat, seeing no one on my way.

He sat enthroned in his office. That's the only way to describe him. So he had abandoned his schedule. It was after ten o'clock, and by all rights, he should have been up on the street with beer and newspaper. As it was, he sat behind his huge desk with the paper open before him and a glass by his left hand.

"Hello," I said, sitting down. I'd asked Charles for coffee on the way through the kitchen and awaited him. "So you've given up working altogether."

"I beg your pardon." He looked up.

"You look so settled there, it's hard to imagine that you'll ever move back to the world of labor."

"Cooking is not a labor but a love. I intend to continue with my duties here." He put the paper aside. "You've read that Italy has joined us? That, at least, is good news. How are you today?"

I told him about Pulis and the telegram while Charles was pouring my coffee. He listened with his eyes closed, leaning back far in his chair. When I had finished, he frowned.

"It would make things much easier if we could ever eliminate someone completely. You say he's going to St. Etienne tomorrow?"

As I nodded, there was a loud, ringing alarm. Lupa reached to a button on his desk and pressed it, shutting off the noise. He calmly opened his desk and took out his pistol, checking to see that it was loaded. "Stay here," he said to me and disappeared into the tunnel. I sat uncomfortably for several minutes before I heard returning footsteps and voices. The curtain came aside and Lupa reentered with Watkins.

"... So it seems possible, though rather a long shot," said the Englishman as he came into the room. "Ah, hello, I didn't realize you were here."

"He's only just arrived," said Lupa. "Would you have some coffee? Tea?"

"Tea, please."

"Fine." He ordered it, and we waited.

"Excuse me," I said, "but what seems possible?"

Lupa closed his paper. "Joseph here has just returned from St. Etienne, where he's been trying to find some information we can use. He's not working at all on the murders, as you are, but only on the arsenal. After the attempt yesterday, I thought things would start to move quickly, but I was wrong. Nothing happened, at least that we know of, at St. Etienne. Joseph believes, however, that he was followed for quite some time, even back here to Valence, possibly by the man who shot at us. He was about to describe him."

Watkins slouched in his chair, looking rather ragged, as though he hadn't slept. The tea arrived, and he sipped at it. Suddenly, when he was about to speak, his eyes became illuminated, and he lost his vacant look. It was amazing, almost as though he were two different people.

"Actually, I never did get a good look at his face. He had brownish hair, I think, dressed plainly, about six foot." He smiled. "Brilliant description, what? Could as well be me I'm talking about." Then he shifted back into himself and sat as though he'd been deflated, sipping at his tea. "God, I'm tired."

"Why don't you get yourself some sleep? Are you going back to St. Etienne right away?"

"I thought I'd go down a bit later, say after dark."

Lupa nodded. "Satisfactory. I'm getting ready to move, to create something if necessary. I've got a good guess who we want. By the way, Pulis is coming down tomorrow morning to deliver. Watch him." He turned to me. "How does he go down?"

"Produce cart, I imagine."

"Good, then he'll be easy to pick up. Catch him outside of town and follow him everywhere. If he meets anyone . . .

well, do what you can. It would be nice if we could use the police."

Watkins stood and moved to the door. "Got it."

"This trip back and forth must get tedious. When you go down, stay until you have something. I have a feeling things are coming to a head."

"Yes, sir," he said and started out.

"Oh, Watkins!"

He stopped and looked back in.

"Don't you think it might be better if you exited the same way you entered? It's just possible that someone might notice you coming out of a building you'd never entered. Also, in the future, why not try coming in by way of the restaurant."

"Right, right, right..." he muttered, crossing the room again. "The plants need watering. I've turned on the lights." He left.

"No olives?" I asked.

"Certainly an oversight. Is there anything else?"

"I was wondering where Anna fits in. In fact, I've wondered about where all of us fit in. I get the distinct impression that there are things you'd rather I knew nothing about, and I'd like to know why."

He sighed. "You're right. There is much you don't need to know. Ideally, you wouldn't know Watkins, but there's no harm in that. For the other things, wait a few more days. You might treat people differently if you knew their alignment with us. For now, you know enough to do your job."

"Well, then, Anna at least..."

"Yes?"

"I'd like to know if Tania's in danger with her being there, or if that was arranged by you."

"Oh, no. Certainly not. I'm concerned, in fact, about any danger Anna may be in."

"Not that again."

"No," he said. "No, not that again. We are simply in different camps on that question, and I'm afraid it won't be resolved until I've seen Madame Chessal's family, perhaps until the whole matter is closed. But Anna...I don't know what to do about her."

"Is she with us?"

"Not in the sense you mean. I've gotten myself entangled with her. She knows generally what my functions are, and sometimes she's a great help, but she works for no government. I think when she leaves Madame Chessal's care, I'm going to send her away. We've talked of marriage."

"Congratulations."

"Posh! A man shouldn't be congratulated when he finds himself trapped. I feel I owe it to her, in a way. She's done a lot for me."

"But that's terrible!" I said. "Don't you love her at all?"

"Oh, love. Come, Jules, let's not be sentimental. Surely, I care for her, but I realize that these things pass. I'm too much my own man to tolerate a woman around for very long. Still," he sighed, "she is a good woman. I suppose there's no help for it. I will send her away for a while." He sat back and closed his eyes. The alarm once more sounded.

"That would be Watkins again. I should show him the switch. Well?" he said after a pause. "Anything else?"

"Yes, there is. Talking of Anna just reminded me. I'm not working with the government any more. I've resigned."

He opened his eyes a fraction. "Hmmm..."

"I expect there'll be some trouble."

"Undoubtedly. Why?"

"Transfer."

"The fools! Don't they believe there's trouble here? Their own agents are dying consistently. So you've quit. Well, good. I'll see if I'll be able to assuage some of their more retaliatory instincts. Don't worry."

"I wasn't," I said, getting up.

"Fine. Wednesday night?"

"Oh, yes, all set with Henri and Tania. Georges said anywhere would be all right with him, and I'm going to see Paul now, so I'll let you know. Oh, one more thing: the police want to see me. They've possibly seen me come here. How well do I know you?"

"Slightly."

"Good, that'll be easy, then. I'll see them this afternoon after I get back." So saying, I turned and left, hearing him calling for Charles to bring more beer.

I'd left the car parked at the telegraph office, so I walked back to it in the still brisk morning, trying again to piece together all I'd seen and heard, and once again coming up with a blank.

Since I'd never been to Paul's house, I had a little trouble getting to it and was totally unprepared for what greeted me. It was set back on a small trail, nearly a kilometer from any real road, and looked like something from a fairy tale. It was tiny and seemed to be perfectly square, no more than ten meters on a side, though it did have two stories. I'd needed to ask directions before I arrived from some children who were playing nearby. All of them knew the place and seemed surprised that I didn't. The roof was sharp-sloping, of the kind you see more often in Switzerland, though it was shingled with the familiar red tile. The house itself was white.

I parked to one side of the trail, walked to the small door, and knocked.

"*Entrez! Un moment.*" Paul's voice came from upstairs. "*Qui est la?*"

"It's Jules," I answered, sitting down. "No hurry."

The first thing I noticed about the inside was the cats. There were seven different kinds of feline lounging over the sparse furniture. I'd never supposed that Paul was so fond of cats; he'd never mentioned them, as cat lovers are generally wont to do. I, personally, did not particularly like them. The other outstanding feature of the room was the plants. There were potted plants in every window and suspended from the ceiling. "Well," I said to myself, "after all, he is a poet."

As though on cue, Paul came down the stairs.

"Jules, good to see you. What brings you around?" We shook hands. His was rather clammy. He was wearing American blue denims and a shirt he called his *chemise de l'Ouest,* a white affair with sloping pockets and mother-of-pearl buttons. "I'm just making some lunch. Will you have some?"

"Just coffee would be fine, thanks."

He walked back to another room, which appeared to be no bigger than a closet. He called me in.

"You've never been here before, right? Right. Well, it surely won't do to have you leave without the grand tour. This room here's the kitchen."

Compared to my own kitchen, it didn't seem even minimally adequate for cooking. There were a pair of burners set on a drain and two or three shelves with a very few condiments lying in disarray upon them. The coffee pot was black with carbon, and looked as though it hadn't been cleaned, ever. There was no sink. He went outdoors to a pump for the water. On the walls were faded posters of "Buffalo Bill Cody's Wild West Show" and one of "Ringling Bros. Barnum & Bailey Circus (The Greatest Show on Earth)." He dumped several measures of coffee into the water and set the whole thing on a burner to boil. I wondered what Lupa would have had to say about the operation.

"Don't worry about the grounds, Jules. There's a filter inside the spout."

Not clearly reassured, I waited, making small talk until the water was boiling. He poured us two cups, took himself a bit of cheese, and we went back into the sitting room. As soon as he was settled, two cats came and sat on his lap and, as we talked, he broke off bits of the cheese and fed them.

"Now," he said again, "what brings you 'round here?"

"I said I'd get back to you about Wednesday night. You

think you'll be able to make it? We'd like to have it at La Couronne, since everyone feels the way you do about my place. What do you say?"

"Why'd you pick that place?"

"Monsieur Lupa offered it." I shrugged.

"He's coming again, is he?"

"Yes. He said we could use his kitchen, which is large and private. I've already sent over lots of beer. He seems anxious to meet us all under better conditions, and I've talked to him once or twice since... since Wednesday."

"Why's he so anxious to get together with us again?"

"I don't know. He didn't really say that. I just got the impression."

"Hmm..." He drank the coffee, which wasn't, finally, as bitter as I'd expected. "Seems a mite strange. But then..."

"*He* is, as you say, a mite strange. But then, I've never been here before, and I find it quite, er, unorthodox. I've never really trusted men who liked cats, if you'll pardon me for saying so. And I find it funny that I've known you all this while, and never would have suspected that of you."

He smiled. "Well, do you trust me less now?"

"It's really not a question of trust or mistrust. I simply find it odd that your fondness for cats doesn't somehow show. Cats seem more of a woman's pet, and you're certainly not what I'd call effeminate."

"Shucks, no." He laughed out loud now, nudging the cats playfully behind their heads. "Well, now you know I like cats, but that doesn't show any more than if I smoked hashish or wore buffalo skin underwear, which, by the way, I don't."

I sipped at my coffee. "Well, yes, but..."

"No. You just can't tell. Take all this stuff about Marcel. Now, I'm sorry and all to see him dead, and I'm sorry for you because you were his friend, but how much did we know about him? Hell, I didn't even know where he lived. What if, for example—and don't get mad—he was having an affair with Tania, and you found out and killed him. Or if he had recently gambled everything on some adventure, and lost, and for that reason killed himself. No way to know. Or if he was a spy of some kind, like some of the others said, and the whole thing had nothing at all to do with him personally, though I myself don't credit that one much. He just didn't seem the cloak-and-dagger type. 'Course, there I go again doing what I'm yappin' at you about. He didn't seem the cloak-and-dagger type, and I don't seem the cat-lover type, though I am, isn't that right, Esau?" This last was addressed to the large black tom seated sedately on his lap. "When you come down to it, and be honest, would I strike you as a poet?"

"I must admit . . . no. Though more so here in your house than elsewhere."

"Because here I'm more eccentric?"

"I suppose, yes."

"But that's just another cliché, you see. The eccentric, sensitive poet. I lived just this way for years before I wrote my first poem. Cats, plants, and all. You want some more coffee?" I shook my head no, but he got up and walked to the kitchen for some of his own. He yelled from there. "Gotta brew up some more. It'll be a minute."

I saw Paul walking outside toward the pump. At the same time, one of the small kittens jumped from a chair and scampered to the foot of the narrow staircase. When I moved to see it more clearly, it bolted up the stairs, then turned to look back at me. Alarmed at the height it had attained, it began whining piteously, and I got up intending to hold it until Paul's return.

But I must have spooked it again, because it turned and disappeared up into a room at the top of the stairs. In all innocence, I followed it into Paul's bedroom-cum-workspace, with a cluttered desk and an unmade bed. Over the bed were more dusty prints of American shows, and the wall over the desk was covered with books along its entire length and breadth. There were two large windows, one just to each side of the bed, and in the corner a stepladder leading to a square hole in the ceiling.

Forgetting the cat and feeling guilty, I nevertheless crossed to the desk and silently opened the top center drawer. It was filled with well-nibbled pencils, yellowing bits of paper with fading snatches of writing barely visible—in short, exactly what should have been there. Glancing at the books in front of me, I found the titles entirely commensurate with my expectations. Possibly he had a hollow book up there, but suddenly that struck me as highly unlikely. The room just didn't *feel* like a hiding place, and I was beginning to feel foolish and slightly embarrassed for having invaded Paul's privacy.

He would be returning shortly with his coffee, and I re-solved to get back downstairs as quickly as I could, when the kitten whined again, this time from the hole in the ceiling. Somehow it had made it up the stepladder and now was truly frightened. I moved over and looked up while the crying continued.

"Come here, kitty," I said, my foot poised on the bottom rung. As I've mentioned, I'm not much of a cat person, and my technique in calling was not effective. In fact, the animal disappeared back into the opening. "Come on," I repeated, "good kitty, come here." I climbed the few steps and looked around.

As my eyes became adjusted to the darkness, I was dumbfounded by what I saw. The attic looked like an arsenal. The walls on both sides under the pitched eaves were covered with rifles and pistols of every size and description. The cat forgotten, I crawled up into the small space and stared. Boxes of ammunition for the various guns sat open on the floor. I noticed a few bullet molds near a low table, what appeared to be a lead smelter, cleaning rags, the usual paraphernalia.

In my shock, I must have lost track of the time. Paul's voice echoed faintly from below, and then almost immediately I heard his bounding footsteps on the stairs. I had no time to cover my indiscretion.

"I'm up here, Paul," I said feebly, "in the attic."

"What the hell...?" he began.

I looked down at him. "I was trying to rescue a cat."

As though on cue, the kitten crawled to the opening and looked over, meowing at the sight of its owner.

Paul stood on the balls of his feet as though poised for action, the coffee steaming in his right hand. I watched his face carefully and even went so far as to make sure my own pistol was within easy reach. But after a moment of consternation, he seemed to reach some decision and smiled at me, his insouciant air returning.

"Well," he said, "I guess you've found me out."

"I had no idea you had such an interest in guns."

He grinned. "Another surprise. First cats, then plants, now guns."

"But so many?"

He shrugged. "It's a hobby."

"You'll pardon me if I say it's a strange hobby, especially at this time. Do the police know about it?"

"I doubt it," he said, "or they'd have probably arrested me in spite of the fact that Marcel was poisoned."

"But what do you do with them?"

"I save them, shoot them, clean them, make ammo. It relaxes me. Takes my mind off the jungle of literary life. Besides, guns fascinate me, always have."

"Aren't you worried about being discovered?"

"God! You talk as though I'd done something. No, not at all. I never let the kids up here, of course, and the few friends to whom I've shown the place can be trusted. I figure if you can trust me with your beer, the least I can do is reciprocate. No, I'm not worried."

"Do you shoot them often?"

"Sure. In fact, yesterday I packed a few of 'em away and went off shooting. Got a couple of rabbits, though I got the first one with a buffalo gun. If there weren't so many of the damn pests, I suppose I'd feel unsportsmanlike, but it's good practice."

"Are you a good shot?"

"In all modesty, Jules, I am a crack shot."

"Yet another thing I'd never have guessed."

"Amazing, isn't it? And there's probably a lot more. I've got quite a few tricks up my sleeve. You know, I was in Alaska when I was a boy, looking to get rich on gold. Picked up a lot of useful knowledge there, not to mention most of my adult interests. Probably that's why I like the kids here so much and take the time for them. Lots of old men helped me out up there, and it wasn't so easy to get by." He stopped abruptly, remembering, drinking his coffee reflectively, his eyes far away. "But come, Jules, take a look at what I really do."

I had to turn my back to him to come down the ladder and I felt a surge of trepidation as I began, but it was quickly over. He led me to the desk and picked up one of the stacks of paper, covered with what was, to me, an illegible scrawl. Americans write in a strange hand.

"My first retrospective," he said proudly. "Collected best poems from my other books. They're even allowing me to pick the material. I'm a little nervous because I've decided to include twenty-three new poems. They asked for a collection of published stuff."

I picked up the bundle. "Looks like a lot of work, but it's impressive, Paul. I'm sure they won't mind the new work."

"I don't really see why they would, but you never know."

"You know," I said, "I'd like to read your work correctly translated someday. I always enjoy it but I'm afraid I miss nuances in English. And the poetry must be very good if they want a collection."

He shrugged. "It's a living. Beats looking for gold." He sat in the chair behind the desk and stared out the window. "I understand, though, that this will be translated into French, so you may get your chance. I'll autograph a copy for you."

I thanked him and saw an opening for more questioning. "Where do you get your ideas, Paul? What does a poet do on an average day?"

The subject seemed to interest him. "Yesterday wasn't my average day, what with the shooting and all, and neither is today, since you've come. But generally I get up around dawn and drink coffee, write for two hours, and go after food. When I get back I have lunch, then go up to the studio and work on my hobbies. Usually, the kids come by. I'm kind of the neighborhood character. They all love coming over here, and we go out and fool around, exploring or whatever. One of the boys got a motorcycle not so long ago, and we've been doing a lot of fooling with that. Lots of fun. You ever ride one? No? Well, you wouldn't believe the speed. Then I generally go to town and have dinner with one of my friends, then home, a little more writing, and bed. Doesn't sound eccentric, does it?"

"Not to me," I admitted. I stood up and walked over to the plants. "You know one of Lupa's fetishes is plants, too?"

"See?" He came over to where I stood and began plucking dead leaves from some stems. "I never would have figured that."

"*Mais c'est vrai,*" I said. "Have you heard anything new about Marcel's death?"

"Have they arrested someone? I'd be happy to see that. It's a real pain reporting every day to the *flics.*"

"No. One of the investigators has been found dead."

He went to a chair and sat down.

"Well, I'm damned! Looks like a bad business."

"Very," I agreed. "He'd just been to see Henri."

"The poor bastard! You think he did it?"

"I've no idea. I'm trying to keep out of it as much as I can. Haven't seen the police yet."

"Probably a good idea. In fact, thinking about it, I'm not sure if it's such a good idea meeting with everyone on Wednesday. Why not put it off a week?"

"I should give you a reason, but it's really more of a personal thing with me. We've, most of us, been friends for so long that I thought it would be good to get back together, lay any suspicion to rest."

"You're right, I suppose. It *would* be good to see everyone back to normal." He stood again with his coffee cup in his hand and clapped me heartily on the back. "Well, Jules, rest assured. I don't suspect you of anything, except that I instinctively mistrust cat-haters." He laughed.

"Then can I expect you on Wednesday?"

"Sure as shootin'."

"Comment?"

"That means, yes, count on it."

"Ah," I nodded. "Have a good day. *Ciao.*"

Paul showed me out, and I walked back to the car. He had raised many more questions for me than he'd answered. He'd been out yesterday with a rifle. But of course, if he were a crack shot, he wouldn't have missed. Then again, possibly...

Hell, I thought, possibly anything.

I got in the car and started off toward the road. I rounded a turn and came upon a group of youths running alongside a boy on a motorbike, heading back toward Paul's house. It was still a bit chilly, and I'd left my windows up, so that as I passed the boys their voices were muffled and indistinct, though shrill, and blended with the noise of the motor. I had the uneasy feeling that I'd heard those same voices before.

13

Jacques Magiot and I had been acquaintances for over forty years, and a mutual antipathy had developed between us over the course of time. When he was beginning his career with the police, I was a gadabout. He was a few years older than I, and before we'd finished *secondaire,* we'd had many of the same friends. Our fathers, as a matter of fact, had been quite close. After they had retired, they spent most of their afternoons together playing bola. So it was more or less assumed that we would become friends. It never happened. Once he tried to recruit me to the force, and I'd laughed at the notion. From that time, the condescension with which he'd always treated me—friendly condescension, to be sure—turned to subtle derision. I think he always considered me a do-nothing, and it no doubt angered him when I began to increase my

father's already substantial fortune through my own re-
sources. Still, we would meet at parties occasionally and exchange pleasantries. As a policeman, he was competent for
routine problems, entirely without imagination, and through
some admixture of luck and obstinancy had arrived at the
position of police chief of Valence.

The police headquarters building was a large, neo-classic
monstrosity in the center of town. Arched and pillared, it
might have been made by a blind, one-armed Roman. It was
the largest building in town, built *sans doute* on the theory
that if might makes right, big makes beautiful. *Tant pis.*

I was ushered down the hall from the front desk to the
room of one of the subordinates, a M. Procunier. He was a
short, heavy, bald man with a large nose and a florid complexion. He sat behind his desk and bade me sit facing him.

"Nice of you to come," he began sarcastically. "We've been
by your house several times. Have you received that message?
There have been some murders lately, you realize."

I nodded. "My good man, Monsieur Magiot knows where
he can find me, and no one said there was any urgency.
Indeed, there couldn't have been, or you'd have stationed
someone at the house and brought me here as soon as I
appeared. Now. I'm here, voluntarily, to answer questions,
I presume, and I have little use for sarcasm. Let's get on with
it." I smiled. "By the way, will Monsieur Magiot be in?"

"He's in now. He's to see you when I'm through taking
your report."

"Fine. I'm at your disposal."

He asked me the same questions they'd asked the previous
Wednesday, adding only a reference or two to Chatelet's death.
Did I have any suspicions? Had anything out of the ordinary
happened to me since Wednesday? I didn't know what Fritz
might have told them, so I mentioned the episode with the
rock and left out yesterday's shooting incident.

"You think it was a prank?" he asked.

"Without any doubt. I heard children's voices."

"Would you like a police escort?"

"Good God, no! Whatever for?"

"Protection."

So it went. How well did I know the people at the gathering? What was the purpose of the meeting? Did I know that if more than three people met at any time, it could be construed as a subversive gathering and was forbidden?

"Thank you," I said, "is that all?"

He directed me to Magiot. Jacques was dealing with some of his men when I entered, and I stood quietly by the door while he finished talking with them. After they'd filed out, he reached out his hand.

"Jules," he said. "Good to see you. It's been quite a while. Nasty business, this, eh? I'm awfully sorry about Routier. He was a good friend of yours, I understand. Do sit down. Cigarette?"

He carried his age very well. Though he was not compelled to by regulations, he preferred to wear his uniform while on duty, and it was well tailored. His dark hair was in a military cut over a disciplined and impassive face. He sat gripping his pipe lightly with both hands over the bowl, his elbows resting on the desk.

I took the cigarette, and sat. "How are you, Jacques? Your man Procunier is quite a personality."

He waved it off. "Oh, sorry about that. I've just been so busy lately I'd rather have him take the routine things. You made a statement?"

"*Oui.*"

"Good. To tell the truth, I was a little concerned about the circumstances of the death at your place. Several foreigners, that sort of thing. You know gatherings of that size are forbidden."

"To drink beer?"

"I know, I know. In your case, it's rather silly. But there

are reasons, as I'm sure you'll understand. There have been rumors that Routier was mixed up in some international matters. Would you know anything about that?"

"Nothing whatever. We'd been friends for a long time, and he never mentioned anything to me. Also, Jacques, between us, he didn't really seem the type, did he?"

He smiled condescendingly. "Yes. Well, I thought I'd ask." He shifted in his chair and, looking down into the bowl of his pipe, said rather softly, "We think we know who did it."

"Really," I said. "Who?"

"How well do you know this Auguste Lupa? That was the first time he'd been to your house, wasn't it?"

"Not exactly. He'd been there that morning. As to how well I know him—hardly at all. I only met him last Tuesday, and he seemed a nice enough chap. He's really an excellent chef, you know."

"So I've heard. That's one of the reasons we find it strange he was there. He should be working at night. We've gone by La Couronne several times and have failed to find him. Why wouldn't he be there during working hours?"

"I don't know," I replied. "It does seem suspicious."

"Suspicious, ha! Damned suspicious, I'd say."

"But, Jacques. You haven't been able to get in touch with me either in all that time, and there's nothing suspicious about me, is there?"

"I hate to bring it up, Jules, but you don't work like your common man. Your hours are your own to order."

I smiled to myself. Probably my wealth would gall him forever. "So you suspect Lupa?"

"Look at the facts," he said. "Lupa's the only new man at the party. He's a foreigner, from Belgrade or somewhere—"

"He's an American citizen," I interrupted.

"—all right, America. Doesn't change the fact. Then, Routier's sitting in Lupa's seat and even drinking from his glass when he keels over. Lupa hadn't even taken a sip from that glass. In the confusion of Lavoie's glass breaking, Lupa dumps cyanide into the glass and arranges it so that Routier goes back to his seat. We don't know exactly how he did that, but it seems reasonable. We've also got some problems with motive, though this international angle might come into play there. Then Lupa can't be found when we want him, he refuses to cooperate at all, and..." Here he paused for effect. "... We went to see Vernet, the owner of La Couronne, and got Lupa's papers, and they're forged. Cleverly, but definitely. We're going to pick him up tonight."

I sighed. "Well, that's certainly a relief, Jacques. I'm glad you've found him. It does look rather bad for him. Forged, you say?"

"Without doubt."

"What about your inspector? Him, too?"

"We think so. He's got no alibi. We figure Chatelet—that was his name—was onto something. He questioned Lupa, and Lupa panicked. With his size, he could have strangled him easily, and probably did. He hadn't reported back to us yet, but his itinerary that morning had him seeing Lupa after the funeral, then the others, and none of the others saw him. He must have seen Lupa first, and been killed before he could see anyone else."

"But couldn't it have happened that when Chatelet saw that Lupa'd missed the funeral, he changed his plans and took off on a new tack? In that case he might have run into someone else altogether."

"Yes, that's true. But why would he change his plans? Did anything strange happen at the funeral? Anything to make you suspicious?"

"No," I said truthfully.

"Well, then."

"Just a thought," I muttered.

"You just let us handle this, Jules. It's what we do best."

I got up to go. "Well, good luck, Jacques. I hope you get him. And thank you."

He shook my hand warmly. "It's a pleasure to set the mind of an old friend at ease. Don't worry about a thing. We'll have everything straightened out and back to normal in no time."

I walked out into the cool evening. If that's what they did best... I smiled grimly to myself. So no one else had seen Chatelet, which of course meant that Henri had lied to the police. Understandable, but certainly neither wise nor wily. I decided to go to Lupa's, to warn him. He wouldn't be any good at all from inside a jail trying to convince a man like Magiot of his innocence. Magiot thought I was supercilious. I shuddered to imagine what he'd think of Lupa.

It wouldn't do to go directly to La Couronne from the police station, so I walked to my car and drove several blocks back toward my house, checking to see that I wasn't being tailed. I wasn't. I parked and began walking, then, back in the direction of Anna's shop. I knew it was a bit risky entering that way, but it would be better than just dropping in, especially if the police had already arrived.

The walk took me nearly a quarter of an hour, and it was completely dark when I arrived. The door was locked, as I might have expected if I'd been thinking of details, such as Anna lying wounded at Tania's house, but it presented no problem. Once inside, I crossed to the back door, behind the screen, and opened it. The smell of the flowers rising to meet me was once again overpowering but pleasant as I picked my way back to the tunnel entrance. I remembered roughly where Lupa had reached to turn off the alarm and, after fumbling along the darkened wall for a short while, got it and clicked it to what I hoped was off. The walk was becoming nearly familiar, and I covered the distance to Lupa's room in less than five minutes. Magiot had said that they were picking up Lupa tonight, and it was now night. There wasn't much time to waste.

I stood at the curtains and listened to see if Lupa had guests. There was a faint glow around one edge of the curtain, so at least one of the room's lights was on. I heard no sound, so I quietly pulled the curtain open and stepped in. My training had not entirely deserted me, and I could still move quietly and effectively if I had to. Lupa sat at his desk, absorbed in some reading. He turned a page, and I cleared my throat.

Normally, a man surprised in that manner will start. Lupa didn't move a muscle. Without the merest glance at me, he closed the book and stared ahead of him. Finally, he turned his head to see me.

"How did you get in here?" he snapped.

"Spontaneous generation."

"How long have you been here?"

"Under a minute. Now relax. It was necessary. You're in a lot of trouble, and we've got to move right away."

"So the tunnel's been unguarded for ten minutes... pfui." He reached for the button on his desk and activated the alarm again.

"You can check all that later," I said. "Get Charles in here, and Vernet as soon as he can be reached. I've just come from the police, and you're to be arrested tonight for Marcel's murder."

He glared at me. "The fools!"

"I couldn't agree more, but that doesn't matter much at this point. We've got to get you out of here and covered before the police arrive."

"The fools!" he repeated.

"Yes," I said. "It seems that they've checked your papers and discovered the forgeries, and that Henri has denied seeing

Chatelet, and naturally they assume, then, that you killed him before he could have seen anyone else. Now, does Charles know about the tunnel?"

"Yes. So does Vernet."

"Anyone else?"

"Besides you, Anna, Watkins, and myself? No. Not that I know of."

"All right. Let's get you out that way then. Call in your men."

"No," he said. "No, I'm not leaving here. Simply impossible. I'm a marked man, and I've decided to stick it out here, and I will do so. I'll call the others."

"But how..."

He cut me off by ignoring me and calling out into the kitchen. Charles appeared shortly, clad in an apron and chef's cap, smiling. He was surprised to see me, but nodded courteously.

Lupa began talking. "Close the front door immediately and go fetch Monsieur Vernet. We are closed for business tonight due to the loss of our chef. I beg your pardon, Charles, but it does have nothing to do with you. After you've gotten Vernet here, continue on out to Monsieur Giraud's house— you remember where it is? Good. Talk to his chef, a Fritz Benet, and tell him to stop whatever he is doing and come along here as quickly as possible. Tell him Monsieur Giraud is in trouble, and we need him. Bring him through the back way. Try to do all this in under an hour, and start now." Charles already had stripped himself of accoutrements and stood ready to go. Lupa turned to me. "You have a car, n'est-ce pas? Bien. Give the keys to Charles. You can drive, can't you? Use the car. Speed is everything. Va-t-en! Go!"

When he'd left, Lupa excused himself and left me sitting wondering what he planned to do. I heard him moving about in the adjoining room, evidently rearranging things in some way. In a short while he reappeared, carrying two beers in each hand. He set them on his desk and opened two, offering one to me without a word. Then he sat with his eyes closed and breathed deeply for what seemed an hour but was actually probably less than a minute. Finally he sat up, opened his eyes, and glanced at the beer glass, presumably to see that the foam had settled adequately, and drank. When he put the glass down, it was empty, and he immediately reached for another beer. He looked at me after pouring.

"So."

"If you don't mind my asking, what are you planning to do? You can't stay here, and every minute we sit here threatens you more. Why don't we just go over to my place, or at least through the tunnel? Here you are too vulnerable."

"Nonsense. What I did in the outer room just then will prevent any interference from the police. The huge tapestries covering the other walls? Well, for such an eventuality as this, I've another on hand. I've simply covered the door to the office and the wall surrounding it. No one will suspect there is a room there."

"But if they search, it's transparent."

"Why would they search? If they're capable of thinking me guilty of Marcel's death, they are no danger to me. They will look in the rooms that remain, which are certainly ample for one man living alone. They won't suspect a hidden room. Why should there be one? Monsieur Vernet will tell them he fired me because of my papers, and Charles will corroborate. Then, of course, there will be a new chef, newly hired, and living in these quarters."

"I suppose that would be..."

"Exactly. Fritz." He drank more beer, and I joined him.

"Did it occur to you that I might not approve of this? That perhaps Fritz is my private chef and of some worth to me, both personally and professionally?"

"Certainly, my dear Jules," he smiled. "That's why I didn't want to discuss any of this with you before sending Charles on his errand. I didn't want to waste the time. You see, there really isn't much choice. I can be very effective here, and I intend to remain. Come. It won't be for long. Enjoy your beer."

I sat and thought in silence. He was right, but it was aggravating. What was I to do with Fritz gone? Suddenly I realized what had begun to nag me.

"I gather, then, that you've cleared Fritz? You might have mentioned it to me."

He did not respond in any way.

"Well?" I said.

He sighed. "There are simply some matters that I can't disclose at this time, even to you, Jules."

"That's ridiculous!"

"Patently, it is not."

"Might I ask why?"

He searched for the least objectionable way to phrase it. "You are a valuable ally, Jules, and becoming a good friend, but there is a certain ingenuousness in your character that I can turn to my advantage. I must ask you to trust me in this."

"I find it highly insulting."

He got up from the desk and crossed over to me, placing his hand on my shoulder. "It is not that, I assure you." He leaned his huge bulk back against the desk. "My father, Jules, had a companion for many years—a very good man of impeccable character and great bravery. But his goodness was so ingrained, his honesty so natural, that he was absolutely incapable of dissembling. My father knew this, of course, and occasionally had to leave this man in the dark, or in a few cases actually mislead him, so that he might not unwittingly tip a winning hand."

Again, his hand came to rest on my shoulder. "Jules, forgive me, but you are not an actor. You are an agent, and a valuable man of action, but if you were closing in on Marcel's murderer, I doubt if you could altogether suppress your feelings until the optimum moment. And that, in this case, is essential."

"But Fritz...?" I began.

"For the time being, let Fritz be my problem. I will say this much: if he is our man, what better place to monitor his activities than under my own roof?"

I was not completely happy or convinced by his rationale, but I could see that his mind was made up. He went back around his desk and sat, and we waited for the others to return. Lupa opened the last beer, poured it for himself, and had nearly finished when Vernet entered.

He was of average height but distinguished by a full, red beard and, incongruously, piercing dark eyes. It was an odd combination, which his dress reinforced. He wore an English derby hat and a large, plaid overcoat which, when removed, gave way to a more conventional attire—a dark suit and tie. The color scheme of his face became even more bizarre when he took off the hat, revealing a head of gray hair. He entered by the tunnel, so of course we'd been warned of his entrance.

"See here, Auguste, what's this about closing down the restaurant? I realize that 'M' and Altamont have asked me to cooperate in every way I could, but we're beginning to lose customers, what with Charles's cooking and your irregular hours. What's the explanation this time?"

Perfectly unruffled, Lupa introduced us.

"Now, sit down, monsieur. I am sorry, but it's really unavoidable. We should be open for business again within the hour, but in the meantime I am going to need your help. Will you have some beer? Cognac?"

The owner sat and nodded. "Courvoisier, *s'il vous plait.*" To my surprise, Lupa attended him. When they had both been seated, Lupa began again.

"We have a real problem, though we could possibly have foreseen it, given the way the police have handled everything so far. They've reached the inescapable conclusion that I am Monsieur Routier's murderer. Monsieur Giraud has just given me that report, and the police are supposedly to be here this evening to arrest me. Unfortunately, that would be most inconvenient, so I've covered over the door to the office and have decided to remain here until I've settled this matter. Let it look to the police as if I've run. That's fine; in fact, it suits my purposes, since now the heat will be off the actual murderer. They'll of course question you as to my whereabouts, and you should tell them that you dismissed me immediately upon learning that my papers were forged and you haven't seen me since."

"Fine," said Vernet with impatience, pulling at his beard, "but who's to be the new chef? How did I find him? And, above all, can he cook?"

"On the last point, you may rest assured. His name is Fritz Benet, and he would be worthy to be my own chef, were I ever in a position to be able to afford one. Maybe after the war... but that's irrelevant. He's been the chef for Monsieur Giraud for quite some time. However, for these purposes Giraud fired him because he suspected him of complicity with Routier's death."

"Now, wait a minute, Auguste..." I began, but he waved me down.

"That puts him in no danger. Believe me, it's perfectly safe. The police have checked him thoroughly."

"But why should I suspect him?"

"He poured the beer." He shrugged. "It doesn't have to make sense to us. It merely has to be plausible to the police. They've apparently settled on me. That you might suspect Fritz will have no bearing."

Vernet sipped at his cognac. "So I will once again have a restaurant."

"Barring difficulties."

That seemed to palliate him. His face relaxed and he looked

at me. "I asked for this when I decided to accommodate our friend here. At least it's not dull."

Lupa picked up the book he'd been reading when I entered and, without so much as a "by your leave," became engrossed again. Vernet and I discussed Fritz's merits until the alarm sounded again. Lupa distractedly pushed the button, and I, seeing that he was taking no precautions, got up and walked into the tunnel, my pistol ready. After a few moments, I heard Fritz's voice and returned to my chair.

When they entered, Fritz crossed over to me.

"You're all right?" he asked.

"Perfectly."

"What's the trouble?"

Lupa spoke. "Hello, Fritz. Please take a seat."

Within a quarter of an hour, the thing had been settled, and Fritz was in the kitchen, getting acquainted. Vernet waited for the police in the bar upstairs, and Charles, somewhat miffed at his demotion, nevertheless was assisting Fritz whenever necessary. Lupa and I sat in the office, discussing the war.

"I still say that it will be over soon. Now that Italy has joined us..."

Lupa shook his head. "Jules, you are deluded. This war will continue for years."

"Years? Don't be ridiculous!"

"Mark my words. You talk of settling down and growing your vineyards in peace. In two years, you'll be wondering if you'll be able to hold on to your land. The government will need every man, every resource, and it will take them. Your hobbies, which you so treasure, and rightly so, will fade to insignificance. There will be no good food available. Everyone will join in the effort. Watkins has brought me the news that they'll soon be hiring women at the munitions factories."

"No!"

"Yes, indeed. Every man will be fighting. Factory workers, sick men, even older men will be forced to the front, and it will be to no avail. The war will drag on. Keep in mind, Jules, it's only been ten months. There's still adventure and idealism in the thought of war. Give the world two or three or five years of it, and you'll see everything you know change. After this case is over, I'm quitting myself, though my uncle will disapprove. I may have to go to America to escape this war, though I fear that even the Americans and their pacifist Wilson will have to join. Luckily for France, they'll support her."

"Not exactly a Utopian, are you?"

"No, a realist. They don't go well together."

Knowing that cynicism and youth were constant companions, I was not unduly depressed by his opinions, though it saddened me to see such an intelligent man obviously unaware of the military realities. Germany was strong, but we'd been beaten in 1871 and had learned from it. The Kaiser was no Bismarck. That was the point to remember. No German army would ever march under the Arch de Triomphe again.

"You French," he continued, "with your *elan vital!* It isn't will that wins a war, it's firepower. This war won't be settled by men being pushed against other men on the fronts but in the countries themselves—where every effort of the economy, the government, the citizenry itself will play a part. And it will be at least two years before that fact is realized. No, Jules. Prepare yourself for a long siege."

"And you," I said, "how will you avoid conscription?"

He sat back. "I am willing to die, I suppose, for freedom, and I am more than willing to devote my talents to serve the Allied cause. But I could never, never serve on the front as one of the thousands who are important because they are bodies. My ego would never permit it. And honestly, Jules, would yours?"

I looked down at my hands. "I'd rather not serve at the

front, if that's what you mean, but in my case it's more a question of age than conceit."

He shrugged. "Call it what you will. Are you getting ready to go?"

I'd gotten up, alerted by noises upstairs. He put his fingers to his lips as he crossed over to me, and together we listened at the door to what sounded like Magiot himself talking to Vernet.

"You expect me to believe that he left here this afternoon and left no hint of where he was going?"

"I expect nothing, monsieur," Vernet replied. "I merely tell you what happened. I dismissed him. He left. *C'est ca. C'est tout.*"

Magiot asked a couple of questions about Fritz and then, angry but satisfied with the responses, left. So it had worked.

Lupa walked back to his chair and sat. "Satisfactory. Jules, you're going home this evening? Good. Would you check something for me?"

"Of course."

"The table in your sitting room, in front of the fireplace, I'd like you to look at it carefully and describe it to me in detail when you return tomorrow."

I left him exactly as I'd found him, sitting over a book at his desk. I found my way out easily through the tunnel, walked to the car, and began the drive home. It had been a long day. Only as I turned off the light near my bed to sleep did I remember that the telegram from Georges hadn't arrived.

14

Tuesday, May 25, 1915. The day broke cool and clear. I threw the comforter off and got to my feet. Downstairs, the kitchen was spotless as always but, without Fritz, seemed lifeless. I made my own coffee, which was not good, and ate one of yesterday's croissants, which was worse. I hadn't seen Tania since Sunday after the shooting, and so I decided to pay her a call.

The walk to her house was always pleasant for me, and no less so this morning. The greens were vibrant, and I'd gotten started early enough to hear the birds chirping. It was not quite cold, though I walked with my hands in my pockets.

Danielle answered my knock and stood wringing her hands in the doorway.

"Is Madame in?" I inquired.

She shook her head back and forth and looked at me helplessly.

"What's the matter, Danielle?"

I brushed past her and on into the foyer. "Tania!" There was no answer.

"*Elle est partie.*" Danielle had come up behind me.

"Where's she gone to? When did she leave?"

The domestic only shook her head, tears coming to her eyes.

"The other woman? What about her?"

"She's also gone."

"When did they leave? Have you no idea?"

"They were gone when I got up this morning. They were here last night. Oh, Monsieur Giraud, I'm so worried. I don't know what could have happened. Everything was normal last night, and now they are gone. There is no note. I heard nothing."

She was becoming hysterical, so I walked her to a chair and we sat down. I took her hand.

"Now look, Danielle. Try to remember. Did anyone come last night? Did Madame act strange in any way? How was the other woman?"

"Last night she was walking around, of course with the bandage still on her head. But we talked, and she seemed well. The madame had dinner and went up to bed early, complaining of a headache. No one came to the house."

"What time did you get up this morning?"

"At dawn, monsieur, *comme d'habitude.*"

"Were there any signs of trouble? Struggle of any kind?"

"No."

"All right. Wait here. I'll look around."

So saying, I left her in the sitting room and went to Tania's room. The bed had been slept in. Her cosmetics were neatly arranged. Her brush had some hair in it—since Danielle cleaned daily, it was likely that Tania had taken the time to comb out her hair. Everything was in order.

On Tania's bureau there was a framed photograph of herself, her husband, and the four boys formally posed around their sitting room mantle. The focus was clear, all the likenesses visible. From the age of the boys, the picture had been taken within two years. I remembered Lupa's directions and my hand reached out to take the thing. But then I stopped. Could I do this to my lover? Were there no limits to this intelligence gathering? How would Tania react to the missing picture? Turning abruptly, I left the room empty-handed.

In the other rooms, I looked at windows for signs of forcible entry, for scuff marks in the hall which might show where a struggle had taken place, but I found nothing. Anna's bandage lay in a wastebasket near her dressing table, but she may have had it changed. I came back down to find Danielle as I'd left her, but now dabbing at her eyes more frequently. The girl was not yet twenty and no doubt was easily upset. "There, there," I said, which was patently no help. She cried for another small time before I could quiet her by suggesting that she go to my house, until further notice, and try to keep the place in order. Even as I said it, I cursed to myself. I'd forgotten to look over the table near the hearth. Still, it was no great matter. I was worried about Tania's disappearance. If nothing else, it was badly timed. What would Lupa say when he heard that Anna had disappeared? I didn't care to think about it.

As we were about to lock up the house, I excused myself for a moment, trudging wearily back up the stairs to Tania's room. Carefully I removed the family portrait from the frame, rolled it, and placed it in my coat pocket. If it would serve to clear her of suspicion, she would have to do without it for a time. On the way back down the stairs, I tried to rationalize my guilt by telling myself that, had she been there, I would have asked to borrow the picture, and she would have acceded. It was small consolation.

We carefully locked up the house and walked together as far as the road. I was in a hurry to get to Valence, though I couldn't have said why—perhaps I was as much concerned with getting out of Danielle's presence. Nothing upset me more than the whimpering voice of an hysterical teenager. Be that as it may, I left her with my keys and turned to Valence. I found myself breathing hard and forced myself to a slow walk. It would be good if, as Lupa said, this thing was coming to a head. I was afraid I wouldn't be able to stand the pace much longer.

I stopped at the first cafe *en ville* and ordered a double espresso and a newspaper. By the time I'd finished both, it was close to nine o'clock and traffic had picked up on the road. I felt much more relaxed and decided for the moment to put off seeing Lupa. Shut up as he was in his hideaway at La Couronne, he would not be of much help in determining Tania's and Anna's whereabouts anyway. And I was still not at all sure that the ladies were at risk. Walking out of the cafe, I glanced in the direction of St. Etienne and saw sulfur clouds beginning to rise. So the factory was still producing. Things hadn't gotten out of control yet.

I headed toward the telegraph office to check on early telegrams. Perhaps they hadn't bothered to deliver Georges's telegram of the night before, or maybe it had only arrived this morning. No such luck. Nothing had arrived for me at all.

Again out on the street, I turned toward the police station, thinking it would seem logical to Magiot if I showed an interest in whether they'd taken Lupa or not. The way my morning had been going, Magiot might even cheer me up.

I was ushered directly into his office. He rose to greet me, and we shook hands.

"Well, Jules, what wakes you so early?"

I'd play his game. "Curiousity, Jacques. I wanted to see if eight o'clock came twice a day. Someone told me it appeared in the morning, and I wanted to check it out for myself."

He smiled tolerantly.

"But," I said, "I really thought I'd drop by and see if you'd picked up Lupa or gotten anywhere with this thing. I had a devil of a time sleeping last night, what with all your talk of international affairs. Have you got him? Did he confess?"

Magiot arranged some papers on his desk, taking his time. He got out a cigarette, offered me one which I refused, and lit it. "No," he said finally, "we didn't get him. He'd left La Couronne by the time we'd come to arrest him."

"Lupa left? When did he go? I saw him there only yesterday morning."

"Evidently Vernet fired him outright when he learned of the forged papers. He packed up and left immediately. You know they've hired your man—Fritz, isn't it?—to take his place?"

"No. No, I didn't know that."

"By the way, Jules, why did you fire him just at this time?"

I shrugged. "I found myself not trusting him. It wasn't anything specific that brought it on, but since he'd brought in the beers that night, it occurred to me that he'd had as good a chance as anyone to poison one of them. I kept getting more and more nervous as mealtimes approached, until finally I wasn't enjoying his cooking, so I let him go."

"But I understand he brought the beers in on a tray from which everyone selected..."

"True. As I said, it wasn't anything specific. I just can't have a man in my house whom I don't trust completely. He could have arranged it, possibly."

"Yes, from your point of view, possible. I think you've been unjust, though it's your right."

I shrugged again. "There are other chefs. But what are you doing about Lupa? Have you any ideas?"

"None, really. He didn't leave by train. At least, no one saw him leave by train. He could really be anywhere. We've wired all the neighboring towns and asked for their hotel lists, though of course he'll change his name. He may have sheafs of forged papers. Still, I think we'll get him. You can rest assured."

"I hope so. Why, though, did you wait until last night to go for him? Surely you could have picked him up at any time."

"We'd already been by in the morning, if you remember what I told you yesterday—it must have been after you had talked to him, because he wasn't there. We reasoned our best chance to find him was during dinner hours. With the force so short-handed we couldn't leave someone there to cover the doors at all times, so we gambled and lost."

"A shame," I said, sincerely.

"Damned right," he agreed, stubbing out his cigarette. "And now, old friend, if there's nothing else, I should be getting on to routines. I'm glad to see you showing some interest at least. Do drop around later if you have any more questions. We should have him within the week."

"Yes. Well, thank you for your time, Jacques. I know the way out."

Out in the corridor, I allowed myself a smile. Passing through the lobby, my hands in my pockets and my head down, I heard a familiar voice. The American accent echoed unmelodically off the marble walls. I stopped and saw Paul leaning over the reception desk, obviously angry.

"But I've been reporting at St. Etienne every day for a week now! I can't be there tonight. Don't you understand? I can report here just as well..."

The gendarme replied in a low voice.

"Well, all right then, arrest me, but at least let me..."

I tapped him on the shoulder. "Paul," I said.

He stopped and turned. "Jules, thank God. Listen, can you help me? These people don't seem to realize that I can't report to St. Etienne this evening."

"Why not?"

"I received a wire from my publishers telling me to meet their representative tonight in Valence. So I thought it would be a simple enough matter to report here, but this man here keeps telling me that it's against the rules. If I were told to report in St. Etienne, then I must report in St. Etienne. It's insane. What's the goddam difference?"

"Why don't you just wire your publishers to meet you in St. Etienne?"

"He's already left by now, Jules. If I'm not here, they won't take it lightly."

"I imagine not. All right, let me talk to him."

I leaned over the desk and pointed out to the *flic* that since they already had a suspect, it was rather pointless to keep hounding everyone else involved. Perhaps Monsieur Magiot would see the logic of my position. At the mention of the chief's name, the desk guard looked down and mumbled that perhaps something could be done to accommodate the monsieur. I told him I sincerely hoped so, and turned, taking Paul's arm, and walked out the front door.

Out on the stoop, I put my arm around him. "Well, how are you?"

"Fine, now, thank you. Let me buy you a drink."

"*Volontiers.*"

We settled in a cafe, and I surprised both Paul and myself by ordering a Vichy water.

"What were you doing in the station?" he asked. "I certainly didn't expect to run into you there."

"Oh, the police chief here is an old acquaintance of mine. Yesterday he told me they were going to arrest Lupa, and..."

"So it was him. I'm damned."

"Not necessarily. The police have decided it was him, and he's left town..."

"Well, that clinches it."

"Well, yes, it appears so. Anyway, I was at the station to see if they'd got him and found all this out. Seems his papers were forged, too."

He sipped at his whiskey. "Doesn't surprise me any, though."

"No?"

"No. Look at it like this, Jules. We'd all been meeting there at your place for a long time, and if anybody wanted to kill Marcel they could have done it any old time. But everybody liked Marcel. 'Course there's other reasons for killing than having it be personal. But anyway, this Lupa fellow comes in, and right off Marcel is killed, and then Lupa runs away. Didn't he have to register every day? He was foreign, too, wasn't he?"

"I suppose they asked him to. But no, since he was in town, they only requested that he not leave."

"Well, there, now. I hope they hang the bastard."

We were sitting on the sidewalk, and the talk turned to other matters. It was a fine day, and we chatted until noon and then decided to have a bite.

Halfway through our ham sandwiches, Paul looked up across the street and spoke. "It's old home week at Grand Central." He motioned with his head to a couple walking toward us on the other side of the road, as yet unaware of us. It was Georges and Madame Pulis. When they were abreast of us, Paul called out to them.

"The secret's out now about you two. Come on over and join us and maybe we won't tell Henri."

They stopped abruptly, waved, and waited for the traffic to let up. Georges took her by the arm and, limping nimbly, guided her to our table. They ordered drinks and, while waiting for them to arrive, Georges continued the teasing.

"Now that it's known, my dear, why hide it any longer?"
He winked at us as Madame Pulis flushed crimson. Taking
her hand, he gave it a gallant kiss. "Or is it to be *au revoir?*"
He turned his head away in mock despair.

"Oh, Georges, stop." Madame Pulis was rather heavily
set, but not unattractive when she wasn't crying. She smiled
broadly and took us all in. "Georges came by to see Henri,
but he's off delivering somewhere, so Georges offered to
accompany me to the market. That's all there is to it."

"What's the line about the lady protesting too much?" asked
Georges, laughing.

She blushed again as the drinks arrived.

"What brings you back so early, Georges?" I asked. "I
thought you weren't due in Valence until tomorrow evening."

"Luck," he said. "Two appointments cancelled. Just as well.
I could use the time off."

"You've heard the news, haven't you?" Paul piped in.

"What's that?"

"Last night the police went to arrest Lupa for Marcel's
death, and he'd left town."

Georges sipped at his Pernod. "So, it wasn't one of us. I'm
relieved."

"You didn't really think it was?" Madame Pulis asked.

He shrugged. "No one really knew too much about anyone
else in our group. When I heard the rumors about the espionage angle, I must admit I became concerned. I didn't suspect anyone, but then I couldn't completely trust anyone
either. Now it's a relief."

"It will make tomorrow night much more pleasant," I said.
"By the way, it's going to be at La Couronne, where Lupa
worked, coincidentally. None of you mind, do you?"

"Not at all," Paul replied. "At least, I don't. Anybody
else?"

Georges spoke up. "*Moi non plus.* But why there?"

"Because the owner there, Monsieur Vernet, is a friend of mine, and I've loaned him Fritz until he has time to find another chef." I didn't see any harm in telling them a different story than the one I'd told Magiot. "In return for which I eat there *gratis* myself. Believe me, I'd never have let Fritz go if it would have meant eating my own cuisine, if you could call it that."

Paul called for the waiter and ordered another round of drinks, and Madame Pulis said she really had to be getting on to the market.

"Shall I join you?" asked Georges.

"Thank you, no. I'm perfectly happy to go alone. Good day, gentlemen."

"A charming creature," said Georges after she'd gone.

"What's she going to the market for? Doesn't Henri own a store?" Paul was relaxing with his third *demi*.

Georges shrugged. "The company, I suppose."

"I hope we didn't embarrass her too much," I said. "She doesn't seem to enjoy that kind of humor."

"Oh, she's fine. Henri and I tease her like that all the time. She just doesn't know you two so well." He paused. "I'm afraid I have a bit of sad news, however. This will be my last Wednesday beer party. I've been transferred to Algiers."

Paul put down his beer. "Well, as you fellows would say, *merde!*"

"You echo my sentiments, but there's nothing I can do about it other than quit, which I can't afford. It's going to be hard. I've come to like this place very much. Not to mention *mes amis.*" He lifted his glass to us.

"When are you going?"

"The ship sails from Marseilles on Sunday, so I thought I'd take the train on Thursday or Friday, probably Friday. I'll have some packing."

"It's lucky the police have decided on Lupa," I said. "Otherwise you might have a problem leaving here."

"Yes," he said, "now that you mention it, it is fortunate. I didn't mention this matter to the company, of course. They'd probably object to one of their salesmen being suspected of murder." He smiled feebly. "Well, at least it's over."

"Not really," put in Paul. "They haven't got him yet, and until they do, I'm not going to rest easy. You don't know it, Georges, but he also killed a police inspector last week."

"Have they proved that, too?"

"Yep. Strangled him right on the road."

"Mon dieu!"

I decided to join in. "I feel I must apologize for inviting him. Possibly all this could have been avoided if..."

"Oh, nonsense, Jules. How could you have known? If Lupa were a spy of some sort—mind you, I'm not saying he was, but if he was—there'd be no way any of us could have known. Don't blame yourself. All of us only got to know you, and each other as well for that matter, because of your nature, because you trust the people you like."

"Exactly," Paul said, "like we were sayin' yesterday."

"But do they have any evidence that Lupa *was* a spy?" Georges asked.

"Either no, or they won't say. You've got to know this man, Magiot, the police chief, to appreciate him. They don't, at least from my talks with him, have any case to speak of against Lupa. Of course, his running won't help him any. They certainly don't have a motive, except this nebulous espionage thing. Magiot needs to solve this murder, and he will, even if he has to get the wrong man."

"So you don't think it was Lupa?" asked Paul.

"I just don't know."

"Then who do you think it was? One of us?"

"No. I really don't think that. It was undoubtedly Lupa, but Magiot's case on him is so weak that to try and prove anything by it would be folly."

"Except that he ran," offered Georges.

"Except that he ran," I agreed.

"And it might be that Magiot just didn't tell you everything he knows, *n'est-ce pas?*"

I also agreed with that.

Having finished his beer, Paul stood up. "Well, I must be going along. Try to get some sleep before my meeting tonight. You say Fritz is cooking at La Couronne? Maybe I'll meet my publisher there."

"You're not going back to St. Etienne?"

"No, no. I took a hotel in town for today."

Georges and I thanked Paul for the drinks. I'd stuck with Vichy throughout and felt good. Paul was a bit tipsy, and Georges offered to walk him to his hotel. They left, saying they'd see me the following night.

I got up and began walking toward Anna's flower shop. Too many things were happening too quickly, and I was becoming very worried about the two women. It was comforting to agree with the others talking about the solution to the murders, but of course Lupa hadn't done it. One of my friends had. I felt for my pistol, tucked close under my armpit. I was glad I hadn't been drinking.

It was not yet late afternoon, and I still didn't feel like seeing Lupa, so I walked aimlessly past the flower shop. No one was inside. I strolled on through the town, past a group of training soldiers in their red pants and blue tunics, out to where the buildings grew more sparse and the fields began. Under a large oak that was beginning to bud, I sat and thought of Tania.

She had gone, left me without a note or a word, and I could put off the inevitable thought no longer. It was beginning to look as if Lupa had grounds for his suspicions. It was entirely possible that Tania had used me, used Ponty, used even her husband before us. And now she had disappeared, along with the secrets that she had said we never kept from one another. I understood then the real reason I hadn't rushed to consult Lupa—I could barely stand to confront myself with my gullibility. Lupa's reaction to the disappearance, whether it was scorn or compassion, would be unbearable.

A great world-weariness came and settled over me. I leaned back against the tree, defeated, and closed my eyes.

The sun was setting when I awoke with a start. Something from a dream had bothered me, and realizing what it had been, I woke up. It had been a clear day when I'd begun to doze, and looking in the direction of St. Etienne, I should have seen the familiar pillars of sulphur smoke rising over the city.

There had been none.

15

Though I moved quickly, the walk back to Anna's shop seemed interminable. Dusk had settled over the town completely by now, making the unfamiliar section of town even more so. Once again the door was locked, and I quietly slipped the lock and stepped inside. This time I let the alarm sound, though of course I couldn't hear it.

Lupa was behind his desk again. He was, as usual, dressed in brown and yellow. It was as though he hadn't moved since the last time I had seen him, except now that he expected me, he was looking at the entrance to the tunnel as I entered his office.

"Getting pretty sure of yourself, aren't you?" I said. "Suppose that hadn't been me?"

He smiled. "Then I should have had to shoot you." So

saying, he lifted his hand above the level of the desk. It held his pistol. "Thank you, though, for the warning. I appreciate it."

With what seemed a great effort, he pushed back the chair and standing, reached out his hand. It was, I realized, our first handshake. "Where have you been? I was beginning to get worried."

"I wanted some time for myself," I said, "and I ran into most of our suspects."

"Indeed?"

"Paul and Georges. We had a fine time. They'll both be coming tomorrow night. But I have news."

He was sitting again. "So have I. Will you have a beer?"

He reached up to his left and pulled a cord which had been newly strung along the ceiling. Two quick pulls. I looked at him questioningly.

"For Fritz," he explained. "We've worked out a code so that I don't starve or die of thirst. Two pulls for beer. If anyone else is about, he unlatches the bell."

As he finished speaking, the door opened and Fritz entered with a tray. Seeing me, he smiled. "Hello, sir. Good to see you."

Lupa spoke. "Fritz, Monsieur Giraud would also like some beer, and he'll be dining with us. You will, won't you?"

"Of course."

When Fritz had brought the other beer and gone, Lupa poured for both of us, waited for the foam to settle in his glass, took a large gulp, then looked at me. "Well?"

"There's no smoke rising over St. Etienne."

He sat immobile, his face showing nothing. With his left hand, he drummed his fingertips on the desk top. He sighed deeply.

"So. In that case, we can do nothing about it. Watkins should be here before long with a report. Did you check the table?"

"No. I forgot."

He drank. "Hmm... well, I have news."

"So you said."

"I've gotten through to my uncle about your retirement, and he's persuaded your people to accept your decision, though if you were younger..."

I nodded. "You needn't say it." If I were younger, I wouldn't have to worry very much about my future; it would be very short.

"You said you met Paul and Georges today. I had understood that Georges wouldn't be back until tomorrow. And what is Paul doing in Valence?"

I reported on my day from the time I reached the police station. He listened without moving, leaning back in his chair with his eyes closed. He might have been asleep. When I'd finished, he opened his eyes and, seeing his glass empty, poured another.

"So they're all happy to believe me the culprit. Understandable, I suppose. Anything else?"

"Well," I hesitated, "yes, actually. Tania and Anna are missing."

He then did something I never thought I'd witness. His glass was on its way to his mouth when I spoke, and he arrested it midway and set it back on the desk.

"When did you find this out?"

"This morning."

"Why didn't you report it immediately?"

"What could you have done? You're effectively a prisoner here." I began defensively, angry at myself for not having come by sooner, for allowing myself to be lulled by my smaller duties, my social obligations. After I had run into Paul and then Georges, I'd felt as though I might stumble upon some solution. Twice I'd headed to La Couronne to see Lupa, and twice I'd decided against it. My suffering self-esteem had needed—stupidly, I now realized—to present him with answers, not questions. I had wrongly persisted in viewing Tania's (and Anna's) disappearance as my own problem, not our common problem.

"I'm sorry," I said, "I retract that."

"No need to," he said. "It's close to the truth."

"No, I should have come immediately. If anything has happened to them..."

A trace of humanity appeared in the hard eyes. He, too, knew both sides—the concern and the suspicion. "Tell me about it now," he said, "and we'll try to make up for the lost time."

I filled him in on my search of Tania's house, how there appeared to have been no struggle. The only inexplicable thing was their failure to tell Danielle.

"Don't you consider that strange?"

"Yes, rather."

"Everything else was in order?"

"Perfectly. Oh, and one other thing."

I took out the photograph and handed it to him. He unrolled it and placed it flat on the top of his desk, staring at it intently. "Yes," he said absently, "satisfactory. Just as I suspected." So saying, he rerolled the picture and placed it in his desk drawer.

"What?"

"In good time, Jules. In good time."

He ruminated for a while. Finally, he straightened in his chair, reaching for the nearly forgotten beer. He drank it off in a gulp. "Well, they *are* women, given to all sorts of odd whims, and there's nothing to be done at this time. Let's see if they return this evening. If not..."

He was interrupted by the alarm. He reached for the switch and turned off the sound, and this time got up to check the tunnel himself. "That should be Watkins," he said. "Would you ring for more beer?"

While I did so, he disappeared. Fritz entered almost immediately, the tray laden this time.

"How do you like it here?" I asked.

He shrugged. "It reminds me of my apprenticeship. The orders are too large, and I spend too much time catering to uneducated palates. Of course, I'm excluding Monsieur Lupa's. I hope this situation won't last for too long. What have you eaten today?"

I told him, and he shuddered. "I could arrange to have Charles deliver fresh croissants and, as for coffee..."

"Really, Fritz, that won't be necessary. I'll survive, though I also hope this charade doesn't go on much longer. I suppose you should know that Danielle is now watching over the house."

"A woman in my kitchen?! You'll have to watch her, sir. Don't let her use any of..."

I raised a palm. "It's all right, Fritz. I'll try to keep her under control."

One of the conditions I'd met in hiring Fritz was a guarantee that I wouldn't let a woman meddle in his affairs in the kitchen, but this seemed to be a special case. "She'll be gone by the time you return."

Lupa returned with Watkins and told Fritz that we'd now have three for dinner. Watkins looked the same as when I'd first met him, complete with swollen cheek, except that he was dirtier. There were smudges on his clothes and face. Lupa dismissed Fritz and he left.

"Suppose someone sees him going out?" I asked.

He looked at me with impatience. "He locks the outside door before coming in. Ah, more beer." He sat, and bade us do likewise. After we were settled, he turned to Watkins. "Well?"

He emptied the olive pits into his hand, then dumped them into the wastebasket next to the desk. "It's blown."

"Yes. We know. Report."

He looked at us, surprised. "But how could you know?"

"There was no smoke," I replied.

"But that's the funny thing. The stacks stopped smoking nearly an hour before the explosion. I thought at the time..."

"Enough!" Lupa bellowed. "Begin at the beginning."

"Yes, sir. This morning I got up at dawn, as usual, and when I got to my post, there was already activity around the factory. Evidently today there was a big shipment scheduled. By the way, last night I was followed again, at least back to my hotel."

"Same man," Lupa asked.

"Yes, sir. I'm sure of it."

"Did you get a better look at his face this time?"

"Yes, sir. I think I could identify him."

"Satisfactory. Go on."

"So I stayed my ground until nine o'clock or thereabouts, and a chilly ground it was, though not so bad as yesterday. Anyway, then I made it out to the road to Valence and waited for Pulis. He showed up in about an hour by horsecart, loaded with supplies. I kind of expected him to dawdle around, but he rode directly to the loading gate and left the cart with the guards while he crossed the street and had some coffee."

"He never went inside the gate?"

"No. They don't allow it."

"How long did the unloading take?"

"No more than a quarter hour. Then they sent a man over to get him, and he picked up the cart and started back out of town. I followed him back to where I'd picked him up, but he looked like he was just heading back here, so I let him go. I didn't like leaving the factory unwatched for so long. Then I got back and watched them arranging things for shipment for a time. Old Ponty kept running in and out, wiping his forehead and giving directions, but otherwise nothing happened for the next hour. Then, around noon, a woman came to the gate, and I recognized her as the one you, uh, you've been seeing."

"Tania was there?" I asked.

He nodded.

"Was she alone?"

"She came alone and went inside. Then, a few minutes later, she left with Ponty. They were gone maybe an hour for lunch, or I suppose it was lunch."

"How were they acting?" put in Lupa.

"I couldn't say, sir, I was too far away."

"All right. Continue."

"They returned at about one, as I said, and both went back inside. After only a few minutes, she came back out and left. I was tempted to follow her, but you'd only said to follow Pulis if it looked promising, so I stayed. I'm glad I did. For about an hour, it was the same story of loading and unloading, with Ponty running around again—and then, all of a sudden, the stacks stopped smoking, as I said. Everyone was so busy I doubt if they even noticed. No matter. I stayed put and waited."

"Good," Lupa said. "Did anyone enter or leave after Madame Chessal?"

"No, sir, only the janitor."

"When did he go?"

"Maybe ten minutes after the smoking stopped."

"Is that his normal quitting time?"

"I can't say for sure, sir. The other times I've been there, he's left at all different times. Last night he was evidently still on duty when I left, and that was late. Maybe his schedule varies on different days."

"All right." Lupa nodded, and Watkins continued.

"About three o'clock, then, Ponty came out to check on something at the guard's gate. Some of the trucks had started their motors, and things appeared to be getting under way, when all of a sudden the whole place just blew up from inside. It was something to see."

"I'd imagine so."

"When things settled a bit, I ran over, as if I were a bystander, to see if I could help. The whole building had been leveled, but outside, things weren't so bad, not so bad as I'd imagined from the size of the explosion." He reached into his pocket—"Anyone care for an olive?"—and continued. "Ponty was already up and around, trying to help wherever he could, and he did get a few of the trucks on the road, but, generally he was running around in circles, and I can't say that I blame him. There were an awful lot of dead and hurt, so I moved back so as not to be in anybody's way. Before too long, the troops came and cordoned off the area, but I got friendly with one of them and found out that they thought it was the ammunition room that had blown. So I came here."

"Satisfactory," Lupa said. "You did well." He turned to me. "You told me that the ammunition room was impossible to enter."

"It seemed to be."

"Hmm..." He leaned back and closed his eyes. Watkins and I watched him thinking for nearly a minute, though it seemed much longer. Finally, he sighed and sat up.

"Yes," he said. "No doubt of it."

There was a knock at the office door, and I got up to open it. It was Fritz, announcing dinner.

We cleared the desk to make room for the dishes. Fritz brought in a bowl so that Watkins could wash himself, and then began bringing in the courses. Being in danger didn't seem to have any effect on Lupa's appetite. I hardly touched the oyster bisque, and though the shad roe was superb, even for Fritz, I found it difficult to get it down. Lupa, on the other hand, ate with relish, talking animatedly about the new book he was reading, the socialist Jaure's *L'armee Nouvelle*. I tried to steer the conversation back around to the explosion, but he insisted we leave it until we'd dined.

"Business during meals upsets the digestion. In this case especially, there is nothing more to discuss." He continued unperturbed through the crème caramel and coffee, while Watkins and I glanced at each other from time to time, shaking our heads.

He rang for Fritz to come clear the service, but there was no response. Evidently someone else was in the kitchen, and he'd unlatched the bell.

Lupa moved everything to one side, poured himself another cup of coffee, and sat back in his chair. I lit a cigarette and stared at him.

"Yes?" he said finally.

"I was casually wondering what we should do now."

"You're sure that everyone will be here tomorrow?"

I nodded and he sighed contentedly.

"Then there's nothing else to be done. You may as well go on home. This affair will conclude tomorrow night. Indeed, it is over now—there only remains to wrap it up and deliver it to your friend Magiot."

I thought he was kidding me. "Oh, fine," I said. "Should I call him now?"

"I think not. It would be premature. Tomorrow will suffice. I'll take care of it."

I humored him. "Why do you want Magiot here at all?"

He sipped at his coffee. "So that he'll be convinced not to harass me." He tried the bell again. "Now, I suggest that tomorrow you see no one until you arrive here, and of course mention to no one that I'll be present. Our man no doubt thinks the heat is off. It would be instructive to watch him react when he discovers he's wrong."

"Yes," I said, "and, just for the record, who should we be watching?"

He looked shocked. "Is it possible you don't know? I'm

sure it will be clear if you reflect on it. Ah, Fritz, excellent! You were right about the cognac in the bisque—far more delicate than the sherry. I salute you."

Fritz, who had just entered with his apron, bowed. *"Merci."*

"Who was in the kitchen just now?" Lupa asked.

"Monsieur Anser. He wanted to see where the meeting would be held tomorrow night, so I showed him my quarters. He's dining upstairs."

"He's not alone, is he?" I asked.

"I believe so, sir. Should I check again?"

"That won't be necessary," said Lupa. He looked at me. "It makes no difference. As I've said, there's nothing more to be done."

When Fritz had finished clearing, I stood to go. "Have you any ideas about the ladies?"

"Yes. I have an idea that they are in no danger. I would not be surprised if they were back in Madame Chessal's home this very minute."

"Well, then, *à demain.*"

Not much mollified, I turned to go. Watkins held the tapestry aside for me. As I walked through the tunnel, I tried to think of what I had missed that made everything so obvious to Lupa, but to no avail.

I skirted the entrance to La Couronne on the way back, since Lupa had asked that I avoid the principals. The road was very dark, and it was beginning to get brisk again, so I walked quickly and was abreast of Tania's house in under a quarter of an hour. It was still, to all appearances closed up. Stopping to light a cigarette, I decided, principal or not, I wanted to see Tania, and so I walked up the drive to the front door.

It was still locked. I pushed the button by the door and set off a chorus of chimes. No lights, no sounds. I rang once more to the same effect, then shrugged and went back to the road. Lupa had been wrong there, and if he were wrong once, he could be again. The night seemed to get chillier.

The light was on in the sitting room of my own house, and I entered to find Danielle sitting on the settee by the front window. She smiled weakly when I entered.

"Evening, sir." She stood, looking much calmer than she had been in the morning. "Have you heard from the madame?"

"Not directly," I said, "but one of my friends saw her today in St. Etienne, so she's probably on her way back now." I wished I could have believed what I was saying, but it would do no good to upset the child. "I'm sure she'll be home by tomorrow evening and wondering where you are."

She brought her hands to her face. "Oh, sir. Then I must be off. The madame would be very upset to find me gone."

"It's all right, dear, I'll take care of it. She wasn't there yet when I passed just a few minutes ago. She'll be all right without you for one night."

"You're sure, sir?"

I smiled. If I could do without Fritz... "Yes, yes, I'm sure. But for now, have you eaten?"

"No, sir."

"Well, come, that won't do." I led her into the kitchen and found some eggs, cheese, and a few dried mushrooms. Remembering my promise to Fritz, I decided to cook her dinner myself, though it scandalized her.

"What would people say?" she asked. "Monsieur Giraud cooking my dinner?"

I laughed. "What *would* people say now? Just sit down and relax. Would you care for some cognac?"

"Oh no, sir, I couldn't."

"*Au contraire,* you could. I wish you'd join me."

While the omelette was setting, I went and poured us two snifters. She took a sip and made a face. "I usually have spirits with water."

I turned the omelette. "Not tonight," I said. I wanted her

to go off to sleep. She ate slowly and carefully. I don't think she tasted a thing.

When she finished, she was drowsy, and I sent her up to my bed. Fritz would never approve of letting a woman into his room alone. I took down a comforter Tania had made for me, turned out the lights, and lay down on the settee to sleep.

Just before I dozed off I became wide awake, and swore. Getting up and lighting a candle, I walked over to the table by the hearth. I set the candle down and looked carefully. The only mark was the small depression that the detective had noted the previous Wednesday.

"Sir?"

I started. Danielle stood wrapped in a blanket in the foyer.

"I heard you moving. Are you all right?"

"Perfectly," I said. "I'd just forgotten something."

She remained, awkwardly shifting from foot to foot.

"What's the matter?" I asked. "Can't you go to sleep? Would you like some more cognac?"

"No sir, only..." she stammered.

"What's wrong, child? Speak up!"

"Well, sir, I just don't know why she wouldn't have left me a note." She started to sob, then turned and ran up the stairs. I went back to the divan and pulled up the comforter.

Neither do I, I thought. Neither do I.

16

The next day I awoke early, had coffee alone in the arbor, then worked in the garden, weeding. At noon, I sent Danielle over to Tania's to see if she'd returned, but she hadn't. It was quite warm. At about two o'clock we took a sparse lunch of tomatoes, pâté, and bread, after which I napped while she did some laundry. Finally, when the sun had just set, she helped me load three cases of beer into the Ford, and I drove to La Couronne.

I entered via the front door and asked Charles if he'd help me unload my cargo. A few of the patrons looked up as we passed. It was certainly irregular to make deliveries through the dining room, but no one complained. I was evidently the first to arrive.

Lupa's quarters had been rearranged to accommodate a crowd, with chairs brought down from above and set around the walls. Fritz was busy with dinners, and I watched him for a short time until I became restless and moved back to the apartment for a beer. Generally I waited until some of the group arrived before I drank, but tonight I made an exception.

The next to appear were Georges and Henri—together, as they usually were. Henri was more relaxed than I'd seen him in the past week. We shook hands, and his grip was dry and firm.

"Georges tells me they've arrested Lupa."

"I think not yet," I said.

"But he did it."

"It appears so."

He breathed out. "That's a relief. I was sure they were going to arrest me because I was a foreigner—but then I forgot," he smiled. "So are Lupa and Paul."

Georges walked up and laid his arm across his shoulders. "I kept telling him last week not to worry. If he'd escaped the arrests last August, the authorities didn't suspect him at all." Georges was referring to the *Carnet B* arrests of suspected foreign agents, which took place upon mobilization. "The same went for Paul, but Lupa—aren't I right, Jules?—came to Valence after August."

I nodded. "That's so. Why don't you have a beer, Henri? And you, too, Georges? I'm sure it's been a hard week for all of us."

We sat, and they began to drink. Henri wiped the foam from his drooping mustache, letting only a few drops fall onto his old faded frock. Georges was dapper in a blue suit and tie. He drank neatly.

"Did Paul make it to the hotel yesterday?" I asked only to make conversation.

"Oh yes." Georges smiled. "Tipsy but in fine spirits. Speaking of which..."

Outside, there was a slight hubbub, and in a moment, Paul entered, beaming. "A fine howdy-do this is!" he said. "Starting without me again." He said his hellos all around and picked up a beer. "Good news, friends, my book is sold! Here's to poetry!"

We drank the toast. He turned to me. "They took the new poems. Isn't that great?"

We agreed it was, and he insisted we all open more beer. In the middle of passing them out, he stopped. "Hey, where's the lady?"

I had been worrying about Tania since I'd arrived but was still hoping she would appear. "I don't know," I said, "but I'm sure she'll be around."

We pulled our chairs into a small circle and began to talk about Paul's good fortune. No one seemed disposed to discuss Marcel's death, and since I had no idea of Lupa's intentions, I decided to wait. Finally, there was a knock on the doorsill, and I turned to see Tania.

"Am I late?" she asked sweetly.

I walked over and embraced her. "Where have you been? I've been worried sick."

She didn't get a chance to answer me, because the other men had come over and bombarded her with their stories of Lupa's guilt and Paul's publishing. So I went and opened a beer for her while she removed her coat and made herself comfortable. When the din had subsided somewhat, she offered her own tidbit: "I've just come from St. Etienne."

The news, of course, had been in the paper that day, and I'd been a bit surprised that no one had brought it up before, but each had had their own personal matters, which were of some importance.

She continued. "That's why I was late, and I'm sorry, but there was much to do. I'd gone yesterday to have lunch with Maurice—he's so lonely, I feel I owe him at least that, Jules— and afterward, planned to go shopping with a friend. It was horrible, really horrible. I'd like that beer, please." I handed it to her.

"Do you know what happened?" asked Henri. "I was there yesterday morning."

"Only what you've read, I presume. The ammunition room blew up. The guards were killed instantly, so they don't know whether someone succeeded in getting in."

"Grisly," said Georges.

"Very," she agreed. "I should have been back last night," she said to me, "but I stayed behind to help with the nursing."

Fritz came to the door, knocked, and entered, closing the door behind him. "Excuse me," he said, "but would you all mind stepping into the office for a moment. Monsieur Giraud has arranged a surprise for you." So saying, he crossed to the tapestry and removed it, showing the door. I felt to make sure my pistol was available and, reassured, sat back in the chair. I took Tania's hand while the others watched and waited for Fritz to open the door. As they filed in, Fritz seated them, and I spoke to Tania.

"Where is Anna?"

"She went to St. Etienne with me. She was feeling much better."

"Well, I don't understand why you didn't leave a note with Danielle. We were both very much concerned."

"But, Jules," she said. "I did leave a note. Out on the coffee table outside where she always serves me breakfast." She smiled and patted my hand. "I know all about it. When we returned and discovered the house locked up, I went to your place and found Danielle, and she told me the whole story. It had been chilly yesterday morning, and she thought I'd rather take my coffee inside, so she never went out to the table. Come," she said, standing, "the others are waiting. What's the surprise?"

I shrugged nonchalantly. "If I tell you, it won't be."

Fritz had me seated to the left of Lupa's desk, facing the others. Tania sat opposite me, and next to her, Paul, then Henri and Georges, with Henri on my far right. Fritz exited. No one spoke. In another moment, the door opened again, and Fritz asked me to help him bring in the cases of beer. I went back out to the apartment, and he closed the door behind me.

Lupa came out from down the hall and motioned me quiet with his finger to his lips. "The table?" he whispered.

"Only that small depression—looks like a spider web."

He smiled. "Yes, I thought I remembered that. Satisfactory. It closes the circle. I'll be right in."

Fritz and I took the beer inside and set it behind the desk. I sat again and Fritz walked out, leaving the door ajar.

"What's the surprise, Jules?" asked Paul. "The tension is killing me."

"Tension rarely kills," said Lupa, appearing in the doorway. "People kill." He closed the door behind him. The lock clicked into place.

They were all on their feet. Lupa ignored the commotion, crossed to his desk, and sat. As he reached for a beer, the noise died down.

"What's the meaning of this, Jules?" asked Georges, but they all shared the sentiment.

"Please, please," Lupa admonished, opening his beer and pouring, "let us be civilized. I've arranged it, through Monsieur Giraud, that all of you would be here tonight. Last week, one of your friends was killed in our presence. The police have witlessly concluded that I am the guilty party, and this is not the case. The purpose of this little meeting will be to expose the killer, which is one of you."

"But you're the killer," Henri exploded.

"No, sir," Lupa replied. "I am not. Most assuredly."

"I won't stay," said Paul.

"Oh, but you will. The door is locked. Besides, what have you to fear? If you are innocent, no harm will come to you. If not, well..."

"I'll tell you what we have to fear," said Georges. "We have *you* to fear. Last week you killed Marcel and that inspector. Tonight you might kill any one, or all, of us."

"Oh, tut, sir." He looked around. "Please, all of you, relax. Would any of you care for more beer? I nearly forgot to have it brought in."

There were no takers.

He leaned back. "Now, then, where to begin? We may as well get at the facts." He sighed, then drank, then began.

"The rumors you have heard about this case being an international affair are perfectly true. Since I will be long gone, and certainly in no danger from any of you, I can afford to tell you this. I am an Allied spy."

He paused for the effect to sink in. "Now, then. I was sent here just after the war broke out to try and learn the identity of one of Europe's most dangerous minds and, having done so, to stop him.

"I'd been having no luck until last Wednesday, when Monsieur Giraud fortuitously invited me to your weekly gathering. The person I sought undoubtedly knew me, since I'd chased him through Eastern Europe for several months preceding my move here to Valence. He kept eluding me precisely because he knew who I was, though I changed my identity and papers in every location. Finally, when I learned that he'd come to Valence, I decided to come here as a worker, find a job, and stay hidden and anonymous until he acted or made a mistake. However, nothing happened for so long that I began to fear he'd left.

"In desperation, I accepted Monsieur Giraud's offer to be seen in public. My luck was extraordinary. The man I was trailing was at that first gathering. Of course, not knowing him put me at a distinct disadvantage, which he decided to capitalize on immediately. He tried to kill me."

He paused to look at the assemblage. "Of course, you're

probably wondering why he chose that drastic method when, in the past, he'd simply run."

"I was wondering that," said Paul, drily.

"The answer is, as my father would say, elementary. He had to remain in Valence until some other job was completed. Last week I learned and yesterday it was verified that that job was the destruction of the St. Etienne Arsenal. So he had to stay, and he had to elude me. When, by mistake, he killed Monsieur Routier, he put me hot on his trail again, for the first time in nine months.

"I resolved not to lose him again, and I haven't. Killing Routier was an act of panic, provoked by seeing me. If he'd kept calm and done nothing, he would have succeeded in his mission at no danger to himself. Monsieur Routier, by the way, since he is dead and the knowledge can do no harm, was himself an agent of the French government, seeking this same man."

A murmur ran like a current through my friends—"What? Marcel? *C'est impossible!*"

Lupa continued, oblivious to their reactions. "I surmise that at the time of his death, Routier's cover was still intact, which means that his espionage connections were still unknown, even to his murderer. That much by way of prologue. Are you sure none of you will have more beer?"

I looked at the faces of my friends. The men all were wary, and Tania was furious.

"I'd like another beer," said Henri.

"What about Monsieur Giraud, here?" Tania said. "Why is he helping you? Is he a spy, too?"

Lupa looked at me. "Him? Don't be silly."

"Then why are you helping him?" Paul asked me.

"Marcel was my best friend," I answered. "After he was killed last week, Monsieur Lupa took me into his confidence, and I believe him. I want to see his killer punished, even if it is one of you."

"It is," interjected Lupa. "What you don't seem to realize is that any of you could have sat in the seat I vacated last week. Whomever sat in that seat would have been poisoned."

They eyed one another, a hint of suspicion finally creeping into an expression or two. Henri sipped his beer and wiped sweat from his brow; Paul leaned with his elbows on his knees; and Georges stiffly crossed one leg over the other. Tania was still angry.

"All right," Lupa went on, "so my first problem was who to suspect, and at first that, too, seemed simple. Suspect Monsieur Lavoie, since he's the only one who was not in Valence during the time I was chasing someone in the East. I saw the flaw in that almost immediately and cursed myself thoroughly, I assure you. The murderer, assassin—call him what you will—rarely did his own work. I hadn't been chasing him all that time, but rather his agents. I checked with another of my contacts on that point, and he agreed. So I had two scores to settle with this man: he'd tried to kill me, and he'd made me look a fool."

"Then how did he recognize you right away?" asked Paul again.

"Photographs." He drank some beer. "You're listening carefully. That's a good sign."

"You still look a fool to me," said Henri.

Lupa nodded. "Perhaps, but let's go on. I was left suspecting everyone, so I had to eliminate. Madame Chessal." He looked at Tania and she met his gaze. "I'm sorry I suspected you for so long, but it began when I entered Monsieur Giraud's house last week. I'm sure you didn't realize it— indeed, you couldn't have—but you, in your close observation of me, changed your position as I did all evening, even after the murder. If I crossed my legs, you crossed your legs, and so on. And so you gave away your interest in me. At the time, I had no idea what could cause that interest, except of course the obvious."

He opened his desk drawer and pulled from it the photograph I had delivered earlier. "Only yesterday did I learn that I closely resembled your eldest son."

"Damn," I said, "he does." Tania's son had a mustache and was much smaller than Lupa, but the face was very similar.

"Where did you get that picture? Jules," she turned to me, her mouth taut, "did you have anything to do with this?"

Lupa butted in before I could speak. "Monsieur Giraud is more your friend than you know, madame. The point is, do I or do I not remind you of your son?"

Tania, still fuming, lowered her eyes. "Yes," she said coldly. "I saw it then."

"Precisely. And you've been piqued at me ever since because your son is in the war, at the front, and I'm not." He leaned slightly toward her. "Be assured, madame, that I too am fighting this war." He continued. "Later, when you came to question me about missing the funeral, I was on my guard and so was perhaps unnecessarily abrupt. I now apologize. And I thank you for your help with Anna's wounds."

The others looked quizzically at us.

"Last Sunday," Lupa went on, "another attempt was made on my life, this time wounding a woman I was with and barely missing an associate. I have been extremely fortunate, I admit. At the time, I thought it possible that my pursuer had hired an assassin and wanted to be sure he'd done his work. Shortly afterward, I realized that that was folly. A hired assassin would have killed me. No, my man was terrified, and was acting as his own agent. In the past, he'd avoided being the center of suspicion because he'd avoided direct action. Now, once he'd acted, the inexorable pull of events would lead to his downfall.

"So I finally rejected you as a suspect, and happily. Monsieur Giraud was most unwilling to believe you guilty."

"Thank you for that," she said to me.

"Monsieur Pulis," he said, turning his gaze full upon Henri. "I'm surprised the police haven't arrested you, since you've acted the most like a guilty man. When the police discovered cyanide in your house, you panicked, and have been on edge since that time. Monsieur Pulis's son is a photographer," he explained to the others, "and cyanide—Prussic acid—is used in the developing process." He wagged a finger at Henri. "You should have immediately offered yourself for thorough investigation, but instead you were terrified that the police would arrest you because you are not French, and you tried to hide, distorting some facts, lying about others. You should never have lied about seeing Inspector Chatelet, for example. That made me suspicious of you, and it had nothing to do with your nationality. Last Wednesday, you were blatantly unhappy to see me. Actually, that worked in your favor, since the man I sought would never have shown himself so openly. I finally discounted you when I couldn't see any possible way that you could bring destruction to St. Etienne, despite your deliveries there. Though it wasn't crucial, I also found it difficult to believe that the man I sought had a high-strung wife and six children to support.

"That leaves the bachelors. To be fair, let's start with Monsieur Giraud. He convinced me of his innocence by his actions late the night of the murder, and if that wasn't enough, Routier's recommendation was."

This last, of course, was nonsense, but I kept my silence.

Lupa half turned in his seat and reached for another beer. Opening it, he stared at the two men sitting directly opposite him. Paul shifted nervously in his chair. Georges lit a cigarette.

"Mr. Anser. I was loathe to suspect you originally because you share my country of citizenship. But consider these facts: you were sitting next to me last week, and were in the best position of anyone else in the room to simply switch glasses with me during the commotion over Monsieur Lavoie's hand. You are an amateur geologist and as such have access to, or have had access to, cyanide. You are a crack shot, by your own admission. You are not French and you live in St. Etienne. The circumstantial evidence against you is, therefore, impressive. On the other hand, last week I sent one of my own men to try and 'cross over' with your help. He was most persuasive and most subtle, and came away convinced that you had no idea what he was hinting at." Lupa turned to me. "That, Jules, was the mysterious man you saw with Mr. Anser when you went to St. Etienne." He went on. "Still, that you refused my man by no means completely cleared you. You might have recognized my ploy and acted accordingly. No, it wasn't until I discovered that Monsieur Lavoie was the man whom I sought, and that wasn't until yesterday afternoon, that I listed those circumstantial facts concerning you as coincidental."

All eyes were on Georges. He sat calmly, smoking.

"I take it," he said to Lupa, "that you are accusing me?"

"Yes."

Georges chuckled mirthlessly. "This is rather tedious, you know."

Lupa shared the grim humor. "I don't really find it so, but perhaps you would like another beer. It may be your last for a long time. Still no? Well. It was admirable the way you arranged to be out of town during most of this week. It did serve to divert attention from you for a time—long enough for you to go about your special tasks.

"Let's begin with last Wednesday. By the way, consenting to be a regular guest was an admirable choice of covers. Whether it had begun by design or by coincidence, you wasted no time in recognizing the value of this particular group to your ends. They were a singularly respectable, though eccentric, group of citizens. Your presence among them established your *bona fides* in an especially effective manner. To

214 JOHN T. LESCROART

the rest of the community, your status as newcomer—and hence a natural object of rumor and suspicion—was substantially mitigated. Then, too, among a group with so many foreign connections, you stand out as passably French. It was a fine decision on your part."

"Thank you," said Georges sarcastically.

"Don't mention it. But to continue, when you saw me enter Monsieur Giraud's sitting room last Wednesday, you immediately recognized me, as I've said. Perhaps my small deductions that evening were a misplaced show of bravado, but in any event you wasted no time, since an agent like yourself is always prepared. I am, too. While the others were preparing for their toast, you slipped from your pocket a mercury fulmonade cap which you'd earlier procured, no doubt, by prying it from the back of a bullet. Much smaller than a *petite pois*, it was an admirable weapon. You placed it on the table and brought your beer bottle down on it, causing it to explode and cutting yourself. The explosion, by the way, left a small but recognizable mark on the table.

"You then excused yourself to dress the wound and, passing my seat by the door, took advantage of everyone's being grouped around the spilled beer, as you knew we would be, to drop the poison—stolen from Monsieur Pulis, I assume—into my glass. You didn't even have to break your stride.

"When you returned and found that Routier had inadvertently returned to my seat and drank the poison intended for me, your panic increased. Please correct me where I may be wrong."

Georges sat quite still. "Every word is wrong."

Lupa smiled. "Of course. I didn't suppose I'd catch you with that. Still, there were other endeavors to which you were committed, and you had a timetable to follow, so the next day you had to go to St. Etienne and deliver an excessive amount of gauze to the arsenal. That you entered and met Monsieur Ponty was incidental. What was not incidental was his comment on learning of your trade. He said, 'I hope we can keep your deliveries small.' Monsieur Giraud, here, has an admirable memory and repeated back to me your conversation with Ponty. That comment aroused my suspicion, and I fell on it like a hungry dog.

"From that moment on, you were my prime suspect. But you had worked well and left few clues. When Chatelet was killed last Friday night, I was tempted to cross you off, but then my associate in St. Etienne had reported that he'd been followed back to Valence and, by his description, I assumed it had been you. The man who followed my agent, by the way, did not have a limp, but we'll get to that. So, in fact, you hadn't gone south on business, but had remained here, hoping to get a chance to kill me.

"Chatelet, with a bit of terrible luck for both of you, ran into you on the street as he interrogated Pulis Friday night. Worse yet, Pulis then introduced you to the inspector. Of course, between Henri's being your friend and Pulis's deep suspicion of me, it never crossed his mind that your presence was questionable."

Henri, his face red now and dripping with sweat, looked wide-eyed from Georges to Lupa. Again and again he seemed to be trying to swallow, but the dryness of his mouth wouldn't allow it. Remembering his beer, he sucked at it like a man dying of thirst.

Lupa pressed on. "Still, Chatelet presented you with an immediate danger. He wouldn't even have to suspect you of anything. Merely his knowledge that you were in Valence would have condemned you."

Georges still smirked. "Why, exactly, would that be?"

"Because in questioning the other suspects, possibly including myself, that fact would have come out. In other words, you were not in St. Etienne where you were believed to be. In fact, you had followed my man to Valence."

"Fascinating," Georges said.

"Not really," Lupa answered. "So Chatelet presented too great a risk, and you did away with him.

"On Sunday, you followed me to the woods where I was to have had lunch. When you saw your opportunity, you fired three times but, luckily for me, you missed. That must have been particularly galling for you. When Monsieur Giraud and I gave chase, you ran, and you escaped."

Lupa leaned back and pulled the bell for Fritz. "That," he explained, "was my signal for Fritz to get Magiot and his men."

"That'll be the end of you, then," said Georges levelly.

Lupa drank his beer. "We'll see. Well, to get on with it, yesterday you succeeded in your primary mission, which was to blow up the arsenal. To do that, you used one of your agents—I'd be curious to know how you recruited the janitor, since all the employees there had 'Top Secret' clearance, but that's another question. Reasoning told me what he had done. My man in St. Etienne, who'd been watching the place all day, noted that the smokestacks had stopped functioning about an hour before the explosion. Shortly afterward, the janitor had left the building.

"What he had done was to enter the boiler room in the fifteen or twenty minutes when, according to Ponty, everyone in the building, including the men stoking the boilers, was acting as a 'pack mule.' He opened the doors to the boilers and stuffed them with as much of your excess gauze as he could fit. The boilers are located, or were located, directly adjacent to the ammunition room, and an explosion of the boilers would of course set off the highly unstable dynamite in the next room. The gauze effectively stopped up the pipes, creating intolerable pressure within the boilers. It also stopped their smoking for at least a half-hour before the pressure became critical.

"There was your flaw. There is no other explanation for the smoke stopping just prior to the explosion. You thought it would go unnoticed, and for the most part it did. Only my agent there noticed it. Otherwise, it was a brilliant plan. You were having lunch with Monsieurs Anser and Giraud while the pressure was building in those boilers. But you should have stayed with directing your agents. When you act on your own, you make mistakes. My agent, you see, swears that he can identify the man who was following him. He didn't know it was you, but now we'll give him a chance to say if it was. Watkins!"

Watkins seemed to magically appear out of the wall as he pushed aside the tapestry and stepped out of the tunnel. Everyone gaped.

"How many secret entrances does this place have?" Tania asked.

"None any more. You've seen them all." He turned to Watkins. "Is he here?"

"Yes, sir."

"Kindly point him out."

He pointed at Lavoie. I reached inside my jacket to be near my pistol just in case it would be needed.

"That's all very clever," said Georges. "It's a neat little theory, with the minor drawback of being completely false. You can't prove a word of what you've said."

Henri cleared his throat. "You were here . . . I mean we did meet you, the inspector and I . . ."

Georges smiled at his friend. "I never denied it, Henri. The point never came up, did it?"

Henri, confused, leaned back in his chair.

"Monsieur Lavoie is right," Lupa said to the group. "I could have paid this man to come in here and identify him. There is no proof. And so, now, I'm going to ask him to do something which will undoubtedly demonstrate his innocence."

"Certainly," Georges said, his smile ice. "I'd be glad to end this farce."

"Well, then. The man who trailed Monsieur Watkins, here, had no limp. I contend that you have no limp but rather a substantial lifter in your left shoe. You can easily demonstrate which of us is right by taking off your shoes."

"This is ridiculous!"

Lupa shrugged, then leaned back in his chair. "Go on, Georges," Paul urged. "Let's get to the bottom of this."

Georges looked around at each of the group, and the sentiment was unanimous. I saw his glance at the tapestry from behind which Watkins had entered, and my grip tightened on my pistol.

Finally, he came to some conclusion and reached down as if to undo his shoelaces. How he did it I don't know, but by some slight of hand, he reached into his jacket and came out with a pistol which he trained on Lupa, the hammer cocked.

"All right, now," he said calmly, "no one is to move."

But I had already moved. My pistol was out. "Georges, drop it!"

He turned toward me and fired at the instant I did. I was hit under the left collarbone, and spun backward and to the floor. Tania screamed and crossed over to me. I felt her place my head in her lap.

"Jules, are you all right? Jules."

I couldn't speak, and the room began to spin before me. There was a pounding from outside, then the sound of a door opening and boots on a wooden floor. I opened my eyes and tried to focus them. It looked as though Magiot and his men had entered. They gathered around Georges, who lay prostrate on the floor.

Lupa spoke, the words coming to me as though through wads of cotton or gauze. "There's your man, inspector. He's dead."

I passed out.

17

It is now August, and we are entering our second year of war. I write in the sitting room, propped on the settee with a pad before me. It looks as though Lupa was right. The war may drag on for a long time.

Miraculously, the bullet did no major damage, and the doctor estimates that I'll be completely recovered in another month. In all, it's been a pleasant recovery period. I've used the time to write this report of my last case. Really nothing formal, of course. Something to read in my advancing years and with which to recall the way it all had been.

Lupa has written twice, from Corsica. After that last Wednesday meeting, Magiot took him in for questioning, but released him after Tania went in and spoke for him. Within twenty-four hours he was gone, taking Anna with him. His first letter was written obviously in the first flush of relaxation. He said it was his first vacation in four years. The second letter, however, showed signs of restlessness, and I wouldn't be at all surprised if he were to return to the fray before long. There was no talk of marriage to Anna, though I gathered that they were together still. Watkins is back in England, presumably with his olives.

There were several strange offshoots from the Lavoie case. Paul and Henri both decided to enlist, and even though Henri was rejected, it brought forever to an end our beer gatherings. And Tania...

Tania lost her second son three months ago, and for a time she fell back into thinking herself old and useless. Her eldest son, the one resembling Lupa, received furlough and came home to comfort her. After that she recovered a bit and began nursing me daily. Fritz complained about constantly having a woman in the house, but I was happy to have her. One day, she entered my bedroom early in the morning and threw back the curtains, letting the sun stream in. She was beaming.

"Monsieur Giraud?"

"Oui."

She came and sat by the bed.

"I'm afraid my fears of approaching old age have been groundless."

"That's what I've always said, my dear."

"But more than you know, love. To avoid a scandal, I'm afraid you're going to have to marry me." Our laughter shook the house.

And so, six weeks ago, Madame Chessal became Madame Giraud. We hope our child will be a girl.

After Tania and Danielle moved in, Fritz eventually moved out, but there were no hard feelings. He'd been in touch with Lupa constantly, and planned to go home to Switzerland for a while, and then on to Corsica. Since they'd begun the rationing of food in earnest, losing Fritz wasn't the tragedy it might have been.

Perhaps strangest of all, Magiot has been around to visit. He's apologized several times for his earlier opinion of me. He'd no idea I was, in his words, "such a man of action." He's even gone so far as to say I deserve my retirement.

We had the Pulises and the Magiots around for dinner the other night, and Magiot said he'd heard I was to receive the *Legion d'Honneur*.

Though I had by now earned his respect, he couldn't resist the opportunity to get in one last dig.

"Do you really think, Jules," he asked, "that the medal is for your efforts in the Lupa business? It seems a rather grand gesture for what was really a rather insignificant episode. Compared to the larger war, I mean."

"My dear Jacques, there's no doubt in my mind that the recognition is for what I do best."

"And that is?"

"I'll tell you what that is," Henri said. "It's for making the finest damned beer in France."

"Hear, hear," said my wife.

I beamed all around and raised my glass with my good arm. "I'll drink to that," I said proudly. And so we all did.

RASPUTIN'S
REVENGE

To Maurice E. "Les" Lescroart,
father extraordinaire,
1920—1986

*"It is hard to know whether
war or peace makes the greater
changes in our vocabularies,
both of the tongue and of the spirit."*

M.F.K. FISHER
"How To Cook A Wolf,"
revised edition

PREFACE

Someone once defined a Russian novel as a book in which people with unpronounceable names do nothing for 362 pages, at which point someone's aunt dies.

I trust the present work will not fall into that category, although Russian names do present certain difficulties which the reader can overcome by keeping the following in mind:

—the suffix "vich" means "son of." Thus, the czarevich is the son of the czar. Likewise, the suffix "ovna" means "daughter of."

—almost all names have a formal and a diminutive form, often characterized by the suffix "sha" or "shka." Thus, Rasputin's first name is Gregory or Grishka, the Empress is Matushka, or "little mother," and so on.

The titles "czar" and "emperor" are both correct and interchangeable, as are "czarina" and "empress."

In 1918, Russia discontinued use of the old Julian calendar and began using our own Gregorian one. Because the events in this book took place in 1916 and 1917 and the documents are often dated, I have retained the Julian dates, which are thirteen days behind our own. This is especially important in regard to Rasputin. It is often asserted that his death on New Year's Day, 1917, cursed the year to tragedy. If it did, the lesson escaped most Russians, since to them he did not die on January 1, 1917, but on the night of December 16, 1916.

Rasputin had several nicknames—the starets, Grishka, the black monk, tyemniy, or "the dark one," and many more. Interestingly, the name Rasputin itself is a nickname for the man born Gregori Efimovich—it means "dissolute" or "depraved."

I used many sources in researching this novel, but three works stand out: "Nicholas and Alexandra," by Robert K. Massie; "The Guns of August," by Barbara Tuchman; and "The Life and Times of Gregory Rasputin," by Alex de Jonge. Any liberties I may have taken with historical facts and characters—and there are many since this is a work of the imagination—are strictly my own and cannot be traced to these excellent historians.

I would like to thank Frank Seidl for sharing with me both his expertise regarding fine wines and his superb company in sampling so many of them.

Lastly, I tip my hat to Sir Arthur Conan Doyle, the creator of Sherlock Holmes, without whom this book, or its predecessor, would not exist.

PROLOGUE

The box arrived in late June. It gave evidence of having once been carefully wrapped—in brown paper and secured with twine. But the customs people evidently sensed something suspicious about the parcel—perhaps some scent of the Kremlin—and it had been re-wrapped at least twice, rather less expertly each time.

Nevertheless, by the time it arrived in California, shipped from my publishers to whom it had been addressed for forwarding, its contents still appeared to be intact. The cover letter read thusly:

Dear Mr. Lescroart:

My name is Mikhail Vayev. I hold the position of Chief Historical Research Analyst in the United Soviet Archive Library, Politburo Special Section (PSS)32.1. I am 56 years old and have held my position for sixteen years. (I was given the job because of my skill with languages—besides most of the dialects of Russian, I am fluent, or reasonably so, in Mandarin, English, French, German, Dansk, and Urdi, as well as Yiddish and Hebrew.)

As a young graduate historian in Khrushchev's administration, my first assignment was to change the names "St. Petersburg" or "Petrograd" to "Leningrad" in every document filed for the years between the onset of World War I and the October Revolution. I must have performed well, though all I remember from that year is sitting in airless and musty misery, staring at the bureaucratic detritus of a long-dead age. In any event, I was promoted and spent the next few years changing Stalingrad to Volgograd and otherwise excising Stalin's name from our history books. (Eventually, I purged Khrushchev's name as well, only to go back and reinsert them both under Andropov.)

In 1970, under Brezhnev, I was appointed chief of my section—(PSS)32.1. That promotion gave me access to Western publications—newspapers and magazines as well as books of fiction and non-fiction. Recently, your novel *Son of Holmes* arrived at the Archives. Of course, even here in Russia, Sherlock Holmes is commonly known and widely admired. I myself have harbored a lifelong interest in the great detective.

I picked up the book immediately. The argument presented in its introduction—that Sherlock Holmes actually existed and operated in England at the turn of the century—I took to be an amusing conceit. Like most people, I believed that Holmes was a fictional character and nothing more.

It wasn't until I turned to Jules Giraud's manuscript itself that I became conscious of a disturbing sense of déjà vu. I was certain I'd seen the names Giraud and Lupa and encountered that writing style before.

Over the course of the next few weeks, I figuratively rifled the files of my brain, trying to determine where and when I'd seen similar material. Then one evening I remembered. In my first assignment, changing St. Petersburg to Leningrad thirty-four years ago, I was sure that I had "sterilized" a file that contained those names.

Excitement kept me awake that entire night. The next morning found me in the bowels of the Kremlin, six floors below the street. I first checked the catalogues for "L" and "G" to no avail, then unsuccessfully tried "A" for Auguste Lupa. Under "J," I came upon something that looked hopeful. I walked to the shelf, and with trembling hands pulled down the dusty folder (Kremlin File No. JG 0665) and began examining the documents it contained.

A hasty perusal confirmed my initial feeling, but a more careful study would be needed if I were to be sure, so I packed the folder into my briefcase and brought it home that night.

As I read, I realized that I had stumbled on the most important discovery of my career—a wealth of material, including Giraud's diaries and prison memoirs, of the events leading up to the abdication of Czar Nicholas II in 1917. Just as important—perhaps ultimately more so—the file utterly convinced me of the actual historical existence of Sherlock Holmes. After reading the material, his role in those events—and that of his son Lupa—could no longer be seriously denied.

Alas, there are certain restrictions in my country that would keep even a find of this importance from being published. The file itself—JG 0665—is still classified. Nevertheless, as an historian, I feel strongly that this story should be told.

Accordingly, I am sending you the enclosed in the hopes that it will at least see publication in the West. It will need editing and translating, but those efforts seem minimal indeed compared with the importance of this find.

Good luck, and thank you.

Sincerely,
Mikhail Vayev*

At first I suspected a hoax. Since I'd translated and researched the background of Giraud's earlier manuscript, I'd run into my share of skeptics and charlatans to whom the entire Holmes issue was an elaborate myth or, more gallingly, a joke.

I had grown tired of the debate, other issues had become more prominent in my life, and I was loath to start the process again by essaying the translation of any purportedly genuine manuscript, regardless of its historical importance.

Nevertheless, I was intrigued, and couldn't resist glancing at the documents. One look at Giraud's diaries and prison journal confirmed their authenticity. I still had the originals of his other manuscript, and the handwriting alone was enough to convince me—it was identical.

---

* At his request, Vayev's name and title, as well as the original file name, have been changed to preserve his privacy.

I struggled with the language and faded ink, reading far into the night. But the French manuscripts ended at a crucial moment—with Giraud in jail about to be executed for espionage. Following that was a startling manuscript in English. The further documents contained a variety of Continental hands that I found incomprehensible. They might have presented no problem to Vayev with his flair for language, but they left me in a state of almost unbearable suspense.

Early the next morning, I had the package copied and brought the original to my friend, Dr. Don Matoosian, a Russian scholar at the University of California at Los Angeles. Guardedly enthusiastic, he told me he would review the Russian documents for authenticity and would assemble a team of graduate students to take on the task of translating Giraud's manuscripts and the other documents. He expected to have his report to me within a month.

It took all of that—thirty of the longest days of my life. But finally the validation came. Dr. Matoosian even asked me to donate the original file to the UCLA Library for Russian studies, which is where it now resides; in another library but, unlike the catacombs where the file lay hidden for seventy years, this one remains accessible.

The events recounted in the documents constitute an essential record of the last months of the Romanov dynasty. Beyond that, this story brings down the curtain on one of history's most incredible vendettas, one whose shadow threatens to hide the sun even up to the present time.

PART
ONE

1

[KREMLIN FILE NO. JG 0665-4600-4668; PSS ACCESS, CLASSIFIED]
OCTOBER 7, 1916

It is a mystery to me.

Not that Freddy Foch and I hadn't been friends since he had been my instructor in the War College, but his regular army training and my espionage work were not always in perfect accord. And now, at his bidding, I am in St. Petersburg, or Petrograd as it has recently been re-named, my retirement having lasted a little over one year.

My role here is straightforward—I am to present a renewed French offer of arms and money to Czar Nicholas II in an effort to keep him fighting on the Eastern Front. So long as the Great Bear of Russia can keep two or three German divisions occupied in the East, the Allies stand a chance of holding off the Huns until we can mount our new offensive in the Spring, perhaps even with American help. If, as seems likely now, the Czar sues for a separate peace with Germany, the stalemate will likely be broken in the Kaiser's favor, with tragic results for France and for civilization.

The three-week trip here by ship was nerve-racking but proved uneventful. We disembarked from Bordeaux in mid-September and steamed up La Manche* into the North Sea,

* The English Channel

constantly on guard against the regular German fleet patrolling those waters, at the same time hoping to avoid the submarines lurking beneath us. As we entered the Baltic, a fog enshrouded us and by the time it lifted we were in Russian-dominated waters with Helsinki behind us. A couple of days in the Gulf of Finland finally brought us to port.

And what a port! What a city! St. Petersburg, the Venice of Russia! Nothing in my briefings had prepared me for the grandeur of this place. In my mind, Russia has always been gray and stolid, its architecture vaguely Eastern, its people a race of unrefined, good-natured peasants. That may be the Russia of Moscow and Kiev, but here in St. Petersburg, I am in Europe.

Marble buildings in pastel tones front either wide tree-lined streets or canals that are cleaner and wider than those of Venice. The city's main street—the Nevsky Prospekt, for example—is as smart and as modern as the Boulevard Haussmann in Paris. French is the main language I have heard spoken, though I have yet to venture from the Winter Palace.

After three weeks aboard ship, the food I had for dinner last night tasted wonderful even if by French standards it was little more than fodder—borscht, some sort of cold fish in sour cream, rubbery crepes they call blinis, and a poor bottle of Bordeaux.

Now it is midday and I have determined to keep a daily record of my mission here—however it comes out, Foch will need a report, and I believe a diary will be useful in preserving my impressions, ordering my thoughts and testing my ideas before presenting them in the heady air of the Royal Court.

(I must say at the outset that I have always found it incongruous that France, the most republican country in Europe, has chosen as an ally the most politically reactionary, autocratic monarchy on the face of the earth. But then I will be the first to admit that *Weltpolitik* has never been my specialty.)

Which brings me back to my mystery. Since being awarded the Legion d'Honneur for a really trivial part in another affair, I may have attained some local stature, but a mission of this significance has never before been appropriate to my portfolio. When I'd been summoned by Foch in September, I naturally assumed he would ask me to oversee some espionage activity more in line with my background— and I was also prepared to decline.

My life with Tania and our daughter Michelle had been so serene and domestic, nestled amid my vineyards and oaks in the beautiful Rhone Valley, that I had been all but able to forget the War as it dragged into its third year. I had no desire to re-enter the fray I had so lately abandoned. Too many of my friends, too many of our friends' children, had already given their lives in that fight, and living—the daily, even boring routines of country life—had become an end in itself, each day treasured for its small compensations, its bland contentments.

But Foch had surprised me. At stake, he said, was nothing less than the very future of France. Preservation of the alliance with Russia was our best hope of winning the war. With America becoming less and less isolationist, we needed to hold out until that young giant had come to our aid. Foch had no illusions about Russia's stability, but he thought our offer could delay the inevitable separate peace between Germany and Russia until beyond the Spring, and that might be enough time.

Foch and I had been sitting at a field table over a lunch of chicken and a chilled rosé as he explained the situation to me. Though ten years my senior, he spoke with a fire and conviction that made him seem much younger than me. I, not he, was the old man. I wondered if my will to survive, to merely exist, was the beginning of the process of dying. Surely Freddy had had tragedy enough for any man—his only son and his son-in-law had both been killed in the first month of the war. And yet he didn't retire. He continued to fight. I could do no less.

After he finished, I spoke. "All that's fine, Freddy, but I don't understand why you chose me."

"You are too modest," he said.

"Not at all. This is entirely out of my province. Surely our ambassador..."

"Maurice Paleologue, a good man."

"Surely he is a more logical choice."

Foch stood and took me by the arm. We moved away from his aides-de-camp and walked to a nearby hillock. Smoke hung like mist over the trenches in the distance. Occasionally a volley of shots would carry up to us on the heavy breeze.

"Paleologue is a diplomat. You are a man of action. Do I make myself clear?"

My confusion must have shown, for he continued. "Jules, a diplomat must move in certain prescribed ways. He cannot just drop in at the Czar's Palace and speak with him. As a matter of fact, Paleologue has been denied audiences with the Czar for the past two months. He has met with ministers, with bureaucrats, with clerks, but not with Nicholas. This is no coincidence. Nicholas is contemplating peace with Germany, and he can't bear to face our ambassador."

"Then why will he see me?"

"If Paleologue says he has a new offer from Paris, the Czar will think it is merely a ploy to get an audience. If an entirely new emissary arrives by military carrier, the demands of protocol and curiosity ought to play into our hands. You will see the Czar."

"And then?"

"And then, Jules, then you personally will convince him to accept our offer."

It was a staggering demand and I said as much. How could I accomplish what others, with lifetimes of training in diplomacy, could not?

Foch smiled. "There are few better natural diplomats on earth than yourself, Jules. Also," he put his arm around me, "I trust you, which is why I chose you."

If it was flattery, it worked. I am in St. Petersburg, and someone is at the door.

OCTOBER 7, 1916.

The orderly was polite enough, though the tone of the invitation to the unscheduled and unofficial meeting was unambiguous. It was a summons.

I followed the courtier through the ornate halls, so vast that we walked for nearly twenty minutes before reaching our destination. There appear to be at least fifty separate wings of the Palace, each with ten rooms or more.

At last we came to the offices of Vladimir Sukhomlinov, who had been the War Minister until the first shots of the War were fired. That he still had an office in the Winter Palace was surprising, but I was starting to sense that many things about the Russian capital were not wholly reasonable.

My first impression was that it was too hot. A huge fire blazed at the hearth, and enormous samovars squatted in each of the four corners. Sukhomlinov himself was half reclining on a divan, picking from a chicken carcass that sat on a low table in front of him. There was no desk, no sign of a file drawer. The floor was covered with layers of Oriental rugs, so that I had to step up to enter the chamber. The soft, yielding carpet made a dignified approach next to impossible, but I tried to manage.

When I was announced, the General didn't rise, but nodded vaguely in my direction and gave some signal for the secretary to withdraw. The door closed behind me and there was a long and, I thought, ominous silence, which I used to study the man.

Sukhomlinov has a rounded, cherubic face with the eyes of a ferret. He wears his whiskers in a Van Dyke, in imitation of the Czar. Black boots covered thin legs to the knees, but his torso, bedecked with medals, is ample. No, it is fat.

"You sent for me, General?"

He pulled himself upright, wiping his hands on the linen

tablecloth, and showed me his teeth. "I did, your Excellency," he said. "Can I offer you some tea? Vodka? A plate of chicken?"

I declined. "And I am a simple emissary, General, with no title."

"You are not a minister?"

"A citizen of the Republic of France, a personal guest of Czar Nicholas, nothing more."

To my surprise, this answer delighted him. He clapped his hands and laughed heartily. "Splendid! Wonderful! Please, take a seat. In any event, we must get acquainted." His French, the language of the court, though accented, was quite good.

I sank deeply into an armchair at his right hand, wishing I could loosen my tie. The heat was really quite stifling. He rang a bell and when a servant entered, he ordered a bottle of wine and a tray of cakes. We sat in continued silence while the chicken was cleared and the new service laid.

"There, now," he said at last. "You are French. You will have some wine."

I took a glass and we toasted the Czar. Then I decided it was time to get to business, if it was to be a business meeting.

"How may I be of service to you, General?"

"It is rather the other way around. I believe I may be able to help you."

"I would be most grateful for any assistance you could give me. You know why I am here, then?"

He nodded patiently, with the air of one tutoring a child. *"On sait tout.* One knows everything, I'm afraid. It is more a burden than anything, but especially here at court, it is a necessary evil—if one wants to survive." He savored a mouthful of wine, then continued. "In any case, Monsieur Giraud, I do know the workings of the Czar's mind, and just now it is in a difficult state—not only because of the War, though that goes badly enough, but there are other things..."

"Such as?"

"His son, the Heir, Alexis."

"What about him?"

"He is a bleeder, you know. A tragic disease. It consumes the Czarina with trying to protect him. It also brought Rasputin to the court."

"Rasputin?"

"Surely you know of Rasputin?"

I shook my head no, and the general laughed coarsely, then leaned conspiratorially toward me. "Monsieur Giraud, it is fortunate I invited you here. Talking to Nicholas, or especially Alexandra, without knowing about Rasputin is a dangerous enterprise."

"Who is he?"

"On one level, he is a simple monk from Siberia, a faith healer. On another, he is, after the Czar, the most powerful man in Russia."

I sat back, chuckling. "Surely that's an exaggeration."

Sukhomlinov took his time pouring more wine. "No. No, I don't think it is. His influence over Alexandra is hard to overestimate. Powerful men have fallen because of Rasputin's disapproval—if he were still alive you could ask Peter Stolypin, our past prime minister, about that.

"Don't misunderstand me, Giraud, I myself think Rasputin is a genuine starets—a holy man—so we've had no problems. But with Nicholas at Spala commanding the army, Alexandra rules Russia. And Rasputin rules Alexandra. A wrong word to the wrong person could leave your mission in ruins and yourself in great danger."

"How can that be?"

He popped a small cake whole into his mouth, washing it down with half a glass of wine. "Rasputin has convinced Alexandra that he is the voice of God's will. And it does seem to be true that he has great healing powers. Twice he has laid his hands on the Heir and brought him back from the brink of death—even after the doctors have given up."

"You said danger. You don't mean physical danger?"

Again that condescending laugh. "I see you don't know about the murders either, then."

At my blank look, he went on. "The other reason the Czar is so distressed lately is that three of his closest aides have been killed in the past three months, and not at the front. Here, right in Petrograd."

"Murdered?"

"Two bomb blasts and a cut throat could hardly be accidental."

"And this is Rasputin's doing?"

He almost spit out his wine. "No! Of course not. I hope I didn't give you that impression. That's not even suspected."

"It seemed to follow that..."

"No, no, no. I only mentioned the murders to show that there are forces at work here that may not be obvious—forces that have influenced the Czar's state of mind."

"And you think all this will have some effect on me?"

He sat forward. "Let me be frank. At this stage the Czar is nearly beaten. After our victories earlier this year in Galacia, and then our disastrous rout, his will is nearly crushed, and he longs for a return to normalcy. If he is pushed too hard..." He sighed.

"Monsieur Giraud, in some ways the Czar is like a child. He is sheltered, he doesn't understand the motives of those around him, he is perplexed by the evil in the world. But, like a child, if he is pushed too hard in one direction, he will sometimes go in the other out of willfulness. He is, after all, the Czar, the absolute ruler of Russia, and he does not like to feel that his options are determined by something or someone else."

With some effort, Sukhomlinov rose. We crossed the thickly-carpeted room to a window. "My advice to you, Monsieur Giraud, is to go slowly. Know your quarry before you hunt."

He put his arm around me, enveloping me in the strong scent of his cologne. I was grateful for his information, but another minute in that room with the heat and perfume would have turned my discomfort to true nausea. Fortunately, the interview seemed to be over. A servant appeared and the General shook my hand. I thanked him for his warning, and within seconds was transported over the rolling rugs outside to the blessedly cool corridor.

Though it was just past four in the afternoon, already the lights in the Palace had been turned on. Outside, a pink dusk deepened, and I felt an urge to be out in it.

Unescorted, I found my way to an exit and walked the streets of St. Petersburg until full night had fallen.

The War shows here more than in my native Valence. One building in four seems to have been converted to care for the wounded. From the narrow byways off the main streets comes a continuous low moan, like a threatening wind—the haunting refrain of men suffering.

Beyond the shadow of the Palace, and off the Nevsky Prospekt, beggars—even women and children—hold out their bony hands for kopecks. I gave away all of my coins, though not one hollow eye even acknowledged me.

Thoroughly dispirited, I returned to the Palace, its polished marble surfaces glinting in the light of a nearly full moon.

OCTOBER 9, 1916.

After sending a messenger to Maurice Paleologue at the French Embassy announcing my arrival, I spent the greater portion of two days with a series of books reviewing court etiquette. My reading was for naught. None of the reference books covered anything like the situation with which I was confronted when I first met Nicholas and Alexandra.

I had of course been briefed that the royal family spent very little of their time in the capital, preferring the peace of their accommodations at Tsarskoye Selo, some fifteen kilometers south of the city, yet I was surprised when I was summoned there. I had assumed that state business would be conducted at court, but I was wrong.

If my first impressions are correct, the very seat of Russian government is an icon-bedecked boudoir, decorated in various shades of mauve, a comfortable yet utterly hideous bedchamber reminiscent of little-used guest rooms in any number of British country estates.

But I'm getting ahead of myself.

A servant called at my room just after an upsetting breakfast of cold fish, onions, and tea. (Oh, for a fresh croissant dipped into a steaming bowl of cafe au lait!) The Czar had returned from military headquarters at Spala and would see me at my earliest convenience.

We traveled by train—the railroad line is the oldest in the country—a short distance over swampland and then came to a small village station with a steeply sloping roof. There, surrounded by mounted Cossacks, our car was separated from the train and transferred to another track, which led to the Czar's station.

A double row of trees lined the wide boulevard that led to the two palaces. We passed the larger of the two, skirted a lovely lake, and approached the vine-covered Alexander Palace, an Italianate structure of some one hundred rooms. Even so late in the Fall, the smell of lilacs and fresh flowers from the Crimea made the Palace smell like a summer garden.

I was led through a huge circular hallway, then turned right into the Imperial apartments, which were hung with photographs of children's bicycles! The "art" made a strange impression on me, as though I had entered a children's world of make-believe.

But I had no time to reflect on that feeling. At the door to the Czar's private study, two huge black men in the flowing robes of Arabia stood watch, huge scimitars crossed between them. They further reinforced my sense of the unreal nature of things at court.

In a moment I was being introduced to Nicholas II, Emperor and Autocrat of all the Russias; Czar of Moscow, Kiev, Vladimir, Novgorod, Kazan; Astrakan of Poland, of Siberia; Sovereign of the Circassian Princes; Lord of Turkestan; Heir of Norway; Duke of Schleswig Holstein, etc.—his various titles in my etiquette book cover fully half a page.

In the flesh, Nicholas is less imposing. Short of stature, with the mildest and friendliest of expressions, and dressed in the uniform of a colonel in the Russian army (though he is its active Commander-in-Chief), he could be anyone. Certainly he projects no imperial aura.

We sat on leather armchairs quite close to one another and he offered me a cigarette, which I declined. For his part, he smoked continuously during our interview.

Thinking to heed Sukhomlinov's advice, I didn't plan to press my immediate objective, preferring to simply take the tenor of the man. I was not even able to do that. We'd barely finished exchanging pleasantries when a lady-in-waiting interrupted us. She whispered something to the Czar and, chuckling good-naturedly, he turned to me.

"It seems there are no secrets, M. Giraud. My wife, the Empress, has heard of your arrival and would like to meet you."

"Of course," I answered, "I would be flattered."

He rose. "We'll have to go to her. Now that I'm home, she's taking a much-needed rest." His faintly apologetic tone, filled with a wry humor, impressed me. He might be Czar of Russia, but he was first a human being, a husband and father, and he had the courage to show it.

We passed through a billiard room, across a corridor, and then through what looked to me to be the royal bedchamber. Beyond that, we entered the darkened mauve room I've earlier described. And on a mauve divan, covered to the waist with a blanket, reclined the Czarina Alexandra, Empress of Russia.

"Good morning, Sunny," the Czar said in English, leaning over and kissing her. "How are you feeling?"

The scene was so intimate as to be embarrassing, although neither of their Royal Highnesses seemed to notice. Nicholas said to his wife, "May I introduce Monsieur Jules Giraud."

I stepped closer and took her proffered hand to kiss. No sooner had I done so than I felt a pressure that prevented me from releasing her.

"*Vous etes francais, n'est-ce pas?*" she asked with an execrable accent.

"*Bien sur, Madame l'Empress.*"

Now she took my hand in both of hers and stared deeply into my eyes. I felt compelled to meet her gaze, and struggled to maintain my composure in the face of such intense scrutiny.

None of the rumors I had heard about Alexandra—that she was haughty, unfriendly, reserved—prepared me for the warmth I read in her eyes. She had a lovely face, perfect skin, a slim yet buxom figure. And lastly, as she reached some decision, a beautiful smile.

I felt myself drawn to her, wanting to protect her, and I believe I got an indication of what the Czar must feel as her husband. There might be a certain surface reserve there, but this was a woman with deep feelings and a passionate nature.

She released my hand, then, and turned to her husband, who had been standing by passively. "Oh, Nicky," she said, again in English, "our prayers have been answered."

The Czar pulled up two chairs and motioned for me to take one. "Which prayers are those, Sunny?"

"For Alyosha, as our Friend predicted."

"Ah." Nicholas sat back and lit a cigarette. Alexandra looked at me.

"Monsieur Giraud, your arrival has been foretold. I saw in your eyes that you are a good man, a kind man. And last week our son's tutor, Pierre Gaillard, was taken down with cholera. We pray for him daily, but he is contagious and cannot go near Alexis." She reached out and took the Czar's hand. "Do you remember, Nicky? Last week Gregory said a Frenchman would arrive in court to take Pierre's place?"

Nicholas responded gently. "M. Giraud isn't here to tutor Alyosha, I'm afraid."

But the Empress would not be gainsaid. She reached her hand out to me. "M. Giraud?"

It was not professional. It was possibly not even smart, but I'd not been sent as a professional diplomat, and the opportunity to become close to the Royal Family seemed rich with potential for my mission. I looked into Alexandra's eyes and saw there a great reassurance.

"I am your Majesty's humblest servant," I said, not exactly striking a blow for the spirit of republican France.

But in reality I was acting from the most French of motives—the desire to please a woman. And the Czarina is already, after but one meeting, first a woman, and only incidentally Empress of Russia.

I was invited to stay on here in Tsarkoye Selo whenever I would prefer. My suite is on the top floor of one of the many houses for nobility that line the boulevard leading from the train station to the Alexander Palace. The house itself—as are all the houses—is guarded by Imperial troops in the most outlandish of costumes. Blue sashes and swinging sabers.

In all, I'm not dissatisfied with events thus far. True, I haven't gotten any commitment from the Czar, but then I haven't tried. It is no small thing to become an intimate of a royal family, and I am well on my way to that position.

Tomorrow I am to be introduced to Alexis and to his sisters, the Grand Duchesses Olga, Tatiana, Maria, and Anastasia. But tonight I will be attending a soiree of some kind at the house of a woman named Anna Vyroubova, who I gather is the Czarina's only personal friend. Alexandra mentioned that she would not be surprised if a special guest were present—the man who "predicted" my arrival at court, who has healed the Heir Apparent on at least two occasions, whom Sukhomlinov called the most powerful man in Russia.

I am very much looking forward to the party. I am beginning to have a strong feeling that my success will depend to a great degree on the support of the Friend—Gregory Efimovich Rasputin.

2

(OCTOBER 10, 1916.)

I am exhausted, but I must try to get some of this down.

It is perhaps fortunate that the days here are so short. By five o'clock, full night had arrived, and I took a rest for nearly three hours before the party. Without that sleep, I would not have lasted through the night.

Tsarkoye Selo after dark is, if possible, even more a fairyland than it appears during the day. Two sets of trees, now leafless, line the main boulevard and bracket the road like supplicating hands, their thin fingers splayed to the night sky. As it happens, tonight there was a full moon, and its reflection on the lake and the structures surrounding it—the Turkish bath house, gazebos, monuments and arches—imbued the scene with magical overtones.

Unescorted, dressed against the chill, I walked to the Old Palace—an enormous blue and white building that I preferred to the royal residence. Dinner would be served there, and afterwards a private group would retire to Anna Vyroubova's.

The ostensible reason for the dinner was the Czar's return from military headquarters at Spala some eight hundred kilometers away. I will do well to remember that he is in fact the active leader of the Russian army. Though he seems the least warlike of men, Commander-in-Chief may be the title he is proudest of.

Because of the diplomatic nature of the dinner, it was extremely well-attended. Even as I approached the Palace, a long line of carriages and limousines were depositing guests at the door. Most of the male guests were in the uniforms of Russian officers—medal bedecked and colorful in bright blues and reds. The women might have come from Paris, and in fact their dresses in all likelihood had. Décolletage is quite the fashion, and since many of the women tend to be Rubenesque, the effect is striking and daring, *très haute monde*.

And jewelry!

The incredible jeweler Fabergé has his headquarters here in St. Petersburg, and his work is everywhere—tiaras, necklaces, bracelets, clasps and pins of every description glittered out of hairdos, between breasts, off throats and wrists. On every table were gem-encrusted ashtrays, cigarette cases, and knick-knacks, each of which could supply a regiment with food for a week.

As it happened, I had just removed my overcoat, feeling underdressed in evening clothes, when I heard a familiar voice behind me. Vladimir Sukhomlinov had entered the room, escorting a lovely woman whom I took to be his daughter.

"Ah, Monsieur Giraud," he boomed on recognizing me, "you have made the party lists already. A good sign, a very good sign." He crossed over to me, kissing me on both cheeks. He seemed already to have been drinking. "May I present to you my wife, Katrina."

As much to keep from staring as out of politeness, I bowed over her hand and kissed it. Mme. Sukhomlinov was stunning. Moreover, she could not yet be thirty!

But before we could get involved in any discussion, a short portly man, dressed simply as I was, smoking a long cigar, came through the door into the receiving room. Again Sukhomlinov boomed. "Ah, Maurice! *Vien ici*. Come and greet your fellow countryman."

With some show of reluctance to which the General seemed oblivious, the man came over. "But surely you know one another?" Sukhomlinov asked. Upon seeing that we didn't, he continued. "Your latest minister to court, Maurice. Jules Giraud, the French Ambassador, Maurice Paleologue."

I was delighted to make Paleologue's acquaintance under these circumstances. It was far better than the sometimes stilted etiquette that determined behavior in so many of the world's embassies. Still, he seemed to be on his guard—his dark eyes revealing nothing of the man within. "I believe my staff extended an invitation for you to come to the Embassy just today," he said. "They told me you had left the Winter Palace."

"I'll be staying here in Tsarkoye Selo from time to time," I said. "The Empress had a chore or two for me." I thought I would keep my actions suitably vague. Neither Sukhomlinov nor Paleologue need to know that I will be tutoring the prince.

"Alexandra is a great woman, another Catherine the Great," Sukhomlinov said. "She is Russia's savior."

The Ambassador smiled coldly. "She has certainly been the savior of some Russians," he said.

The General's face hardened and began to turn red. His wife tugged at her husband's sleeve. "We must get settled at the table, dear. Come along." Stiffly, Sukhomlinov bowed to me and turned on his heel without another glance at Maurice.

"What was that about?" I asked.

Paleologue took me by the arm and we moved toward the dining hall. "I hope you are not too close to that man."

I shrugged. "He seems a nice enough fellow."

"He is Russia's greatest living traitor."

"Sukhomlinov? He is past Minister of War, isn't he?"

The Ambassador laughed coldly. "He is also less than two months out of jail for treason. Freed by Alexandra Fedorovna, the Czarina."

"Why did she free him? Was he guilty?"

"Oh, *sans doute*. But he is also a friend of the Friend." He stopped me before we had joined the queue, punctuating his words with stabs from his cigar. "Rasputin!" he hissed. "Those are the kinds of men he favors—sycophants, hedonists and fools—and Sukhomlinov falls into all three categories. Did you meet his wife?"

I nodded.

"His fourth. A beauty, is she not?" Without waiting for me to answer, he went on, his voice rising. "And obviously aware of it herself. She spends more than our entire Embassy. And where did her husband get the money to keep her in the style which she demands? From systematically plundering the War Treasury for nearly two decades while he was Minister."

I thought Paleologue was getting a little carried away, perhaps out of some personal motive such as jealousy or the General's influence with Alexandra. His little black eyes gleamed with intensity. I backed away a step and looked at him levelly.

"Those are strong accusations, Monsieur."

The Ambassador seemed to retreat. He visibly softened, taking a long puff at his cigar. Holding the smoke in and closing his eyes, he finally exhaled a plume toward the ceiling, permitting himself an almost embarrassed smile. "Why don't we sit down and talk for a moment? If you are going to have any success here at court, you must at the very least know whom to avoid."

We moved to a small salon off the main entryway and sat on two of the burgundy-colored velvet stools that lined the wall. "I am afraid I have no patience left for that man, and I shouldn't let it show so blatantly, but this is one topic where my diplomatic training deserts me. I've distrusted and disliked Sukhomlinov from the moment I met him. How did he get in touch with you?"

"He invited me to his office at the Winter Palace. He said he wanted to give me some advice to help my mission."

Paleologue chuckled drily. "Do nothing or, if you must do something, do it slowly, *n'est-ce pas?*"

"*Exactement.*"

"Well, as his old associate Sazonov told me, 'It's hard to get him to work, but to make him tell the truth is well-nigh impossible.'" He shook his head. "The man is so blatant he amazes me; he might as well wear a German uniform."

"But what has he actually done?" I asked.

Paleologue straightened, his back against the wall. "What has he done?" He grimaced slightly. "Well, before the war, he amassed his own fortune by his mastery of the art of the expense account. He would go on troop inspection tours to Vladivostok—thirteen thousand kilometers round trip—for which he was compensated by the distance traveled, and never get off the train. He actually bragged to me about this. He also would only approve contracts to those who feathered his nest.

"But those are only the petty, personal things. I suppose they are common enough, especially here in Russia. More important, but still probably not criminal, is his legendary and colossal stupidity. He believed until hostilities actually erupted that this war would be a chivalrous affair, fought with sabers and bayonets, the infantry and cavalry charge. He wouldn't hear of the word firepower—machine guns were unmanly. And the result? Even now Russian factories are only producing 35,000 rounds of ammunition per month, while the army needs an estimated 45,000 rounds per day. No wonder eight million of these poor people have already died in battle. How do you defend against a German advance when you have no bullets in your guns?"

He grew silent, puffing at his cigar. "And still we haven't touched upon his treachery. He is a known confidant of German agents, doing everything in his power to convince the Czar to seek a separate peace."*

"But does the Czar listen to him?"

---

*If anything, Paleologue understates the General's treachery. In 1925, when he published his memoirs, Sukhomlinov's original dedication was not to Czar Nicholas, whom he had served for so long as War Minister, but to ex-Kaiser Wilhelm of Germany.

The Ambassador sighed. "Old Vladimir has always been able to charm Nicholas with dinner prattle. And that is what policy seems to be based on lately—small talk, lip service to autocracy, and acceptance of Rasputin."

"But why does the Czar... ?"

He cut me off. "It's Alexandra, not the Czar. Rasputin is the power..."

But he was not to finish. A gong sounded and servants appeared to usher us out of our salon and into the main dining hall for the entrance of Nicholas and Alexandra. Before he went to his assigned place, Paleologue shook my hand. "We will talk again tomorrow, but be careful. Trust no one. Nothing in St. Petersburg is as it seems."

If, after my voyage here and my first few meals, I had begun to think that I would eat nothing but cabbage, fish and potatoes until I returned home, tonight proved me happily mistaken.

Although the Romanovs are known to be the least social and sophisticated of royal families, the buffet at tonight's dinner could have come directly from the table of the Sun King himself.

As they began wheeling the trolleys from the kitchen, I forgot for a moment the court's intrigues and my mission here, and found myself remembering with fondness my colleague Auguste Lupa. After our last case together in France, Lupa and I had stayed a while in communication. But then with the birth of our daughter and his probable involvement in other cases, we had lost touch. A brilliant chef in his own right, Lupa would have been a boon companion to share in this meal—no one I had ever met enjoyed eating as much as he did. And the food tonight would have delighted him.

The fois gras was not from Strasbourg, but was excellent nonetheless. The caviar, Beluga, was the best I'd ever had, served up in obscenely large silver goblets with lemon, grated onion and hard-boiled eggs. We had Perrier-Jouét

Brut '74 with these courses, and drank several toasts to Nicholas and to victory.

After the toasts, the waiters brought plates of trout and sturgeon, sorbets, then a richly fragrant, clear amber turtle soup. There was another ice, then suckling pig with horse-radish (a special treat for Nicholas), racks of venison and boar, filet steak, pheasant and quail. For red wines, we could choose between the Grand Echezeaux '87 or Margaux '93, though for whites there was only Meursault '06—the only indication of shortages caused by three years of war.

Dinner went on, with its usual banter, for over three hours, with the Czar and Empress making the rounds of the tables, each one of which had a setting for them as they moved among the guests.

The courses continued—some noodle dish with sour cream and strips of beef, thickened fish veloutes, mounds of truffled eggs, mushrooms, fat white asparagus and flawless green petite pois. And then the coup de grace—fresh framboise from the Crimea for dessert, served chantilly with a Chateau d'Yquem '74. Lupa would have been in heaven.

At midnight, Alexandra appeared at my side, and re-minded me of the party to which she'd invited me at Anna Vyroubova's after the dinner. I had forgotten all about it or, more honestly, could not believe that anyone would be at-tending it at this hour. After such a meal, I'd been looking for the earliest opportunity to excuse myself and come back to my room to sleep. But one does not refuse an invitation from an empress, so I ordered three successive demitasses of Ital-ian coffee and bolted down the burning liquid. A few min-utes later, Nicholas and Alexandra left the dining room, signaling the end of the evening.

I put on my coat and walked out alone into the now truly bitter night. Turning off the tree-lined boulevard, I followed a bridle path for several hundred meters until I came to a small white house set back into a stand of trees.

The moon had set. The only light in the blackness of the

night came through the frosted windows of the house, across which figures moved like puppets in a shadow play.

The coffee had done its work. I was no longer tired.

There could not have been a greater contrast between the dinner I'd just attended and the soirée at Anna Vyroubova's. The hostess herself set the tone. She was an enormous, potato white woman dressed in a flowing white dress. Something like a nun's habit covered her head. Her lips were thick and red, her face, under the pasty complexion, blotched. A thoroughly unattractive person, she can only walk with the aid of crutches, though I don't know whether it's because of her weight or some accident or illness.

She was gracious enough in greeting me, though I was somewhat surprised that she spoke Russian—fortunately my command of that language is reasonable—and we moved from the lobby, where I had my coat taken by one of the Arabian Guard, to a large sitting room that was already crowded. A table along one wall groaned under the weight of two samovars and thirty cakes. A fire blazed in the hearth, servants moved to and fro dispensing tea and sugar—the room itself was decorated with the same overstuffed furniture as the Empress's mauve bedchamber, and the walls were similarly covered with religious portraits and icons.

Through the tobacco smoke, I noticed that most of the guests had congregated in one corner of the room, and someone was holding forth from that quarter, though the crowd blocked my vision.

The woman Vyroubova asked me if I'd like some tea or Madeira, and I took a glass of the wine. The Empress hadn't yet made her appearance—if indeed she was coming—and while I waited for her arrival, I moved back against a wall and surveyed the scene.

Many of the sixty or so guests had, like myself, just come from the dinner, so there was a smattering of uniforms and formal gowns. For the rest, and it was the majority, dress was simple—in fact, it shocked me that people would dress so

informally in the expected presence of the Empress. The
men, of course, wore ties, but some had removed their dinner jackets, and several of the woman appeared to be no
more than peasants, in ill-fitting dresses of minimal design.

I must mention one exception to all of the above. While I
was standing taking in my surroundings, I noticed a woman
standing pensively by the hearth, her arm resting casually on
the mantle. Even now as I write I can see her clearly. She
wore neither the crinolined fluff of the society women nor
the flaxen bedsheets of the peasants, but a lovely silk or taf-
feta flowing dress of light blue and pink floral print. Though
modest in style, it managed to show off her slim yet womanly
figure to great advantage.

Her chestnut hair was gathered at her neck into a soft bun,
and wisps of it had escaped the coiffeur's comb and hung
charmingly at her temples. In profile, her face was an ivory
cameo, with a proud chin and dainty nose. With that sense
people have when they are being watched, she turned toward me and smiled shyly, then looked down and back toward the fire.

I mention this woman only because she was so completely
out of the cast of the rest. That feeling of unreality that I had
experienced in a number of settings here dissipated as I
gazed at her beautiful face with its clean lines and untroubled
brow. If someone so innocent yet so vital could exist here in
the court, perhaps there was still hope for the Czar's entourage and for all of Russia.

I had almost made up my mind to go over and speak to her
when the doorbell rang and Vyroubova shuffled past. In seconds, Alexandra Fodorovna was standing next to me in the
doorway to the salon. Gradually, as the presence of the Empress was felt, the talk in the room died down. Soon the knot
of debaters at the far end of the room had all turned and
bowed—all except one figure who now loomed above the
group, smiling at the Empress as though (forgive me the
thought) she were his lover arriving at a tryst.

Rasputin!

I will never forget that first vision of him—the crowd actually parted before him as he came toward Alexandra—dressed in a bright blue satin shirt, open halfway down his chest. On his feet were heavy peasant boots, into which he had tucked his pants. His unkempt black hair is parted in the middle and hangs to his shoulders. The dark beard is also long and full yet matted, as though he doesn't wash it. In physique, he seems a peasant—strong shoulders, thick hands and neck. His nose is broad though his cheeks are hollow.

But what struck me the most were his eyes. A pale, unearthly blue or blue-gray, they seemed to dart wildly until they alighted on something, and then their intensity could be frightening.

After greeting Alexandra with a kiss on the hand and the word, *"Matuska,"* or mother, he fixed those eyes on me. I think the Empress must have said something to introduce us, but I really have no memory of it. One moment I was standing there, looking at Rasputin, trying to form an objective opinion of the man, and the next thing I knew, he had taken my hand in both of his, and was looking deeply into my eyes.

I cannot describe clearly what I felt, but suddenly it was as though I were floating somewhere high above the crowded room, with Rasputin at my side explaining the world as though through his own eyes. How long he held me in this manner I couldn't say—it mustn't have been for too long—but I had to force myself finally to break away from the trance.

It was an unsettling and unique experience that gave me an immediate insight into this man's power over the Royal Family. Yet, strangely, I felt nothing sinister. It may have been excessively intimate, but I could see where his inclusion of one into his world could, under the right circumstances, be comforting.

Whether that sort of comfort is appropriate between an Empress and a peasant is a question I will not try to resolve.

In any event, when the bond between us had been broken, he smiled at me, showing a mouthful of dirty teeth, and spoke to the Empress again. "The Frenchman?"

"Yes, Gregory, the one you saw."

"Alyosha will be pleased. I am pleased."

Rasputin then escorted Alexandra, taking her arm, to a settee where he sat at her feet as she reclined. The scene was really too cloying for my tastes and I went to the refreshment table while most of the rest of the crowd gathered around the royal couch.

I was searching for something less sweet and stronger than Madeira when a voice came from behind me.

"Almost had you, didn't he?"

I turned to face a uniformed Commissar around my own age, with a ruddy complexion and black hair. He spoke French but in that loud, bluff style I was beginning to associate with all Russians. "Boris Minsky," he said, shaking my hand and nearly breaking my fingers with his grip. "Your first meeting with our holy Gregory?"

I nodded.

"What do you think? The greatest man in Russia? In the world, perhaps?"

"You don't like him?" I asked.

For a response, Minsky actually spit on the carpet, wiping it in with his boot. He reached into his tunic and pulled out a flask, which he uncorked and drank from. "Would you like something to drink?" he asked. He looked witheringly at the table. "Tea and Madeira! And only Madeira because Rasputin likes it."

I held out my glass and Minsky half-filled it with vodka. "Is he so bad?" I asked.

Minsky pointed back to where Rasputin and Alexandra sat. The monk was starting to speak more forcefully, addressing not only the Empress but the group gathered around them.

"Is that right?" Minsky asked. "Is it right for the Queen of all Russians to be on a loveseat after midnight with a peasant?"

Minsky's complaint sounded familiar—more jealousy over

his own lack of influence. As tactfully as I could, I said as much to him.

He drew himself up to his full height—considerably more than mine—and seemed to come to some decision. "Monsieur Giraud. You just illustrated one of the most insidious things about that man. He seems to have a knack for deflecting criticism by calling into question the integrity of his accusers. In my case, though, I'm afraid your defense of him falls apart."

"I didn't mean to be defending..."

"No, that's all right. It's common enough. But I am not without some influence myself. I have been the Czar's friend since before his coronation. We served as officers together while he was in the Army, and we still ride together nearly every day. I have his ear. I am not jealous of Rasputin's influence, though I very much fear it, and there is a great difference."

Chagrined, I just nodded and sipped at my vodka. It was much preferable to the Madeira. Minsky seemed to hold no grudge though, and, his earlier point made, he started in again.

"I'll tell you why I resent Rasputin's influence—not because I dislike him, though I do, and not because he is undermining people's respect for Nicholas and Alexandra, though he is—but because he does not understand policy or issues."

"But surely he doesn't make policy."

"Ministers cannot remain in office without his blessing. He judges people by whether they are 'good,' not knowledgeable. And his definition of good is probably not yours or mine. He has convinced Alexandra that any criticism of the Czar or any of his policies is 'bad.'

"So, though we are losing battles, the poor have no bread, and the army has no bullets, no official minister dares tell Nicholas these things. To do so would be disloyal!"

"I see the problem," I said.

"Take this vodka," Minsky said, continuing. "Before the

War, production and sale of vodka was controlled by the government. It brought in thirty percent of the government's income. Then one of Rasputin's ministers decided that soldiers might get drunk on the night before an important battle, so he recommended to the Czar that vodka be outlawed for the duration of the War. Nicholas didn't think much of the idea, but every other minister went along with the suggestion. The result? On the verge of the greatest war we have ever fought, we cut our budget by one-third! I ask you, Giraud, can a country survive this madness?"

"But we're drinking vodka right now." I said.

"That's the hell of it! Of course we have vodka. Now every shopkeeper and potato farmer makes it illegally, and the government gets no income from it."

"But surely," I said, "if you know this, you can tell it to the Czar."

Minsky took a huge pull at his flask. Then he shook his head sadly. "No, Giraud, I am a farmer fighting a flood tide. The small seeds I plant get washed away before they can flower."

"Can nothing be done?" I asked.

He nodded toward Rasputin, now holding forth. "Against that? Listen to him."

Even across the room, every word in the staccato rambling was clear. Rasputin sat, one knee on the floor, the other leg curled on the divan, and beseeched Alexandra to talk to the Czar.

"You must, *Matuska*, you must. The peasants. The starving. All they need is your prayers to the Czar. For bread, sugar, butter. Stop the trains. The troops are all right for now. The people need bread. All St. Petersburg. Everyone."

"What's he saying?" I asked.

"The same harangue he was giving us before Alexandra came in. He wants to have her ask the Czar to stop all troop movements to the capital, and to use the trains instead to bring in bread, sugar and butter." Minsky was starting to slur.

"Why? Is there a shortage of supplies?" That seemed impossible after the meal I'd just been served.

"That's the problem. The food is rotting in warehouses. It doesn't seem to find its way into town." He took another pull at his flask. "Last week they discovered three hundred head of cattle starved in boxcars. Someone just forgot them on a siding. They had to be used for glue."

There was a silence from across the room and we glanced there. Alexandra was just handing the monk a glass of Madeira. It looked as though she were waiting on him. With the merest nod of acknowledgement, Rasputin took the glass, emptied it in one gulp, and continued his monologue.

Minsky swore violently under his breath. Then he raised his voice. "Father Gregory!"

Rasputin looked at him mildly. "Yes?"

"Why don't you just have one of your ministers give the order for the trains? No need to bother the Czar."

All other sounds in the room abruptly stopped. Minsky took a few lurching steps toward the divan. "In fact, why don't you just wave your hands and make food appear? Can't you do that?"

The Empress spoke up. "That's enough, Boris."

Minsky exaggerated a bow. "Pardon, your Majesty, but it's not enough." He faced Rasputin again. "Can't you do that? Can't you talk to God and get food and bullets and while you're at it, have the Germans surrender?"

Two Imperial Guardsmen entered the room from the hallway and began moving toward Minsky. He didn't even see them, turned as he was toward the Empress. "He's a fake, your Highness. Can't you see that? He's no more a man of God than I am! Look at him. Please open your eyes."

One of the other officers in the room spoke up roughly. "Minsky, you're close to treason."

The Commissar exploded. "Damn this talk of treason! I'm no traitor! It's no treason to speak the truth. Your Majesty, please, you must listen. You must..."

Rasputin gave the Empress a look and something seemed

to pass between them. Suddenly Alexandra snapped at Minsky. "You will be silent! Enough!"

The guards weren't needed. Minsky looked at the couple on the couch, shook his head in defeat and, bowing as graciously as he could, made his way out to the hallway.

The incident provided me with any proof I might have needed for Rasputin's hold over Alexandra. It was clear to everyone in the room. He told her when and how to act, and she did his bidding immediately, without question.

Suddenly very tired, I waited a few moments for some other guests to leave, then said my good-byes to the Empress. She was graciousness itself, the problem with Minsky apparently forgotten. Rasputin, still next to her, asked if he could accompany me tomorrow when I meet Alexis, or Alyosha, the Heir Apparent. Alexandra thought that would be a wonderful idea.

In the hallway, I noticed Minsky slumped in what looked to be a drunken stupor, attended by the beautiful woman I had earlier seen by the fireplace. She was sponging his forehead, trying to bring him around. I don't suppose he could have been in better hands.

Tomorrow will be a long day. Now I must sleep.

3

[PORTIONS OF THE FOLLOWING ENTRY IN GIRAUD'S DIARY, NOTED BY ELLIPSES, ARE ILLEGIBLE. IT IS PRESUMED HE WROTE IT IN HASTE ON THE TRAIN FROM TSARKOYE SELO TO ST. PETERSBURG.]
(OCTOBER 11, 1916.)

... some explanation for his presence, but he didn't have time. He mentioned a dinner later in the week. Paleologue may be right about nothing being as it seems.

In any event, I was up by daybreak, which was nearly nine A.M. I was groggy from last night's food and drink, but a breakfast of tea and some harsh ...

... to the rail station. The chill had deepened and the sky hung low and gray, presaging snow. The nobles' houses that lined the boulevard, that only yesterday had looked so impressive, now seemed to squat depressingly under the impending force of nature.

In front of one of them, a small crowd had gathered—several children with their governesses, five or six members of the Imperial Guard, perhaps *une douzaine* of townspeople. I passed closely enough to hear someone say the name Minsky, and that stopped me. Curious, I went to the stoop and inquired as to what had happened.

266

"The Commissar is dead," someone told me.

"Minsky?"

"Da."

"But how?"

No one seemed to know. We all stood shivering, waiting for the inspector who was within to come to the door and tell us some news. Other passers-by stopped and gathered until there was quite a crowd. I was supposed to be on a train to St. Petersburg to meet Rasputin and Alexis, but I decided to wait. There was no sign yet if it was a murder, but I found it hard to believe that the vital man I had spoken with last night had simply died in his sleep.

And if it was another murder, it would undoubtedly play some part in the timing for my own mission. I had to know.

But the crowd was beginning to get restless. Catcalls and jeers rose on the morning air as an additional six Imperial Guardsmen, mounted with sabers drawn, appeared from out of nowhere, it seemed, to encircle us. I must say they did nothing to provoke any disturbance, but their presence, and the resentment it caused among the townspeople, was an indication of the tenuous nature of the civil peace...

... specifically forbidden on the streets, even here among the nobles in Tsarkoye Selo. That this chance gathering at the scene of a death could provoke a political demonstration didn't speak well for the stability of the Romanov reign.

Some signal must have been passed from the mounted guards to those sealing off the house, for someone went inside and in only a few moments an extremely old, crooked and bald gentleman appeared in the doorway. His blue pants were pleated, baggy and threadbare, and his open shirt needed to be ironed. Yet when he addressed the crowd, his voice, remarkably shrill and clear, was the very soul of authority.

"You are all asked to disperse. We have an unfortunate situation here involving the death of Commissar Minsky." He turned and spoke to someone in the house, out of my vision. Unfortunately, his words were easily heard. "They don't have to know that. We don't know that."

"Don't have to know what?" someone yelled from the crowd and as though with one movement, it began to press forward. "What's Nicholas hiding now?" someone else cried.

"Please, remain calm! There is nothing to know. Commissar Minsky appears to have had too much to drink, much too much. He died in his sleep. Now..."

From behind the old man came a deep bellow that chilled me more than the autumn wind. Though it had been months since I'd heard that voice, it was as familiar to me as my own name. It said one word, in English. "Rubbish!"

And next to the inspector, dwarfing him and filling the doorway with his presence, loomed the immense bulk of Auguste Lupa. Since I'd last seen him, he'd gained perhaps twenty kilograms, but he still looked powerful rather than fat. He looked out over the crowd for a second, then turned to face the other man. "Minsky was murdered," he said quietly, though his voice easily carried to where I stood.

"This is not the proper time," the inspector answered.

"It never is!" a man beside me...

"...that he didn't walk to his bed."

The two men didn't even seem aware of the growing commotion at their feet...

...quiet down. Instead they disappeared back into the house. As the guards began to show signs of spurring their horses into the crowd, it began to break up of its own accord. I waited, lagging behind, while the rest of the people went their ways. Finally, I mounted the stoop and asked one of the guards if I might speak to Lupa. Somewhat to my surprise, he knew the name, and waved me in.

I could hear a discussion continuing as I walked through the hallways to the back of the house.

"Here," Lupa said, "these black marks to the bed."

"They could be anything," the higher voice said.

"In fact, they could be nothing except what they are—the signs of being dragged by the armpits while his bootblack lined the floor."

I got to the door.

The inspector spoke. "I don't even grant that. But other than that, what is there?"

"There is the fact that he is lying in bed, neatly covered by his bedsheet, but with his boots still on. Anyone who is so drunk that he falls into bed with his boots on does not first turn down the bedsheet and crawl under. Further, as you well know, someone called his guards to escort him from the party at Vyroubova's. When they arrived, he'd already gone, and was in bed when they got here."

"That's circumstantial."

"And how did someone so drunk find his way home alone?"

"He may have simply gotten impatient."

Lupa shook his head. "A man whom, you contend, had drunk so much that he would shortly die from it? No, Inspector, you can't have it both ways. He was either sober enough to walk home alone, in which case he wouldn't have died from the drinking, or he was brought here, already in a stupor, by his murderer."

Lupa turned from the dead man on the bed and was looking directly at me. His face broke into what was, for him, a broad smile—his mouth lifted perhaps a centimeter. "Ah, Jules," he said, "satisfactory."

This greeting totally mystified me, but I didn't have time to reflect on it since he immediately went back to the topic. "Would you like more?"

"Da. You would expect a white crust around his mouth, would you not? That is a symptom of arsenic poisoning, not alcohol."

"Pah!" Lupa exclaimed, including me in his response. "Everyone who's read 'Madame Bovary' thinks he's an expert on arsenic. It is child's play to wipe off the residue." He faced the old man. "No, Monsieur Dubniev, it is irrefutably arsenic poisoning. Come here, closer."

Dubniev approached the bedside. Lupa, rather forcefully I thought, pushed the man's face over Minsky's. "Now inhale," he said. As the inspector did so, Lupa pressed on Minsky's chest, forcing out the tidal air.

"What do you smell?" Lupa asked.

Dubniev straightened up, his face twisted in revulsion. "Garlic," he said.

Lupa's lips curled again in his peculiar smile. "Exactly, sir. Garlic."

The old man looked confused. "Is that a telling point? I'm afraid I miss its significance."

Lupa put an arm against one of the bedposts and leaned against it. "The smell of garlic is indicative of arsenic poisoning."

The inspector laughed. "It's also indicative of a taste for escargots."

"True," Lupa admitted, "and in another country at another time, the smell of garlic on a corpse's breath might mean nothing. But here in Russia, in the Fall, after three years of war," he ticked off the points with his fingers, "there is no garlic."

"How can you be . . . ?"

"I spent last night cooking in the Czar's kitchen. Believe me, sir, there is no garlic. None, not a clove. I would not have missed it."

"That doesn't prove . . ."

"Excuse me, but of course it does. If the Czar's kitchen doesn't have a spice, you may rest assured it is not available in all of Russia."

Dubniev looked down, defeated by Lupa's knowledge. "I will order the autopsy," he said, sullenly, and I sensed that my friend had made an enemy.

But he was not excessively jubilant at his victory. "It doesn't matter. Someone killed him—the autopsy will merely confirm it." He turned to me. "Jules, it's good to see you. How was the Baltic?"

The question seemed plausible only because I was used to Lupa's deductive ability, though I don't understand how he could have known I made the trip by the northern route rather than the more common one through the Mediterranean and the Black Sea, then up by train from the Crimea.

Dubniev bowed rather stiffly and asked Lupa if there was anything more to be done before he returned to his headquarters.

After a moment's hesitation, Lupa nodded. "Have some breakfast, Monsieur. It will put things in a better perspective."

I knew Lupa well enough to know that he wasn't being flip, but the response seemed to strike Dubniev badly. Without a further word, he turned and marched from the room.

"That was..." I began.

Lupa shrugged. "It's understandable. The man is completely beyond his depth. He is, in fact, near panic, and of all times, now he should be rested and well-fed. Instead, he stays up pondering, forgets to eat..." He sighed. "It's no wonder he feels threatened, but he should realize that I'm here to help him, not take his job."

"You're working here then?" I asked.

Lupa nodded. "I have only just begun." He cast a fleeting glance back at the body on the bed. "It is a bad business. But come," he said, "there's nothing more to be done in this room. How about you? Have you eaten? There's a kiosk down by..."

...his third cup of tea and the last of his sixth or seventh piroshki.

He leaned back against the wall of the train station, arms crossed in front of him, his eyes nearly closed. I was being closely scrutinized, and decided I would take the opportunity to turn the tables on my friend. Fifteen months before, when I'd first met Lupa, he had carried himself with an air of youthful enthusiasm. Now, though still a young man of perhaps twenty-seven or -eight, his experiences as an agent behind the invisible front of this terrible war had obviously aged him.

There is a gravity now recognizable in him, underscored by the physical weight he's added to his frame. His face is at once ruddier, more healthy, and wearier, more strained. The paradox lends the whole a great deal of character that was not as obvious before. He still combs his dark brown hair straight back, emphasizing the strong high forehead, the heavy brows.

"Your life has agreed with you, then," he said at last. "With Tania. And you've had a child?"

I nodded, smiling. "A girl, Michelle."

"Ah, congratulations. You're doing your own cooking?"

"It was impossible to replace Fritz," I said. "I didn't even try."

"Yes," Lupa agreed. "He is brilliant. We've stayed in touch."

"So have we."

Lupa's eyes gleamed with humor, and I suddenly realized why. Accustomed as I was to his displays of deductive virtuousity, I could think of nothing in my dress or bearing that might have given away the fact that I'd had a child and did most of my own cooking. Obviously, Fritz had filled him in on those details, and he was enjoying his charade that he had deduced them. Noting my look of understanding, Lupa nodded, his lips curling a fraction of an inch in a smile.

"It's very good to see you," he said.

I uttered some similar sentiment, but was curious about his presence in the capital. If he was investigating Minsky's murder, he might be involved with the other Palace slayings, and if that were the case, it could affect my own mission.

In answer to my questions, he was, I thought, surprisingly forthcoming. "Just so, Jules. These killings are having their effect on the Czar. Minsky's death might push him over the edge, though I pray not."

"Over the edge to what?"

He shrugged. "Abdication or a premature suit for peace."

"Do you think he might actually abdicate?"

The train's whistle blew. It would be leaving shortly for the short run into St. Petersburg. Lupa accompanied me as I walked to the platform. "He is in a precarious state. He might do anything."

"And have you made any progress?" I asked. "Does there seem to be any connection between the murders?"

"That's what I hope to find out. And you . . ." He paused, then continued in a different vein. "Well, there have been four murders now. The first, Dieter Bresloe, was the Czar's confidant and bodyguard. He was blown to pieces in his room. Next was Sergei Lubovitch, a member of the Imperial Guard and the Czar's chess partner. His throat was cut. The last before Minsky was Duke Pavlaya Beretska, Nicholas' second cousin and Lord of the Hunt. Nicholas loves to hunt."

"How was he killed?"

Lupa looked disgusted. "Another grenade, this one at the Winter Palace after he'd been to visit the royal children."

The train whistle blew again; the wheels began to turn. I stepped aboard. "So they were all close to the Czar?"

Lupa walked alongside as the train gathered speed. "That's all," he said. "It's not much."

I started to say something as the train let out another tremendous shriek. The words were lost. Lupa raised a hand in farewell. While I watched, he turned and went back into the station, head down, lost in thought.

Rasputin's flat at 20, 63-64 Gorokhavaya Street was a short walk from the train station, just opposite police headquarters. Last night, the monk had instructed me to take the back way up from the internal courtyard to his apartment, and when I got to the landing three flights up, I understood why. A line of visitors already had formed behind a velvet rope that was tied across the hallway.

A man stood at the door, controlling who went in or out. When I told him who I was, he consulted a list on which appeared to be scribbled names and appointment times, and then ushered me in and closed the door behind me.

I felt somewhat at a loss since the flat appeared to be empty. It was still long before noon, and I thought perhaps, after staying late at Vyroubova's, the starets wasn't yet awake.

Walking through the antechamber, I became aware of some presence but I can't really say how I noticed it. Did I smell something, sense movement? Was there some almost unheard sound that registered?

To my left was a large bare chamber with chairs arranged around the walls and a samovar in one corner. Religious icons were the only decoration. On my right was a dining room with a table on which sat a bowl of fresh fruit and several vases of flowers. The furniture was of that same style, or lack of it, that characterized the Mauve Room and Vyroubova's house.

Now I heard a definite sound through the door beyond the dining room. Pushing it open, I realized I had intruded into Rasputin's bedroom, and I would have backed out at once had what I saw not arrested me.

Rasputin, completely naked, stood facing away from me. His back was already covered with red welts, and as I watched he continued to flog himself, slowly and regularly, with some sort of weighted leather thong.

Of course, flagellation is an important part of some religious sects, but I'd never seen it practiced before and it horrified me. Reflexively, I backed away a step, knocking into the door. At the noise, Rasputin stopped abruptly and turned to face me.

Just as he did so, however, there was another noise from still another door off his bedroom. That door opened, and a woman stepped out of what must have been a bath or dressing room. Her hair was in disarray and her skin blotched, but otherwise she was dressed like a noblewoman.

In my career I have been in many types of situations, but never before had I been in a room with a woman and a naked man. Acutely embarrassed, I made to leave, but Rasputin stopped me.

"No!" He turned to the woman. "You! My cassock, then go."

Obediently, the woman grabbed his robe and handed it to him. Then, without a word, she brushed quickly past me and was gone, closing the door behind her.

When I turned back, Rasputin had donned the cassock and was smiling at me. "Sin is the first step to holiness," he said, without a trace of apology. "To Alyosha, yes? Tea? Here or there?"

I am getting used to his staccato way of talking. I was beginning to feel the man might be mad, though subsequent events today make me hesitate to try to label him. He has some power—that is certain. I must reserve my judgment. I sense that he would be the worst possible enemy to have at court.

He didn't really seem to care about whether I wanted to go directly to the Winter Palace. He, it seemed, was going to have tea. We went together into the bare room I'd seen earlier, and he poured two cups from the samovar. He drank like a Russian peasant, through a lump of sugar held in his front teeth.

The moment of relative silence gave me time to collect my thoughts and somewhat recover my sangfroid. Though he had handled my unexpected arrival in his room with great presence of mind, I thought it would be instructive to see his reaction to other events.

"Have you heard?" I said as casually as I could between sips of tea, "Commissar Minsky is dead."

At first, he made no response to my statement. He took another sip of his tea, then looked at me as if wondering when I had arrived and what I was doing there. Gradually, those frightening eyes widened, then narrowed, and he slowly took the lump of sugar from his mouth and placed it in his saucer. "What did you say?"

"They think it was murder."

"Murder," he repeated, as though it were a word he'd never heard before. He stood up, then walked to the window and stared down into the back courtyard. "This will be hard for the little father."

"The little father?" I noticed the change in his voice pattern. He was speaking in sentences, not phrases.

"Nicholas," he said abstractedly, "the Czar."

"Forgive me," I said, "but I got the impression last night that you and Minsky were enemies of some sort. At the least, that you had grave differences."

He turned back from the window, his eyes blazing. He was clearly sensitive to even the mildest of criticism.

"Minsky was a friend to Nicholas, and the little father needs his friends." Then, as though remembering that he was out of character, he went back to his babbling. "His burden. The War. Killings. Blood everywhere. No one will survive it."

"Be that as it may, you argued."

He stood up straight, pounded on his chest with one hand. "We are Russians! We drink, we fight, then we forget. Minsky was a patriot, a true Russian. He loved the Czar!"

"But he didn't love you."

"I? Who am I? A simple peasant. I don't matter."

Oddly, I felt that he truly believed what he was saying. My feelings about the monk were shifting as quickly as his moods. One moment he appeared nearly insane, raving and making pronouncements, and the next he was in fact a simple peasant, somewhat awed by the position in which he found himself, and naturally possessive of it, but withal an honest and concerned Russian with a deep commitment to the Czar and Czarina.

It is good to remember here that love of the Czar is the definition of loyalty. Truer here and now even than it was when Louis XIV uttered his famous *"L'etat, c'est moi,"* Nicholas is the state.

While it is a fact that Russia has a legislative body, called the Duma, it is only a decade old and has no real power. By that I mean it has no power to enact legislation. In fact, all law is directly the will of the Czar. All appointments, all pardons, positions, expenditures—in short, every decision on every conceivable topic is ultimately the Czar's to make. Even if there are laws covering some situation, that law can be overridden by the simple expedient of petitioning Nicholas.

And here, I'm beginning to understand, is the root of Rasputin's power. To use Minsky's phrase, he has the ear of the Czar—or in his case, the Czarina, which may be more effective in that he is at one stroke proposer and lobbyist.

We finished our tea. Perhaps in the time we'd talked, Rasputin had seen something in me that he finally decided he trusted. Though I questioned him rather closely about Minsky, I accepted most of his explanations. Perhaps he came to see that I was not a critic, merely a questioner. In any event, when we had put down our cups, he came and stood in front of me, taking my arms in his incredibly strong hands, and stared into my eyes as he had last night.

I didn't look away, but neither did I feel the almost hypnotic power in his gaze. As a matter of fact, after a moment I smiled at him, rather as man to man, as if to say "Enough of this nonsense. Let us do our work."

And he in turn smiled at this understanding, clapped me on the shoulder, and said, "Your heart is in the right place. Come, we'll meet the prince."

He disappeared into his room for another moment, and reappeared wearing heavy boots and black pants under his cassock. Another royal blue shirt peeked from under the black religious robe. If there was a contradiction there, he seemed as oblivious to it as to the rest of his actions.

Interestingly, from this time on he spoke to me normally. I think the two-word phrases and staccato delivery either must be nervousness or an act he delivers for the benefit of those who might be moved by it. When he saw it had no effect on me—it certainly did not make me feel that he was any more holy or inspired—he dropped the pretense entirely. At least that made for easier communication.

We ducked out of his apartment via the back stairway. The people waiting on the landing behind the rope pressed forward, but Rasputin merely blessed them and led me quickly away.

"They are sheep," he said. "They all want something. They will wait until I return."

A light, wet snow had begun to fall. We walked out through the courtyard, past a group of lounging men in greatcoats, who bestirred themselves as we came abreast of them and fell in behind us.

"Who are they?" I asked.

The starets didn't even turn to look. "Detectives," he said. "Beletsky, one of our ministers, thinks I ought to be protected. I humor them."

"Protected from what?"

We had come to the Neva, the shortest and coldest of rivers, and turned up toward the Winter Palace.

"Assassination." He waved his hands as though pushing away the idea. "It is a conceit. I am being watched, spied upon. It is ludicrous."

"Why do they do that?"

He was setting a pace I found difficult to match. The snow was beginning to fall heavily now and we were quickly outdistancing many of the detectives.

"They want to discredit me with Alexandra. But the Czar already knows I am a sinner. And I keep their son alive."

I glanced sideways at him to see if there was any trace of irony or humor in that statement, but I could see he meant it literally.

I wanted to question him further on that but the foot traffic in the street had become heavier as we came nearer the Palace, and people had begun recognizing him. The first was a boy, no more than twelve, who ran up next to us, imploring "Father Gregory" to give him some food. Without breaking stride, Rasputin produced a small loaf of bread and an apple from his cassock.

In a city with a starving populace, such largess doesn't go unnoticed, and before long a small crowd of children had attached themselves to us, calling out and begging almost in a chant.

Rasputin stopped at the entrance to the Winter Palace. I was ready to duck inside when I saw that he had no intention of avoiding the young mob. Instead, he turned and raised his hand in a blessing.

The children all knelt in the swirling snow and listened to Rasputin talk softly to them. As he spoke, he motioned them forward one by one and gave each a bite to eat—some fruit, bits of bread, pieces of cheese. His message was simple, delivered over and over in his staccato manner. "Russia needs your prayers. Go home. Be with your mothers. Pray for the Czar. There will be bread."

It seemed to be a different Rasputin, a glimpse of a real holy man. Through the snow I could see a few of the detectives who had stayed with us watching the scene. When the last of the children had been fed, and had gone—presumably home to their mothers to pray—Rasputin took me by the arm and we entered the Palace.

"I wonder if that will make it into their reports to the Czar," he said, and immediately my sense of his goodness was marred by doubts over whether he had somehow orchestrated a charade.

Paleologue's words came back to me with renewed force: "In St. Petersburg, nothing is what it seems."

I have already commented on the size of the Palace. As Rasputin and I walked toward the children's quarters, I realized that what I had thought was one of the largest and most complex structures I had ever been in was really only half of it. The building is actually in the shape of a huge rectangle with a courtyard within it. The long side of the structure, against the river, houses offices of people such as Sukhomlinov and quarters for visitors like myself. It also affords a view across the river to the Petropavlovskaya Krepost', the Fortress of Sc. Peter and Paul, a walled prison said to be so impregnable that even the bones of those who die there never get out.

The street side of the Palace is the more heavily guarded. It is the city residence of the Czar's family and, as such, like Tsarkoye Selo, it is almost a city in its own right. Under the high ceilings are myriad booths dispensing goods for the royal table (which Rasputin told me were wasted—Nicholas, Alexandra and the children all ate simply). Nevertheless, the shops seemed to be flourishing. The contrast with the poverty in the streets outside could not have been more complete. There were also stores—storerooms might be a better word—with furniture, bolts of cloth, hardware, bric-a-brac. So well-provisioned did they appear to be on this side of the Palace that I briefly entertained the amusing thought that they could mount a seige on St. Petersburg from within.

Of course, we had no trouble entering this enclave. Rasputin and I were admitted without a show of identification. Presumably anyone in the company of the starets was considered safe, a notion I find potentially quite dangerous.

When we had gone through the public area, we came to another checkpoint, and here again we entered unmolested. I asked Rasputin if he had really predicted my arrival.

He stopped and looked at me as though surprised at the question. "The matushka was distraught. I told her that her son would soon have his French tutor."

"And she took that to mean me?"

The lids came down, half covering his eyes. "Did you not?" he asked. It was the same tone he had used when he told me that he kept the Czar's son alive, and I haven't yet decided if he is merely a brilliant opportunist, claiming successes for coincidences, or whether he really does have some powers of healing or foresight that he may not fully understand and yet fully believes in. Certainly what happened next speaks well for the latter.

We had just come into a rotunda off which led several hallways when we heard a regular, drumlike tattoo followed immediately by the sustained screams of young girls. Wasting not a second, Rasputin ran for the sound, his cassock flowing. I was only a step behind him.

At the end of the hallway, we stopped at the entrance to what might have been designed as a grand ballroom. Now, the marble floors of the huge chamber were covered end to end with straw, and over the straw was galloping an enormous Arabian stallion, nostrils flared and panicked, squealing like a pig.

On the magnificent animal's back clung a small boy in a soldier's uniform. Across the room, four girls in white dresses huddled together around another figure. As the horse came upon them, it rose up on its hind legs, turning from the wall, and the girls screamed, panicking the animal even more.

Without any hesitation, Rasputin ran to the middle of the room and began whistling, yelling, jumping up and down, anything to get the horse's attention.

As the stallion turned from another headlong rush at the distant wall, the boy added to the cacophony with a scream of his own. He was holding to the pommel with both hands, his feet miraculously still in the stirrups. The reins dragged between the horse's flying hooves, and foam flecked its distended mouth.

"Griskha!" the boy yelled. "Grishka!"

Grishka is the diminutive of Gregory, and I realized the boy had seen Rasputin and was yelling for help.

The horse put its head down now and charged at the monk. But as soon as he knew that the stallion had seen him, Rasputin stopped his wild gesticulating. Instead, he stood stock still with outspread arms, and began a kind of singing in a deep voice that echoed from the gilded walls. The words were pure gibberish, or perhaps some peasant dialect that I didn't know. Maybe, in fact (when I reflect on it now), he was speaking in tongues. In any event, it seemed that it would be his last action, since the charge showed no sign of slowing. We all watched horrified as the animal bore down upon the holy man. Surely he would be trampled to death!

Rasputin stood his ground. The horse galloped down the length of the room. Then, suddenly, when no more than ten meters separated them, the stallion visibly slowed. It was too close to stop, but the animal passed by Rasputin, who turned as if he were a matador executing a madrilena, without a cape.

Following his lead, the horse seemed to be struggling to come to a full stop and get back to the starets. It finally did so, then turned around, dropping its proud head, and shuffled almost lazily, snorting, until it came and nuzzled its nose into Rasputin's bosom.

Immediately, a rough-looking man with a huge mustache, dressed in a sailor's uniform, ran up and took the shaken Heir Apparent from the saddle. Rasputin continued to stroke the stallion's face, speaking quietly to it. He took yet another apple from the bountiful cassock and fed it to the beast. The girls rushed up to surround him as I approached from the other side. But no one said a word. No one dared interrupt.

Only when satisfied that the horse was calmed did Rasputin look up. He seemed genuinely surprised by the crowd surrounding him. The sailor, who on closer inspection looked even more like a thug, handed Alexis to Rasputin, who chucked him gently on the chin and smiled.

"You did well not to fall," he said.

The boy, a well-formed, even handsome twelve year old, beamed. "How did you stop it?"

With no hesitation, as though he believed it to be the truth, Rasputin answered. "God wanted it to stop. He wanted no harm to come to you."

The sailor spoke up. "It is too late for that. He'll be bruised."

Rasputin put the boy down and glared at the man. "The bruises will not be serious."

"They don't have to be! You don't know the..."

"Enough!" It was a woman's voice. The horse blocked my vision of who had spoken. "Derevenko, it might be better if you took his Highness to be examined."

Rasputin bowed meekly to the command, though I thought I sensed irony even in that action. "As you wish, Elena. It couldn't hurt." He looked at me. "As it turns out, the tutoring will have to wait."

"Oh, is the new tutor...?"

From behind the stallion stepped the graceful figure of the woman I had seen last night at Vyroubova's. When she saw me, she smiled as if secretly pleased at something, then extended her hand with a natural self-possession I couldn't help but admire.

"Hello," she said, with a flawless British accent, "I'm Elena Ripley."

If she had been an enigmatic and distantly lovely vision last night—a precious and untouchable cameo—today she radiated a wholesome freshness that was nevertheless somehow consistent with the earlier image. Her beauty was so transcendent it makes style seem wholly irrelevant.

And yet she wasn't intimidating. Rather, without being in the least forward, she projected warmth, invited friendship. She must have been aware of the potential power of her beauty—her imperious tone to Derevenko and Rasputin was evidence of that—but I could see it was not her way to wield it.

Elena, drama tutor to the Grand Duchesses and governess to Tatiana, introduced me to the four of them—Olga, Tatiana, Marie, and Anastasia. Finally I met Alexis, who, now that the immediate danger had passed, seemed high-spirited and intelligent.

As soon as the introductions began, Rasputin took the horse by the bridle and walked away with it. Elena was apologetic that my tutoring of Alexis would have to wait, but she demanded that Derevenko take the boy to his doctors to be checked. Evidently, internal bruises are as serious as cuts for him—and this morning's ride would have bruised nearly anyone.

As soon as Alyosha and Derevenko had gone, all four of the Grand Duchesses began coaxing Rasputin to rejoin them. They seemed genuinely fond of him, asking him to tell them what must have been a familiar story of Russian peasant life. When he came back over to us, leaving the horse with a servant, Elena separated herself from the group. Her distaste for the monk was obvious, but she was too well-bred to show it overtly.

I listened to the first few words of Rasputin's story, but I really had no interest in it, and if I wasn't going to be instructing Alexis today, I had other appointments to keep. Waiting for a natural break in the tale, I bowed and bid them all adieu.

4

Last night's dinner must, indeed, have been a special occasion. Supplies here in the city are so low that Paleologue and his staff share their meals and their servants with the English embassy!

I have nothing against the British. They are brave fighters and loyal allies. What they lack in élan and panache is more than compensated for in their contributions to, among other things, world literature, for example.

But their food! Ugh!

It must be one of Paleologue's greatest hardships to bear with this arrangement in the name of international cooperation. I was invited to lunch, but upon seeing the greasy sausages, cold toast, radish or beet sandwiches, tea with milk poured into it, not a green vegetable in sight, I said that I had just come from a huge breakfast and couldn't eat a thing.

When we left the dining room, Maurice told me that the kitchen prepares English food one day, French the next, and that I had arrived on the wrong day. Not, he added, that the French food was that much better.

"Surely there must be a huge difference," I remonstrated. We were in his office having cigars. Fortunately, he had somehow contrived to have his samovar play a part in creating a passable blend of coffee. After merely viewing the British clotted cream, I was happy to drink something strong and black.

Paleologue stroked his pointed chin. "No, Giraud, there is not much difference. We don't have supplies, you see."

"But surely last night..."

"Last night was a state dinner for the Czar."

"But the food was excellent."

"Sublime," he agreed. "But come here. Look."

I stood and walked over to his desk. With a key, he opened a cabinet that had been built into it. Within was a platter laden with many of last night's staples—a bowl of sugar lumps, another of butter, three loaves of bread, several apples and pears, a brick of cheese. At my questioning look, the ambassador smiled. "Our greatcoats are good for more than fighting the cold."

I was shocked to see the official representative of my country stooping to such levels, and probably did not hide my feelings adequately. But Paleologue was immune to my scruples. He closed and locked the cabinet, motioned for me to sit again, and gave me a little speech.

"Don't make the mistake which is ruining this country, Giraud. Don't let yourself be cut off from reality. The palace is an unreal world where nothing is wrong, there is plenty of food, the Czar makes no mistakes, and the people are all happy and simple peasants.

"There is no way that I can overemphasize the seriousness of the situation here. There is very little food. The people are quite close to revolt. Mismanagement, incompetence, plain stupidity are rampant here, as are greed, fear and panic. What you see at Tsarkoye Selo and here at the Winter Palace is the last flicker of the Nineteenth Century, of the world you and I grew up in.

"Now it is not merely a new century, it is a different world, and there is no place in it anymore for the finer sensibilities—gentility, honor, charm. It pains me to say it, but what we are doing, especially here in St. Petersburg, is slogging through, trying our best to survive, and survive alone."

"But surely," I said, alarmed at his pessimism, "survival alone is no goal. Without what you're calling the finer sensibilities, what is the point to living?"

"Ask that question and you won't live to enjoy the answer," he said. Then, realizing his harshness, he continued. "Giraud, I don't mean to attack you. Maybe I've been here too long. I forget that there is another world—a Paris, for example, even a..." But, choked with emotion, he couldn't finish.

"I'm sorry," I said.

He waved it off, puffing at his cigar. "And now to business. The offer?"

"First there is something else that might bear upon it. Have you heard about Minsky?"

He thought a moment. "I don't believe I know a Minsky."

"He is a Commissar, one of the Czar's equestrian guard. I met him last night. In his own words, he is the last personal friend of Nicholas at court—all the rest defer to Rasputin."

"Well, what of him?"

When I told Maurice of the murder, he first had no response other than to close his eyes and draw reflectively on his cigar. He remained in that attitude so long that I wondered if he had perhaps forgotten my presence.

"Sir?" I asked.

Slowly, it seemed unwillingly, he pulled himself up and out of his reverie. With a deep sigh, he forced himself to speak.

"You are correct, Giraud. This will bear upon your mission."

"What do you think I ought to do?"

He stood and began pacing back and forth from the bookcase to the fireplace. "It is hard to say. Initially, I was going to tell you to get to Nicholas and force a commitment as soon as possible. He is newly back from Spala, and in the past it has been after those tours as Commander-in-Chief that he has been most enthusiastic for the War. Now, though... now I am not sure."

"You think it might be wiser to wait?"

"Not exactly. I think he simply may not be prepared to make decisions. And there's no point in showing our hand until we can bet it."

"But now would seem ideal to me. If we present a strong argument, in his preoccupied state he might commit before realizing all the implications."

Paleologue sat on the edge of his desk. "No, no. You don't know Nicholas. He doesn't act that way. These murders— there have been three before this, you know—have worked on his will. Of all rulers, he is the least aware of the position he is in. His immediate family is his life. In mentality, he is extremely petit bourgeois. Have you seen his apartments? The furnishings?"

He stopped, checking himself. "Well, that is irrelevant. But he rules Russia as though he were running a small business. This is not to say he is a bad man. To the contrary, he is simple goodness personified."

"But they call him 'Bloody Nicholas.'"

"He has had bad luck." Perhaps realizing how apologetic that sounded, the diplomat covered himself. "Not that he hasn't made mistakes, Giraud. He has. But they almost always have been out of naiveté, out of wanting to do the right thing and simply lacking the sensitivity to see what it is.

"It began," he continued, "on the day of his coronation. The peasants showed up in such numbers for the celebration that they couldn't fit into the area arranged for them. Then the word went out that they were running out of beer. You know how that is. Well, hundreds of people were killed in the ensuing crush."

I started to interrupt, but he stopped me. "No, that wasn't all. What made our Czar 'Bloody Nicholas' is that he was advised to attend the Coronation Ball that night. The smart move, of course, would have been to have canceled it in sympathy for the dead, but Nicholas' uncles persuaded him that it was essential that he not disappoint the visiting foreign guests who were looking forward to the ball. Needless to say, the peasantry took his attendance there as the utmost callousness on his part. Hence, Bloody Nick."

"And that, I take it, isn't an isolated case."

"Not at all. The man just moves along from crisis to crisis, always seeking to do what is right. But the nature of government is that it needs a guiding policy, and he has none, other than belief in the autocratic principle that he can do no wrong and, astoundingly, that he doesn't want his wife mad at him."

"You must be exaggerating."

"How else do you explain Rasputin?"

I thought about it and conceded that he might have a point. "But where does that leave me and my offer?"

Maurice went back around his desk and sat down. "I think it makes us very vulnerable. He might very well refuse."

"But why?"

"Because, Giraud, he is sick of this war. He is losing in the North and he knows it. And now his friends are being killed. Remember what I just told you—his family life, his intimate circle, is his reality. And now the War is encroaching on that.

"This latest murder—though any of the previous ones might as well have done it—might be the nudge he needs to sue for a separate peace. Once that is concluded, then at least he could concentrate on his family again and, to a lesser extent, on the reforms this country needs so badly. It is ticklish. I'm not sure he'll react that way, but I think it's possible that if we urge him too strongly in the one direction, he'll feel like he's being manipulated and go the other way out of contrariness, or, as he'd put it, out of exercise of the Royal Will. But I'd bet my last franc that pro-German forces are behind these killings." He paused. "And it seems to me they know their man."

I considered mentioning Lupa's presence to Maurice, but decided to hold my tongue. My knowledge of the moods and intrigues of the court is still extremely limited. Even Paleologue, in spite of his official position, is untested. He might have known the Czar's chess partner or hunted with the Lord of the Hunt. No, until I had a little more background, I would keep Lupa to myself.

Suddenly Maurice swore violently and pounded his small pudgy fist on his desk. "Damn Sukhomlinov and his meddling! If you'd presented our case to Nicholas only yesterday you might be on your way home today."

"And now?"

"Now it seems we're forced to take his advice and wait. We can't push Nicholas. Maybe in a week or so he'll be receptive again, but now I can't permit it."

It may have been good policy, but hearing his decision, I was struck with a disturbing sense of déjà vu. "Excuse me, Maurice," I said, "but that, nearly word for word, was exactly what Sukhomlinov recommended. And last night you violently opposed it."

Paleologue chewed thoughtfully on his cigar. Finally an ironic glint appeared in his eye. "It's galling, I admit. My only defense is that since last night we've had another murder. It's changed things, at least for the short term. We'd be foolish to deny it, and doubly foolish to push Nicholas just at this time." He looked at me across his desk. "We can only hope to get some hiatus between now and the next disaster."

"Or that the murderer is found."

"Yes," he said, "or that."

Outside, the gray sky matched my spirits. Flakes of snow had begun to fall and the heavy clouds portended a major storm. I found myself wishing Lupa had accompanied me into the city. The more I was learning about Nicholas, the more these murders loomed as the major stumbling block to my mission, and no one was better equipped to get to the bottom of them than my friend, Auguste Lupa.

My thoughts turned back to our earlier adventure together in Valence. When that had begun, I hadn't known the man at all, other than by reputation. But that reputation was impressive. Though working as a chef and not yet 25 years old, Lupa had already established himself as the best espionage

agent in Europe. When my friend and fellow agent Marcel
Routier had been killed, Lupa and I were forced to work
together, to confide in and trust one another, and out of that
experience was forged a mutual respect and—perhaps unlikely, but true—a friendship.

Now, in this foreign setting, I felt that Lupa had been on
the verge of confiding in me again while we talked at the
train station, but that for some reason he had held back. That
was cautious and reasonable, but given the importance of my
role here, and the necessity to understand the Czar and his
court, it is also frustrating.

He must have his reasons. And, as everyone seems to
agree, I must be patient.

But walking back to the train in the swirling snow, thinking of the shopkeeper mentality of the ruler of one sixth of
the earth, I once again encountered a crowd in the street.
Everyone was rapt with attention, though unnaturally quiet.

"What is happening?" I asked a woman who craned her
neck to see over the heads in front of her. I could make out a
phalanx of Cossacks on horseback but beyond that, nothing.

"They've arrested four men for stealing."

She climbed to the parapet of a lamppost. Over the bitter
wind, I heard a hoarse voice giving what sounded like military orders.

"Who are they?" I asked.

"Peasants," she answered, then added with heavy sarcasm.
"The Czar loves his peasants."

The voice of the commanding officer carried over the
crowd, informing the people that theft in wartime is treason.

"What did they steal?" I asked the woman.

Then came the terrifying word. "Prigotov'tes'. Gotovy?
Ready, aim . . ."

"Bread!" the woman shouted down at me. "They stole
bread."

"Ogan! Fire!"

The volley shattered the afternoon's peace.

A moment of utter stillness was broken by the woman

above me. From her perch above the street, she raised an arm into the air and let forth a call, thick with rage, that was taken up by the mob. As I backed away, the smell of gunpowder stinging my nose, my ears rang with the cries. "Long live the revolution! Down with the Czar! Down with Bloody Nicholas!"

5

(OCTOBER 15, 1916.)

The storm let up last night. I sat it out here at my little window desk in Tsarkoye Selo, trying with little success to fathom the first hectic events of my stay here. Communication with the outside world has been impossible, though I do have a telephone that connects me with the immediate community.

I haven't had to return to St. Petersburg. Rasputin was right about Alyosha's bruises—they simply never developed, although Czarina Alexandra called me twice to tell me that the boy would not be able to take his lessons until it was determined there was no bleeding. Evidently the doctors are now satisfied, and I am scheduled to go in tomorrow. Rasputin's reasoning—how he could have known that Alexis would not bleed internally—still eludes me.

Tonight I am to see Lupa again. It is not a moment too soon. I have grown extremely restless in these two days of storm-enforced confinement. Even if it is too early to present my case to the Czar, I would like to be involved in something interesting and Lupa will likely provide that opportunity.

This morning I received an invitation from a woman named Anastasia, the wife of Grand Duke Nicholas, to come to dinner. I have no idea why she would ask for me, but one glance at the guest list, which was enclosed with the invitation, was enough for me to decide to attend. Lupa was on it.

But aside from the opportunity to see Lupa and my restlessness at being shut up alone in my quarters, there was another reason to attend the dinner. The governess Elena Ripley was also to be there. Irrationally, my heart beat faster at the prospect of seeing her again.

This shamed me enough to spend the better part of the afternoon writing a letter to my wife, Tania. It is hard being apart from her for this long, knowing that a continent at war separates us, and that we may never hold each other again.

Paleologue's comments about the modern world have been haunting me, locked up as I have been without distractions. Certainly I am no longer the same bon vivant who dallied in espionage a mere two years ago. Before hostilities began, it was all a game, albeit a serious one. Or, more precisely, one we all took seriously. But there still was a feeling that there was a "gentleman" class that took care of events and kept them in some kind of balance. In that club, it was bad form to cheat or lie. The prevailing belief was that war was a naturally occurring phenomenon whose primary function was to rearrange borders and provide a surcease from the monotonous tedium of domestic life.

Every generation should have a war! Build the character of the young! Splendid idea!

But now the rot of this War has spread to every part of society and, worse, has entered the most secret places of men's hearts. Gentility is not worth the trouble. Commitment is a practical joke urged upon fools by charlatans. There is a new word for scoundrel—it is "realist."

I am not immune to it myself. I have been dreaming not of my loyal and lovely Tania, but of a governess whom I don't even know.

The excuses come readily to hand. Tania is far away and need never know. I am lonely. Life is too short and too hard, and what harm is there is a little comfort?

And of course all this is ridiculous. I've spoken no more than a hundred words to the woman, and what would a young and vibrant beauty like Elena Ripley see in a middle-aged courtier like myself?

I write it down to note its absurdity. Now I must dress for dinner.

I had to laugh upon being admitted to Anastasia's house, which is less than a hundred meters from my own in Tsarkoye Selo. In neat Cyrillic script over the door to the cloakroom is crocheted the legend: "Rasputin not spoken here!"

The woman herself was formidable. Handsome, dark and buxom, she greeted me with a gaiety and force I hadn't encountered since leaving France.

"Jules! I must call you Jules. How good of you to come. Your friend Auguste has done nothing but sing your praises. Oh, I'm so looking forward to this evening! Can I have someone get you a drink? Here, let me help you with your coat."

Somehow getting a word in, I pointed at the embroidered sampler. "Is that enforced?"

She smiled. "It is more a joke now, but when I had it done, I was quite serious. We introduced him to court, you know."

"We?"

"My sister Militsa and I. Surely you've heard of us, the Montenegrin nightingales?"

"Of course," I lied, "and I'm delighted to finally meet you."

Knowing that Lupa had been raised in Montenegro, the connection that had led to my invitation here was becoming more obvious. She gushed on. "We were totally taken in. But then, one makes mistakes, *n'est-ce pas?* Ah well, it can't be helped. There are bounders everywhere, I suppose. It can't be helped. Do you like whisky?"

She put a crystal glass in my hand and pushed me into the house proper as someone else knocked at the front door.

Though not large, the drawing room was sumptuously appointed. Two chandeliers glowed brightly overhead, a string quartet was playing a selection from Prokoviev. Armchairs and settees in royal blue and red, not mauve, velvet were tastefully arranged over a turquoise Oriental rug. Fine art adorned the walls—not an icon was in sight. The effect, if slightly overdone, was nevertheless pleasing.

But again, the focus of my attention became the woman who sat demurely, a wine glass in hand, listening to the music with a faraway smile playing at the corners of her mouth. I had arrived early, and we two were thus far the only guests.

I crossed the room and lowered myself onto the far end of the couch on which she sat. Sipping my whisky, I tried to concentrate on the music, but my mind was elsewhere. Elena had her hair down, chestnut tresses falling below her shoulders. Her dress was the light yellow-orange of high clouds in a dawn sky. Eyes closed, rocking her head slightly back and forth in time to the music, she did not become aware of my presence until it ended.

"Oh," she said, charmingly flustered. "I'm sorry. I didn't hear... I wasn't aware..."

I smiled. "You like Prokoviev?"

"I adore him. It is so romantic. It takes me..." She paused, seeking the right word, "...it takes me home."

Though she said it lightly, I felt the pain in the admission.

"Where is that?" I asked. "Home, I mean."

"Originally it was Maidstone, a little town in England, in Kent. Now, I don't know. I don't know if any of us will have a home again."

I moved closer to her on the couch.

"Now, now, Miss Ripley, I'm sure we will. The War can't drag on forever."

She sipped at her wine. "It seems they've been saying that forever."

I had to admit she was right, but there was no point in belaboring that unhappy topic. "What brought you here in the first place?" I asked. "Kent is a long way from St. Petersburg."

She smiled. "I am, or rather I was, an actress, Monsieur Giraud..."

"Jules, please."

"Thank you. Jules, then. And I am Elena."

"And you are an actress?"

A wistful look. "Was, I'm afraid. I haven't been on the boards in nearly three years."

"When you came here?"

"Yes. I was in a command performance for King George, and he commissioned the company to come here and perform for his cousin, the Czar. Do you know how alike he and King George look? It is truly startling."

"I had no idea."

"Well," she sighed, remembering, "it was all very grand and exciting, coming to Russia to perform for the court. But then the War began. A few of the company decided to get out right away, but back then the general feeling was that the whole thing wouldn't last so long."

"I remember it well. In France we thought it would be over by Christmas."

"Then you know. Anyway, I was young, ambitious, perhaps foolish...I didn't know when I would see Russia again, and I didn't want to leave before I'd experienced it. Do you know what I'm saying?"

The questioning glance, the need for approval for her actions, was touching. "Of course," I said. "It would only be natural."

She rewarded me with another smile. "But then, of course, it was too late. There was no getting out. When the Czarina heard that I was left behind, she graciously asked me to tutor the girls—excuse me, the Grand Duchesses—in drama and to be a sort of governess. It has been," again that fetching pause, "rewarding."

"But not acting."

There was real gratitude in her eyes, as though she had finally met someone who could understand. "No," she said, "it's not acting."

The band started another song and a young man in uniform came into the room. I heard the booming voice of Sukhomlinov out in the entranceway and realized that my private talk with Elena was at an end. Just before we stood, she touched my hand and nodded shyly.

"It's really not so bad," she said. "Thank you for listening to my silliness."

"Now you are being silly," I said, "it was my pleasure."

We stood to greet the young man, Ivan Kapov, as Anastasia bubbled into the room behind Sukhomlinov and Katrina, his wife. Though Lupa hadn't yet arrived, she directed us into the dining room where an array of hors d'oeuvres had been laid out—caviar, smoked salmon, patés of every description, iced vodka, whisky, and champagne. Though I don't normally like to mix grape and grain, I switched to the Moët.

As I took a slice of toast covered with the luminous grey pearls of Beluga, I felt a momentary pang of guilt over the fate that had put me in this room rather than on the streets of St. Petersburg, where even our ambassador was reduced to hoarding. The memory of the executions the other day over a few loaves of coarse peasant bread rendered the first tastes of the rich fare flat and tasteless.

But with Anastasia in a room, there could be no sustained introspection. She flitted from topic to topic, from Court scandal to War news, with the unflagging enthusiasm of a schoolgirl. I learned that her husband, Grand Duke Nicholas (not to be confused with the Emperor), had been the Commander-in-Chief of the Russian army before the Czar had taken over only six months ago. I had of course known of the Duke—he was a personal friend of Freddy Foch. Almost a giant and dashingly handsome, he is revered still by the army, and is presently commanding the modestly successful campaign in Galacia.

Anastasia was recounting her husband's latest exploits

when Sukhomlinov interrupted crudely: "When will he be coming back to the capital to claim the throne, dear?"

"Lashka, don't talk nonsense." Katrina, his wife, did not want to discuss the subject. Looking at her face, which had been so pretty three nights before, I was struck by how wretched she looked, as though she'd been crying continually for hours.

"That's not nonsense, it's treason," Anastasia said. "No one is more loyal to Nicky than my husband. You know that, Vladimir."

Ivan Kapov, who'd been conspicuous by his silence until then, spoke up. "It's not really a question of loyalty. The Czar has lost the confidence of the people, and . . ."

"That's not true!"

Kapov took Anastasia's hand. "My dear Annushka, of course it's true."

He was a young man, not yet thirty, with long blond lashes over blue-green eyes. His ruddy, clean-shaven face glowed with health and good humor. The blue-sashed uniform bulged impressively over his chest, and tapered to a waist that many women might envy. He seemed to have the ability to quiet Anastasia by looking into her eyes. Now, kissing her hand almost intimately, he said quietly. "Admitting the truth isn't treason. Neither is criticism."

Sukhomlinov laughed loudly. "She's in a difficult position, Ivan. Of course she wants her husband to return and take the throne, so she has to protest."

"Too much, methinks," Kapov said in English, darting a glance at Elena.

If she noted the allusion, she kept it to herself. Her loyalty was to Anastasia. "All the same, we really should watch what we say in front of the servants."

It was a remark so typically British, so understatedly humorous and yet so apropos, that we all found ourselves laughing. Watching Elena as she too joined in, I was sure she saw both the irony and the pith of the statement.

However, Anastasia was not one to let any sort of silence

develop in the midst of a party. "Well, then, Elena, whatever shall we talk about?"

Elena deftly included me into the conversation. "Perhaps M. Giraud can tell us about the Friend's latest miracle?" There was a bite to her voice in the reference to Rasputin.

"Are we allowed to discuss him here?"

"With suitable disclaimers," Elena said lightly.

As simply as possible, I recounted the story of the monk and the runaway stallion, ending by saying that strange though the actual taming had been, more inexplicable to me was Rasputin's conviction, proven true, that Alexis would suffer no bleeding.

"But Jules, surely the explanation is simplicity itself."

I whirled around at the familiar voice. Auguste Lupa stood framed in the doorway holding a tray on which was arranged an impressive display of canapés and other finger foods.

"Ah," he said, looking over the hors d'oeuvres table, "I see the first courses are appreciated. But then how can one fail with simple and unadorned natural ingredients?" He put his tray on the table and motioned everyone forward to it. "But these!" he said, nodding at the platter, "these creations are a better test of a chef's mettle. Come, come, while they are hot."

Anastasia broke in to introduce Lupa to the rest of the guests as we gathered around to sample the fruits of his labor. In the months since I'd worked with him, his deductive abilities had overshadowed the brilliance of his cuisine in my memory. But that wasn't just. The man was possibly a better cook than he was a spy, and he was the best spy in Europe.

The array was spectacular in range as well as in depth. Crayfish restuffed into their shells with a dill mayonnaise, escargots en brioche (if pastry of such airy texture and flavor could be called brioche) with Pernod and, I noticed, no garlic, julienne breast of squab wrapped in pancetta, cod cakes with a marron onion dressing, a spicy Periwinkle and black pepper bisque served in vodka shot glasses, tiny sausages of such subtle complexity that they defy description...

The champagne flowed like water. Lupa was truly in his element as the plaudits for each new taste exceeded the last. Only Katrina Sukhomlinov seemed immune to our high spirits. She held her glass of champagne stiffly in front of her, her face a mask. She looked almost ill, and I wondered fleetingly why she had come to the dinner if she wasn't up to it.

When we had disposed of the hors d'oeuvres, we sat down to dinner. Lupa, it seems, had prepared his Plateau Royale as a sort of tour de force. He was not Anastasia's chef, so he sat down to dine with the rest of us.

After we'd been served our first course, sturgeon in aspic, I brought the conversation back to Lupa's solution to how Rasputin could have known Alyosha's bruises weren't serious.

"But Jules, there is only one possible explanation."

I glanced at Elena, saying that I didn't see it.

"Nor do I," she agreed.

"That is, of course, true. Both of you looked at something without seeing it."

I smiled. "What should we have seen?"

"First let's establish what you looked at. There was a horse running wild with Alexis in the saddle, as you put it 'holding on for dear life.' When he saw Rasputin, he called out to him. Is that all?"

Both Elena and I said yes.

"So your assumption was that Alexis, because he was screaming in panic, was somehow as out of control as the animal."

"But he was," Elena averred.

"No, madam, he could not have been. Unless he were perfectly in control, he would have been thrown to the floor. He might have been scared, but he was riding correctly— holding on with his hands, riding with his haunches flexed and off the saddle. It's the only way he could have stayed on the horse. Where you, Jules, and you, Miss Ripley, saw the panic and madness of the beast, it seems that Rasputin saw the control of the rider. He also saw the fear, but fear doesn't cause bruises."

Anastasia said, "So there was nothing miraculous about his prediction. Another fraud!"

Sukhomlinov answered. "Not at all. He never claimed a miracle."

"But neither did he deny it," Elena said hesitantly.

The general chuckled. "Who can blame a man for taking advantage of other people's false perceptions?"

"It's not particularly honorable," I said.

He shrugged as though that concept had no meaning for him. "But he did, after all, calm the animal in the first place, didn't he?"

"For that," Lupa said, "I have no explanation."

"And with that," Anastasia said, "let's drop this topic. Surely there must be better things to discuss than Rasputin."

Elena took the cue. "Jules, can you tell us what brings you to St. Petersburg?"

Possibly I'd had too much champagne. At any rate, I was entirely forthright in my response.

"Oh dear," Anastasia said when I'd finished, "first religion and now politics. How can we enjoy our dinner?"

"Rasputin is hardly 'religion,'" Katrina said. They were her first words since she had chided her husband.

"I really am going to forbid his name being mentioned if this continues." Anastasia's party was turning all too serious. "Ivan, surely there are other things to discuss."

But she had appealed to the wrong man. Kapov smiled thinly, and addressed himself to me. "You realize, Giraud, that if we keep fighting, as you propose, then we are doomed. But of course," he added sarcastically, "that doesn't matter if France can survive."

"Oh, dear," Anastasia said again.

Lupa interjected. "And if you stop fighting you will get a peace from Germany that will make what it did to France in '70 seem mild."

"And that was rape," I added hotly. Both Elena and Anastasia were shocked at the word, but it was appropriate for the reparations Germany had forced on us, for annexing Alsace-Lorraine, for marching its army through l'Arc de Triomphe.

"Nonsense," Sukhomlinov retorted. "You have no appreciation of the ties that bind the Kaiser and the Czar. They were allies against Japan, you remember, less than a decade ago." He stabbed some food on his plate, but continued speaking. "You republicans forget the value of blood . . ."

"What an unfortunate turn of phrase," I said.

Kapov joined in again. "The General means blood relationships. Nicholas and Wilhelm are cousins, after all."

"And ten million people have died," Lupa said blandly. "Just imagine if they didn't like each other."

"Events took over," Sukhomlinov said.

"So it would seem," I responded. "And now what we're trying to do is help Russia until we can fortify the Western Front. America will be joining the War in the Spring."

"Wilson will never join a war," Kapov said.

"And even if America does," the General said, "what will it matter? They've never fought in Europe. Untested armies don't win battles."

"Neither, it would seem, do unarmed ones," Lupa said. It was a direct blow to Sukhomlinov, who had failed so miserably while he had been Minister of War to put Russian factories to work making munitions, with the result that brave Russian troops often went to battle without weapons, with instructions to loot the battlefield for arms as they came upon them.

The General flushed deeply as Kapov started to say something in his defense. But evidently Anastasia had had enough. She rose from her chair and fairly shouted "Gentlemen, please!"

Kapov, who had risen halfway out of his chair, bowed in deference to her wishes and offered a tight-lipped apology. The Grand Duchess nodded her acceptance, smiled formally at each of us, and sat down. "Now," she said, striving against the current for the earlier light tone, "I think we'd all be happier discussing something else. Auguste, won't you entertain us with one of your little conclusions?"

I was proud of Lupa. Two years before, I doubt if he would have responded so gallantly to a request to treat his tremendous ability as a parlor game. After all, the question was comparable to asking a trained assassin to demonstrate his garroting technique over dinner. For surely Lupa's deductive ability was as deadly a weapon as any bullet, wire or blade.

But he nodded graciously, even going so far as to apologize again to Sukhomlinov and Kapov for upsetting them. He then turned to our hostess. "What should be my subject, madam?"

At that moment one of the servant's entered with a fresh bottle of wine. I was closest to him and he poured a sip for me to taste. At my approval, he began filling glasses. As he reached Lupa's end of the table, Anastasia whispered "Leo," indicating that he would be Lupa's subject. When he reached the Grand Duchess, she touched his arm and addressed him. "Stand up straight and let M. Lupa look at you." The man was identical in dress and manner to every servant we had seen that night.

"That isn't necessary," Lupa said. "I've seen the man."

"And?" Anastasia said, dismissing Leo to the kitchen.

"Beyond the obvious facts that he is newly married, deaf in his left ear, scrupulously honest, and plays the balalaika, I see nothing very distinctive about the man."

There was a general murmur around the table. Elena was the first to speak up. "But how?"

I said, "I think I understand newly married. The ring?"

Lupa nodded. "Of course. Still shining, completely unscratched. He cannot have worn it over a month."

"Leo was married three weeks ago," Anastasia confirmed.

"But the rest?" Elena asked. "How could you see all that?"

"When Anastasia said the man's name while he was pouring my wine, he didn't respond in any way. Surely he didn't hear her. His left ear was facing her. Therefore, I presumed he'd lost the hearing in it."

"And the honesty?" In spite of himself, Kapov was intrigued.

"He offered M. Giraud the first sip of wine from a full bottle. Many a servant will take the first nip, thinking it would never be noticed."

"It's true," Anastasia said. "I've heard the other servants tease Leo for his honesty. When he finds coins that have fallen between the cushions in the furniture, he always returns them to me."

"And the last, the balalaika?" Kapov said.

"Callouses on the tips of his right-hand fingers." Lupa, slightly embarrassed by this public display, tried to make light of it. "Really nothing very complicated, you see?"

But Elena was impressed. "Do you see that much in all of us?" she asked. "It's really rather frightening."

Throughout the display, Sukhomlinov hadn't said a word. Now he spoke up. "Yes," he said, "it is rather frightening. What does a chef do with such a skill?"

The ever-effusive Anastasia answered. "Oh, M. Lupa is not here as a chef. He is here for the murders."

"The murders?" Elena said.

"You remember," Anastasia said, "while you were in the Crimea with the girls?"

"Oh yes, for the first one anyway. I remember."

"And I'm afraid I have news on that score," Lupa intoned. "It's been determined that the total has now reached four, the latest being Commissar Minsky. He was murdered last night, here, in Tsarkoye Selo."

Kapov raised his patrician brows. "Indeed?" he said.

At the mention of the Commissar's name, Katrina Sukhomlinov, who had been so withdrawn all evening, suddenly burst into tears, covering her face with her napkin. After the first heart-rending sob, she excused herself and rushed from the room.

Her husband, struggling to retain his aplomb, rose stiffly, bowed to all of us, and followed her.

"Oh dear," Anastasia said again. "I'm afraid this isn't going very well."

Kapov took it as a cue himself. "I confess that my appetite has also deserted me. Will you please accept my apologies?" So saying, he got up and left us.

Just then, Leo entered with a crown roast of venison. Lupa beamed. "Your highness," he said to our hostess, then nodded to Elena, "Miss Ripley. Jules. Since those of us that remain appear to be of like mind, may I propose a toast to victory?"

We lifted our glasses. "And to the Czar," I added.

Elena looked at Anastasia. "And to your husband's safe return."

We drank the toast and when Leo had served us, Lupa took a tentative bite of the venison. After a thoughtful pause, he said, "I think the classic hunter sauce benefits from a taste of red currant. Don't you agree, Jules?"

6

When I first heard the truth of it, I was furious. Now I am not so sure.

Dinner was most pleasant, with Elena and Anastasia doing most of the talking. After the disputes over Rasputin and government policy, it was nice to eat and listen to the women gossip over local affairs. Also, after my black thoughts earlier in the evening, it was good to remember that normal life does go on. All is not intrigue, treachery, and dishonor.

But Lupa had, after all, invited me to the dinner, and we had barely finished dessert when he indicated to me that it was time we leave. Thanking our hostess and bidding adieu to Elena, Lupa and I walked out into the frozen wonderland of Tsarkoye Selo.

The sky in the North glowed with the shimmering aurora borealis and the frozen crust of snow crunched under our feet as we walked the length of the main street of the Czar's enclave. It was cold, but with the food and wine we'd consumed, I was comfortable.

We shared a few moments of small talk. Since leaving Valence, Lupa had spent some time in Corsica, done a job in Italy, and then had settled back in Montenegro. There, his relationship with his fiancée Anna Dubrov had come to an end. It had been regrettable, but for the best, since women, he said, could not understand his methods or his work.

Finally, I said, "It's a wonderful coincidence to run into you again here in St. Petersburg."

There was a moment's silence, broken only by our quiet footfalls over the snow. "Yes," he said at last. "Yes, it's extraordinary."

After a few more paces, I noticed that he was chuckling.

"Would you care to share the joke with me?" I asked.

"There is no joke, Jules," he said. "I am amused at times by the amount of coincidence you are willing to credit."

I remembered his first words upon seeing me at Minsky's—"Ah, satisfactory!"—as though I'd been expected. Suddenly I felt like a pawn being moved by unseen and powerful hands, one of them Lupa's, whom I'd always viewed as a friend.

"Did you arrange this?" I asked coldly. "And if you did, why?"

"Don't be angry, Jules."

"I'm sorry, but it doesn't seem wrong to ask what I am doing here."

"Come," he said, "let us sit down. We need to talk."

We had reached a gazebo on the banks of one of the rowing lakes that hadn't yet frozen over. Lupa motioned me inside and we sat on wooden benches along one of the walls. The gentle lap of the water, the susurrus of the breeze through the bare trees, the shimmering sky to the North— all might have been soothing on another occasion, but tonight all I felt was a sudden isolation from my fellow man. The stark, lonely setting seemed the mirror of my soul.

Far off, a bird screeched, then we heard a muffled crack, like a gunshot, followed by a rumbling noise.

"What's that?" I asked, too upset to think for myself.

"It sounds like a tree breaking under the weight of the snow," Lupa replied, and he was right.

"I'm afraid I'm not thinking too clearly," I said.

"You are angry," Lupa repeated.

I raised my voice. "I am five thousand kilometers from my home, away from my wife and child. I have risked my life to get here because I believed my mission was essential to our war effort. Now I am told that I've been duped, and by the very people I believed I could trust. What kind of fool wouldn't be angry?"

The big man put his hand on my shoulder. Knowing how he disliked physical contact of any sort, it was a powerful gesture. "Jules, your role here is critical. That much is true."

"But I am not to get my commitment from the Czar?"

"Oh yes, as far as that goes, that's also correct."

"But there is more."

"Let's just say that your official status ties in neatly with your real purpose here."

"And that is?"

"And that is to help me try to save Russia."

I stared at the younger man, his face sober in the silver shadows. There was no trace of the arrogance that his words would imply. "And you must know," he continued, "that upon that salvation rests the future of France."

I leaned back against the cold, unfinished wood. If I could still be of help to my country, any sacrifice would be worth it, but my pride still smarted. "If my work here is so crucial," I asked, "how is it that I could not be told about it?"

Lupa folded his hands in front of him, elbows on his knees. "Because, my friend, I perceived that you must have a legitimate and important reason to be here in your own right, and you do. I wanted to give you several days to establish yourself in your official capacity before recruiting you to my work."

"But you had no confidence that I could carry off the deception."

"That's not the point. Why burden you with it? Even now, you could refuse to help me and you would still have an important function here at court. We are both working for the same thing—to keep Nicholas on the throne and his troops at the front."

After another minute of wrestling with myself, I saw the logic of his position. There was even, I realized, an admirable economy about it. It was better that I remain ignorant until I was ready to play an active role—what I did not know I could not reveal, either intentionally or *par hazard*.

"All right," I said. "Why are you here? To investigate the murders?"

"Of course."

"And Anastasia sent for you?" I didn't see a connection there.

We left the gazebo and began walking along one of the many bridle paths that wound back around the palaces. "Not directly," Lupa said. "Actually, the Czarina sent for me. She sent the messages through Anastasia, who is the daughter of King Nikita of Montenegro. He, in turn, appealed to me."

"And I?"

"I knew I would need you. Since I would be an official investigator—in effect a member of the police force—I expected that people would try to hide things from me. But I needed eyes and ears where my presence would not be sensed. You are the most skilled undercover operative I've worked with. I therefore determined to have your help."

"But conveying the message to me? How did you accomplish that?"

He chuckled again. "That was rather fine. Anastasia's husband, Grand Duke Nicholas, is a close friend of General Foch. I remembered that you and Foch were also on good terms."

"And my offer to the Czar?"

"That, Jules, is genuine. Originally, it was to be offered through Paleologue, but Foch thought a special emissary would be more effective. And he agreed that you were the ideal choice."

I had to laugh at all the flattery. "All right, but why did Alexandra send for you in the first place?"

He nodded. "She saw the effect the first killings had on Nicholas. She reasoned, correctly I think, that someone is launching a personal terror campaign against him. And she also thinks that, unless it's stopped, it will succeed."

"But succeed in what, exactly?"

"In forcing Nicholas to sue for a separate peace."

"Does she really care so much about that? She herself is German, isn't she? One would think she'd quite favor it."

"No." Lupa shook his head. "No, even though her enemies believe that, I'm sure it's not true. Her loyalty is to her husband, and to passing on the Romanov line through Alexis, and she is fanatical about that. Otherwise, she is quite naive politically. Her main concern is the personal effect the War, and these murders, have on the Czar."

"That ties in with what Paleologue told me," I said, and explained the ambassador's characterization of the royal family as petite bourgeoisie. But another thought occurred to me. "If these murderers simply assassinated Nicholas, wouldn't that get the job done?"

"No, I don't think so. The throne would pass to Alexis, under the Regency of Alexandra. The people, as they always have in the past, would probably rally to the Romanov line, and the War would continue."

"So the ultimate object of the murders is to get Russia out of the War?"

Lupa slowed down. "I don't know. It seems the most logical answer."

"But...?"

"Yes, Jules, but..." He stopped and took a huge gulp of the freezing air, as though he were clearing his head. "I'm not sure. It's perplexing. Knowing that doesn't narrow the field at all."

"But surely..."

Lupa shook his head. "No, Jules, not at all." He ticked off the points with his fingers. "The Royalists want a separate peace because so long as Nicholas keeps losing on the battlefield, the monarchy loses prestige. The democrats want the same thing because they believe that a demoralized Czar would grant concessions to the Duma. The Communists want the men now fighting the Germans at the front to be home to start the revolution. About the only people that don't want a separate peace are the Allies and, thus far, Nicholas himself."

We'd come all the way round behind the Alexander Palace. Lupa pointed out the lights in the upstairs window that marked the bedroom of Nicholas and Alexandra. As we watched, the shadow of a man came to that window, seeming to bear the weight of the world on his slumping shoulders as he stared out over the glittering snowscape.

Lupa must have felt the same way I did—we had intruded upon a private moment. He touched my arm lightly. "This walking has given me an appetite," he said. "Perhaps we can get a bite in the Czar's kitchen."

"Oh, yes," I answered sarcastically. "After ten courses at dinner, I'm famished. Let's just nip into the Czar's kitchen and have a snack."

But Lupa was already moving. "If you'd rather not, we'll meet again tomorrow," he said over his shoulder.

I followed him. "Do you have entrée to the kitchen?"

"Of course. Do you think I'd agree to come to such a God-forsaken corner of the world as St. Petersburg without making some demands for my own comfort?"

"But the Czar's own kitchen?" I caught up with him just as we reached the back door to the Palace. He had a badge or pass of some sort that got us past the Ethiopian guardsmen, who in any event seemed to know him.

"It is not so outrageous. After all, I do have some small reputation as a chef, so I put myself in a place where I could satisfy my own desires and also be of some help."

I remembered the state dinner I'd attended the other night, and how, unbidden, I had thought of Lupa as the food had begun to appear. I recounted the experience to him.

He nodded. "Just so. I've always admired your palate, Jules. It doesn't surprise me you recognized my touch. Any chef worth his mettle leaves a signature on his work."

We had come to another checkpoint. Inside the palace, every new hallway had a brace of the Ethiopian guardsmen.

They are a unique feature of the court here, brightly dressed
in blue and red, scimitars in their belts. Their role, however,
ostentatious though it may be, is not for show.

And Lupa is evidently not only known but liked. We were
waved by after the most perfunctory of exchanges.

"How long have you been here?" I asked him.

"It will be three weeks tomorrow."

"You seem to have made friends already."

"Yes, they're good men. I like to experiment, as you know,
and someone has to eat what I prepare."

"But surely you're not the chef de cuisine?"

"No, no, not at all. That is Max—Maximilian—Pohl, the
hope of Russia."

I laughed, thinking it was typical of Lupa to accord that
honor not to a general or a statesman, but to a cook.

But my friend stopped and faced me. "I'm not joking,
Jules. Pohl is a great chef, but he is also a great man. He
possesses that rarest of qualities—one which seems to be
entirely missing here—of balance. It shows in his dishes, of
course, but more in the way he lives and in his politics.

"Do you remember how we were saying that everyone except Nicholas and the Allies want a separate peace? Well,
there is one other exception—those who believe that there
is enough goodness in the Russian heart to overcome these
troubles. Pohl is such a man. He knows the Czar well—
Nicholas will often come down to the kitchen at midnight
and boil up some mushrooms in a little tin cup. They talk.
They are friends.

"And Nicholas, he says, is ready to include the people in
the government. It was he, after all, who created the Duma
only ten years ago. But first he wants to win the War. If he's
forced to negotiate a separate peace, he will be weakened
and the people will probably revolt, and that will result in
chaos."

Except for food, I had rarely heard Lupa speak so passion-
ately about anything. Pohl obviously made a strong impression on him. I wanted to question him further. I had, after

all, seen things outside the palace, on the streets, that indicated the time for balance had passed. I wondered if Lupa
and Pohl, cooking here in the palace, had much sense of the
tension that pervaded the capital.

But we had come to the kitchen and heard voices raised in
anger. We pushed open the doors in time to see one man,
nearly as big as Lupa and armed with a butcher knife, lunge
at another.

The smaller man ducked out of the way, pulled a ladle
from a rack over his head, and threw it at his attacker.

"Max, watch out!" Lupa yelled.

The ladle missed its mark, clattering loudly into the pans
on one of the stoves. The armed man—Pohl—again attacked, and again the other man evaded him, then turned
and rushed toward us, toward the doors.

"Auguste, stop him!" Pohl yelled.

Though dressed in his greatcoat, my friend didn't hesitate.
He took a couple of steps, then threw himself horizontally at
the fleeing figure, hitting him above the knees. The two men
fell to the floor in a heap. Still, Lupa's quarry did not rest,
but continued to struggle trying to free himself.

"Jules, get help!" he cried.

Immediately I turned and rushed back toward the last
checkpoint. But the guards had already heard the noise and
were descending upon the kitchen at a run even as I pushed
through the doors. They might wear scimitars, but both of
them carried revolvers as well, and had them out.

It was over in seconds. The guards covered the other man
as Lupa struggled to his feet, rubbing his head. Pohl walked
up to him with the knife in his hand and held it in front of his
face. "I ought to cut your throat," he said.

If this was the balanced and mild hope for Russia, I
thought, the country was beyond hope.

"Put the knife down, Max," Lupa commanded.

The guards, knowing both Pohl and Lupa, seemed inclined to let them do whatever they wished. The chef

seemed to struggle with himself, then slowly brought the knife to his side.

"Get out of here, Karel. I never want to see your face again."

The small man fairly spit at his attacker. "You'll see my face in your dreams 'til you die, you coward!" Laughing horribly, he continued. "What I've already done ought to haunt all of you palace rats long enough."

Then, without so much as a glance at Lupa, myself, or the guards, the man dusted off his coat and began walking out of the room.

"It's all right," Pohl said to the guards, "let him go. It was a personal matter."

"I would hardly call that personal," Lupa said coldly.

We were seated at a small table in the back of the kitchen, drinking the best beer I had tasted since my last sip of my own home brew back in France.

"Karel Borstoi was the best friend of my youth, Auguste." The Czar's chef spoke calmly. He is the size of my friend, but the resemblance ends there. Where Lupa is dark, nearly swarthy, in appearance, Pohl could be a Swede. His hair is pure white, almost as though he powders it with flour. In spite of having no eyebrows, a thin ascetic nose, and an overbroad sensuous mouth, there is yet something attractive about his face. He smiles easily, and there is in those blue eyes a sense of joy in life, of understanding beyond his ken—even, as Lupa would have said, of balance. "I will not see him rotting in jail."

"You were about to kill him half an hour ago."

"Death is release. Prison is its opposite. There is no comparison."

"Don't quibble with me, Max. He tried to kill the Czar. You just admitted that."

According to Pohl's story, it was true. Borstoi had come into the kitchen as he had often done before. After all, he was a personal friend of the chef. The two men had been sitting drinking, and when Pohl had gone for more beer, Borstoi had taken the opportunity to try and put arsenic in the Czar's sugar bowl. Pohl came back a little early, discovered his friend's betrayal, and the fight had started.

"He won't be admitted here again."

"It may already be too late. What was that he said just before he left, about damage already done?"

He waved it off. "That's just his way. There's no sign he's done a thing."

"Which could also be a sign he's done it rather well, don't you think?" Lupa didn't have to mention it aloud. He and I both knew Minsky had died of arsenic poisoning.

Pohl finished a glass of beer and poured himself another. "You mean the murders?" He shook his head. "You don't understand, Auguste. This is a personal thing between Karel and the Czar and, now that he's betrayed my trust, between me and him. It has nothing to do with the other murders."

"How could someone like Borstoi be personally involved with the Czar?" I asked.

Pohl shook his head sadly. "It really has been a tragedy, but for Karel to blame Nicholas personally is an overreaction."

"What happened?"

"Karel's father published one of our small evening newspapers. At the beginning of the War, he started printing articles by Communists and other revolutionaries. As the War news got worse, the articles got more and more strident as the censors got more powerful. He was finally told to stop printing." The chef sighed. "Well, he wouldn't do it. He said the people needed to know the truth. Finally the secret police came and arrested him, tried him for treason, found him guilty, and shot him."

The chef appealed to Lupa and me. "I did everything I could, but Karel just won't believe it. Nicholas was in Spala when his father was arrested. And from arrest to execution took only two days. What else could I have done?"

"Certainly Karel doesn't think it was your fault?" I asked.

"He thinks I could have somehow gotten through to Nicholas, and I tried. There just wasn't time. So now he blames both of us, the Czar and myself. Really he blames everyone and everything. He says the system itself is rotten and has to be replaced."

"Starting with Nicholas," Lupa said.

"Evidently." The chef finished another beer. He drank more quickly even than Lupa. "And now he is tempting the same fate as his father, publishing the same paper, directly calling for open revolt."

"Why haven't the police stopped him?" I asked.

Pohl laughed bitterly. "That's the great irony. When Nicholas came back from Spala last time, I told him about the execution and he felt terrible. After looking over some issues of the paper, he decided it wasn't treasonous." He put away half of another glass of beer. "There's an example, Auguste, of what I mean when I say he's starting to listen to the voice of the people.

"So today Karel is publishing his paper with the Czar's blessing. And now, in my opinion, the articles are treasonous, much worse than anything his father ever printed. That's why I asked him to come here tonight—to try and reason with him, ask him to be a little more moderate. Before tonight, at least we'd always been able to talk." The poor man shook his head. "I had no idea he hated me so much. If he'd succeeded in poisoning Nicholas, who do you think would have been blamed?"

Lupa nodded and laughed thinly. "Now there," he said, "there is a simple deduction."

A few minutes later, when the talk had turned again, as it always seemed to, to food, I excused myself, saying that I had to be up early to tutor Alexis. Lupa and Pohl remained, drinking beer and exchanging recipes.

Coming home last night, I wrote a while, then went to bed and slept fitfully for a few hours. This morning I rose groggily and finished my last entry.

Now, save one solitary wagon unloading supplies at the Alexander Palace, Tsarkoye Selo is quiet. The sky, through heavy snow clouds, is beginning to show a hint of light in the east, but the street lights are still on, their small flames sputtering in the freezing gusts.

I realized that I never told Lupa I would work with him. If he is right about the murders weakening Nicholas' resolve to fight on, then of course they must be stopped. My original mission and his work toward the same goal, and any help I can give I must offer.

And yet I am filled with foreboding, as though the force of this Russian winter now so lately begun will defeat us all, as it has so many others before us. Perhaps it's simply fatigue, but I can't escape the feeling that none of us will live to see another Spring.

7

(OCTOBER 16, 1916)

After a busy morning and an early afternoon nap, I am feeling much better. Lupa sent a note in my absence saying that he'd be coming around at six o'clock to make some plans for our investigation. That is still an hour away, and yet night has long since fallen.

I was in St. Petersburg at half past eight this morning. The snow had been swept from the main streets and I took the Nevsky Prospekt up to the Winter Palace, charmed anew by its style and grandeur. The country may be ravaged, the city itself starving, but there is no sign of it on this boulevard. I passed four boulangeries as I walked and stopped into one for a good croissant. Here the wealthy send their servants to buy bread, and here they come themselves to shop for clothes and imported goods, to have their hair done and, I would presume, to gossip.

Braced by the bite to eat and the sharp morning chill, I felt prepared to meet my young charge. I was ushered upstairs to a book-lined chamber and told by a servant that His Majesty was finishing his breakfast and would be along shortly.

His Majesty! I mulled over the phrase, struck by its irony.

And then, noting my surroundings, the Palace itself, the tutors, bodyguards and retinue attached to this boy, I recognized the reality behind the term. There was a majesty inherent in his position, but for a boy, it must be a lonely and daunting one. And was he not, after all, still just a boy?

The door opened. I was lost in my thoughts, and the Heir Apparent was in front of me before I could move. Behind him lurked the menacing bulk of Derevenko, whose job (I discovered this morning) was to keep Alexis from falling, bumping into things, cutting himself, or in any way getting bruised. It must have been an exhausting and thankless role, but even so, his dour expression surely was overdone.

Alexis, in his own sailor uniform, marched straight up to me and addressed me imperiously: "When the future Czar of Russia enters a room," he said, "it is customary to stand."

I stared at him for a long moment. This was clearly a test, and my reaction would determine whether or not we would get along.

I remained seated. "In France," I said, "a student bows to greet his tutor."

"We are in Russia."

"We are studying French."

He eyed me levelly. If there was any trace of humor in those gray-blue eyes, he hid it well. Suddenly I looked into the space behind him, shouted, "Look out!" and held up my hands as if warding off a blow. "Down! Get down!"

Immediately Alexis dropped to the ground, covering his head with his hands. Derevenko went to one knee, partially covering the boy against the expected attack.

Still in my chair, I said quietly. "Abject prostration isn't necessary. A simple bow would do."

If I made an enemy in Derevenko, I made a friend in Alyosha. The prince raised his head, looked around behind him, then up at me. The startled look gave way slowly, but when he'd realized what I had done, he broke into a sheepish grin. Finally he began laughing aloud, and I joined in.

Derevenko glared and muttered, but I barely noticed.

Helping the boy to his feet, I extended my hand. "A republican compromise," I offered. "My name is Jules Giraud. We met the other day."

He took my hand, a surprisingly firm grip in one so young —he was almost thirteen—and shook it warmly. Derevenko, fuming, got up and dusted himself off. He glared at me with ill-disguised anger.

"It's all right, Rudi," Alexis said. "No harm was done."

"And if harm was done, whose fault would it have been?" the man asked. Then, to me, "Do you want the boy's death on your hands?"

"Rudi, that's enough! You can go. We'll start our lessons now."

The big sailor's words seemed muffled through his heavy mustache. "I'll be just outside."

When the door closed, Alexis giggled again. "Don't mind Rudi," he said, "that's just how he is. You did take quite a risk, though. How could you know I wouldn't order you shot?"

I shrugged. "I didn't. Could you?"

He smiled. "I don't know, actually. I've never ordered anybody shot. I don't think I'd like it."

"No, I should imagine that pardoning those who are about to be shot would be more fun."

"My father does that," he said proudly, "quite often."

We'd naturally been speaking in French since he'd come in, and he might have been a young *bien élève* from Paris. His accent, which he'd probably picked up from his last tutor, the Swiss Pierre Gaillard, was slightly thick, but passable.

"Well," I said at last, "I must confess I've never been a tutor before. Is there some sort of routine we're supposed to follow? Did you and Monsieur Gaillard leave off somewhere?"

"We usually left off with me sleeping." He laughed, then sat down, and spoke more seriously. "We were supposed to have conversations. Every day Pierre would come in and say,

'Today we discuss Molière,' or 'Eh bien, the migration of salmon is a fascinating topic, don't you think?"

"And they didn't interest you?"

"Occasionally, but for the most part, no. Pierre wasn't, isn't, very clever. Even the interesting subjects seemed a little dull. And he would never discuss the most important thing of all. He was afraid, I think."

"And that was what?"

His young face lit up at the thought. "Politics. The world. My father."

It was an interesting string of words, I thought. Rubbing my chin, I asked drily. "Why do I sense a challenge here?"

Pleased, he nodded. "A glove Pierre would not have felt."

I was beginning to be impressed with the boy's intelligence and subtlety. "Or perhaps would choose not to."

"Perhaps, though I think not." He lowered his voice, and suddenly he seemed years older. "Monsieur Giraud, can you tell me about my father? Do you know what's happening here?"

I pondered the question. It was most extraordinary that I hadn't been briefed before coming to this tutoring. And even as that thought occurred to me, I realized that there may have been reason, not oversight, behind it.

Surely the royal couple would have told me to avoid certain topics if they had wanted to keep them from Alexis. That they hadn't done so argued that I might be a conduit to pass feelings and impressions between parents and son. And even if such weren't the case, the opportunity played directly into my own role here.

Interpreting my silence as hesitancy, Alexis solved another problem that had begun to occur to me. "If you are worried about being overheard," he whispered, "follow me." He covered his mouth with a finger, then led me back through the study, away from the entrance where, presumably, Derevenko sat sulking.

Opening a door without a sound, we darted unseen across a hallway, closed another door behind us, and moved into a furnished suite, through a sitting room and then what must have been Alyosha's bedroom. Against the wall of that room was a large closet.

Pulling the door to, Alexis turned on an overhead light, then pushed aside the clothes. There, a ladder led up to a skylight.

Alexis pulled down a heavy coat and put it on. Then, still whispering, he told me to take one for myself. There might have been compelling reasons for this kind of stealth, but it was becoming more and more clear to me that here was simply a boy enjoying a secret getaway from the adults. The fear of actual spying gave the game an added piquancy, but in essence I believed we were doing nothing more than playing hide-and-seek.

In another moment, we had climbed the ladder, pushed open the skylight, which was partially blocked by snow, and were out on a landing on the roof of the Winter Palace. The area, perhaps three meters square, was walled to just above Alyosha's height on the three sides facing the city. On the last, the roof fell gradually away, though the inner courtyard still couldn't be seen. And hence, I realized, no one in the courtyard could see up here. It was an ideal hiding place.

The spot was empty except for a chair and a shovel, and Alexis wiped off the former and bade me sit, while grabbing the latter, removing his coat, and shoveling the snow off onto the roof. He evidently relished the physical exercise, taking after his father, famous for loving to chop his own firewood.

When he'd finished, a light film of sweat covered his face, but he was beaming happily. The sun had come out, and while still far from warm, the walls blocked a good portion of the wind, and it was quite comfortable. Alexis, like a good boy remembering a lesson, put his coat back on and looked up gratefully at the sun.

"This is very fine," I said. "Did you and Monsieur Gaillard come up here often?"

He shook his head. "Never. No one has ever been up here but me."

"But..."

"I don't know," he said simply. "You took a chance with me this morning. I'm doing the same with you. Things aren't as much fun when there's no one to share them with. And besides," he added, "we can talk freely here. Pierre was always worried about being overheard. I think that's why he never said anything interesting."

"Aren't you being a little harsh on him?"

The boy sighed. "Maybe I am, I don't know. He's a nice man, and he has taught me French."

"Rather well."

"Yes, all right. But I'm at an age now where my regimen is ruining my life." He held up a hand. "No, I'm not being melodramatic. I know I'm a bleeder—I may die. I'll take it further. I will die. But so will you. And these efforts of my mother to make my life, um, insulated—well, the effect is that I don't feel like I've got much of a life. How would you like to have a Derevenko hovering behind you at all times in case you fall down?"

"You are, after all, the future Czar. It makes sense to protect you."

"My sisters are protected, and yet they're allowed to live. No one seems to believe it, but I'm getting to the point that I know what will hurt me."

"But what about that episode the other day?" I asked. "With the runaway horse?"

The boy shrugged. "I'd ridden that horse a hundred times, a thousand. It's never happened before."

"Still, it's fortunate Rasputin happened along, or ..."

"Rasputin! Are you already in his power?"

The question stunned me—not only its virulence but its sentiment. I thought the boy worshiped the starets.

"No, I'm not. But it did seem that he calmed the animal, and I thought you cried out his name when you saw him."

The boy thought a moment, then a light of understanding came to his eyes. "I never saw Rasputin until the horse stopped. All my attention was focused on Grishka." Then he laughed charmingly. "Grishka the horse," he said. "The horse's name is Grishka. I was calling its name."

Was anything as it appeared here in St. Petersburg?

"Then you aren't close to the starets?"

It was obviously a difficult question. "He doesn't belong where he is."

"Which is where?"

"Advising my mother, even trying to influence my father. I'm sure it's he who convinces my mother I need to be so protected. It's to his advantage." Frustrated, he slapped at his leg. "I don't need that kind of protection anymore. If I die, I die, but I will die having lived."

"Dum vivo vivebo," I said, smiling.

"What's that?"

I stood up. "It's Latin. 'While I am alive, I will live.' It's been my motto since I was about your age."

"What is it again?"

I told him, and he repeated it a few times, setting it to memory. He asked seriously, "Can I take it as my own?"

Inordinately flattered, I looked in his eyes for any trace of irony, but there was none. *"Bien sur,"* I said. "Of course."

He went to the chair and stood upon it, facing out over the city. "You see down there?" he said. "This view is why I come up here. I can be alone anywhere—I mean away from Rudi and the girls—but here I can see my people."

He pointed down to the street. "See there? That line. What are they doing there?"

"Waiting for bread, I believe," I said.

The answer seemed to verify something he'd been thinking. "So it's come to that."

"The city isn't in very good shape," I said. "Supplies are very low."

"I've seen the demonstrations from here, too. Of course no one tells me what they're really about, but I've figured it out. Are we losing the War, M. Giraud? Is my father all right?"

Again I was struck by the personal identification the boy had between his father and the state, but before I could respond, he continued.

"You know, I've gone to Spala with my father several times since he's taken command of the army. Every night we would take a long walk around the compound, and you know what he tells me?"

I shook my head no.

"He says that, no matter what, I should strive to learn the truth. And, he says, in our position that is the hardest thing to know because no one will tell you the truth."

"I will," I said, and I mean it.

He paused. "Then, if you do, you will be the most valuable ally I have ever had."

"But, of course, you can't trust me yet."

His young eyes were filled with the awful truth of that knowledge. "I know."

"Let me ask you something," I said. "Do you know about the murders?"

He sat back down on the chair. "I know my father seems to be..." He hesitated. "Well, to answer your question, there have been three, n'est-ce pas?"

As gently as I could, I told him about the fourth, about Minsky. The news hit him hard. I watched his innocent face contort with emotion. Then he stood up and walked to where the gentle roof sloped down to the courtyard, facing away until he had overcome the struggle.

"Uncle Boris and I rode together with Papa every day at Spala. He treated me like a man." He took a deep breath and swallowed hard, then put his own emotion behind him. "How is my father taking it?" he asked.

"I haven't seen him since it's happened. I don't believe anyone has."

He nodded as though the answer was expected. Suddenly he looked up and said in Russian, "God, don't let him give up!" Then, back to me in French, "at least not for that reason."

"What reason?"

"That he feels so alone."

That response, from a boy, impressed me. "What do you mean?" I asked.

"He is the Emperor. The nature of command is being alone. Even I know that." He paced the edge of the enclosure. "Don't you see what they're doing?"

"Yes," I said calmly. "I think I see quite clearly. Someone is trying to make your father so personally unhappy that he is no longer able to be the Czar, or, more accurately, to act as the Czar should act."

After a minute of reflection, he looked me in the eye. "That's exactly right," he said. "If I could see him and talk to him, I could tell him that."

"Why don't you try?" I said, suppressing any guilt at the manipulative question.

"I am going to, M. Giraud. I really am."

The wind had suddenly turned cold. It came in gusts and we saw clouds beginning to gather in the North. "We should be going back down. Derevenko will be worried," I said, smiling.

Back in his room, he stopped and extended his hand formally. "Thank you, sir. On the first day, you have taught me something important."

"And what is that?" I asked, shaking the royal hand.

He grinned boyishly, but there was something very mature behind the expression. "Dum vivo vivebo. If I don't live to become Czar, that is my fate. But while I am alive," his eyes shone with the promise, "while I am alive, I will live."

We managed to get back to the study without being seen, and after arranging a few props so it looked as though we'd been going over some books and taking notes, Alyosha summoned Derevenko and the first "lesson" came to an end.

Feeling very pleased with myself, and with the boy's intelligence and manner, I was leaving the children's quarters when I heard a gentle sobbing from an alcove off the main hallway.

I stopped to listen. Something about the sound was oddly familiar, so I peeked into the darkened recess, not wishing to intrude but curious nevertheless.

A thin ribbon of dim light came through a narrow window. Within its beam, motes of dust hung in the still air like sequins, now catching more, now less of the weakening sun. A dozen votive candles in red holders burned before a statue of some saint.

Kneeling in profile at the side of the alcove, weeping into a handkerchief, was Elena Ripley. Torn between wanting to console her and not wanting to intrude, I stood in the entranceway and finally cleared my throat. When she looked up, I moved a step into the room.

"Who's there?" she said in English. She had been crying in the darkened room. With the bright light behind me, I was probably no more than a silhouette.

"It's Jules. Are you all right?"

Sighing once, bringing herself under control, she sat back in the pew. "I don't know," she said. "I just don't know." A fresh wave of tears broke, and I came and sat next to her.

"There, there," I said, patting her gently on the shoulder. "It's all right. Come on now. What is it?"

She had never looked younger, more vulnerable, more beautiful. Her lips were slightly swollen, almost bruised looking, her eyes glistening with her tears, the color high in her cheeks. After dabbing ineffectually at her face, she regained control enough to whisper to me.

"It's Tatiana."

Immediately the murders came back to mind and I thought the worst. Could they be striking now directly at the Czar's family?

"Is she all right?"

She nodded, and I breathed a sigh of relief.

"What is it then?"

She sniffed, swallowed hard. "We've had a fight. We've never before had a fight."

I almost had to laugh. With the War going badly and murders in the court, a tiff between two young women hardly seemed the stuff of tragedy. Still, it would be coarse to seem to take it too lightly, so I again patted her on the shoulder. "I'm sure you both will work it out. What was it about?"

"It's the first time," she repeated. "She's never been that way before."

"Calm down now. Just tell me what happened."

She nodded and sniffed again. "I was trying to coach her Cockney. She was doing a reading of Eliza in *Pygmalion*. Do you know the play? No? It's a Shaw, and the whole point of it is class and accent.

"And she was reading the Cockney parts with her mother's perfect British. Her great-grandmother was Queen Victoria, you know, and she prides herself on her accent. All I did was try to explain that in this case the Queen's English was not called for, and she was frustrated anyway because she couldn't get the Cockney, and we started yelling at one another. I got very upset and said she couldn't understand the point, and she said I evidently understood the lower classes all too well, and we kept going and now..." she stopped, another sob breaking from her, "and now, and now they'll put me out on the street."

She broke down again, leaning into me and crying. I put my arm around her, grateful that she couldn't see my smile. "Now, now," I said. "I'm sure they won't put you on the street."

"But what would I do, Jules? People are starving and rioting. I wouldn't survive."

"I'm sure they won't turn you out, Elena. I'm sure."

She straightened up again. "How can you be sure? You don't know Tatiana. She's really angry."

"She'll get over it I'm sure, if you will."

"But I'm not even mad anymore."

"There. You see? I'm sure she's not either."

"But what if she is?"

"First, 'what if' is not ever anything to worry about. And second, too many other people love you and will intercede." Then, because the whole affair was silly to me, I tried a joke. "You could even try Rasputin. He..."

But she reacted as though she were burned, pulling away and nearly shouting. "No, never! I'll never do that!"

I reached for her hand. "I'm teasing, Elena. Just teasing."

"But..." she began.

"Look at the friends you have here. There's nothing to worry about. I could even go to Alexis. Or Anastasia could help. You won't be turned out."

"You don't think so?"

I smiled, squeezing her hand. "I'm sure of it. Now, come on, let's wipe those tears from your pretty face."

She looked at me gratefully. I took the handkerchief and carefully dried her cheeks, around her eyes. "There," I said firmly, striving for my most avuncular tone, "much better, don't you think?"

Somewhat embarrassed, she nodded. "I'm sorry," she said. "But I am worried. I don't know what I'll do if they turn me out. I don't know where I'd go."

"You don't worry. That's all. I'm sure it'll all be over in a day or two, and if there's still any problem, I'll help you. I promise."

"You don't have to do that."

"Shush." I touched her lips with my finger. "No more of it, all right?"

She looked into my eyes, then briefly pressed her lips against mine. "Thank you," she said, "you're a good man."

I can't pretend the kiss didn't affect me deeply. Trying not to show it, I took her hand and lifted her to her feet. "Come," I said, "I'm on my way back to Tsarkoye Selo. Walk with me."

Back in the hallway, in the light, my heart returned to its

even beating. We strolled easily side by side, talking about trivial things—Derevenko, her relations with the other Grand Duchesses, with Anastasia, a few words about Lupa's deductive display the previous night. Finally I ventured a few thoughts on my formal mission. We had come to the exit to the children's quarters, and she stopped and took my hand, looking at me steadily.

"I'm glad you're here," she said. "If anyone can convince the Czar to do what is right, it is you. I'm sure of it."

I bowed stiffly, wrestling with the effect this young woman had on me. I felt anything but a paragon of virtue and goodness. Strange as it seems, I can't escape the feeling that somehow, unlikely as it may be, Elena is attracted to me.

It is disconcerting.

In any event, we shook hands and I left, walking under a newly-overcast sky to the train station.

8

When Lupa arrived, he suggested we go into St. Petersburg for dinner, and though I'd only returned from there a few hours earlier, I acquiesced. The train ride is really only a minor inconvenience, over almost before it begins.

Lupa had heard that the Villa Rhode boasted an extremely delicious solyanka d'esturgeon and he had made a reservation there. The restaurant, on the extreme outskirts of the city on the right bank of the Neva, was a good long walk from the train station, and on the way there, as the first flakes of a new snowstorm began to fall, Lupa had the opportunity to outline his suspicions.

"In a way," he began, "we are fortunate. The court is such a tightly-knit unit, and in general so closely watched, that our murderer must be one of a relatively small group of people."

"Have you narrowed it down at all?"

He nodded. "It's odd. The murders have been by poison, bomb and knife. They could almost have been committed by different people."

"Or directed by a different intelligence?" I offered.

"Exactly. I've thought of that. But I tend to discount it."

"Why?"

We rounded a corner onto the Nevsky Prospekt, and the

bustling street of earlier that morning was nowhere in evidence. The storefronts were boarded. Only an occasional automobile rumbled by in the swirling snow. The street lights hissed as we passed beneath them, their little pools of yellow light doing little except marking the curbs.

Lupa turned up his collar against the wind. "I am going on the assumption that our motive here is the one we've discussed. Are you still willing to stand by that?"

I nodded. "I think so. Before I knew you were here, Paleologue told me about the killings, and believed their aim was to weaken the Czar's will."

"There's no doubt it makes sense," he said, "but is there another possibility?"

"Of course. There is always another possibility."

I heard him chuckle under his greatcoat. "Just so. Well said, Jules."

"But in this case," I continued, "nothing else makes much sense. Especially since you've been sent for. Alexandra must believe it."

"All right, then, if we agree on motive, and we do, then there remains..."

"Means and opportunity."

We had passed by the Winter Palace and were crossing the Neva. Snow clung to its banks, but the gray water had not yet iced over—we heard its churning flow around the pilings under us. Then the Fortress of Ss. Peter & Paul loomed ahead, and I swear I could feel the despair of the incarcerated through the thick stone walls. How many of them, I wondered, had committed any real crime? And how many would live to be free again?

"I'm sorry," I said, realizing Lupa had been talking. "Could you repeat that?"

"I said the bombs ought to narrow things down. Who could get access to bombs?"

I thought about it. "Or who could make one?"

Lupa shook his head. "No. I think not. These were a small

and very efficient weapons. Since I wasn't here to examine the victims, I can't be sure, but the reports I've read seem to point more to grenades than to true bombs."

"Well, then, wouldn't anyone in the army...?"

Lupa stopped. "In France, it's true that anyone in the army would have grenades. But what have we heard about supplies here in Russia? That even bullets are hard to come by, *n'est-ce pas?*"

He was right.

"Then we might expect," he continued, "that only someone with real access to munitions might..."

"Sukhomlinov," I said.

"It's a thought. Or someone in a similar position. Ah, I believe we are here."

The street in front of the restaurant was lined with black automobiles, attesting to its popularity. From inside came the sound of gypsy guitar music. Lupa stood outside the door for a moment sniffing the air.

"The first test of a restaurant," he said. Seemingly satisfied, he pushed open the door and held it for me. Inside, the warm air was suffused with the aromas of a well-stocked and professional kitchen. As our coats were taken, Lupa gave his name, and the maitre d' rushed up to shake his hand.

"Auguste Lupa," he said, "this is a great honor."

Lupa bowed. "The honor is mine, Monsieur Muret. May I present a friend, Jules Giraud."

Muret took us to a booth in the back of the crowded room, and I surveyed the scene. It was not the most plush of restaurants, catering as it did to those who fancied gypsy music. Still, there was a genuine sense of enjoyment in the atmosphere. Talk was loud, the ambience robust.

When the waiter brought a large pitcher of beer for our first courses, I knew Lupa had picked the right place. We both share a fondness for beer—it had been the basis of our original acquaintance—and we drank the first glasses in companionable silence. The solyanka d'esturgeon turned out to be a variation of the fish stew I'd had two or three times since my arrival here, although at the Villa Rhode it was made of the best ingredients. With black bread and fresh butter, it was quite good, although I would never understand Lupa's rapturous praise for the dish—it paled beside the simplest saffron-laden bouillabaise.

But then, I remind myself, we are a long way from France.

Five pitchers of beer had come and gone, along with our stew, when the owner Muret approached our table. Lupa was effusive in his compliments over the dish and I feigned enthusiasm as well. We invited him to join us, and when he sat down he ordered a round of schnapps.

The gypsies were playing louder. During dinner, three men had been strumming guitars on a small raised platform in one corner of the room. Just before we'd finished eating, an old woman, with a voice of exceptional pathos and power, had stilled the room with a stirring rendition of "The Swan Song." Now, as the schnapps arrived, she began another song, with more of a beat, and the crowd began to respond by swaying and clapping.

"Is that Varya Panina?" Lupa asked.

Muret nodded. "The greatest living gypsy singer. We are fortunate to have her."

We listened to the song, its raw yet plaintive melody forcing its way into the consciousness. I found myself moving in time to the guitars, and when the singing stopped, it was as though I was coming out of sleep. The woman—who was quite ugly—had created something that was transcendently beautiful and nearly addictive.

As we finished applauding, there was a commotion in the back of the room. A door to a private dining area had flown open and a small party of diners, seemingly quite drunk, issued into the main salon. At its center, with what looked like common prostitutes on each arm, was Gregory Rasputin.

He called out loudly. "Another, Varya! Another!" he yelled as he staggered up toward the stage. "Let's have another song." He sat himself down in the midst of the performers and called for a bottle of Madeira.

Lupa leaned over to Muret. "Who is that cretin?" he asked in a whisper.

Muret shushed him. "Be careful what you say. That is Rasputin."

The monk had his wine, and was trying to prod one of the members of his party into singing along with Varya. The other diners seemed to take this display in stride. Indeed, I got the feeling that some might have come for just such a show. Lupa, however, did not find it entertaining.

"The man's a fool, and he's drunk," he said.

"He may be drunk, but he's no fool," Muret responded.

"The gypsies are robbing me! Somebody help!" Rasputin had fallen backwards on the platform, and three or four gypsies were endeavoring to help him up. "They're picking my pockets! Stop them!"

It all had the quality of being rehearsed, and I must say the monk, the diners, even the gypsies appeared to be enjoying themselves. The guitarists struck up another round of chords, and Rasputin began singing, loudly and out of key, urging the rest of the crowd to join in, which many of them did.

I noticed, though no one else appeared to, that Varya Panina had left the stage. Lupa tapped me on the shoulder and indicated that he, too, had had enough. As we were getting up, Muret shrugged, clearly saying that events such as this were out of his control, that he wasn't happy, but the patrons seemed to enjoy themselves, and he had a business to consider.

Lupa bowed, muttered a perfunctory thank you, and marched through the crowd across the room. I trailed behind by a few steps. At the cloakroom, we paused for another minute, listening to the "most powerful man in Russia" lead the room in a chorus of vulgar song. Lupa didn't even wait inside to button his coat. As soon as it was handed to him, he pushed impatiently at the door and was outside.

Down the street from the Villa Rhode, we passed a lone figure huddled under an awning. Lupa stopped before we'd quite come to it, then walked over and extended his hand.

"You were magnificent," he said. "I am sorry for that . . . for that embarrassment."

Varya Panina raised a tear-stained face to my friend, then took his hand and smiled feebly. "It will be over in an hour, then I will sing again. We get our strength from our pain. Rasputin, like everything else, will pass."

There was nothing more to say. We nodded to the singer and made our way back toward St. Petersburg in a brooding silence, the wet snow thickening under our boots. On the bridge across the Neva, a black limousine came roaring by us, much too close to the curb. We were spattered with slush and someone leaned out the window, laughing and yelling obscenities.

Lupa and I wiped the snow from our coats. When we had gone another fifty meters, my friend suddenly spoke without breaking his stride. "It could be we are already too late," he said. "Russia may be lost."

I had to be in St. Petersburg in the morning again, so I elected to stay at my room in the Winter Palace. As in my own case, Lupa had been given suites in both Tsarkoye Selo and the Palace and he suggested we stop by his rooms before going to bed.

There, he offered me some tea with lemon. Though I was tired, the long walk had given Lupa time to think. He had evidently overcome his feeling that it was too late to do anything about saving Russia.

"I'm curious about Borstoi's comment the other night," he said. "You remember when Pohl was having him thrown out of the kitchen? He said he'd already done a great deal of damage. I wonder what he meant by that, if perhaps you'd be able to find out."

"Do you think it could be Borstoi?"

Lupa shrugged. "We're just beginning. It's wise to suspect everyone. Minsky was poisoned and he was in possession of poison."

"But by the same token, Auguste, Pohl seemed quite ready to use a knife on Borstoi. And one of the killings was a cut throat, *n'est-ce pas?*"

Lupa sat back in a wing chair. "I have no suspicion of Max, although you're right, I should have." He seemed to mull over that possibility for a moment, then straightened in his chair and continued. "But let's still find what we can about Borstoi. If anything, he has a surfeit of motive—personal on two levels—as well as political. I wonder if he could have had access to a grenade, or if he is friendly with anyone else at court besides Max. It's worth pursuing."

We decided that the best approach would be for me to pretend that I was sympathetic to his cause. He would probably be convinced of my sincerity by the very fact that I had come to visit him. That alone could be construed as a treasonous act, given my position with Alexis and my public mission to the Czar. If that were not enough to gain his confidence, Lupa and I would come up with something else later.

I had finished my tea and was ready to go to bed. "So," I said, putting on my coat again, "we have Sukhomlinov, Borstoi and Pohl."

"In fact we have nothing," he said. "But it would be wise to keep in mind everyone we might suspect."

"There are others besides those three?"

"Surely you didn't think Katrina Sukhomlinov acted normally at Anastasia's? Did you see her reaction when I mentioned Minsky? She ran crying from the room. No, she is involved in something we're not aware of."

"But could she have killed Minksy?"

He shrugged. "Both she and her husband were at Tsarkoye Selo that night. It is hardly significant that they weren't at Vyroubova's party."

Frowning, he went on, stirring what remained in his cup with his forefinger. "And we might as well include Ivan Kapov. Think of his comments at Anastasia's. He left me with the strong impression that he would stop at nothing to get the separate peace, and he seems to be a man of action, not just rhetoric."

He drained his cup in a last swallow. "More tea? No? You're right, it's late." He put the cup down. "But it's still too early to make any judgments. We could even include Elena Ripley since she was with Minsky at Vyroubova's just before you left."

"That's ridiculous!" I could listen to him include anyone else, but that was too farfetched for me to accept.

Lupa's eyes narrowed. "Is it? Have you asked yourself why it is that a simple governess seems to be a fixture at so many parties?"

I was surprised at the violence of my reaction—it was almost as though Lupa were attacking me personally. "Elena is far from a 'simple governess,' as you call her. She is a brilliant stage actress—young, single, and extremely beautiful. She would grace any party. And on top of that," I continued, "perhaps you have forgotten, but she was in the Crimea with the Czar's daughters when the first murder occurred."

"That is true. You're right."

"Thank you," I replied stiffly.

"But it is also true that you are smitten with her and it might affect your judgment."

"I'll be sure to guard against it!" I replied with some heat. "I am a married man, and I have been faithful to Tania."

He held up a hand. "I never said you weren't. Come, Jules, calm yourself. Elena has no discernible motive, but she did have opportunity in Minsky's case, and anyone, male or female, can plant a bomb or cut a man's throat in his sleep. I only mention her for the same reason you included Pohl. Until we have some evidence, everyone is suspect. Everyone must be."

Still angry, I retorted. "What about Alexandra? Why not suspect Rasputin while we're at it? At some point the field must narrow. We can't suspect an entire city."

Lupa sighed deeply, and suddenly his own fatigue seemed to match mine. "Jules, let's get some sleep. If it makes you any happier, I don't suspect Alexandra. Or, for that matter, Rasputin, though I don't come away from my first sight of him very impressed. In fact," he added lightly, though there was no misreading the venom in his voice, "I would gladly strangle the man for what he did to Varya Panina."

"It was insensitive," I agreed.

Lupa eyed me with a strange intensity, as though a thought had just struck him. "Do you think it was Rasputin in the limousine?"

I'd of course heard stories of the starets driving a black automobile through the streets of St. Petersburg at night, shooting beggars at random, setting fire to houses, raping women and defiling churches, but his notoriety in the city and at court was such that those types of rumors were inevitable, and I told Lupa as much.

He seemed to find that explanation reasonable. Tomorrow, he said, he was going to interview Katrina Sukhomlinov. And after I saw Borstoi, we could meet again and see if we'd made any progress.

Exhausted, I finally said goodnight, walked to my suite, and immediately fell asleep.

9

"I've been thinking," Alyosha said, "and I'm not so sure that Rasputin is good for my mother."

When I'd arrived to see the Czarevitch that morning, he'd delighted me by bowing as he greeted me. Now we were up in the "secret place," even though a light snow was falling. Alyosha had already cleared away the night's drifts with his shovel—it was a task he never overlooked, he said. Clearly, it was very important for him to be outside and away from the presence of Derevenko rather than sit in the warm and airless study. Also, I think the act of escaping was a game he rather enjoyed, and selfishly I realized that sharing it with him created a bond I couldn't manufacture any other way.

"How is that?" I asked.

Alyosha scratched a smooth chin, no doubt imagining himself with a Van Dyke like his father's. "I remember what we were talking about yesterday, how for someone in my father's position, or even in mine, the truth is the hardest thing to know."

"Yes?"

"Well," he hesitated, as though this discovery were a difficult thing for him, "I think Grishka," he smiled, "Rasputin, not the horse, wants to protect my mother too much. In the same way that she wants to protect me."

"Why do you think that?" I asked, impressed with the boy's insight.

"I don't know for certain. Or I'm not sure." He grinned disarmingly. "*Sont—elles les mêmes choses?* Are they the same thing?"

"Not exactly. Go on."

"Well, I know Gregory is a great solace to my mother, but it somehow doesn't seem right to me that an Empress seeks solace over understanding."

"And what should an Empress seek?"

He stomped around in the light snow. "That's what I've been wrestling with. With Papa at Spala, my mother has been running the government, or controlling appointments, which amounts to the same thing."

"And you think Rasputin has . . . ?"

"I know," he interrupted. "I know that Rasputin has no political training, and that he still tries to persuade my mother over appointments. And then she writes to Papa and the things are done." He shook his head, as though trying to understand something beyond him. "With Papa trying to direct the War, M. Giraud, he has come to rely on Mama's intuitions and advice. And that was all right when it was Mama speaking for herself. But now I believe she is afraid— afraid for me and afraid for Papa. And Gregory makes her feel better."

"And there is something wrong with that?"

He pondered a moment, then smiled, "Ah, *la methode Socratique*." It was a joy to watch him switch from boy to man, from prince to student. The man-prince continued: "No, not in itself. I just wonder if the truth gets hidden when there's only one version of it."

"And your mother only chooses to see one?"

"I think so. That's what concerns me."

It was my turn to pace across the enclosure. Last night's vision of Rasputin, drunk and obnoxious, threatened to crowd out my other thoughts. Suddenly it was very obvious to me why the monk was so roundly hated. Society saw him as I did last night and also knew that he had the Empress' ear. The relationship did not inspire confidence in the wisdom of the Romanovs. "Alexis," I said at last, "if you remember one thing when you become the Czar, this would be a good one."

"It's the same thing my father says, but why can't he see that he's not doing it?"

I looked at the confused face, so serious and so aware. He will be a good Czar someday, I thought, if only he could live so long. His hands were in his pockets and he was starting to shiver in the cold. "As you said, it may be up to you to tell him. Will you be seeing him soon?"

He said that his parents were coming into the city for Minsky's funeral, and that he had already requested a private, formal audience with his father. Oddly enough, that seemed entirely appropriate to me, though I'm certain that only days before I would have scoffed at the idea as childish bravado.

I said that I was getting cold and asked Alexis if he would mind if we went back down to the study where it was warmer. In some strange way, I sensed that he was putting on the mantle of Czar with me—it wouldn't do for him to admit that he was cold. That would be weakness. Or, more exactly, it would be showing weakness. If his struggling was telling him anything, it was that rulers are allowed moments of vulnerability in private, but in public they are not.

If only his father could make that distinction, I mused. Perhaps Alexis, in his formal interview, could begin to get the point across. If it could be done at all, I was sure Alexis would find the way to do it.

Back in the study, I changed the subject. Did he know Elena Ripley? I asked casually. Had he heard about the fight between her and Tatiana?

He seemed almost relieved to gossip, as though the burdens of his future responsibilities were weighing heavily on him. He hadn't heard about it yet, but volunteered the opinion that Tatiana was too sensitive and far too headstrong to take criticism well.

"Takes too much after her mother," he said sardonically.

"Do you think Elena will be let go?"

He laughed, as though at himself. "Do you think we are consulted over those things? Do you think I'd request a Rudi Derevenko? No, it will all blow over. It always does." He sighed. "It seems to be the nature of our little closed-in world that these flareups occur. I think they're the only things that keep boredom from killing us."

Karel Borstoi was setting type in the tiny back room of what had been his father's newspaper office. It was early afternoon, and I'd left Alexis—reassured over Elena's security—about forty minutes before, crossing the city on foot under still-overcast skies.

In spite of the cold outside, in Borstoi's shop it was sweltering. He worked shirtless and his wiry body glistened in the light of several bare electric bulbs. He was a small man, but his muscles rippled like a thoroughbred's as he lifted heavy trays of type from the set table to the press. I stood in the doorway watching him for several minutes before he noticed me.

"Eh, what do you want?" he said in almost-guttural Russian. Then, "Do I know you?"

I stepped into the brighter light of the room, loosening my coat. "We've seen each other before."

He moved back a couple of steps, while I continued unbuttoning my coat. I looked down for a second, and when I faced him squarely he was holding a hand ax, evidently prepared to use it.

"I'm here as a friend," I said. "I was at the Czar's kitchen the other night."

Still wary, he glanced behind me. "You're alone?"

I took my coat off and draped it over a chair, then sat down. "Yes, of course. And unarmed," I added, raising my hands, "as you can see."

"What do you want?" Poised and tense, he stood on the balls of his feet, the ax gripped so hard his knuckles shone white. "Did Max Pohl send you?"

"Would Max Pohl send a friend? I said I was a friend." I used the word *priyatel'*, friend. Then I smiled thinly, taking a chance. "In fact, I am *tovarishch*, a comrade."

His eyes darted from me to the open room behind me.

"If you're so worried about it, why do you leave the doors open? Come, sit down, we should talk. It's Karel, isn't it?"

He nodded, and I introduced myself.

"How is it you were with Pohl?" Still, his stance didn't change. He was ready to attack or defend in an instant.

"I might ask you the same thing."

"Stay right there," he commanded. Giving me as wide a berth as the small room allowed, he checked the front office. I admit that while he was behind me, I was not altogether sanguine. The small breeze of his passing made the hairs stand on the back of my neck. If he was a murderer, if he thought I was hunting him down, it would be a short work for him to end his worries.

I felt him reenter the press room, and sensed him hovering behind me. "Listen to me," I said, as casually as I could, "my position at court can be very helpful to you. If I'd wanted to harm you I could have done it easily when I arrived."

He came around the front of me again and I let myself breathe. Though he still held the ax, now it was more as a prop than a weapon. He pushed himself up backwards onto the edge of the press and relaxed. I reached into my breast pocket, took out a cigarette, and offered him one, which he took, smelled, put in his mouth.

As I struck a match, he smiled coldly. "Do you mind if we switch?" He gave me his cigarette and took mine.

I laughed. "At some point, this becomes ridiculous."

He inhaled deeply, nodding. "You're right," he said, "and we are not at that point."

I shrugged. "*En tout cas*, I came here. I thought we could help each other. Perhaps I was wrong." Standing up, I took my coat.

"What are you doing?"

"I am leaving. There are other cells. It will just take a little more time." I started to turn for the doorway.

"You know about the cells?"

I stopped. "We have a Party in France."

He considered that. Then, "How can you help me?"

"I am at court. I have an official position. I am tutor to the Heir. The question is, how can you help me? The other night, you seemed very bold. Today I meet a man terrified of a cigarette. I made a mistake. Good day," I paused, spitting out the last word, "*tovarishch*."

He wrestled with it so long that I thought it hadn't worked. I walked out of the back room and through the front office, and was already preparing how to word my failure to Lupa, when he caught up with me on the street. A dirty brown woolen shirt was his only protection against the cold, but he seemed immune to it.

"It's not unnatural that I should be cautious," he said, hurrying along next to me. "My father was abducted out of that office, and now Max..."

"Max let you go the other night," I said harshly. "That's the reality. We must think clearly at times like these. Paranoia stifles action. It's the mother's milk of cowards."

"I'm no coward!" he answered hotly.

I stopped and faced him. "All right, Karel, perhaps not. But I am not a spy for Bloody Nick."

"And I have no proof of that."

I conceded the point. "All right, I'll get you proof. In the meanwhile, don't you think that someone with my access at court might be worth knowing?"

It was his turn to smile as if he were hiding something. That smile bothered me. In it I could read the bitterness of his struggle—here was no dreaming idealist fueled by hopes of a new Russia, a better society, but a profoundly hate-filled and unhappy young man, driven by thoughts of revenge and violence.

"Yes," he said, "it's good to know people at court." All at

once he started to shiver as the freezing wind gusted around us. I suggested we return to his shop.

In the sweltering press room, he poured himself a cup of tea, holding it in both hands, blowing on it and inhaling the warm steam as it rose. When he'd finished, he put down the cup, gave one tremendous final shiver, and boosted himself back onto the press, facing me. "Now, comrade," he said, "how can we work together?"

He poured two more cups of tea and we spent the next half hour discussing my official role here. His understanding of the international situation was severely limited by his blind hatred of the Czar, and I came to the conclusion that his Communist beliefs would easily give way to any other political view so long as one of its main tenets was overthrow of the Romanovs. In essence, he is simply an anarchist, and a dangerous one.

But the long discussion did accomplish one purpose—a superficial friendliness developed between us. At least, on my side it was superficial. From Borstoi, I sensed the almost frantic reaching out for friendship and approval that one often encounters in insecure, haunted men. In the end, he asked me if he could take me to lunch at Cubat.

"Isn't that rather extravagant?" I asked. Last night, Lupa had mentioned it as one of the most exclusive dining places in the city, one he wanted to try himself before our investigation was completed.

But Borstoi grinned conspiratorially. "I'll take care of it." He went to a closet against the back wall of the press room and took out a white linen shirt, cravat, coat, and greatcoat. When he saw me looking at him with surprise, he quickly spoke up. "From my days at court. It's a helpful uniform in certain circumstances."

As we walked to the restaurant, I used his reference to the court as an introduction to expressing my thoughts on the murders, though I omitted any mention of Lupa, or my connection to him. I said that I understood Pohl was one of

those suspected of murdering Minsky. As I was about to go
into the reasons—access to arsenic and so on—Borstoi interrupted me.

"I never doubted Max did it."

In some shock, I asked him to repeat what he'd just said.

"I said of course Max killed Minsky. He all but told me as
much the other night."

"But Max is a Czarist, isn't he?" I remembered Lupa's
opinions regarding the chef, his loyalty to Nicholas, his belief
in orderly progress through the monarchy.

Borstoi stopped and looked at me as if I were a madman.
"What do politics have to do with Minsky's killing?"

I briefly outlined it—expressed as my own original idea—
that the murders seemed to be directed somehow at the
Czar, to weaken him, to make him lose his taste for continuing the War.

"Yes, yes, of course that," he said impatiently, "in the case
of at least one of the first three. But Minsky had nothing to
do with the Czar." Then he added, "but it is wonderful if it
adds to the man's miseries."

I choked down my natural response. "But you think
Minsky wasn't part of that?"

He laughed. "I know, or all but know it."

"But then . . . ?"

"Giraud, there are other issues in the world besides politics."

"Did Pohl admit killing him?"

"No, no. Not even to me. He's not that stupid. But I suppose Sukhomlinov could have done it, too. They both had
the motive."

I was greatly confused, but we had just arrived at the restaurant. The Cubat was so elegant it made the Villa Rhode
seem like a bohemian boîte. We had our greatcoats taken by
the maitre d' and were seated, at Borstoi's request, in the
back of the establishment. His manner to the captain was
appropriate, and he appeared perfectly at ease in the midst
of this society. I also noticed a vast improvement in his Rus-

sian as he spoke to the waiter—no doubt his unfinished accent up to this time was some attempt at consistency with his proletarian stance. But I was too curious to press any side issues. As soon as we were seated and our waiter had left us, I grabbed Borstoi by the arm. "What do you mean, Pohl and Sukhomlinov had the same motive?"

He looked down at my fingers and I loosened my grip. "Why is your interest so great, Giraud?"

Afraid that I had betrayed myself, and rather than go on the defensive, I attacked. "Because, you fool, I'm operating on certain assumptions in trying to play my government against the Czar. It's a very subtle game. I have to read Nicholas exactly, and if Minsky's murder hasn't shaken him, then now might not be the right time to pressure him, and I was under the impression that it was."

The arrival of our wine provided a moment's respite, and it was enough for Borstoi to digest my words. "It's wonderful," he said, convinced by my anger if not my argument, "it probably has had that effect."

He took a sip of the wine, smacked his lips appreciatively, and whispered to me. "But Giraud, Minsky was having an affair with Katrina Sukhomlinov. Her husband is beyond himself with jealousy, and, to make it more interesting, Pohl is also in love with her. If that's not why he died, I'm a royalist."

The room almost whirled before me. As soon as he said it, it was so obvious that I wondered how it had never occurred to me or to Lupa. It explained so much, not the least of which was Katrina's behavior at, and tearful exit from, Anastasia's party. Just to be saying something, I protested. "But surely Max would know it would have such a powerful effect on the Czar?"

"So what? What's that to him?"

"I understood he was, I mean politically he was ..."

"Max?" Borstoi laughed coarsely. "Max is the least political man I've ever known. He doesn't care about anything but himself. If you wanted a job at court, what would be your politics? Of course he says he pro-Romanov. Anything else would put him on the street."

The waiter came again and Borstoi ordered for us both as I tried to assimilate what he'd been telling me. He might have earlier appeared unwashed, bitter, insecure, even foolish, but his analysis of how things worked in St. Petersburg made more sense at the moment than all of my own imaginings and all of Lupa's finely-deduced theories.

"And the other killings?" I asked when the waiter had gone, "were they jealousy, too?"

Again that mirthless laugh. "Katrina Sukhomlinov is a very passionate women, and her husband is old. She is not the only one of her type at court." He paused, considering something, then went on. "But at least one killing was aimed at weakening the Czar. I'm certain of that."

"How is that?"

It was as though a warning sounded somewhere. He looked away across the room, then back at me. Clapping me on the back with forced gaiety, he switched back to his gutteral accent. "You bring your proof to me and I may tell you."

During the rest of the meal, I tried to make conversation though my mind was reeling with the possibilities uncovered by Borstoi's news about Katrina Sukhomlinov. What if Lupa had been summoned here and there was no plot? What if the entire city and court ran on tracks of personality, greed, jealousy, mysticism, and there was in fact no coherent political thought directing anyone's actions in any direction? Certainly, the Romanovs themselves were singularly domestic and parochial for a royal couple. It wasn't too farfetched to assume that their style had imprinted itself on the fabric of Russian life from top to bottom. After all, Nicholas had been Czar for nearly two decades.

These thoughts made me feel completely useless here, and yet I saw no other course of action but to press on. It was even possible that Nicholas would be relieved to learn that the murders had no relation to the War or to himself. Of course, the deaths of his friends would still be difficult to bear, but he could escape feeling that he was somehow to blame, that ending the War would put a stop to the deaths of his retinue.

Karel Borstoi became more and more animated as he ate and drank. I sipped one glass of wine during the lunch and let him down the rest of the bottle, after which he ordered another. He was excited about the War news, about Minsky's death, the Czar being back at the capital, the effect Rasputin was having on the populace, undermining all faith in Alexandra's judgment, and all belief in the Czar's essential goodness.

Finally, as I knew he would, he asked me about Lupa. Who was he? Why had I been with him in the kitchen? What was his relationship to Pohl?

It was easily explained, and most of it truthfully. Lupa was a special investigator assigned to the murders. I had a legitimate interest in the progress he was making. Lupa was an amateur chef and had struck up a friendship with Pohl. It was the right time to tell him—the explanation went down as easily as the wine.

The young revolutionary finished his meal and excused himself for a minute. I sat drumming my fingers on the tablecloth, anxious now to get to Lupa and impart this new information. Through the window, I could see that out in the street, the snow was again falling heavily. A waiter came and refilled my glass, and I wondered, not for the first time, how Borstoi was going to pay for this meal.

And that thought brought on other doubts about my would-be comrade. Why had he not been conscripted into the army? Did he have enough connections at court to protect him from that? Was he planning another assassination attempt on the Czar? How reliable was anything he had told me? If he didn't believe my ruse as his co-conspirator, he would be wise to feed me false information and hope it would further muddle affairs at court.

But before I'd come to any conclusions, he returned in a state of high excitement. He began babbling about the work of a friend of his, Vladimir Ilyich Ulyanov.

"You mean Lenin," I said, and could tell from his reaction that I had passed another test of sorts. He went on to say that when he published the latest paper he'd received from Switzerland, the revolution would begin at last.

I started to say something appropriate when there was a commotion in the hallway behind us. First we heard loud voices, then the sound of running feet, pots banging. The maitre d' scurried past us to the kitchen and returned almost immediately.

In the center of the room, he clapped his hands once, and when he had everyone's attention, spoke calmly. "I'm sorry to have to interrupt your meals, but I must ask that we evacuate the restaurant immediately. There is a fire."

Fortunately, no one panicked, though we were beginning to smell the smoke while we stood waiting for our coats near the front door. We got outside just as the first of the fire fighters arrived, klaxons blaring. I wanted to stay and see if I could help, but Borstoi pulled me away rather roughly. Then he began chuckling.

"What's funny? A fire could destroy half the city."

"Let it," he said. "It's the rich half anyway. Let the bastards burn!"

But I couldn't let it go at that, and I pulled away from his grip, about to go back and help.

"Giraud! The fire won't spread. It's confined."

"How can you know that?"

He grinned. "Because I started it." When I looked at him incredulously, he shrugged as if it were a small matter. "And they say there's no such thing as a free lunch. Ha!"

10

After leaving Borstoi, I wandered again through the back streets of the city. I felt I needed to get away from palaces, intrigues, and conversations and sort out my thoughts. The wind swirled snow in the doors and alleyways and every other building seemed to sport the red cross of the field hospital. I don't know whether it was because of the muting effect of the snow, or because suffering men moan more at night, but I heard none of the sounds that had haunted the streets on my first walk through them.

As I pushed through the unswept knee-high snow, I had to remind myself that it was only October. The proper winter was still months off. Seeing the hopeless resignation on the faces of women and children pressed against the frosted panes as I passed, I began to believe in my heart that the country could never survive another winter of war and defeat.

It might almost be better, I thought, if Nicholas did give up, if the murders and lack of supplies and battlefield losses convinced him that the seemingly doomed effort was not worth it. At least then the immediate suffering might be lessened.

But then I remembered the brave sons of France, England, even Italy, who were dug into trenches from Amiens to Strasbourg, of the losses they'd sustained and the suffering they'd already endured. I thought of the eight million Russian boys who had already given their lives for the Allied cause. Shall all of that have been in vain?

No, it could not be. An afternoon with the likes of Borstoi was a glimpse of an uncivilized world, and I firmly believe that our cause is no less than civilization's itself. Nicholas must not give up! His brave troops had already once saved my country—during the first weeks of the war as Germany had to shift two regiments to the Eastern Front just when it seemed they had us overrun. And now we needed them again. It was a hard truth, but undeniable. The Czar's commitment was our greatest, and only, hope. But what, I wondered, was Russia's?

My wanderings had taken me again to the river, and I stood mesmerized by the heavy gray water as it flowed through the city out to the sea. The snow fell and the wind whipped white and frozen flecks of foam onto the dirty snow-covered banks.

And I got my answer. As I leaned over a rough stone parapet, from one of the closed up houses behind me I heard what sounded like a hundred children all at once. Turning around, I saw that a school of some kind had released its charges for the day. The young boys and girls spilling from the doorway were like their counterparts everywhere— whistling, playing tag, jostling one another. Four girls, bundled in near-rags, held hands and began skipping away, singing a folk song.

And there, I realized, was Russia's hope—its children, its songs, its culture, even its bleak winter were its own, not Germany's to dominate and dictate to. There is still strength here, even in the country's great suffering. If only the Czar can remember it, I thought, turning my steps back to the Palace.

Lupa sat behind a great desk in a tapestry-shrouded room near his sleeping quarters in the Winter Palace. He hadn't come in from his own investigations until well after nine o'clock.

In the meanwhile, I had eaten dinner (cold fish again) in my own room and waited, reading Chekhov, until I'd received his summons.

There was a full pitcher of beer on the desk, and three empty glasses lined neatly along its edge. More impressive were the half dozen vases of flowers that bloomed in all colors on the desk, suffusing the room with their aromas.

"How . . . ?" I began.

"I mentioned my love of flowers to Alexandra, and she kindly has provided all I could want. They have been changed daily. Wonderful, aren't they?"

I couldn't deny it, but neither could I understand where they'd come from.

He finished his latest beer. "Oh, they arrive twice a week by train from the Crimea. Normally, they are for Tsarkoye Selo, but . . ." He shrugged.

The critical thought came unbidden, but I could not ignore it. One had to question the Romanov's priorities and sensitivity when meat and butter for their people rotted in side-tracked boxcars, while their own personal flowers arrived on schedule twice a week from halfway across a ravaged country.

But Lupa had motioned me to a chair and I could see something was on his mind as well, so I held my tongue.

"I am enraged," he said quietly. "Can I pour you a beer?"

Another glass appeared from somewhere in the desk, and he slid it over the desk to me. It was very cold and delicious.

"I don't blame you. Where did you get this?"

His shoulders moved a millimeter. "Alexandra again. It is Pohl's beer. She's had a cask sent down from Tsarkoye Selo."

In spite of myself, I laughed. "You don't do without, do you?"

"To what point?" He drank again, dismissing that subject and moving on to our real topic. "Then you know."

"Katrina?"

He nodded. "Women, Jules. I've said before that they are

of two types—foolish or dangerous. I think our Madame Sukhomlinov may be both."

I reported on my talk with Borstoi, mentioning his opinion that Minsky's murder had nothing to do with a plot to weaken the Czar. Then I added, "Borstoi thinks your friend Pohl killed Minsky," I said.

"Katrina thinks her husband did. Did Borstoi tell you that he was the second lover of hers to be killed?"

"The second?"

Lupa nodded, seemed to consider something, then went back to his beer, finishing it in a gulp. He immediately reached for the pitcher, took a fresh glass, moved the empty one into the line along the edge of the desk, and poured. "At least the second," he said. "The woman's taste is apparently," he paused, searching for the word, "catholic. Her husband, Minsky, Pohl, half of the rest of the cabinet. My God, Jules, is it possible this entire affair is over that woman's favors?"

"I considered that all afternoon," I said. "The possibility of coincidence gets a little remote, don't you think?"

He drummed his fingers on the desk. "She received me in a peignoir. Did she think I wanted . . . ?" He shook his head.

The thought amused me, and I sipped my beer to cover my smile. "Did you know about she and Pohl before? Borstoi had nothing good to say about him."

Lupa glared at me witheringly. "Consider the source."

"Yes, but even so, what he said made a great deal of sense."

He lapsed into silence, drummed his fingers more. "The woman didn't mention Max by name. As a matter of fact, she didn't even hint at any suspicion of him. Her main concerns were her husband and Minsky."

"Would the General have killed him?"

Lupa shook his head. "One fact argues strongly against it, and that is this: Minsky was not her only current lover."

"Maybe Sukhomlinov doesn't know about the others."

"I get the impression the former War Minister knows about everything."

I thought about my first meeting with the man, his comment that "one knows everything, I'm afraid." I tried to recall if there had been an undertone of real sadness in that statement, as though he knew of his wife's indiscretions. It had been nothing, I was sure, but a world-weary ex-diplomat's lament, and I told Lupa as much.

"So where does that leave us?" my friend asked.

"Well, Borstoi did say he was sure that one murder was political."

"Did he say why?"

I told Lupa that he demanded more proof of my sincerity, and then went on to describe my lunch at Cubat, the fire, and so on. When I'd finished, he merely shook his head and drank more beer, as though I'd confirmed something he'd already decided.

A hidden clock chimed somewhere, and seconds later we heard the churchbells throughout the city echoing the refrain. I looked at my watch. It was ten o'clock.

"What should we do next?" I asked. "If the motive for these killings is possession of Katrina Sukhomlinov, I may as well make my proposal to Nicholas and prepare to go home."

Lupa stared at a spot behind me for so long that I turned to see if something were there. He closed his eyes and pursed his mouth in the manner I'd come to recognize as a sign that he was deep in thought.

"No," he said at last, as if to himself. "No, I can't accept it." He sat up straighter, finishing yet another glass of beer, and pushing it to the line at the edge of his desk. Surprisingly, he did not immediately pour another. "Just because we have a possible second motive does not necessarily eliminate the first. As you say, the odds of coincidence become remote, but in fact, given Katrina's promiscuity, they are not all that

"Women, Jules," he said simply after he'd gone through his usual ritual of watching the foam settle and taking his first sip. "My father was right having nothing to do with them."

I crossed my legs, relaxing. It appeared our business for

the night was over. "Your presence here indicates he had something to do with at least one of them."

He sighed, closing his eyes. "Yes, my mother." His brow clouded.

"We needn't . . ." I began, but he stopped me.

"No, that's all right. A painful memory, that's all."

"Your home wasn't happy?"

He snorted quietly. "Home? I had no home, Jules."

I sat back in my chair. Lupa had rarely offered even a glimpse of his personal life or history to me before.

"My father and mother . . ." He stopped, sighed, went on. "My parents were both famous. Their careers kept them apart, and neither career was conducive to raising a child. Mostly I traveled with my mother—do you remember the opera star Irene Adler?"

"She was your mother?" I was shocked. Irene Adler had been a world-renowned contralto in the '80s and '90s. Almost as famous as her singing had been the scandal of her involvement with the King of Bohemia. Looking at Lupa, I wondered if he were perhaps an illegitimate prince.

"Yes, she was my mother. She deserted me when I was eight."

I tried to remember, and recalled that Irene Adler had died in a train accident around the turn of the century. I mentioned this to my friend.

"Yes, I survived that wreck."

His choice of words went a long way toward explaining Lupa's antipathy toward women. If he considered his mother's death a "desertion," there was much the young man hadn't resolved.

"And your father?"

He sighed. "The pattern had already been set. I traveled with my mother. By the time I was two, they'd separated. To this day, I don't know if they were ever married. After my mother," he paused, began again, "after the accident, I couldn't very well move in with him, though of course I visited him. In fact, I spent many summers with him. Scotland,

France, Norway. England, he said, was too dangerous for me. So I was raised by a succession of 'aunts' and 'uncles' all over the Continent."

"And you never saw your father except on these vacations?"

He waved a hand. "Don't get me wrong, Jules, I learned a lot from my father. He is a brilliant man, very analytical. But a child wouldn't have fit into his life."

In spite of Lupa's protestations of understanding, I could sense the bitterness underlying his words. "In fact I know most about my father from reading about him. I frankly believe that I was merely a responsibility for him, little else."

"And now?"

He shrugged sadly, draining his beer. "Now it doesn't seem to matter anymore."

Though it was clear to me it did.

"We've gotten out of touch since the War. I suppose he is happily raising bees in Sussex, perhaps dabbling in some monographs now and then. I don't know. It doesn't really matter."

I had to ask. "Then he is not the King of Bohemia?"

Lupa actually laughed. "Ah, the well-known scandal. No, Jules, he is not the King of Bohemia, though he is probably better known."

Another chime sounded in the still room, and suddenly the spell was broken. Lupa looked around as though unaware of where he had been, then laughed rather too loudly, as if to cover his embarrassment. He clapped his hands together.

"Well," he said. "Enough of that. How did we get on that topic? Tomorrow we see if we can make some real progress."

He stood up, signaling the end of our interview. "I think I'll have to speak to Max. By the way, Sukhomlinov may have a private stockpile of weapons. His wife hinted as much. I'll have to see him. Have you made another appointment with the Czar? He is coming into town tomorrow, you know."

I'd never heard Lupa rattle so aimlessly. Obviously the memories of his childhood had stirred up emotions which

were still difficult for him to understand or control. I held my
hand up to stop him.

"Why don't we get some sleep, my friend? It is late."

He stopped, nodded, sat down, more vulnerable than I
had ever seen him.

"It's all right that it matters," I said. "About your father, I
mean."

He looked at me, his expression blank. Then, in a hoarse
whisper: "You know, we have even worked together. He
helped me in Valence, the last time I worked with you. But
none of it is personal. He has never cared about me."

"I'm sure he does," I said, aware of how weak it sounded.
In truth, I wasn't sure of anything. "It will look better in the
morning."

He remained seated, and I said goodnight. I had just gotten to the door when he stopped me. "Jules!"

I turned. "Thank you."

With a lump in my throat, I nodded and walked into the
hallway, closing the door behind me.

11

Lupa's discussion of his background made me think of my own home, my wife Tania and daughter Michelle. In my room, I took the last letter Tania had written, which I'd received before I had even left France, and began to read the elegant script. It was full of the domestic trifles that made up our pleasant life in Valence. Michelle's teeth had started to come in (when I see her again, there will be a mouthful of them!), our own vendange had started (for next year's vin de table—and now the pressed juice was halfway to nouveau beaujolais), Tania had cut her hair. What were they both doing now? And how soon would it be until I could be with them again?

I poured myself a tumbler of vodka, not quite remembering how the bottle had come to be in my room. Taking my pen up, I resolved to write a note to Tania. But no sooner had I sat when I became suddenly drowsy—the images of Tania and Elena Ripley began crowding one another in my thoughts. A few desultory lines appeared on the page. I tried to remember Tania's face, but could only see Elena's profile in the reddish light of the alcove in the Winter Palace. Now, as I wrote, was she under the same roof as me?

I stood up, walked to the window, and looked out across the courtyard that separated the two sides of the building. Across the way, only two or three windows showed any light. I shook my head, went to my valise, and drew out the photograph of Tania I had brought with me. Staring at it, my eyes burning with fatigue, I fancied I could hear her voice and her laugh.

Somehow reassured, I poured another small tot into my glass and prepared for bed. With the photograph propped on the lamp next to me, I chuckled at my imagination. But as soon as I had extinguished the light, it began plaguing me again. I realized I hadn't finished the letter, but couldn't quite force myself to move. Sleep came and engulfed me.

I was already awake when the messenger knocked the next morning. Nicholas and Alexandra had arrived in the city for Minsky's funeral. They planned to remain at the Winter Palace for at least several days to see to some diplomatic matters, among which I was included.

When the messenger had gone, I glanced at the unfinished note to Tania with its few scrawled lines. I bunched it up and threw it away. I would write a real letter when I had the time.

I stopped by Lupa's rooms, thinking he would have a better breakfast than I had come to expect, but he had already gone out. So I had to forego eating. It didn't really bother me.

In spite of all my drinking the night before, I felt remarkably lucid. The freezing air as I walked across the half-dark courtyard further braced me for the morning, and by the time I arrived at Alyosha's study, where a servant gave me a bit of pastry and a cup of tea, the dark thoughts and doubts, even the foolish imaginings of the day and night before had passed. Thinking of my audience this afternoon with the Czar had restored my motivation and my sense of perspective.

The smiling face of Alyosha as he marched into the study further lightened my mood. In his blue sailor suit, even with the frosty bulk of Derevenko shadowing him, he was a heartwarming sight. I stood when he came in, we exchanged salutes, and then he bowed to me, clicking his heels in military fashion. His eyes shone as we sat in wing chairs for the day's chat. Without discussing it, we both knew we wouldn't be going up on the roof—the imminent arrival of the Czar had charged the atmosphere.

"Dum vivo vivebo," he said to me as soon as he'd dismissed his bodyguard. "And today I begin. I have an appointment with my father before the funeral."

"And I see him this afternoon."

He cocked his head questioningly. "What are you seeing him for?" he asked. "Something to do with me?"

I realized I hadn't told the boy anything of my real purpose here, and I briefly outlined it. Instinctively, I felt he would be sympathetic to my cause.

He cocked his head sideways as he listened to my explanation, a smile playing at the corners of his mouth. "I should have known you were not a mere tutor. Have you been poisoning me with Republican ideas in these sessions? All without my knowledge."

"No doubt yes to the first part. As to doing it without your knowledge, one would be hard pressed, I think, to accomplish that."

He looked pleased yet embarrassed at the compliment. Then suddenly he grew serious again. "I did make it a point to find out who you were," he confessed. "And I never sensed that you have tried to manipulate me."

"I never have," I answered truthfully.

"We said that if I could come to trust you, you could become my most valuable ally."

"That's true."

"I think I have almost done that. Will you keep telling me the truth, even if it is hard?"

"Of course."

He reached out his hand. "As gentlemen, let us shake hands on that."

We did so.

It might have been easy in other circumstances to laugh at the boy, but this was no pose, and there was nothing funny or unseemly about it. Here was a young man struggling with the duties and forging the kinds of alliances that would consume his life as an adult.

"And now," he said, "can I say anything to my father that will help you?"

I shook my head. "I don't think so. It's your first formal meeting with him, isn't it?"

He nodded.

"Well, then, I think you'd do well to remember what we talked about yesterday, about his personal life interfering with his public one. Frankly, that will play into my hands, but I don't want to push him."

"Why not? Don't you believe in your mission?"

"Yes. I believe in it, but pushing too hard might drive your father in the other direction. Better to let him come to the decision in his own time—then he'll be more committed to it, and that, in this case, is essential."

He sat still a moment, rubbing his chin thoughtfully. "Well," he announced, "I will say my piece, and we will see if it has an effect."

He stood up and walked to the window, his small hands clasped behind his back. "Monsieur Giraud?" he said, without turning around.

"Oui?"

He turned and faced me. "I don't think I understand war. I know my father hates it. He tells me that Uncle Willie—Kaiser Wilhelm—likes it. I don't understand it. It's not even really fighting for what you believe in. The fighting becomes an end in itself. Isn't that true?"

"Sometimes it seems like that."

"So who is right?"

I looked at the innocent and open young face, asking me the question of the ages. "Maybe that's something you should ask your father," I said. "It's a question he ought to consider."

Elena was praying in the alcove.

I walked down the aisle and knelt in the pew behind her,

and finally touched her shoulder with an outstretched finger. She jumped at the pressure, twisted her head, and then smiled to see me. Half turned, she sat back on the bench.

"You're still here, I see," I said, then added, "I'm glad."

The smile became shy, then faded altogether. "But Tati hasn't seen me yet, and today the Czarina meets with her daughters."

I patted her arm, which rested along the back of the bench. "Don't worry. She's not going to turn you out."

"I wish I could be so sure."

"You can be sure. I talked to Alexis this morning, and he said his sister was just sulking, that's all."

"He really did? He said that?"

"And if that's not enough," I continued, wanting to impress her, "I'll mention it to the Czar when I meet with him this afternoon."

Her eyes widened, flecks of pure gold in the green irises. "You're seeing the Czar today?"

I told her about the summons and my worries over the outcome of the meeting. Immediately, she seemed to forget her own troubles, and directed all of her concern to me. "Oh, Jules, you must go then and prepare. Don't waste any more time with my foolish worries."

"Time with you is never wasted, your worries are not foolish, and there is nothing more to prepare." Even in the dim light, I could see the slight flush to her cheeks. I realized I might scare her away with my tendency to excessive gallantry, so I continued speaking in a more neutral vein. "It is all a question of how he's taken Minsky's death."

"Yes," she whispered. "Yes, that was terrible. But how does that affect you?"

I told her, though it was clear to me that the nuances of politics were unimportant to her. Nevertheless, she listened politely, and questioned me when I'd finished. "If only these murders would stop, then, it would help you, wouldn't it?"

"Theoretically it would help my mission, yes. Or at least we're working on that assumption."

"We?"

I saw no harm in mentioning my connection to Lupa and his investigation. Its goal was intimately connected to my diplomatic role.

"But Jules," she said, her hand coming to rest over my own. "That means you are coming into contact with suspected killers. Oh, please be careful. I didn't know..."

I patted her hand. "Now, now. It's not all that dangerous." I told her about my "free" lunch with Borstoi, about Lupa's interview with Katrina in a negligée.

"But they may not be the guilty ones."

I shrugged, making light of the whole thing. "I'm not doing much anyway," I said. "It's mostly my friend Auguste Lupa. There's no danger."

"I wish I believed you."

I was touched by her concern, but there was really nothing to be done. The investigation with Lupa was part of my job, and if it became dangerous, then so be it. I stood up and asked her if she'd like to accompany me as far as the courtyard. Though I wouldn't be attending Minsky's funeral, I felt that I could serve both diplomacy and statecraft by paying a call on Paleologue before my audience with the Czar.

As we walked the length of the corridor, Elena and I talked of my hopes for my mission. If the Czar accepted our offer today, then it was finished.

"But will you stay on," she asked, and I don't flatter myself to have read the hope in her eyes, "at least to continue helping your friend Lupa?" she added.

I stopped and took her hand. "Elena," I said softly. "I would probably go directly home to my wife and child. Lupa is committed to finding the killer, but I am only interested insofar as it concerns the Czar's plans for continuing the War. If he commits to that, I will be going."

She looked down, her eyes unable to meet mine. "I understand," she said, and she squeezed my hand.

Then she pulled herself upright and forced a brave smile. "Then let me, if you will, give you a kiss for luck in your meeting today. Whatever will make you happiest, that's what I want for you."

I told myself it was a harmless gesture, and I leaned over for *une petite béquetée*. Elena came up on her tiptoes, put her arm around my neck, and the peck turned into a true kiss. When we separated, I found myself trembling, holding the beautiful young woman still tightly in my arms.

Her eyes had opened wide. I could feel her heart pounding strongly through the thin fabric of her blouse. A flush had risen in her cheeks, and a startled but pleasurable smile flickered at her lips.

Quickly she hugged herself against me, then lightly brushed my cheek in another kiss—this one as the first should have been. "For luck," she whispered breathlessly.

And then somehow I had let her go and she was half-running, half-skipping back down the corridor without a look back while I leaned against the wall, recovering my composure, the touch of her lips still fresh in my mind, aware that I was—I am—courting not just a woman, but disaster.

Paleologue's words were not heartening, although in the state I found myself, nothing more than an armistice or Lupa revealing the murderer could have buoyed my spirits.

Grand Duke Nicholas, Anastasia's husband and the Czar's cousin, was experiencing setbacks in the campaign in Galacia, which heretofore had been the only bright spot in the Russian war effort. Maurice wasn't sure if the Czar had received that intelligence yet—he himself had only found out from a "leak" in the British staff at the shared embassies. The Ambassador was of the opinion that more bad news of the war would only dispose the Emperor further toward a separate peace. Therefore, it was essential that I make as strong a case as I could today.

I countered with the argument we had earlier adopted, that if we pushed too hard we might lose the match, but Paleologue, after first saying it was of course my decision to make, strongly felt that the risk was worth taking.

I took a carriage from Embassy Row back to the Palace, my thoughts a tangled skein of motivations, impressions, and doubts both personal and professional. Why had Lupa ever picked me for this mission? And why would a brilliant man like Foch go along with that choice? I was old, ineffectual, seemingly unable to control either my emotions or my actions.

Paleologue had offered me lunch at the Embassy, but upon learning that it was "English" day, and remembering the quality of the food prepared in the embassy kitchen, I declined. Thus, by the time I came back to my room to dress formally for my audience, I was famished.

But fate decreed that I should miss lunch as well as breakfast. As a manservant and I struggled with cummerbund and cuffs, I reminded myself of the men at the front who were suffering, starving, dying of wounds, and I chided myself for my softness. Many men fasted before strenuous mental tests, and though Lupa might never approve, I resolved to use the unaccustomed discomfort to test my own mettle.

The antechamber to the courtroom in the Winter Palace was a small, book-lined study. I arrived a half-hour early for my appointment and the secretary—a tall, black American who introduced himself as John Tucker Wilson—escorted me into the room and offered me tea, which I accepted. I must have stared overlong at him, for he volunteered the information that if he looked somewhat familiar to me it was because I had seen him before at Tsarskoye Selo, as one of the "Ethiopian guards."

Here, dressed impeccably in a suit of British cut, he presented an entirely different figure, and I wondered if that formality would extend to the Czar in our interview. If so, it would be a far cry from our earlier, intimate meeting in the mauve bedchamber. The question bore forethought, and Wilson was sensitive enough to leave me alone with my tea to ponder it.

Some time passed. I heard raised voices from behind the

closed door, and I wondered who could be in there that would have the effrontery to shout at the Czar of Russia?

Five minutes later I found out as Ivan Kapov, the royal cousin, came through the door to the Czar's office in full military dress.

His handsome young face had high color. In fact, his entire bearing showed signs of excitement—eyes shining, steps light, chest puffed out.

I stood upon his entry and he stopped to look at me as I bowed.

"Ah, Monsieur... it's Giraud, *n'est-ce pas?* How are you today? Seeing Nicky, are you?"

Before I could answer, John Tucker Wilson had joined us. "It will be a few more minutes, Monsieur. His Majesty prefers a hiatus between appointments." He nodded to Kapov. "A successful meeting, your Highness?"

"Very, very, very." A controlled yet strong smiled showed off a gleaming set of teeth. Kapov really was quite a handsome young fellow. The smooth brow furrowed slightly. "Though of course he wouldn't give a definitive answer until he'd thought more about it. But that's just Nicky's way. I think this poor fellow's death has just about done him in."

Suddenly I remembered Kapov's politics from the night of Anastasia's party. I couldn't help but interrupt.

"You mean Minsky?"

"Is that the fellow's name? Yes, I think so."

"Excuse me, but may I ask what you've just seen the Czar about?"

The secretary began to protest, but Kapov stopped him. "No, it's quite all right in this case." I got the impression that he also suddenly remembered my politics from the other night. His blue-green eyes flashed gray-green, the shade and temperature of the Baltic in winter. It was the briefest look, but it convinced me that this man was no mere royal playboy. His every pore breathed a commitment that, in the quiet formality of the drawing room, seemed to verge on the fanatical.

"I'm afraid, sir," he began, his sarcasm thinly veiled, "that your own interview might bear upon the same issues with different results. Dear old Nicky has completely lost his heart for this war. He believes that someone is killing his friends to make him stop fighting. Since he can't seem to win on the battlefield, he sees his only chance to save lives—real lives of people he cares about—is to give up. He's terrified his family might be next. I shouldn't be surprised if he wires Willy tonight suing for peace."

"But it's absurd," I said. "The War isn't a personal matter at all."

Kapov smiled condescendingly. "Be that as it may, someone has made our Emperor feel like it is, and I applaud them."

"Them?" I asked, jumping on the word.

Was it guilt, suspicion, or mere annoyance I read in his eyes. Whatever it was, he dismissed it. "A figure of speech. I applaud the action."

"And what of the victims?"

He shrugged. "There are always victims in a war."

"Even an innocent man like Minsky?" I knew he was right, but his attitude frustrated and angered me.

His pretty face set in an arrogant mask. "My dear Giraud," he said, "if it would shorten this war by a single day, I myself would kill a hundred Minskys." He paused for his words to sink in. "And then," he sneered, "then I would dance on their graves."

Upon meeting Nicholas for the second time, sitting behind his desk with the mildest of expressions, I realized how much I had let his position impress itself on me. The man had receded behind his office. Now, as I faced him, I was struck anew by his calm, good-natured demeanor, the slightly bemused look he wore, his air of quiet respectability.

I presented my compliments and he asked me to sit, which I did on one of the stiff chairs in front of his desk. After having put the moment off for so long, I felt a great relief to finally be in a position to present my offer, and I came straight to the point.

"Your Majesty," I began, "as you know, both of our countries are struggling to bring this War to a successful conclusion. No one knows more than yourself how bravely your troops have fought, and what price of blood they have already paid. And still the War continues stalemated on both the Eastern and Western Fronts.

"We look back gratefully to your help in the early months of the War, when your loyalty to our alliance, though it meant great suffering for your own country, allowed France to survive.

"I know that your troops are low on weapons and even ammunition. You have lost ground in the North, and are barely holding your positions in Galacia. There are rumors that you may seek a separate peace."

I stopped, watching him carefully, but his face showed nothing more than a wistful interest. "Could you blame me?" he asked mildly, as though my answer truly interested him.

"I don't think the Kaiser's terms would be particularly generous."

He smiled coldly. "No, not if I know my cousin Willy. But what is your alternative, Giraud, a noble annihilation of all my country's manhood?"

"I have been sent to assure you that the fight is still worth it, that victory is still possible, and that France is committed to her alliance with you."

He nodded. "That is very heartening," he said with thin irony.

But I pressed on. "Specifically, your Majesty, I am authorized to present to you an offer of one hundred thousand rifles with bayonets, an equal number of grenades, two hundred fifty heavy guns, five million rounds of ammunition, and whatever other ordnance and supplies you might need to keep your armies in the field until August 1st of next year."

"Next year," he said softly, looking down at his crossed hands, "August of next year." He shook his head. "And what will happen then?"

"There is a chance America will enter the War. The balance of power may shift. It is a hope. It is not defeat."

"No," he repeated. "No, it is not defeat." His eyes met mine. "The offer is generous, Giraud."

He said no more. I waited silently while he took a cigarette from an ornately-carved box on his desk. For nearly two minutes that seemed like an hour, we sat across from one another, the Czar smoking calmly.

Finally he sighed and smiled at me almost apologetically. "You have made quite an impression on my son," he said.

It was an unexpected tangent that nearly caught me off guard. What about the offer? But he had changed the topic, and he was the Czar. There was nothing to do but respond. "He is an extraordinary young man. I like him very much."

He nodded. "It is hard to know where to draw the line between protecting him and teaching him. Hard for me and my wife, I mean."

"I think all parents face that dilemma," I said.

"Yes," he agreed in an abstracted way, "yes, but in his case, with his illness, it is, pardon me, doubly so."

No response seemed appropriate, so I sat and waited while the Czar fumbled with a paperweight and other bric-a-brac on his desk.

"The point is, I suppose, that we should read the signs. For a long while, he was just a boy. And now, so suddenly, he isn't... or isn't quite the same." He laughed in his self-deprecating way. "He let me know rather strongly this morning that he was ready to... to begin his active training."

"It's strange," he continued, musing, "he is so different than I am. When I was his age, I only thought of playing. I thought my father would live forever and somehow, eventually, I would get the training I needed to become Czar. My father seemed to think the same thing—he never appointed me to any government posts or gave me any responsibility, and that all seemed perfectly natural.

"But then he died, and I was Czar." Lost in his thoughts, he stopped speaking for a moment, then pushed himself back from his desk. "Let's have some tea," he said. "Do you mind?"

We walked to the ubiquitous samovar in the corner of the room and he filled two translucent porcelain cups with strong, nearly black tea, then he motioned to a couple of comfortable chairs on either side of a small table, and we retired to them.

"The desk," he said, "is the enemy of communication."

I took that heartily, as a sign that his decision hadn't yet been made. It gave a boost to my patience.

"My wife isn't for it," he said, rather enigmatically.

"What is that, your Majesty?"

"Alyosha. She doesn't think he's old enough. Though of course, she didn't talk with him this morning. He seemed quite mature and determined to me. Said I was confusing my duties as Czar with my personal feelings." He smiled again, but there was flint in it. "Why do I suppose you have some influence there, M. Giraud? Is that what you think? I would not like to think you are criticizing my handling of my office to my son."

I took a sip of the tea to stall for time. This was unexpected, though upon reflection I now realize that it might have been foreseen.

"Alexis is astute enough to ask his own questions, your Majesty. He asked them of me, and I told him to bring it up with you. As far as I recall, I ventured no opinion on the topic."

Those mild eyes stared at me from an expressionless face. Perhaps stalling for time himself, he sipped his tea. "I believe you. It's natural that the boy should grow up. I'm proud that he's showing such concern. But my wife, the Empress, doesn't like it." He gestured helplessly. "She is . . . over-

sensitive, I believe, regarding criticism. When I told her
about Alexis' questions..." He hesitated. "Well, at first she
was all right, just surprised as I had been. Then, after lunch
—we had Rasputin to lunch, he presided over the service for
Boris—after lunch, she was suspicious of you. She cannot
abide disloyalty."

"Forgive me, sir, but with all due respect I am not your
subject."

"But as Alyosha's tutor...?"

"I would never abuse the trust you placed in me, your
Majesty. Or your wife's." I leaned back in the chair, in a
relaxed pose, my teacup perched on my knee. "If you'll allow
me to say so, I think Alyosha has been waiting for an opportunity to speak his mind. He has been trying out some ideas
on me—ideas that I think you'd approve of, even be proud
of.

"It may be that his physical breakouts of the past, eluding
Derevenko and riding runaway horses, for example, were
merely manifestations of the same impetus. He's his own
person, maybe a little headstrong, but I think this avenue of
expression is a safer one, all in all, than a physical one."

Nicholas lit a cigarette and considered what I'd said. Finally, exhaling with what appeared to be a sigh of relief, he
gave me a really wonderful smile. "I will pass your thoughts
along to the Empress. I am convinced and delighted by your
answer."

The Czar stood up and walked to the window, drumming
his fingers on the sill. According to Paleologue, John Tucker
Wilson, my briefings, and every etiquette book I had read
regarding audiences with Nicholas, there was unanimity on
one thing—when Nicholas went to the window and began
drumming, it signalled the end of the interview.

But I could not leave. I hadn't come to discuss either my
loyalty or his son.

I put my cup on the table with a small clatter. No doubt
Nicholas expected next to hear the door closing as I made my
way out. Instead, I went to the center of the room, went to

one knee and remained so, and spoke: "If your Majesty will excuse me?"

It startled him—he spun around and faced me, a scowl darkening his countenance.

"I know I have taken too much of your time, and I must beg your Majesty's forgiveness for my presumption, but we've spoken frankly up until now, and my duty compels me to request another few minutes."

To my surprise and relief, his frown gave way to a bemused smile. "You're an original, Giraud, I grant you that." He stepped away from the window, his hands fluttering like birds before him. "Come, come, please rise. Don't be ridiculous."

I stood. We are almost exactly the same height, and our eyes met and held. He was no fool—there was no question as to why I had stayed or what we would have to discuss. And there was no more denial of the hurts we would have to expose to come to an understanding.

For a terrible moment, I saw in his eyes all the anguish of his position, the responsibility and the fatigue. But that reality was as a palimpsest behind which those eyes limned the enormity of his personal loss.

I cast diplomacy aside. "Sometimes it must seem almost too much to bear," I said quietly.

The man's shoulders sagged. "Most of the time," he began, even more softly, "I am able to put aside these, uh, personal matters." He turned his back to me. "I understand what my son was saying. He was right. But I feel I am at the mercy of events that I can no longer even pretend to control." Again he faced me. "My judgment is affected, Giraud. I can't seem to do anything about it. Aside from my wife, Boris was my closest friend, and many of the things we discussed I couldn't even say to the Empress—man things, jokes, you understand?"

I nodded.

"It didn't take the pressure off—nothing can do that, I suppose—but it was a relief, a tie to normal life." He paused, sighing again. "Perhaps my last. Come, let's sit down."

We went back to the chairs, and I waited while he went through the ritual of lighting another cigarette. Finally, resting his elbows on his knees, he hung his head and continued. "I just don't feel I can take this anymore. I wasn't born for this, like my father, or even like my son. I am a ruler by circumstance only. If they next attack my family, I . . ." He paused. "I couldn't stand it, Giraud. I can't put them to that risk."

So we have lost, I thought.

I felt for the man, but my job was to influence the king. Fleetingly, I wished Paleologue, or Foch, or Grand Duke Nicholas, or even Lupa were here with their strengths, their personalities, their powers of persuasion. But they weren't. It was up to me, and I had no answers, only a redundant empathy and, hopefully still, a soldier's heart.

I could argue the niceties of treaties and alliances, of commitments, promises and common goals, but it would all be wasted. There was no logic left—only feeling.

"I have a family, too," I said. "A wife and a daughter. My wife has already lost her first husband and two sons on the battlefield."

The monarch raised his eyes to mine. "I'm sorry."

I shrugged. "*C'est la guerre*. I would only ask you, as a man, to wait, if you can, just a little longer. Perhaps the murderers can be caught. If you don't, sir, you are not only surrendering Russia to the Kaiser, you are dooming France . . ." I paused, ". . . and my own family."

He gazed at me, levelly and soberly, for several seconds. Then he stood and for the second time went to the window. After a minute, he began drumming his fingers on the sill, and this time, since there was nothing left to say, I bowed to his back, and tiptoed from the room.

12

John Tucker Wilson handed me a note as I exited the Czar's room. It was from Lupa, who had just finished his own interview with Alexandra.

I didn't know what Nicholas would do, whether or not he would sue for peace and so end the War on the Eastern Front within hours. I felt I had failed—and if I had, even Lupa's investigation would be more or less meaningless. In any event, he ought to be aware of the situation. Time was indeed short.

As I hurried toward my meeting with Lupa, I heard the unmistakable sounds of another riot outside. Perhaps word had gotten out that Nicholas and Alexandra were in the Palace. Maybe it was just another outburst over no bread or the cold or another defeat had been announced.

Whatever its cause, the riot could not help but add to the Czar's worries. He would hear it and see it from his window. Would it stiffen his back, I wondered, or break him down further?

In either case, I had to get to Lupa. If there was any hope left at all, I believed it lay with my friend's solution to these killings, if he had one. It is all very nice to have suspects, I mused, but at some point the list must begin to narrow. How close, I wondered, was Lupa to that point?

I burst into his office to see him sitting behind his desk,

surrounded by flowers, reading and drinking beer! He
looked up as soon as the door had opened, and had put the
book down by the time I got to his desk.

"Jules," he said, "satisfactory."

"No it is not," I exploded, venting my pique. "It is not
satisfactory at all. You sitting here reading and drinking as
though you're on holiday, while the War is coming to an end.
I've just seen Nicholas and he's going to capitulate unless you
come up with a suspect in these killings. He may have already done it. What are we going to do?"

The young man glared at me briefly, then grunted in annoyance. "Sit down, Jules, calm yourself. Have a beer."

"I don't want a beer. We have to . . ."

He held up a hand. "Please."

I sat down, waiting.

He finished his glass, pushed it to the side of the desk—it
was the first one there—then took out a clean glass and
poured from the pitcher. After the foam had settled properly,
he took another sip, smacked his lips, and addressed me.
"While I understand your frustration with this, I have done
quite a bit today and I resent your implication that I have
somehow been remiss. Alexandra and I have just had a very
successful meeting, in which she has given me power of subpoena, and now I am awaiting the arrival of our friend General Sukhomlinov."

"But Auguste, time is running out."

His nostrils flared as he slammed his palm flat against the
desk. "Don't you think I know that? What am I supposed to
do? Pull a murderer out of a hat?"

"It might help," I said evenly. "We have to do something."
I went on to tell him about my meeting with Kapov and his
comment about "killing a hundred Minskys," and then the
audience with Nicholas.

He listened quietly, eyes closed, nodding from time to
time. When I finished, he drank more beer and then talked.
"Alexandra led me to believe it wasn't so bad, that she

thought he could hold out for another few weeks—that is, unless there's another murder."

I shook my head. "I don't know. He seemed close to the end to me."

The big man sighed. "Well, if that's the case, Jules, there isn't much we can do. We can only hope that you had some influence on him. And remember, you saw him immediately after Kapov, and Nicholas might still have been reacting to some of his cousin's arguments when you came in."

I had to admit a kernel of truth in that statement.

"In any event," Lupa continued, "we should, I agree, move with haste. Maybe even create a suspect out of whole cloth. It's an idea. But right now," he went on, "I've asked you to be here in more or less an official capacity. Sukhomlinov will be arriving shortly, and I'd like you to take notes behind that tapestry." He pointed to a painted screen that hung over the back half of the room. "I don't want him to know we're working together, but I need an official witness to the proceedings."

At my questioning glance, he explained. "I think the General is capable of casting his own nets in these waters. He is going to want me out of the way—I am, in his view, personally harassing him, and my success here would threaten his separate peace. Ergo, I predict he will launch a campaign of his own to discredit me—perhaps even kill me."

"Do you think he killed Minsky?"

Lupa shrugged and finished the second beer. "I expect to have a better idea within an hour."

Lupa: I have sent for you, General, to ask you some questions relating to the death of Boris Minsky.

Sukhomlinov: Are you accusing me of that murder?

L: No. Not at this time, though it is my understanding that you were not unhappy to see him dead.

S: That is not a crime.

L: So you admit that that's true?

S: And I repeat that it's no crime. The man played at being a soldier, and he filled the Czar's ear with nonsense.

L: And for that he deserved to die?

(No response.)

L: You were at Tsarkoye Selo the night he was killed, were you not?

S: This is absurd, Lupa. I was at the Czar's dinner as everyone knows, with my wife.

L: And afterwards?

S: Afterwards we went to our quarters there.

L: Both of you? Together?

S: Yes, of course.

L: That's odd. I spoke to your wife yesterday, and she said you quarreled, after which you went out alone. What did you quarrel about?

S: I don't remember if we quarreled at all.

L: Wasn't it about Minsky?

S: What about him?

L: (long pause) We'll leave that, General. But you did take a walk?

S: I don't remember. What if I did?

L: If you did, I would ask if you saw Minsky, but since you don't remember...

S: You seem to be implying two different things: that I wanted Boris out of the way for political reasons, and because some issue of honor might also have been involved.

L: That's correct. Two very good and different motives.

S: It's ridiculous. If it were an affair of honor, I would have challenged him to a duel. Politically, there are more important men than Minsky. Who was he? A fly in the Czar's ear. There was no reason to kill him on that score.

L: There is a theory, General, that these murders—and this is the fourth, remember—serve a political end. Have you heard about that?

S: You mean to weaken the Czar's will? It's the silliest idea I've ever heard.

L: Still, these murders began just after your trial for espionage three months ago...

S: Where I was acquitted.

L: Yes, you were. Your timing, from the point of view of my investigation, was unfortunate. And the trial didn't seem to have any adverse effect on your friends, your views, did it?

S: Which views are you referring to?

L: The ones which led to your arrest in the first place— you never seem to have a dinner or social engagement without a suspect agent of the Kaiser in attendance.

S: Many of those men were my friends before the war.

L: And you see no reason to treat them differently now?

S: No. They are not spies. They are writers and businessmen.

L: I can only wonder what legitimate business they might now have in Russia. (Pause.) All right. Now, as to your arsenal...

S: Don't you think that was covered well enough at the trial?

L: Nevertheless, I find it provocative. According to this report, you admit to having over one thousand grenades, four hundred rifles, and at least fifteen thousand rounds of ammunition. As you were Minister of War, I can imagine how you got them, but what use can they be for you now?

S: I came by them legally, and they are for my protection.

L: Legality is an interesting concept, and perhaps even technically accurate. One is led to wonder, though, why the army has such incredible shortages, while your own larder is so well-stocked.

(Pause.) Confound it, sir! Don't you realize that you are the only source of grenades in this city? And the first murders were done by grenade? Have you no answer to that?

S: No. None. It is the least of my concerns.

L: If I find any other connection, I can and will have you arrested.

S: (Laughs.) Then I would be well advised to get you out of the way, wouldn't I? Good day, sir. This meeting is over.

* * *

"Could he do it?" I asked when he'd left. "What did he mean, 'get you out of the way'?"

Lupa, with a look of disgust, fiddled with some papers on his desk. "That was an interesting choice of words," he said. "He is used to having his enemies arrested. That would get me out of the way. Or, if he is our killer, that approach would also work."

"I loathe the man."

His fingers drummed. "Yes, I share that feeling. But what did you think of the interview?"

"I think it got us nowhere."

"Not exactly. It got us somewhere. We can probably eliminate the General. It is almost too obvious. He had two motives, means were no problem, and there was all the opportunity in the world. The man may be venal, but his stupidity would have to be colossal to act so unconcerned with so many facts pointing in his direction, and he is not stupid. He wears his villainy on his sleeve, but I'm not sure I believe he's a murderer."

"And where does that leave us?"

Lupa leaned back in his chair, closing his eyes. For a moment, he was so still I had the impression that he'd dozed off. His only movement was the regular pursing of his lips. So he was thinking.

"Tell me about Elena Ripley," he said at last.

It was an unexpected sally and it must have shown in my reaction. "Come, Jules," Lupa said in response, "she is the last person to have been seen with Minsky. The propinquity alone is potentially damning."

"You're grasping at straws," I said defensively. "Elena knows nothing about all this."

"You've talked to her about it, then?"

"Obliquely."

He leaned forward, concern now written clearly across his features. "And I take it," he said quietly, "that she knows of our alliance?"

"I may have mentioned something about it."

Again he leaned back. Again the eyes closed and the mouth moved. Finally he grunted and settled himself back at the desk. Almost to himself, he said, "Well, it is done. Some good may even come of it."

I thought of his new power of subpoena. "Are you going to be speaking with her?"

He shook his head. "There's no need so long as you are not befuddled."

I assured him I was not, and promised that I would not keep from him anything she told me that might be pertinent to our investigations.

"Anything at all, Jules, please. Pertinent or no. Something could be hidden in the most seemingly casual remark. All right?"

Feeling he was being peevish, and thoroughly disenchanted with the topic, I agreed, though I wasn't sure at the time, nor am I now, whether I intend to or not.

My spirits low, I wandered the corridors of the Palace. It was late evening and might as well have been the dead of night.

After leaving Lupa, I went over to the children's chambers, intending to pass some time with Alyosha, only to find that the royal children were dining with their parents. I thought I would pay a call on Elena, but she, too, had gone out.

Since I'd heard no news of a treaty with Germany, I still entertained hopes that all was not lost, but Lupa's puerile insistence on suspecting Elena and his lack of success with Sukhomlinov, which he had called a triumph of sorts, had sapped my confidence in him and his abilities.

At the end of our meeting, he'd suggested I go see Borstoi again and finally get to the bottom of the "damage" he'd supposedly wrought, but I explained that without proof of my commitment to his cause, my credibility with him would be next to nil. With his characteristic bravado, he assured me that I could plan on seeing the young firebrand tomorrow, and I'd have the proof I needed. He'd see to that. Without the heart or even the curiosity to question him further, I walked from his office.

I don't know what I was thinking or where I was going. Suddenly I could no longer stand the confines of the Palace. Hunger gnawed at me but somehow the thought of food made me nauseous.

Out on the street, the low clouds were visible in the dark sky. The wind had died down, but the cold's grip on the city was still firm. Barricades testified to the earlier riot—which I'd all but forgotten—and their jagged and crossed angles gave a spectral cast to the night's shadows.

My steps, unbidden, took me where they would. The capital was deserted, bundled up, quiet. Occasionally a yellow streetlamp crossed swords with the gloom—always it was a losing battle.

And then, almost inaudibly, I heard the strains of music. It was somehow familiar, though unrestrained and wild, as though melody and meter had given way to noise and frenzy. Looking up, I realized I had wandered to Gorokhavaya Street. The music was coming from the far end of the block, from the window of a brightly lighted room three flights up. As I came closer, I noticed that automobiles lined the curbs. The music grew louder, more discordant—gypsy guitars and tambourines and voices out of key.

I was still halfway down the street when my heart stopped. A hooded figure stepped gracefully from one of the cars and made for the entrance to the apartment. When she half-turned and looked in my direction, I couldn't help but call out.

"Elena!"

But it could not have been her. The face was in shadow, and she showed no hint of recognition of the name, vanishing immediately into the blackness of the stairway.

I came abreast of the building. From my angle, I could only see shadows cast upon the ceiling of Rasputin's flat.

Watching the satyr-like figures dancing in strange contortions, my head swam with all sorts of grotesque visions.

Suddenly the music stopped, the window was thrown open. Rasputin, naked at least to the waist, thrust his black-bearded face into the teeth of the cold. Laughing hysterically, obscenely, he shouted out over the rooftops, and though the words had no meaning to me, in them and the accompanying laughter I heard the thin-edged sound of unmistakable madness, accompanied with what I can only describe as a howl not of insanity but, unaccountably, of triumph.

13

Lupa was at the door to my chambers before dawn, our differences of the day before forgotten. Still in my robe, I admitted him, and he helped himself to my breakfast of tea, cakes and eggs while I made my toilet.

When I returned and poured myself some tea, he commented that I looked tired, and I explained that I hadn't been able to sleep very well. My walk, with its unsettling vision of Rasputin, had depressed me, and I had continued wandering around the deserted and despairing city until well after midnight. Finally retiring, I had lain awake trying to devise a stratagem that would convince Borstoi of my sincerity.

Lupa tut-tutted me, a smile playing at his lips. "I told you not to worry about that, that I would take care of it." To say Auguste Lupa looks smug is more or less an exercise in redundancy, but clearly he was quite proud of himself.

Reaching into his coat pocket, he extracted a rectangular black leather box, about the size of his hand, with a monogrammed "F" tooled into its cover.

"What is that?" I asked.

"Your proof."

He passed it to me and I opened it to one of the great shocks of my life. Nestled in peacock blue velvet was one of the fabulous Fabergé eggs!

"My God!"

"Yes," he agreed. "It is quite a piece of work."

I could do nothing but stare at it. It was at once precious, fragile, and breathtaking, its value inestimable.

I had come across references to these eggs in my briefing notes. The tradition had started in 1884 when Czar Alexander III presented his wife, Marie, Nicholas' mother, with one of them for Easter, the greatest Russian holiday. Nicholas, when he became Czar, had continued the tradition, every Easter presenting one specially-designed egg to the Czarina and another to the Queen Mother.

There are only fifty-six Fabergé eggs in the world! Though I hadn't seen any others, descriptions of them beggared the imagination. Each of them opened to what Fabergé called a "surprise"—gem-encrusted vistas or scenes from Russian folklore and history.

One of the most celebrated eggs was the Great Trans-Siberian Railway Easter Egg, which Nicholas had commissioned for the birth of the then-new century. Its "surprise" was a working model of the Trans-Siberian Railroad, constructed of enamel, diamonds, rubies, pearls, and gold.

The egg I now held in my hand, though much smaller, was no less impressive. The blue-white porcelain seemed more fragile than any real egg. Etched into the top were two Imperial eagles in gold and gold leaf. Twin large, perfect diamonds braced each side at the widest point.

"Squeeze the diamonds," Lupa said.

I did so, and the egg opened to reveal its "surprise." I had wondered at the name of the piece, "L'Aube," which was inscribed in the finest filigreed gold on the inside of the box. When I opened it, however, I saw that the surprise captured the dawn sky to perfection.

Inside the egg, set into its lower concavity, was a scale-model of a typical Russian pastoral scene. Little diamond dewdrops flecked a field of emeralds in the foreground. A ruby sun rose on the upper half of the egg, whose background was a lighter shade of the same peacock blue as the velvet lining the box, brushed with what had to be gold and ruby dust. On the right, the sun cast its golden rays over the shimmering onion-shaped dome of an Orthodox church. The dome was the centerpiece—a flawless yellow topaz the size of a quail egg. On the left, a sapphire river coursed through a meadow in full flower. All this, and the thing was only the width of my hand!

I finally tore my eyes away and looked at Lupa in disbelief. "How did you get this?"

He leaned back sipping his tea. "I asked for it and the Czarina gave it to me."

"Oh, of course," I said. "In that case, why didn't you just ask for two?"

"Jules, don't be angry again."

"I'm not angry. I'm amazed and a little nervous. Mere possession of this thing without permission . . ."

". . . would undoubtedly be a capital offense. But there is nothing to worry about. We have permission."

"And you want me to give this to Borstoi? Alexandra gave her permission for that?"

He paused. His fingers began to drum methodically on my writing table. "Not exactly. I presume she would want it back."

"And so what, exactly, am I supposed to do with it?"

"That, I'm afraid, Jules," he said, sighing, "is up to your own discretion. I left my proposed use of it rather vague."

"But to be valuable to us, as proof for Borstoi, I have to use this some way?"

"You'll probably have to give it to him. We may have to steal it back."

I rested the closed box containing the egg on the table. "This is getting dangerous," I said evenly.

He shrugged. "It was dangerous to begin with. And now, as you pointed out yesterday, time is running out. We have to make something happen."

"And you think Borstoi..."

"...is a good place to start. We know he has tried to kill Nicholas, and he admits succeeding at some other damage already. I need to know what that was."

I agreed. Dangerous or not, if this was the route to progress, it had to be taken.

"By the way, Jules. I had an interesting ally when I met with Alexandra after you left me yesterday."

"Oh?" I said, again taking the box into my hands and looking at it. The thing would probably buy my entire estate in France. "Who was that?"

"Rasputin."

I almost dropped the egg. "That's impossible!" I said. "I saw him at his apartment last night."

"You visited him?"

"No. I saw him. There was some sort of party and I passed under his window."

Lupa shook his head. "Well, I assure you, he was with Alexandra and me in her room not twenty minutes after you left me."

I thought about it, and there had been time. He could have left the Palace after meeting with Lupa and the Czarina and easily made it back to his flat, especially if he drove, before I arrived there. But it somehow disconcerted me. The monk seemed to be everywhere lately.

"What did you think of him this time?"

The look of distaste that twisted Lupa's mouth spoke volumes. "I don't understand his hold on Alexandra."

"Alexis," I said. "She thinks he can keep her son alive. He's evidently done it more than once."

"If you believe that," he began, then checked himself. "What I don't understand," he did say, "is that Rasputin convinced Alexandra to give me the egg. I don't think she would have parted with it otherwise. He stared at her in that fixed way, and put her almost in a trance. Then he said, 'What are mere possessions compared to your husband's peace of mind? If this egg can provide that, it is worth the sacrifice.'

"And that settled it. After the shortest reflection, she walked directly to the case, unlocked it, and handed me the egg."

"I know. He had the same kind of effect on her at Minsky's last party."

Lupa was silent a moment, then shook his head. "Women," he began, and I sensed he was about to launch into his familiar tirade, so I spoke up.

"What are your plans for today?"

"I have three interviews scheduled. By the way, if you see Miss Ripley, you can tell her she is no longer a suspect."

Here, at last, was some welcome news, though I had never seriously entertained the thought. "She wasn't aware that she had been," I said, "but I'm glad you've reached that decision. May I ask what happened?"

"Anastasia. I ran into her yesterday and she told me that Miss Ripley had stayed at her house the night of the party at Vyroubova's. She was escorted by a group of Minsky's brothers-in-arms, and they continued with him to his house."

"Did Anastasia know any of the men?"

"She hardly noticed. It was late, and dark. A group of young officers, she said."

"Kapov?"

He nodded. "The man who would kill a hundred Minskys? Yes, Jules, the thought had occurred to me."

Derevenko, surly as ever, and bolder without Alyosha by his side, tolerated my presence only by an obvious act of will. Though he volunteered nothing, eventually I got him to tell me that my tutoring that morning had been canceled— the dinner with the Royal Family had kept the prince up late, and he would be sleeping in today.

Almost as an afterthought, he handed me an envelope embossed with the royal coat of arms. It was closed with the seal of the Czarevitch and I opened it as soon as I was out in the hallway alone.

Dear M. Giraud:

Please forgive my absence today. My mother believes I need some extra rest. I think she is angry that I spoke so freely to papa, and wants to punish me for a day. I will see you tomorrow.

A.

It was upsetting. If Alexandra was angry with Alyosha and thought I was somehow infecting him, as Nicholas had intimated yesterday, I would be well-advised to keep my "lessons," as my predecessor Gaillard had done, to the milder humanities. I liked Alyosha, very much, but I could not have my position at court ruined by a misunderstanding with the Czarina.

Looking in at the alcove where I had been meeting Elena, anxious to tell her the news of her "acquittal" by Lupa, I was disappointed to find it empty. But then, I realized, it was several hours earlier than we usually met. She was undoubtedly tutoring the girls.

I thought of the woman I had seen outside Rasputin's last night. Similar experiences, I suppose, are commonplace—I mean situations where one wants to believe something so badly that the facts surrounding it come to be meaningless. Last night, I was so tired and lonely that I was seeing Elena in every shadow. I wanted to see her, therefore I did see her. But, in fact, it hadn't been her.

I was beginning to realize how Lupa's decision regarding her had lightened my spirits. Sukhomlinov and Elena were now out of it. Who did that leave? Borstoi and Kapov, and perhaps Pohl, and we would be drawing the net ever tighter today. It was a relief. We were finally moving ahead. Progress was being made. We might, in fact, succeed before it was too late.

My appetite returned with a vengeance. I hadn't eaten a proper meal in two days, so I stopped in at one of the booths in the children's wing of the Palace. I was loathe to walk the streets carrying Fabergé's egg in my pocket any longer than was absolutely necessary. The meal also afforded me time to come up with some plan as to how to best use the egg.

Fortified by strong tea and several sausages stuffed into fresh rolls of black bread, I was ready to begin. I still didn't have a specific idea, but my confidence had returned. I was certain I could read the moment and act accordingly.

I made one last stop at the alcove to see if Elena had finished with the Grand Duchesses, but it was still empty. Then, making sure I was well bundled against pickpockets and the cold, I left the Palace.

Borstoi's shop was closed.

I knocked, then banged on the front door for several minutes to make sure he wasn't hiding in the back. My frustration increasing, I stood in the street as though waiting for the door to magically open. A brittle sun began to break through the high white cloud cover from time to time. Its light was feeble; it gave no warmth. And when it ducked again behind the clouds, as it did regularly, it only served by contrast to make the day seem colder.

But there wasn't much else I could do, so I wrapped my coat around me and made myself as comfortable as I could on a stoop in a covered doorway across the street. It was possible Borstoi would come late to his shop, and that possibility, I reasoned, was worth a few hours of my time.

Fortunately, it didn't turn out that way. The chill hadn't yet worked its way into my bones when a young boy walked up to the door of Borstoi's shop and, without any hesitation, opened it with a key. He leaned over, picked up some papers that were lying on the floor, and reclosed and locked the door. Putting the papers into the pocket of his coat, he began returning the way he'd come.

He'd only gone about three blocks when he disappeared into a building that, before the War, had probably been quite respectable. Now it had gone to seed, as had so much of this part of the city. My first impressions of St. Petersburg as the Venice of the North had been tempered by my wanderings through it. Certainly, the grand boulevards—the Nevsky and the Morskaya Prospekts, for example—were still luxurious and impressive, but the rest of the city had fallen as though from grace, and now seemed all the more sad for its past glory.

The boy came out of the house and walked back past me on his way somewhere else. I waited a few more minutes, then mounted the seven steps and pushed at the unlocked door. The inside of the house was dusty and stuffy, as though its windows had been closed for too long, but well-appointed and clean. The vestibule was wide and its hardwood floors echoed.

"Who's that?" a voice called from a back room.

"Jules Giraud," I answered. "Is that you, Karel?"

"Back here."

There was a short, carpeted hallway with a staircase running off to the left. Just beyond the hall, I came to what must have been the dining room with its huge table and chandelier. Three other doorways opened into it—evidently eating had been a focal point in the lives of those who had lived here.

"In here, Giraud."

Borstoi looked a mess. He was propped up in a makeshift bed in what was normally a smoking room. His right arm was in a sling and his head was wrapped halfway round with gauze, through which blood had seeped. One eye was half-closed and beginning to show purple, and several cuts marked his weak chin.

"Karel! What happened?"

In spite of his wounds, he smiled broadly. "It was marvelous, Giraud, bloody marvelous."

"What was that?"

"The riot! You didn't hear about the riot?"

"I had a busy day. What happened?" I had to remind myself that I was on his side. I sat down, feigning interest.

"Just outside the Palace. It started early—as soon as word got out that Nicholas had come to the city." He grimaced in pain, made himself more comfortable, and continued. "The man's incapable of doing the right thing."

"Nicholas?"

He nodded. "It was a petition, that's all. Five hundred workers asking—asking, Giraud, not demanding—that the bread shops open earlier and stay open later. But of course our Czar couldn't be bothered with his people.

"And what was beautiful, what was incredible, was that when the guard was ordered, as they always are, to fire on the crowd, the soldiers refused." He laughed, spittle coming to the corners of his mouth. Even though it obviously caused him pain, he laughed. "And then the fun really began!"

"The soldiers mutinied?" I asked.

"About two hundred of them. Poor bastards were executed last night." That fact stemmed his ebullience for a second, but then he went on. "But you'll see, the soldiers will join us in the revolution. We're all the same class. They won't fire on their own people."

"That is wonderful news!" I said.

I remembered my meeting with Nicholas yesterday, even while all this was going on, suffering for himself and for his people. I was almost tempted to confront Borstoi with the complexity of the situation, but it was plain that nothing could sway him from his vision of "bloody Nick."

"And I have more that I hope you think is wonderful," I continued, taking the box from my pocket and placing it on the sofa beside him.

"What is this?"

I forced myself to smile into his eyes. "I hope you'll accept it as proof that I am with you in our struggle. You said you needed something." I motioned toward the box. "That is something."

He picked it up and carefully opened it. His eyes widened. "Is this real? Is it what I think it is?"

"Press the diamonds," I commanded.

When he did, the "surprise" had the same effect on him

that it had had on me. He sat mesmerized, just staring, trying to take in every detail. "Where did you get this?"

I shrugged nonchalantly. "I'm afraid I stole it. They're rather careless in the royal apartments. Almost nothing's locked up."

He sat holding it for another few minutes, looking at it from all sides, opening and closing the lid. Finally, he closed it, then the box, and laid it carefully on an end table. He leaned his head back, closed his eyes, and smiled. "It's a fortune, Giraud. It can buy everything we need. Guns, ammunition, printing supplies, bombs. It's the beginning, the real beginning." He opened his eyes, tearing himself away from the dreams, and reached out his good hand. "You must forgive me, comrade, for doubting you. These times..."

"I understand completely," I said. "They call for caution. I would have done the same thing."

As though reassuring himself that it really existed, he again picked up the box and lovingly beheld its contents. "It's unbelievable! A Fabergé egg, here in my house." He tore his eyes away. "Giraud, *tovarishch*, would you be so good as to go to the kitchen and get some glasses? This calls for a celebration."

When I returned, he had produced two bottles of unopened prewar vodka. Taking the glasses, he half-filled them, toasted the revolution, and drained his.

Coughing, he smiled, "The pain is gone, comrade. I feel only joy."

He refilled his glass, this time toasting the memory of his father. Again we clinked glasses, and again he drained his. "You must really forgive me," he repeated. "You didn't seem one of us, somehow. Can you understand? Here, drink more."

In the next hour, he returned to the egg several times as though to reassure himself that it was real. He would be talking, or finishing another drink, then reach over, open the box, and stare at it, energized anew. He had finished two-thirds of the bottle, and was, literally by now, feeling no pain. By this time, we were great old friends. I had been pouring most of my drinks into a cuspidor that rested beside his sofa, and was still quite sober. It was time to go to work.

"Karel, comrade," I said in a controlled slur, "where can we trade this egg in for rubles? It will not be easy, I'm afraid."

Again he reached for it, opened it, took in its beauty. "Never thought..." he began, then bringing his eyes into focus on me, he smiled. "Oh, not to worry, comrade. We have friends, besides you, in high places."

I didn't want to push. "Excellent. Here, let me look at it."

As he handed it to me, he reached for the bottle, dispensing with the glass altogether. It was as though he needed the jolt from the alcohol to keep his good fortune in perspective. He tipped the bottle up.

"Giraud," he whispered hoarsely. "You know Kapov?"

My hands, holding the egg, began to tremble, my heart to pound. To cover up, I stood myself to a shot of vodka.

I nodded, hardly daring to believe I'd heard what I thought I'd heard and that the circle was at last beginning to close.

"I know an Ivan Kapov, but he's the Czar's cousin."

Borstoi grinned crookedly, showing a mouth of gapped and blackened teeth. "Isn't it rich? That's Kapov."

"He is a comrade?"

That really brought on a fit. "Kapov? Comrade Kapov?" He howled at the thought, grimacing as the laughter shook his bruise-wracked body. "Oh, that's good." There were tears in his eyes. "I haven't laughed so well in years. No, Giraud, Kapov is not a comrade. After the revolution, he will be among the first to go to the wall."

He picked up the bottle and drained it, then lay back for a moment to recover his breath. I grabbed the second bottle, opened it, and put it in his hand. The plan I hadn't been able to formulate that morning was now fully developed.

"I don't understand, then, comrade. If..."

"Look," he said, forcing his eyes open. "We want the same thing. Different reasons." I had to struggle to make out the increasingly slurred words. "Using each other now. We both want the War over. Now. After that?" He shrugged. "After that we fight."

"And we can trust Kapov?" I asked.

He opened his eyes full and summoned up all of his lucidity. "Blood pact," he said. Then he laughed. "We started the murders so we'd have it on each other."

"You've been...?"

He waved a finger from side to side in front of his face. "Tsk, Tsk... only the first, Dieter Bresloe, a pig. The Czar's bodyguard. I was bait." He shook his head to try and clear it. "Kapov captures me, locks me in Bresloe's room. Goes to his friend Dieter, says he's caught an anarchist. Bresloe comes back, we overpower him, knock him out, close door, leaving grenade behind." He smiled madly at the memory. "Boom!" He laughed, drinking again.

"How did you get the grenade?"

Borstoi shrugged. "Kapov talked some fool general into showing off his arsenal, and he just pocketed a few and walked away with them."

"Sukhomlinov," I whispered.

Borstoi, now laying back limp as an old rag, made a face. "I don't know. Don't care."

I didn't want to seem so curious that I called attention to it, but I had to know more. "But why did you kill Bresloe?"

He snorted. "Kapov's idea. Stupid. Weaken Nicholas by killing his friends."

"It seems to be working," I said.

He wagged his head. "Too slow, not certain. Kill Nicholas." He laughed weakly. "Kill Bloody Nick himself and the War will end. You'll see."

"But the other murders?"

"Not me. Too risky, too slow."

"Just Kapov?"

He shrugged, belched, swallowed. "Don't know. Probably. Doesn't matter." He looked over at the egg, raised the bottle again to his mouth. "Doesn't matter now," he said, the tone of triumph ringing even through his drunkenness.

I was silent a moment, trying to comprehend what I had just heard. The royalist Kapov and the Communist Borstoi were the strangest of allies at first blush, but on a little reflection I realized that they were no more unlikely than monarchist Russia and republican France. The common goals outweighed the other differences.

Borstoi's snore roused me. He lay back, his mouth gaping open, the bottle cradled in the crook of one arm. As I watched, he shifted, snorted again, settling into the cushions, then moaned quietly. His deep breathing became regular, his eyes opened partway, showing only a jaundiced shade of yellow.

After a quarter of an hour, during which I scarcely breathed, I whispered his name. When there was no response, I spoke it aloud. Then I nudged him. Finally, I made a fist and pounded him on his broken arm. At that, he moaned but remained sleeping. If he'd awakened, I would have told him I was trying to rouse him, but he didn't move.

The second bottle was already half empty, so he'd downed perhaps a litre of vodka himself. They gave less than that to people who were to have limbs amputated.

I picked up the egg, took one last loving look at it, closed the box, and put it carefully into my coat pocket. The sun, outside, cast a topaz glow over the room as it broke through the clouds just before setting. After a last look at my slumbering "comrade," I walked outside to the street, hands in my pockets, whistling.

14

Now it is ten o'clock. The bells have just stopped. I've been writing for over six hours, trying to get it down.

I've sent my man to Lupa's every hour to no avail. Now that the murders are solved, Borstoi and Kapov should be arrested, the egg returned, and Nicholas reassured. The iron is hot and I must strike.

But Lupa has disappeared and I am beginning to feel that I must report to someone. Borstoi could awake at any moment and find the egg gone. Knowing he has been betrayed, he will either run or warn Kapov. If the latter, I am in grave danger. If the former, I could not forgive myself. And the stakes are too great to take any risks.

Now, at least, the truth is committed here to paper. I really can wait no longer. If Lupa isn't in, I will go to Alexandra and tell her myself.

I have made what could be a costly mistake.

After pacing outside Lupa's door for a while, waiting for him to return and trying to decide on my best course of action, I finally chose to see the Empress myself. After all, she was Lupa's employer—he might even be with her—and she was most concerned to find the Palace killers.

I had a small argument with a lady-in-waiting over the propriety of seeing Alexandra without an appointment at such a late hour, but I said it was an emergency, and demanded that she announce me. If the Czarina wouldn't see me, I would abide by her decision, but I was sure she would.

I was right. After a short wait, I was admitted back into the Royal chambers, decorated in the homely fashion of the Palace at Tsarkoye Selo. Alexandra was sitting in a mauve easy chair, wrapped in a purple sleeping gown. Her quite spectacular reddish hair hung down over her shoulders, and she sat with one leg curled under her. She was extremely attractive, with her natural regal bearing softened by the informality of her attire.

It could also have been the contrast. Across from her, in a white formless sheet embroidered heavily with what looked to be rhinestones and brightly colored yarns, sat Anna Vyroubova, pudgy hands clasped in her lap, a cane leaning against her chair, her rather large feet planted solidly on the floor.

As soon as I entered the room and bowed, I detected the chill. At first I thought it might have been the interruption, but then I remembered the misgivings about my tutoring that she had mentioned to Nicholas only yesterday.

And I remembered that Alyosha hadn't been allowed to see me today.

Without thinking too much, wanting to please her and set her mind at ease about her husband and my own loyalty and good faith, I went to one knee.

"Your Majesty," I began, "I beg you forgive me the lateness of the hour, but what I have to say cannot wait any longer."

She looked down on me, not motioning for me to rise. There was in her glare that fixity I had noticed before when she'd been with Rasputin, and it briefly crossed my mind that she might be under some post-hypnotic trance, especially concerning me.

"Yes?" she said coldly. "Go on."

So far was she from the gracious and warm person who had met me and asked if I would tutor her son that I felt I must

have misread her on that occasion. I even looked at the Vyroubova woman for support, which of course was not forthcoming. The peasant woman and the queen were, at that
moment, cut from the same cloth.

Thinking to throw oil on the waters, I changed tack
slightly. "But first," I said, forcing a smile, "I'm sure your
Majesty will be relieved to have this back."

I took the box from my pocket and presented it to her. For
a fraction of a moment, her eyes lit up again, especially as
she opened the box and looked at the egg itself. But faster
than it had come, the expression was gone, replaced by a
sterner displeasure than previously.

"How did you come by this?" Alexandra asked. "I gave this
to Lupa."

"Our plan . . ." I began.

"Our?" Her voice was deep as thunder. "I gave this egg to
Auguste Lupa under his personal assurance that he would be
responsible for it. And now you return it to me."

"Yes, but . . ."

"What other conspiracies are afoot here that no one sees fit
to tell me about?"

"There was, is, no conspiracy, Madam, but . . ."

Her eyes now flashed, the color high in her cheeks. "I am
not 'madam,' Monsieur. I am the Czarina of Russia, and you
will address me properly."

"Yes, your Majesty."

She turned to Vyroubova. "See how they treat me? Oh,
our Friend was right, I'm afraid. It's everywhere." Again she
turned on me. "You think I'm the German whore, don't you?
Some impediment to be gotten around? Well, I am not. I am
my husband's guardian. No one else watches out for him. It
is all traitors and knaves."

"Your Majesty, please."

"Enough from you!"

Vyroubova struggled to her feet and limped across to Alexandra, where she sat at her feet as the queen patted her hair
as though she were a dog.

After a tense little while, she faced me again. "I will determine what's to be done with you and Lupa. Now leave us."

"Your Majesty..." At least I had to try and tell her I had found the murderers. Maybe that would calm her, but she stopped me with another glare. There was no choice. I bowed meekly and backed from her presence.

My hands shake.

On the way back here to my rooms, I stopped by Lupa's and he was still not in. Where can he have gone?

I had assumed he'd told the Empress of our plans, or at least outlined them. Surely she knew my role here was as much with Lupa as with Nicholas or Paleologue. Could it be Lupa hadn't told her? And if he hadn't, why hadn't he informed me of it? Might he have simply forgotten?

What could account for Alexandra's mistrust of me, for such an abrupt and uncalled for change of heart? It really does seem that she is under some sort of spell. Certainly she is not rational. But, as she pointed out, she is the Czarina of Russia. Irrationality in her, in a twinkling, becomes the law.

My hands will not stop shaking.

I've had two small glasses of vodka from the room's bottle. It scarcely helps. Now, in my robe, I sit waiting for a knock on the door—from Lupa, or from the Palace Guard.

It comes.

It is Elena, her face streaked with tears. She waits in my sitting room. I go to join her.

PART TWO

15

[KREMLIN FILE NO. JG 0665–4698–4710; PSS ACCESS, CLASSIFIED]

For all of Alexis' promises, the excitement of his parent's arrival in St. Petersburg evidently overshadowed his involvement in petty domestic issues such as the fight between his sister and Elena. When she knocked at my door on the night I'd been to see Alexandra, Elena told me that Tatiana had refused to see her for the third day running. During the day, she had waited for me to appear with the news that all had been somehow reconciled, but I never showed up.

As the day wore on, she became more and more frantic about the tenuousness of her position. She even thought I had abandoned her. In desperation, she finally decided, on my earlier advice, to swallow her prejudice and appeal to Rasputin because of his great influence on Tatiana.

She huddled deep in one of the chairs in my sitting room, flushed with the cold, with running through the streets back to the Palace from Rasputin's apartment.

(I, in my robe, had admitted her. I am not a young man. It serves no purpose to pretend I wasn't aware of the implications of the situation.)

I brought her a cup of tea from the samovar, and she sipped at it gratefully. She did not sob, and yet tears glistened in her lovely eyes. Occasionally they would brim over.

"It was horrible, Jules. I didn't know people could act like that."

"You don't have to talk about it," I said gently.

"No. I think I should. It might help." She cradled the cup in both hands, blowing on it softly. The room was dimly lit by two flickering gas lamps, one on a table beside the sofa on which I sat, another on the wall behind Elena. In spite of her desire to talk, the silence came to envelop us. Our eyes locked across the room.

Finally I had to speak. "What exactly happened?"

She sighed, then shivered as though with cold. Her voice was low and controlled, as if she feared that if she let a trickle of emotion into it, a torrent would follow. "After I didn't see you, I don't know what happened to me. Suddenly there seemed to be no hope. And I remembered what you'd said about the monk. He did know the girls. Maybe he could intercede for me.

"Still I put it off. You know how I feel about him, Jules. He is so . . ." She let that remark hang.

"Don't dwell on it," I said. "Go on."

"Anyway, finally I didn't know what else I could do. I had even gone to bed, saying that things would look better in the morning. But I couldn't sleep. I kept seeing myself turned out of the Palace, with no place to go and no friends."

"You will always have a friend in me."

She smiled, sniffed, sipped at the tea. "Thank you. But I even came by here earlier and you weren't in."

"I was visiting the Empress."

She nodded, still absorbed in her demon visions. "Then it seemed there was only one hope left, and that was Rasputin. One of the pages drove me to his flat, and I could see there was some strange party going on. But I had come this far, and I brushed aside my misgivings and fears and knocked at his door."

She shuddered, her voice now no more than a whisper. "Jules, half the court was there. People I have seen as courtiers, dukes, ladies-in-waiting—except there they all seemed crazy. The music was wild, people had their clothes off, someone grabbed me and touched me," she paused, embarrassed, "where he shouldn't have." She stopped. "And above everything, I kept hearing Rasputin's laughter. He wasn't laughing at anything, Jules. He seemed out of his mind, insane."

I recalled the other party the night before. "And what did you do?"

She looked down. "I ran. I was afraid. I'm still afraid. I came here, I didn't know what else to do, who else to turn to." She looked at me imploringly. "Oh, Jules, would you please hold me for a moment?"

We both stood, and I held out my arms and encircled her slender, womanly body. I could not help but be aware of her curves as she pressed herself to me, hiding her face against my chest. I've no doubt she could feel the stirrings of my own passion, for suddenly she pulled half away and looked up at me, her eyes wide and shining.

"I'm sorry, Jules. I'll go immediately. I didn't mean this to happen."

A better man might have taken her cue and let it end there. I do not delude myself. She offered me every opportunity to have nothing come of our embrace, and so I have no one but myself to blame for what happened afterward.

Her flushed, tear-streaked face gazed questioningly up at me, her tremulous expression one of fearful wonder. From her breath came the scent of almonds. Her skin, smooth and fine as porcelain, gave off a sublime glow in the sepia light.

Cast under the spell of her nearness and beauty, I could not let her go, but leaned down—seeing myself as though from a great height—and brought my lips to hers, gathering her back into my arms.

I don't know how long it lasted. A second or an hour. But (I realize now, looking back on all that's happened since) it was my own Rubicon. When the kiss ended I was a different man than when it had begun. Any identification I might have felt with the nobler, preWar values was forfeit. It may be the

War has corrupted me, but whatever caused it, I was, I am, now a "modern man," and any thought that I was somehow cut from a finer cloth than, say, Borstoi, can be seen as the baldest conceit.

Elena, breathless, ended the kiss, ran her fingers lightly over my cheek. "Forgive me, Jules," she whispered, "forgive me."

"There is nothing to..." I began, but she stopped me, pressing a finger softly against my lips.

She nodded, as though affirming something to herself. "There is, Jules." She sighed, hesitated, looked deeply into my eyes. "I love you." Tears gathered, then fell over onto her cheeks. "I'm sorry, but I love you."

My head swam. My knees grew weak. Unable to respond any other way, I kissed her again, pressing away the feeble pangs of my conscience in the warm softness of her mouth.

Finally, she pulled away. Taking my hand, she led me back to the sofa. "Sit down a minute, Jules. I'll be right back."

She disappeared into my bedroom. A few moments later she returned, barefoot, wrapped in one of my robes. She carried two glasses and set them on the table next to me. "If you want me to leave, I will go now," she said.

"Elena, I need to think."

"I know it's..."

It was my time to hold up a restraining palm. "No, please. I don't want you to go." She stood in front of me, waiting for some word, but again I was tongue-tied. Finally, she made a decision, leaning over the table, handing me one of the glasses which contained a large drink of vodka. She raised the other glass, which held a small tot, to her lips. Then she touched her palm to my face and said softly. "You look exhausted. I will sit here across from you and we'll talk."

I looked at her gratefully. "I am married. I love my wife. But if I touch you again..."

She hushed me. "Don't say anything. It's all right."

Curling one leg under herself, her hair down, she sat in the same posture as Alexandra had earlier that night. But unlike the Empress, Elena's whole being glowed with warmth and acceptance.

"Has it been a hard day for you, too?"

And suddenly all the suppressed emotions of the past hours welled up within me. In rapid succession, I remembered my frustration with Lupa, my elation over Fabergé's egg, my worry over not finding Borstoi at his shop, then the thrill of hunting him down and so completely gulling him, my incredible faux pas with Alexandra, and finally the anguish and joy of Elena's declaration. For the first time in years, I felt myself on the verge of crying.

Elena, without a word, came and sat beside me. It was not passionate, barely even physical, but she took my tensed shoulders in her hands, turned me toward her, and cradled my head in the fragrant hollow of her neck.

"It's all right," she said. "Why don't you just talk it all out?"

I closed my eyes, and the tension gradually began to ease as she massaged my temples with her fingertips. I started talking, occasionally sipping at my drink. From Foch to Alexis, from Sukhomlinov to Kapov, Paleologue and Lupa, I poured out my soul, sparing nothing.

When I finished, she leaned down and kissed me softly on the lips. "So it is over," she whispered.

"We still must apprehend Kapov," I said.

"But you're sure it's him?"

I rested my head back against her. "As sure as I can be without other proof. Certainly sure enough to have him arrested and interrogated."

"And what about this other man, the anarchist, Borstoi? Wasn't he part of it, too? What will you do with him?"

Fatigue was overwhelming me. Still, I wanted to stay awake, to remain aware of Elena's presence, so I forced myself to speak. "I'm convinced it was Kapov. I'll turn my information on Borstoi to the regular police, and they'll deal with him. But the Palace murders—the ones Lupa and I have been investigating—may be laid at Kapov's feet. I'm all but certain of it."

She hugged me to her, then stood and pulled me to my feet. "Come, Jules." She held to my hand tightly.

Like a sleepwalker, I followed her into the bedroom. She came to the side of the bed, her robe hanging open slightly. Turning, she put her arms around me. She was shaking. We lay down on the bed.

And lying in her arms, it all became plain. Things would work out somehow. When Alexandra found out the murders had been solved, that Kapov had committed them, she would forgive Lupa and I our deception with Fabergé's egg, Nicholas would become assured that his personal world was secure, and would regain the strength to continue the war. My mission would end in triumph and glory, the initial step in the Allies' last and ultimately successful campaign for victory.

Though I don't recall being asleep, I must have already been dreaming.

16

Twice while it was still dark, I was awakened by Elena's movements beside me, and both times she hushed me back to sleep, saying it was the middle of the night.

When I finally awoke to a cup of steaming café au lait served by Elena, she had already dressed and re-hung my robe on a peg against the wall. She sat easily on the side of my bed, chattering animatedly about the upcoming day—my talk with her last night had convinced her that everything would work out with Tatiana, and she was anxious to go and see her royal charge.

In spite of my fitful awakenings, I felt wonderfully rested from the best sleep I had enjoyed since arriving in St. Petersburg. Staring at her, I felt euphoric, confident, strong. Try as I might, I could not remember anything of the night before after falling into her arms.

I tried to control my expression. Had we not, then, consummated our affair? I could not insult her by asking. Certainly, as she brought in the breakfast the servant had delivered, her face aglow—teasing, familiar, solicitous—she acted very much the satisfied new lover.

The vodka bottle, still on my desk, was nearly empty. Had I drunk so much of it? I remembered having a drink or two when I'd come back from visiting the Empress, and then Elena had brought in a glass that had been nearly full. I strained to recall. Was I still, at least technically, faithful to Tania? Suddenly it seemed terribly important to know.

"Is something wrong, Jules?"

I shook my head, having to smile as I gazed at her lovely, concerned face. *"Rien, cheri. Vraiment."*

"I didn't keep you awake?"

I shook my head. "I've rarely slept better."

"Except for the dream, you mean."

I looked at her quizzically.

"I'm afraid I was up most of the night," she said. "I thought my tossing next to you might have . . ." Her tremulous look showed a mixture of embarrassment, fear of my reaction, and, I thought, a strong desire not to displease me. "But sometime after two—I remember the bells had just rung the hour—you sat up, not knowing where you were, who I was." She paused. "I thought you wanted me to leave. You don't remember?"

"I remember waking up," I said, "but not wanting you to go. You didn't go, did you?"

She pouted fetchingly, then smiled. "When I went to put my clothes back on, you wouldn't let me." She blushed slightly. "And I am here still." Serious now, looking into my eyes, she leaned over and kissed me. "It's all right, isn't it? Will we see each other again?"

"Of course." At her questioning glance, I repeated it. "Really, of course."

She walked out of the room. I reclined in the bed for another minute, pensively sipping at my coffee. Then, like a vision, she appeared once more in the doorway, her face now serious, clouded with some strong emotion. "Please don't worry, Jules. Everything will be all right. And I still love you."

Then she was gone.

Lupa had a huge breakfast spread out before him on a table in his room. He listened patiently, chewing and drinking without stop, while I first admonished him for being absent the day before, then told him of my meeting with Borstoi, of the man's confession and implication of Kapov, and finally of the problem with Alexandra. When I'd finished, his only comment was to ask me if I'd eaten yet.

"Yes. I had a light breakfast with Elena Ripley." There was no need to go into any further explanation.

His brows lifted. "Indeed. And how is Miss Ripley?"

I was perhaps feeling defensive about her. In any event, I had no patience for his misogynist leanings.

"Why do you show so much interest in Elena? It's established that she has nothing to do with our investigation. It seems more important to me that we have a confession from Borstoi and a clear culpability from Kapov. Don't you think we ought to begin trying to apprehend them?"

He munched thoughtfully on a bit of roll. "Hmmm. You are right, I suppose. It's only that I interviewed Kapov yesterday and he seemed to have alibis for two of the murders. I was going to check into them today." He finished a cup of cocoa. "But no, you are correct. There's no time to lose. And Alexandra must be calmed."

He stood up and pressed an imaginary wrinkle from the broad expanse of his waistcoat. "By the way, Jules—one last question and then I'll drop it—during your breakfast with Miss Ripley, you must have been tempted to crow a little about flushing out Borstoi and Kapov?"

"Did I mention them to Elena?" I began heatedly. "Yes, but last night." At his glance, I dissembled quickly. "I saw her briefly upon returning from Borstoi's, and I told her then. She was overjoyed."

Lupa leaned his knuckles against the tabletop, closed his eyes and puckered his lips several times. He remained that way for so long that, had he not been standing, I might have thought he'd dozed off. But then, when I was just about to speak his name, he came back to himself and smiled at me. "Let's get a guardsman," he said, "and put Borstoi and Kapov in chains."

He had just come around the table and had draped a heavy

arm over my shoulder, beginning to say something, when the door to the room flew open. It was a captain of the Imperial Guard, out of breath and excited.

"Inspector Lupa, you must come quick. Someone else has died."

Lupa and I exchanged glances.

"The Czar's cousin this time," our messenger gasped. "Ivan Kapov. He's hanged himself."

Nothing could be more obvious, I thought, as we ran through the hallways of the Palace. Borstoi had somehow gotten to Kapov, told him of my duplicity and that, because of his admissions to me, the game was over. Kapov, in despair, and knowing that there was no escape—only humiliation and execution—had killed himself.

His rooms were up another flight of steps, at the far end of the Palace from where Lupa and I stayed. As a royal cousin, he of course had his own suite, but it was really merely a small garret just under the roof of the Palace, to be used mostly for sleeping or, perhaps, for romantic liaisons.

Our messenger escorted us through a small group of other guardsmen who were keeping out a growing number of the curious. As we entered the room, I was surprised to see that Kapov wasn't there. But the guard didn't hesitate. He led the way to a window that looked out over the inner courtyard. When he threw back the shutter, a blast of cold air stung our faces, but nothing could take our eyes from the ghastly spectacle outside.

The body of Ivan Kapov swung gently back and forth from one of the beams that extended out from the roof. The wind gusted and half-turned him so we could see the swollen tongue protruding from the purple mouth, the eyes white and bulging from a contorted face.

"Cut him down!" Lupa commanded.

The guard called for help from the knot of men at the door. Two more guardsmen came in and began wrestling the stiffened body inside. Engrossed as I was in this operation, I didn't notice anyone else enter the room until I heard his voice, shrill and authoritative.

"Why are you disturbing the body?"

It was old, wrinkled Inspector Dubniev, the man who had been at Minsky's bedside in Tsarkoye Selo. "Why are you cutting him down," he asked.

The guards were cowed into silence, but Lupa responded. "Good morning, Inspector, I gave the order."

The old man glared at my friend, furious that his authority had again been usurped. "It is my place to give those orders!"

Lupa reached into his breast pocket and extracted a folded square of paper, embossed with the royal shield. "This is my commission from the Czarina," he said quietly. "As you see, it's been expanded since we last met."

The inspector looked over the credentials and handed them back to my friend without a word. He turned to the guards. "Proceed," he said. Then he bowed once formally to Lupa, turned on his heel, and walking with a stiff, wounded dignity, he left the room. If I'd earlier thought that Lupa had made an enemy of Dubniev, now there was no doubt of it.

But Lupa's attention was on the body being brought back in through the window. As though reading my thoughts, however, he spoke. "It can't be helped," he said. "All will be forgiven if we succeed."

"But we have succeeded..." I began, only to be quieted by Lupa's upraised palm. Instead, he ordered one of the men guarding the door to close it.

The guards put the body on the bed, but Lupa wasn't yet ready to examine it. Rather, he went back to the window, hoisted himself up onto the sill and, balancing himself precariously twenty meters above the courtyard, he leaned out and studied the rope which was still attached to the beam.

As I looked on, he extended his arm, leaning out to touch the end of the beam. Though he seemed completely oblivious to the drop should the perch give under his weight, the guards and I stood holding our breath against his slightest slip.

When he came back down inside the room, he stared at the floor under the window and slowly studied the walls on either side of the window, the shutters, the hinges, everything. Finally he turned and straightened up.

As he had done earlier that morning, he closed his eyes and pursed his lips, rubbing his hands together to warm them. Going to the bed, he leaned over the body and smelled its mouth. Turning its head roughly, which he had to do because of its stiffness, he examined the knot where the rope had bruised the neck.

Kapov had been wearing a purple sleeping gown, cinched at the waist. Lupa lifted it to view the body, presumably searching for bruises. Muttering something to himself, he turned next to the hands, to which he gave special attention. Finally, he straightened up.

I had found the entire display absurd. What did he expect to find? Kapov had hanged himself, and that was all there was to it. Lupa's insistence on studying the body struck me as pretentious foolishness to prolong an already protracted investigation.

"Auguste," I said. "Surely what has happened is obvious." And I explained my theory—indeed, the only plausible theory—about Borstoi's betrayal and Kapov's suicide.

He listened patiently. When I had finished, he spoke to the lead guardsman and directed that Kapov's body be taken to autopsy.

"But..."

"No, Jules. No buts. I want to know his condition when he went out that window. Come," he said, putting his arm around me, "this room is oppressive. There's nothing more to be done."

Out in the hallway, he continued, whispering. "I don't want to say much in anyone else's presence."

"I understand that," I said, "but surely we should go to the Empress and report."

He shook his head. "There is still one untied string. Max Pohl sent a message to me this morning." At my look of surprise, he explained. "I would have told you about it if the guard hadn't rushed in just when he did. Really, my friend, I'm not hiding things from you. In any event, Pohl's note said that he has discovered a crucial fact about the poison used to kill Minsky. Something about being able to trace its source."

"Well, that source probably will lead to Kapov."

He nodded. "Undoubtedly, but I want to hear what he has to say before I take our case to Alexandra."

Though that made sense, I was worried about delaying our report, and I said as much. But Lupa overrode me. "Jules, it's my case. I must conclude it my way."

Reluctantly, I acquiesced, but I did have one other concern. "How do you think Kapov's death will affect Nicholas?" I asked.

Lupa stopped and faced me. "Now there is a point," he said. "Were the two especially close?"

"I saw no sign of it. They were cousins, but otherwise I got the impression their relationship was rather formal."

Lupa chuckled without humor. "All the kings of Europe are cousins."

"So Kapov is the first court death that won't affect the Czar personally. That, at least, is good."

Lupa shrugged. "It is either good, or it is the beginning of a new phase."

"What do you mean?" I asked.

He hesitated, then laughed as though ridiculing himself. "Nothing, Jules, nothing. Sometimes my imagination runs away with me."

With all the events of the morning behind me, I was somewhat startled to realize that it was still early enough to try and call on Alyosha.

After leaving Lupa, who said he was off to interview Pohl, I crossed the courtyard to the children's wing. Halfway across, I tried to determine which of the gables Kapov had swung from, though it was impossible to tell.

My mind was still a jumble of conflicting thoughts and emotions—fear of Alexandra's wrath, relief that the murders had been solved, concern over my original mission with Nicholas, curiosity about Pohl's message, even apprehension at seeing Alyosha again. And, of course, overlying everything, the elation, guilt, passion and remorse of whatever was happening between Elena and myself and—though she wasn't here—with Tania and our child.

And so it was with a sense of wonder that I came upon the Heir Apparent and the Grand Duchesses playing a kind of tag together in one of the outer halls in their part of the Palace. Here was no intrigue, no court foppery, no jealousy or hatred, but five happy young people caught in a frieze of simple joy. Even the dour Derevenko, seated nearby and looking on, wore a tolerant smile. And as I came upon the group, Elena appeared from where she had gone to retrieve a ball.

Seeing me, she waved and called out "Jules!" and my heart leapt to my throat. As moving as Elena's, though, was Alyosha's reaction. He stopped teasing one of his sisters, turned and ran across the length of the hall toward me. Stopping a meter away, he smiled broadly and bowed in our private joke, then he came up and threw his arms around me.

"Monsieur Giraud," he said, "I'm so glad to have you back. I've missed you."

"I've missed you, too, your Highness."

His eyes gleamed. "I have to talk to you about my father," he whispered excitedly. "We had the most marvelous talk."

"We will," I answered.

But before I could say more, Elena had come up, touching my arm protectively. "Alyosha, should we do our surprise?"

The prince nodded and ran back to be with his sisters. I

took in Elena's smiling face. "It looks as though Tati and you are reconciled."

"It's wonderful! This morning it had all been forgotten, as if nothing had happened." She leaned closer to my ear and whispered conspiratorially. "I have a feeling that Alexis talked to her. And I know whom to thank for that." She took my hand to lead me across the hall. "But you? How are you?"

Not wishing to go into it, I said I was fine, and asked her what the surprise was. She grinned happily. "Just a little skit we've worked up, isn't that right, children?"

One of the girls—the prettiest—stepped forward and held out her hand to be kissed. "I am Tatiana Romanovna," she said, with great seriousness, but then a twinkle showed in her eyes, followed by a fetching smile that reminded me of Alexandra's when I'd first met her. I bowed and kissed her hand.

"Since you've swept away both my brother and our governess," Tatiana said, "they've persuaded us to perform for you."

Alyosha spoke up. "And so that I can keep up with my studies, the play is in French."

Thoroughly charmed by the gesture, I said the appropriate words and retired to a chair by the wall while Elena prepared them for the "curtain." The skit was a rendering of the scene of Hugo's "Les Miserables," where Jean Valjean steals the loaf of bread. Alyosha played the young Valjean, and his portrayal was powerful and subtly ironic. I wondered how the children had come to choose that moment, that topic, and whether it had been Elena's influence, or the growing political awareness of Alexis. Whoever had done it, in that setting it was a stirring piece. Even the girls were believable in their parts, although the youngest of them, Anastasia, was a bit of a ham.

Elena, myself, and even Derevenko were generous in our applause when the skit ended. Each of the Grand Duchesses then came by to shake my hand, and I congratulated them. I was especially proud of Alyosha, and ventured a buss on each cheek for him.

"Quite brilliant," I told him. "You could easily make a career of this. Don't you agree, Elena?"

"Beyond any doubt."

He shrugged off the compliment. "I felt the part strongly, Monsieur Giraud. There must be a thousand Jean Valjeans in my Russia right now—good men, driven to desperation. I can't afford to let myself forget that."

What a wonderful ruler he'll make!

But it was time for lunch, and Elena clasped her hands and instructed the children to go with Derevenko to eat. Before they left, Alexis came up to me and whispered "Tomorrow," and I nodded in accord.

When Elena and I were alone, we sat on our chairs by the wall holding hands. "That really was quite excellent!" I said. "And a wonderful theme for royalty to consider."

"Yes." Suddenly she seemed tired, abstracted. Looking at her carefully, I saw that there were dark circles under her eyes.

"Are you all right?"

A weary smile. "I'm afraid I didn't sleep last night." She squeezed my hand. "I was too excited. Perhaps I should go now and try to get some rest."

"I'll walk you to your room," I volunteered.

As we crossed the courtyard, a new snowstorm had begun. I told her about Kapov's suicide and mentioned that Lupa would be reporting to the Czarina after his interview with Pohl.

"But I thought it was all tied up? Didn't you say that Kapov was the murderer? Surely killing himself right at this time is tantamount to a confession?"

I explained Lupa's ridiculous insistence on getting all the facts before making his report. Obvious though the whole thing was, Pohl's information might shed light on some new aspect of the crimes, and if it did, Lupa wanted to know about it.

"I suppose that makes sense," she said wearily.

"Sometimes Lupa's brilliance hurts him, I believe," I said, and told her about ordering the autopsy for Kapov, though the cause of his death couldn't have been more plain.

But I could see all this talk was tiring her more. She lapsed into silence, and her hand in mine went slack. "But come, let's get you to your bed."

We'd arrived at her rooms, and when she opened the door, she looked into my eyes. "Please be careful," she said. "All this worries me so much."

I kissed her lightly. She looked at me questioningly, and in response I turned her around and patted her derriere as I might have done to a child. "To bed, alone."

Looking back over her shoulder, she nodded in acquiescence, and closed the door between us.

17

I had to get out of the Palace. Quite apart from my natural feeling of confinement within its walls, I was loath to run into any of Alexandra's entourage until Lupa had reported to her.

It was, in fact, lunchtime, and I was hungry, so I made my way, for the third time in a hour, across the courtyard, through the other side of the Palace, and out into the street.

The snow was falling hard, and I marveled yet again at the severity of this early Russian winter. It was no wonder it had proven stronger than any number of invading armies. If only it could prevail once more against the Prussians!

I dined at a small but rather elegant restaurant called, simply, Ernest, and treated myself to a full bottle of Bordeaux to go with a dish of chicken, paprika and sour cream. Lingering over a brandy and cigar, my thoughts turned, finally, to my wife.

And strangely, suddenly, I felt a great outpouring of love for her. I foresaw the successful end of Lupa's investigation and of my mission. With a full stomach and good brandy to hand, the emotional strain of the past few days was gone, and I began to view the world in a clearer light.

It was not unnatural that I should be attracted to such a lovely creature as Elena, but my first and true allegiance was to Tania. Perhaps I had been unfaithful—I truly did not remember—but I would not let that temptation befuddle me again.

Elena—young, vital, impressionable and passionate—
would soon recover from her infatuation with me. For what
else could it be? I was to her, as she was to me, a sympathetic ear, a warm and comforting body during a most difficult time. I still felt nothing but affection for her, and I
hoped I hadn't compromised her honor. Upon more reflection, I was sure I hadn't. How would I not have remembered?

In any case, tonight would mark a return to the platonic
nature of our (the word applied) love. It would be better. We
didn't belong together. I belonged with my wife and child.
And the realization of that gave me more contentment than
any I'd known since I'd left Tania's side.

I looked at my watch. Lunch had taken me nearly two
hours! Suddenly I was anxious to get back to Lupa, to see
this thing ended. I looked forward to my interview with Nicholas, smiling to myself as I imagined convincing him that
the time was now ripe for a new commitment to France. It
was a heady vision.

I paid my bill, got into my greatcoat, and pushed open the
restaurant's door into the blizzard. But even the weather
couldn't chill my ardor. As I kicked my way through the
curb-deep snow, I kept my head up, like a horse running to
water. My deepest thirst—that my mission succeed—was
about to be slaked!

I hastened to Lupa's office. The Palace had a strangely
muted mid-afternoon lethargy hanging over it. The storm
must have driven many people to their rooms.

At first glance, Lupa too had been affected by it. He sat—
without beer!—his hands clasped before him on his desk.
Neither were there any flowers. That situation should have
filled me with foreboding, but it did not. Though I couldn't
see his face from the door when I entered, I somehow knew
that his eyes were closed and his lips pursing in and out in
that distinctive way of his when his mind was deeply engaged.

I approached quietly, and when I'd come to my chair, I whispered his name. "Auguste."

Immediately he looked up, and in his eyes I could see that Pohl's information must have shaken him. There was no sign of arrogance or bluster, only a grim determination and sadness, almost one of personal loss.

"What happened?" I asked.

He sighed from the bottom of his soul. "Max outdid himself with lunch for the Czar," he began. Then he sighed again. "No. I won't be flip." He stopped.

"What is it?" I repeated.

"After he'd served lunch to the Czar, Max went back to the kitchen and put a bullet into his head. He's dead."

"*Mon dieu!* It can't be!"

Lupa glared at me. "I assure you, it is."

"But why? Was he . . . ?"

"It would appear so. If he and Kapov had been in it together . . ." He stopped. "Borstoi might not have told you everything either. Perhaps someone else knew about Pohl. I don't know. What else makes sense?"

In my shock, I immediately thought of Sukhomlinov, the last of our suspects. Pohl had been in love with his wife. He had supplied the grenades to Kapov. Strongly pro-German, he'd only escaped conviction as a traitor months ago. And he was still bitter at the Czar for removing him from his post as War Minister.

"There is another possibility," I began, "and it does make sense."

"What is that?"

"That someone killed Pohl, hoping to make it look enough like suicide that it would be assumed he was somehow involved in the plot and, like Kapov, did not want to face a trial and certain execution."

Lupa's eyes shone with a new high anger. "That is plausible," he said. "And who would that be?"

I began to tick off my points against Sukhomlinov. "On

reflection," I concluded, "he had more motive than anyone. He must have been the prime mover."

Lupa heard me out, then stared for a moment into the space behind me. Shaking his head, he spoke softly. "It is my fault. I involved him."

"Do you mean Pohl?"

He nodded glumly.

"Don't be absurd, Auguste. It was Pohl who chose to get in touch with you."

The big man stared dolefully at me for a long second, then hung his head. "It wasn't worth it."

"But it does leave only one person," I said.

"Yes, it does."

We sat, unmoving, for another few moments. As though remembering something of no importance, he mumbled something about the preliminary findings of Kapov's autopsy, but then let that topic drop, as he did his head. We would come back to it. For the moment, I would leave him to his grief, but soon we would have to take action. Even now, Sukhomlinov might be plotting against us.

And as though in answer to my thoughts, there was a knock on the door, followed immediately by the entrance of several Imperial Guards led by old, shrill Inspector Dubniev, and by the ex-Minister of War, the Palace Killer, Vladimir Sukhomlinov.

"Auguste Lupa, Jules Giraud." The inspector's voice cut shrill as a whistle through the room as he formally pronounced his charge. "I'm placing you under arrest for conspiracy, subversion, and espionage."

Lupa nodded calmly, as if he'd been expecting it.

Then we were clapped in chains and led away.

18

How long have I been in this tiny cell overlooking the frozen Neva with the Winter Palace across the way, beckoning and taunting me? Since the arrest, the beatings, the trial—perhaps six weeks. A lifetime. An eternity of cold and hunger.

When I first arrived in St. Petersburg, I remember being amused by the impregnability of Petropavlovskaya Krepost—the government prison. No longer is there anything remotely funny about it. Each day begins with the same terrible litany carrying up to my windows from the inner yard.

"Prigotov'tes', gotovy? Ogon!" And then the volley. It is a horrible way to be awakened. I don't know why it is taking them so long to get around to me and Lupa.

It hardly matters now. One day soon they will come for us. It is almost comforting to realize it.

Dear Tania,

I am assured that this letter will be posted to you.* I know you are a strong and brave woman, and I pray our child will take after you, rather than her weak and ineffectual father.

* It wasn't. It was still in the file.—Editor.

My mission here is a shambles, although Nicholas struggles on blindly, without any commitment to France, but as yet still unwilling to give up. As a military man, he is brave but strategically incompetent—in short, he is the perfect Russian! After the murders stopped... but you don't know about them, and there's no point in going into it.

My darling, I love you. I love our child, our life and our country. Please remember that.

I don't know an easy way to say this—I will not be coming home. There has been intrigue here and I've been in the thick of it. Our old friend Auguste Lupa was here when I arrived, and many things have happened. A few were disastrous. I want you to know that everything I did was in the line of duty and for the glory of France. I was not a coward, and have brought no disgrace on our name. When called upon, I had no choice but to be a good soldier. Now, it seems, a soldier's death awaits me.

Perhaps we always knew, somewhere in the back of our minds, that the firing squad is the ordained end for aging or careless spies. I am afraid I have been both.

Kiss Michelle one last time for me. I love you.

Your husband,
Jules

[KREMLIN FILE NO. JG 0665–4712–4790, CONT.; PSS ACCESS, CLASSI-
FIED]

(I don't know the date. The guard will not tell me. He laughs at the question.)

I don't really understand this impetus to write, as if anything I put down might matter now. Still, it seems important to capture it, to make some sense of it, or reorder the reality and find forgiveness for myself so that I might die in peace. Was it all my bungling, my weakness, my misguided refusal to give Lupa all the facts? I can't be sure. Perhaps other, greater forces were at work that I understand only imperfectly, or perhaps, as I tried to tell Foch when all this began, I was simply the wrong man for the job.

[KREMLIN FILE NO. JG 0665–5111–5350; PSS ACCESS—CLASSIFIED; EXCERPTED TRANSCRIPT OF TRIAL OF GIRAUD, JULES (CROSS REF. —LUPA, AUGUSTE, NO. 0671 FF.). PRESIDING MAGISTRATE GRAND DUKE SERGEI ZOSTOV. PROSECUTOR ANAXAGORAS BERIA. FORTRESS SS. PETER & PAUL, NOVEMBER 8–9, 1916, O.S.]

(Witness Boris Sukhomlinov)

Beria: And Giraud's purpose here in St. Petersburg?

Sukhomlinov: As I said, he was to proffer an offer to His Majesty, Czar Nicholas II, regarding a renewed commitment to France.

Beria: And he mentioned nothing to you about investigating any murders?

S: Nothing.

Beria: When did you first become aware of that connection?

S: On the morning of his arrest. I had been speaking to Inspector Dubniev, and he mentioned the meddling Lupa and his French companion at Kapov's apartment. When I realized he was referring to Giraud, several suspicions formed in my mind.

Beria: And what where they, General?

S: Primarily that two foreign nationals from different countries working together constituted a security threat. Espionage seemed indicated.

Beria: Anything else?

S: Yes. Giraud, in one of my discussions with him, seemed especially interested in my access to weapons.

Giraud: [from the dock] That's a lie!

Beria: [to G.D. Zostov] Your Excellency. Another outburst from the prisoner and I will request that he be gagged.

Zostov: Monsieur Giraud, you will keep quiet. Continue, please.

Beria: And what use would Giraud have for weapons? Did he give you an explanation?

S: No. It was all couched as a matter of interest. I only mention it because I found it provocative.

Beria: So do I, General. So do I.

(Witness Karel Borstoi)

Beria: Your Excellency, this witness is in chains because he has been convicted of murder, attempted regicide, subversion, and conspiracy. His father was executed according to the Holy Czar's wishes for similar crimes. His own execution has been postponed until he could testify in this trial. Borstoi, can you hear me?

Borstoi: (Unintelligible.)

Beria: Borstoi? Guard, give this man some water and revive him. (A pause while this is done.) Now, are you better?

Borstoi: (Nods.)

Beria: Speak up, animal! Answer my questions! Are you able to respond?

Borstoi: Yes.

Beria: Do you recognize the accused, Jules Giraud, in this courtroom, and if you do, please point him out.

Borstoi: Yes. There, in the dock.

Beria: Louder, please.

Borstoi: Yes, in the dock.

Beria: How do you know him?

Borstoi: Communist. Comrade.

Zostov: Quiet in this room! I won't tolerate these displays. Continue, prosecutor.

Beria: You met him as a Communist?

Borstoi: Can't talk. Teeth.

Beria: All right. I'm familiar with your proposed testimony. I will ask and you will answer. Isn't it true that you met Giraud for the first time with Auguste Lupa in the Czar's kitchen, after you'd had a fight with Max Pohl, the Czar's chef?

Borstoi: Yes.

Beria: And then Giraud sought you out in your printing shop?

Borstoi: Yes.

Beria: And why did he seek you out then? Isn't it true that it was because he knew you had just attempted to assassinate the Czar?

Borstoi: I don't know.

Beria: You don't know? Try to remember. Didn't he tell you as much?

Borstoi: If you say it.

Beria: I do say it, but it's for you to swear to it.

Borstoi: Then yes.

Beria: Yes, what?

Borstoi: Yes, I swear to it.

Beria: And wasn't the purpose of his initial meeting with you in your shop to enlist your aid in further subversive, revolutionary acts?

Borstoi: That's what he said.

Beria: That is all for this vermin. Take him out and rid the earth of him.

(Witness The Grand Duchess Anastasia)

Beria: Your Excellency, you know the accused?

Anastasia: Why, yes. He was at one of my parties. I thought he was quite a charming...

Beria: And how did he come to be invited to your party?

A: Oh, there's no mystery there. His friend Auguste Lupa asked me to invite him.

Beria: And why was that?

A: I would assume to tell him about his real role here in St. Petersburg.

Beria: His real role?

A: Yes. To work with Lupa on the murders. Didn't you all know that? I thought it was common knowledge.

Beria: He wasn't sent by the French government?

A: Oh, he might have been, but it was all arranged through Lupa. You see, I asked my husband...

Beria: Please only answer the questions I ask. Is that clear?

A: My good man, there's no need to be rude.

Beria: I apologize, but we are trying to make a specific point here—whether Giraud was in fact an diplomat of the French government, or whether he was an agent for Lupa.

A: Well, if you mean why was he here, then of course it was because Lupa had sent for him. But...

Beria: So he was working as a spy?

A: I think that's a very harsh...

Beria: But wasn't he, in fact, working in conspiracy with August Lupa, under false pretenses, as a spy?

A: Well, I...

Beria: Yes or no, madam?

A: Yes, but...

Beria: That's all. Thank you.

(Witness Elena Ripley)

Beria: Miss Ripley, what is your occupation?

Ripley: I am a drama tutor to the Grand Duchesses Olga, Maria, Tatiana, and Anastasia, and governess to Tatiana.

Beria: And when did you first meet the accused?

Ripley: I met him in the Winter Palace when he first came to tutor the czarevitch Alexis.

Beria: Isn't it in fact true that you met him at the home of Anna Vyroubova?

Ripley: No, that's not true.

Beria: Are you sure, Miss Ripley? It is my understanding that you were both present at a party given there on the night Commissar Minsky was killed?

Ripley: We may have both been there. We did not meet.

Beria: But he was there?

Ripley: I saw him, yes.

Beria: And who did he spend the most time with?

Ripley: I don't know. As I said, I didn't know him at the time, and I didn't follow his movements.

Beria: Isn't it true he spent almost the entire evening with Minsky?

Ripley: I said I don't know. Is Minsky, too, suspected of conspiracy and subversion?

Beria: Miss Ripley. I ask the questions, and I don't like your tone. Monsieur Giraud is one of the most dangerous...

Ripley: Nonsense! He is the kindest of men, and...

Beria: Miss Ripley! I am warning you! (Pause.) Now. All right, we'll leave that night. When did you and Monsieur Giraud become better acquainted?

Ripley: After he'd started tutoring Alyosha—Alexis Nicolaevitch.

Beria: And how did he come by that job?

Ripley: I don't know. I think the Czarina appointed him to it.

Beria: Didn't that strike you as strange?

Ripley: I didn't think about it. He is a native French speaker, as was his predecessor Pierre Gaillard. It seemed reasonable that Alexandra Fodorovna would choose him.

Beria: But was it reasonable that he would accept? (Pause.) Miss Ripley, was that reasonable? (Pause.) Miss Ripley, the Crown commands you to answer!

Ripley: He had a reason.

Beria: Louder, please. We can't hear you. You said he had a reason. Don't nod, answer me!

Ripley: Yes.

Beria: And what was it? Did he tell you? Damn it, I...

Zostov: There will be no profanity in my courtroom, prosecutor.

Beria: I apologize, your Excellency. But this witness is recalcitrant, and I lost my patience.

Zostov: Well, find it again and proceed.

Beria: Miss Ripley, again I ask you. Did Monsieur Giraud tell you why he accepted the post of tutor to the Heir Apparent.

Ripley: Yes.

Beria: And why was that?

Ripley: He said it would help him manipulate the Czar. But he didn't mean...

Beria: He said he was going to use the Heir Apparent to try and manipulate the Czar?

Ripley: Yes, but I'm sure...

Beria: Thank you.

Ripley: But it's not...

Beria: Thank you, Miss Ripley. Please confine yourself to answering questions that I ask. Now, what is your relationship with the accused?

Ripley: We are friends. But that last point...

Beria: Close friends? Miss Ripley, please!

Ripley: (Pause) Yes, I would say we are close friends.

Beria: And is your friendship such that you exchange confidences with one another?

Ripley: Yes.

Beria: And did Monsieur Giraud mention his, uh, relationship with Auguste Lupa?

Ripley: Yes, of course.

Beria: And how did he characterize it?

Ripley: What do you mean?

Beria: I mean, what purpose did it serve? Was it mere friendship? Did it have political overtones? Was there a conspiratorial or secret element to it?

Ripley: Jules told me that he and Lupa were working to solve the Palace murders. That he was Lupa's undercover assistant.

Beria: Undercover? In other words, secret.

Ripley: I suppose so, yes.

Beria: Secret from whom? Everyone?

Ripley: Yes. You see, Lupa thought...

Beria: Even the Czarina? The person to whom Lupa reported?

Ripley: I think so, but that was because...

Beria: Please! Just answer my questions.

Ripley: But you see, you're twisting things up. There was no reason to tell Alexandra about Jules' involvement...

Beria: Miss Ripley, I warn you. I'll have you gagged and make you write your answers if I hear any more of this. Do I make myself clear? Do you understand?

Ripley: Yes.

Beria: Now, in the course of his discussions with you, did the accused ever mention a Karel Borstoi?

Ripley: Yes.

Beria: In what context?

Ripley: Well, the first time was about his attempt to poison the Czar.

Beria: Do you mean to tell this court that Giraud knew about an attempt on the Czar's life and did not report it to the authorities.

Ripley: Well, Lupa was an authority, and Lupa already knew. They both knew about it.

Beria: So both Lupa and Giraud knew of the assassination attempt, and even knew the identity of the assailant, and did nothing to apprehend him? In fact, did they not conspire to meet with him again over the course of the next days?

Ripley: You're making it sound so bad.

Beria: Miss Ripley, we are talking about high treason, subversion, harboring a fugitive, and accessory to regicide, to say nothing of the accused's evasions and manipulations. If it sounds, as you put it, bad, it's because it is bad.

Ripley: But Jules was using Borstoi to catch the murderers.

Beria: I'm glad you brought that up. It brings us to another point. Did Giraud tell you that he and Lupa had solved the murders?

Ripley: Yes. He said Borstoi and Ivan Kapov had done them.

Beria: And when did he tell you this?

Ripley: The day before his arrest.

Beria: One full day before his arrest? Did Lupa have this information?

Ripley: Jules said he did.

Beria: And yet neither of these men, whose defense for
their conspiracy has been that they were working on some
secret mission for the Czarina—though she didn't know
about Giraud's involvement—both of these men knew the
guilty parties for a full day before their arrest, and did noth-
ing to convey that information to the Empress?
Ripley: Well, that's technically true, but...
Beria: And didn't Giraud actually have an audience with
the Czarina after he knew the identity of the killer?
Ripley: Yes, when he returned the egg, but he...
Beria: And, Miss Ripley, did he mention that small de-
tail—that the murderer had been identified—to the Em-
press?
Ripley: No, but...
Beria: Thank you, that's all.
Ripley: No, you're making it seem...
Beria: That's all, I said!
Zostov: Step down, Miss Ripley. You're excused.

(Witness Anna Vyroubova)

Beria: Miss Vyroubova, you are here to depose for Czarina
Alexandra Fodorovna, are you not?
V: Yes.
Beria: And you have a prepared statement?
V: Yes.
Beria: Would you please read it?
V: (Reading) I met Monsieur Giraud in my chambers with
my husband, Czar Nicholas II. On the earlier advice of my
religious advisor, I had been expecting someone to come and
help tutor my Alexis in French. Accordingly, I asked Mon-
sieur Giraud if he would fill that role.
   All seemed to go well, but I became suspicious of him
when my young Alexis began spouting political ideas to his
father. Someone must have put these ideas into his head, and
a Friend suggested to me that it must have been Monsieur
Giraud—he was the only new influence in my son's life.

At about this time, Alyosha also began declining to attend the regular meetings with our starets, Father Gregory Rasputin. This was, and remains, a matter of grave concern to me. Rasputin has always been a favorite of Alyosha's. But now my son has told me that he finds the monk's simple spirituality repugnant to him. He seems drawn to republican, even communist ideals, and my Friend and I attribute this to Monsieur Giraud's influence.

I next interviewed the staff, and from one servant, a loyal man named Derevenko who is entrusted with guarding Alexis from physical mishap, I learned that Monsieur Giraud had forced my son to grovel before him. This is intolerable!

Finally, under the most stringent of restrictions, I permitted one of my greatest treasures, a gift of my dear husband, the Fabergé egg entitled "Dawn," to be leant to Monsieur Giraud's co-conspirator, Auguste Lupa. After Monsieur Giraud delivered the egg to me that evening, I consulted with my spiritual adviser and became convinced that the two men were acting in concert to subvert my husband's will, which is the highest form of treason.

The following day, a beloved cousin and our valued chef were both killed. When Inspector Dubniev and General Sukhomlinov informed me of these tragedies, and stated their belief that Lupa and Giraud were involved in them, I resolved to act, and ordered their arrests.

Trusting in God and all the saints to protect us, I depose and swear that the foregoing is true. Dated this eighth day of November in the year of our Lord 1916.

Beria: Is that the entire statement, Miss Vyroubova?

V: Yes, it is.

Beria: Do you, as your own witness, have anything to add?

V: (Pause.) No.

Beria: Thank you. The Court humbly conveys its thanks and compliments to our most gracious Czarina. You may step down.

(Witness Auguste Lupa)

Beria: State your full name.

Lupa: Auguste Lupa.

Beria: Let the record show that the first words from the mouth of this witness were lies. Do you recognize this document, sir?

Lupa: I do. It is my passport.

Beria: And under what name was this passport issued?

Lupa: Can you not read it yourself?

Beria: Indeed I can. It is made out to John Hamish Adler Holmes. Is that your name?

Lupa: The name I use is irrelevant, as is your entire line of questioning. For this proceeding, my name is Auguste Lupa. Your Excellency, may I address the Court?

Beria: You may not! This is ...

Zostov: Prosecutor, I believe the witness asked me the question.

Beria: Yes, but, your Excellency, it is not allowed.

Zostov: I will determine what is allowed in my courtroom. Monsieur Lupa, why should I consider this request?

Lupa: Because, your Excellency, I hold a commission from the Czarina, a specific commission, and I am ready to fulfill its conditions at this time.

Zostov: And what prevented you before?

Lupa: My arrest.

Zostov: Were you not questioned after your arrest?

Lupa: Most assuredly. But the guards and interrogators here in the prison are not interested in the truth. They are only interested in answers. So I answered them.

Zostov: I, too, am interested in answers.

Lupa: I would hope, Excellency, that you are also interested in the truth. I am not trying to save my own life or that of my innocent companion Monsieur Giraud, but to honor my commitment to Czarina Alexandra. I am still an officer of her court, and I still hold her commission. All of my actions, indeed all of Monsieur Giraud's, are explainable and reasonable only if viewed in the light of the facts I possess. If there is not to be a travesty of justice here in your court, I must be allowed to make my case.

Beria: Your Excellency, this is absurd. This man is on trial himself for the most heinous of crimes. He has perjured himself to this court, our interrogators, and to the Czarina herself. Any testimony he gives must be regarded as purely self-serving.

Zostov: Nevertheless, prosecutor, what he says might be heard. I am interested to see justice done, not just to have questions answered. I assure you that whatever he says will remain very suspect. Proceed, Monsieur Lupa.

Lupa: Thank you, Excellency. First, an explanation of my commission. Alexandra Fodorovna asked me to come to Russia from my home in Montenegro to try and get to the bottom of a series of murders that she felt was weakening the Czar's will to continue prosecuting the war. Contrary to popular belief, she is not at all pro-German. More than anything else, she desires the War to end, but only if it ends with a victorious Russia.

When she initially requested me, there had been three slayings. At the time of my arrest, there were six. Since my position at the court would be official, I determined that I would need another investigator working behind the scenes in a different capacity. As I'm sure your Excellency realizes, an official status is helpful for administrative purposes, but can be a downright hindrance to getting at facts.

I chose Monsieur Giraud for this role. I trusted him and we had worked together before. For various reasons, not the least of which being that I thought it likely he would refuse me if I made my request boldly, I designed a cover mission for him, which was nonetheless legitimate. When he first came here, he was aware only of that mission—to present a French offer of arms and money to the Czar in return for his renewed commitment to France for the winter months.

No doubt it was the Czar's return to Tsarkoye Selo which prompted the killing of Boris Minsky, the first murder after my arrival. It had the required effect, plunging Nicholas into a funk so deep that Giraud could not make his offer with any hope of its being accepted.

At this time, I solicited Giraud's help, and he agreed to it. I did not tell the Empress of Giraud's part in my plan because, frankly, I suspected that she would confide it to Anna Vyroubova, who abhors keeping secrets as nature does a vacuum. Excuse me, Monsieur Beria, but this is common knowledge.

In any case, events began to move swiftly. It is true that Giraud and I were both aware of Borstoi's attempt to poison the Czar's sugar. But—and this is crucial—my commission called for me to find the Palace killer, not potential assassins of Nicholas. Perhaps I erred, but I reasoned that if Borstoi could lead me to my quarry, that would be the greater good. Since he would be denied future admission to the Palace, I assumed that he could no longer be a danger to the Czar. That assumption, by the way, proved correct.

Giraud and I began our investigation into Minsky's death, and the field became rife with suspects. Initially, I suspected Elena Ripley because she had been the last person seen with Minsky, and because poison is a classic woman's murder weapon. Her motive? Jealousy. She was in love with Minsky and he had overturned her in favor of Katrina Sukhomlinov, with whom he was having an affair.

Suk: (from the gallery) That's a lie, Lupa. That's a black lie!

Zostov: Here, here! General, I must caution you.

Suk: Your Excellency, this is slander of the rankest sort.

Zostov: If it proves false, General, I will add slander to the charges against him. In the meanwhile, I will not tolerate interruptions in my courtroom. You, and all of you, are here at my pleasure, and you will be well advised to remember that. Proceed, Monsieur Lupa.

Lupa: Thank you. As I was saying, it was tempting to consider Miss Ripley as Minsky's killer, but the weight of evidence favored our hypothesis that the murders were politically motivated, and Miss Ripley had not even been in St. Petersburg when the first killing had taken place, so I was forced for the time being to exclude her from consideration.

However, the motive of jealousy immediately reappeared, again centering, if the General will excuse me, around Madame Sukhomlinov. It seems that Max Pohl, the Czar's chef, also harbored an infatuation for that woman. He might have killed Minsky to eliminate his rival. Certainly he had the poison at hand.

But in my heart I could not suspect the chef. I knew him well. He was a patriot. He knew how the other murders had affected the Czar, and I didn't believe he would place his own passions over his love of Russia. I hasten to add that while I held this view privately, I nevertheless did not cross him off my list of suspects.

But heading the list was General Sukhomlinov himself.

Suk: Your Excellency! I must insist...

Zostov: General, this is my last warning. Guard, stand by the General and if he speaks out of turn again, remove him from the courtroom. Monsieur Lupa, I also tell you that if this tale leads nowhere, you may expect no mercy from this court.

Lupa: I would expect none, Excellency.

Zostov: That is good. Our justice, though severe, is merciful. Our anger can be very painful. Do you understand?

Lupa: Completely.

Zostov: Proceed.

Lupa: Sukhomlinov had both political and personal motivation to kill Minsky. The Commissar had just returned from Spala with Czar Nicholas, and was about to re-ignite his affair with the General's wife. Sukhomlinov hated Nicholas not only for removing him from his post as Minister of War, but for allowing him to be prosecuted for espionage. His business interests, mostly German, were being subverted by the prolonged War. There were a dozen reasons why he should act.

But Monsieur Giraud had not been idle. And his pursuit of Borstoi—including his brilliant subterfuge involving the Fabergé egg—abruptly changed the focus of my investigation.

My colleague has been much maligned during this trial for his deception of the Czarina. In his defense, I must make two points: First, he had no reason to believe the Empress was not fully informed of his possession of the egg—indeed, that he returned it directly to her proves that. Second, by spuriously presenting the egg to Borstoi, Giraud convinced him that they were brother communists. This resulted in Borstoi's boastful confession to the first Palace murder, and set the stage for the solution to the rest.

Beria: The solution to the rest?

Lupa: Exactly.

Beria: You realize, of course, that Inspector Dubniev has closed the file on those murders.

Lupa: That doesn't surprise me. I assume he concluded that Kapov and Pohl worked together and, when they were about to be found out, entered into a suicide pact.

Beria: There is ample evidence to believe that that is exactly what transpired. And indeed, there have been no further killings—a good indication that the murderers themselves are dead.

Lupa: It might also mean that the killer took advantage of an ideal opportunity to stop. Since the crimes are believed solved, there is no further investigation. Even a dimwit would see that, and we are not dealing here with an idiot. Far from it.

Zostov: Go on.

Lupa: When Monsieur Giraud brought me the information that Borstoi had confessed to committing the first murder with Kapov, it was tempting to consider the obvious—that Kapov had continued the killings, and may have even done so with Borstoi.

But Borstoi's rationale for stopping after one murder—that someone else saw the effect it produced on the Czar, and continued with their own campaign of terror—made a perverted kind of sense to me. Why should Borstoi and Kapov continue putting themselves at risk when someone else was apparently willing to do their work for them?

I must now make a confession, and in so doing I offer an apology to M. Giraud. We are charged with being co-conspirators. And it's true that to a certain extent we worked together. But to a greater extent, I worked alone, and I used M. Giraud for my own purposes. Jules, please forgive me for this.

Zostov: Monsieur Lupa, you will address yourself to this court. We are growing impatient with this story and are unmoved by your apology to the accused. Get to the point.

Lupa: The point, Excellency, is this. Early in my investigation, I had eliminated one of the suspects from consideration. Elena Ripley had been in the Crimea with the Royal Family when the first murder had been committed. She was, therefore, demonstrably innocent. Subsequently, M. Giraud and she formed an attachment. He began confiding in her.

And on a hunch, I began feeding disinformation, through him, to her.

Beria: Disinformation? You mean lies. You lied to your own partner?

Lupa: I won't argue semantics with you. I presented information to M. Giraud as though it were factual when I knew it not to be.

Beria: But what prompted this "hunch" in the first place? If you knew Miss Ripley was innocent... ?

Lupa: I knew, or at least believed, she had not committed the first murder. But I couldn't get away from the knowledge that she was the last person to be seen with Minsky, that poison is a classic woman's weapon, that she seemed to be a fixture at gatherings where a simple governess had no place. But as I say, at the time, it was only the merest conjecture. I had no motive for her, only means and opportunity.

To keep M. Giraud from suspecting anything, although I don't believe he would have been suspicious in any case, I told him that Miss Ripley had left Minsky with a group of fellow officers on the night he was killed. Now doubly assured of her innocence, M. Giraud had no reason not to trust her completely.

Even so, it remained a minor theme while I carried on my regular investigations which, with the exception of Borstoi, were proving exceptionally barren. It wasn't until Borstoi's confession to the first murder—and only the first murder—that Miss Ripley came back under suspicion. It was possible, I reasoned, that there was more than one killer. Then, at Kapov's death—his rather too convenient and timely death—my suspicions grew to convictions.

Beria: But Kapov's death was a suicide.

Lupa: No. That was a murder!

Zostov: Silence! I must again warn the gallery. These outbursts are not acceptable. Proceed, Monsieur Beria.

Beria: You realize that Inspector Dubniev has proclaimed Kapov's death a suicide.

Lupa: And he was about to do the same with Minsky. In both cases he was wrong.

Beria: And I presume you can prove that?

Lupa: The facts allow no other conclusion. I ordered an autopsy of Kapov's body as soon as I examined him, and got the results just before my arrest. He had died of hanging...

Beria: Brilliant! Hanging, you say?

Zostov: Curb your sarcasm, Prosecutor. This is hardly new ground, M. Lupa.

Lupa: New ground will be broken, Excellency. The autopsy showed that Kapov was both drugged and drunk when he died.

Beria: Many suicides find courage for their final act that way.

Lupa: True. But Kapov could not have walked or even moved on his own with the quantity of poisons in his body. It is flatly impossible that he could have fashioned a proper noose, or balanced himself sufficiently on his window ledge to loop the rope over the gable. It's in the autopsy report. Read it, if Inspector Dubniev hasn't destroyed it.

Beria: But that alleged destruction would also serve you well, wouldn't it?

Lupa: Not really, I don't need the autopsy. The captain of the guards who discovered Kapov's body can testify to some other critical points. Kapov's fingernails were broken off—two of them to the quick. The others were bloody and filled with splinters, splinters of the same rough wood that bordered the window. There were matching scratch marks on the shutters.

Beria: That's all? That is your evidence?

Lupa: That's not all, but it should be enough. Taken together, it is damning. Someone drugged Kapov, looped a rope over the outside gable—by the way, I checked and it was near enough that anyone could have done it—then dragged him to the window. When the noose was over his head, Kapov regained enough consciousness to realize what was happening, and put up a valiant struggle, grabbing at the shutters, the border to the window, anything to save himself from that last terrible fall.

Please, let me continue. I know that thus far this has all been conjecture, a pet theory. You need proof, and I needed proof. I got it.

I made up another lie, one that I shall regret for as long as I live. Though it identified the murderer beyond any doubt, it resulted in the death of one of the finest men I have ever known, Max Pohl.

After reaching the conclusion that Kapov had not killed himself, I told Monsieur Giraud that Pohl had news concerning Minsky's murder, something to do with locating the source of the poison that had been used to kill Minsky.

As I surmised he would, Giraud passed this information along to Miss Ripley. It must have been a terrible shock for her. She had just killed Kapov, thinking to end all suspicion surrounding the murders, and now here was a new threat.

She wasted no time. With her position as governess to the Grand Duchesses, she had the run of the Royal Quarters. And being a beautiful woman, she undoubtedly had no trouble seducing Max, who was a very passionate man, into a vulnerable position. When she'd done that, she shot him, leaving the gun in his hand to give it the appearance of a suicide.

But the string of coincidence had by now grown too thin—it could no longer support the weight of Miss Ripley's deceptions.

She was the only one with reason to fear Pohl, with a motive to kill him. No one else knew of his supposed information. I was about to arrest her when I myself was taken into custody.

Beria: This is ingenious, monsieur, but it is still not compelling. It is all "might have been," "should have done." There is no evidence.

Lupa: Question her and depend on it. Elena Ripley is guilty.

Ripley: (from the gallery) No!

Zostov: Madam, I would...

Ripley: Please, your Excellency. It's impossible!

Lupa: It's not impossible. It's established.

Ripley: No! You're saying I killed Kapov. But I was with someone that whole night who can prove I didn't do it, who can testify to my innocence.

Lupa: He would have to be an unimpeachable witness, Madam. He could not, in fact, exist.

Zostov: Miss Ripley! Return to your seat. Get away from the dock!

Ripley: Oh Jules, I'm sorry. I'm sorry, I tried not to tell.

Beria: Are you saying...?

Ripley: I was with your own colleague, Monsieur Lupa. Jules Giraud. I didn't kill Kapov. I was with Jules.

Zostov: Silence! Silence! Miss Ripley, control yourself. Guard, get her away from the accused. Monsieur Giraud, is this true? Giraud, I am addressing you. Answer me. Is this true?

Giraud: (from the dock) *Oui, c'est ça.* (Whispers.) I am sorry, Auguste, but you must be wrong.

Zostov: What did you say? Speak up, man.

Giraud: She was with me. She could not have killed Kapov.

Beria: Your Excellency. This farce must be concluded. Not only can Monsieur Lupa not prove his accusations. The only thing he has proven is that he has a vivid imagination and he is an adroit liar. His own co-conspirator refutes his testimony. This court has been more than lenient with him, with them both. They even lie to one another. For my part, I dismiss this witness. I've heard enough of him. Step down, sir.

Lupa: I would just like to ask Monsieur Giraud...

Beria: I said step down! Your Excellency...

Zostov: I concur. Guards, take this man to his cell!

19

[KREMLIN FILE NO. JG 0665-4712-4790, CONT.; PSS ACCESS, CLASSI-FIED]

This morning the ink was frozen.

I was awakened, as always, while it was still dark, and fed my bowl of gruel. While I ate it, I capped the bottle holding the ink and sat on it. By the time I finished eating, sitting on my cot wrapped in the threadbare blanket, the ink had begun to thaw.

It was still too dark to write. There was, in fact, nothing else to do but listen to this morning's execution volleys—nine of them—each preceded by the clear ringing voice of the captain of the firing squad. *"Prigotov'tes'. Gotovy? Ogon!"* And then the shots.

Though it is more bitterly cold than it has been, for the first time in a fortnight, the weather has been clear for two days running. The sky—now as I write—is an almost purple hue. Sound carries wonderfully. I look out toward the Winter Palace and sometimes fancy I can hear voices. Occasionally a floe will crack on the Neva. Sometimes, when it's very still, one can make out the crunch of footsteps through the crust of the snow.

I find myself entertaining the most morbid thoughts. I know that within a short time, my own body will be riddled with bullets, and I try to imagine where those bullets are right now—in what box, in which room, stuck into which soldier's cartridge belt.

Sometimes I feel grateful that I am in Russia, with its late mornings. Since the executions are carried out at dawn, I vicariously relish the few extra hours I will be given than if my punishment were to be carried out in my native France.

These are ridiculous thoughts, but they weigh heavily.

Yesterday, possibly because it had stopped snowing, they took us to the yard and I saw Lupa. He's lost a remarkable amount of weight in such a short time, but his frame is still strong and robust. We spoke a few minutes before the guards separated us.

Much to his surprise, Rasputin has come to the prison more than once to visit him, although Lupa didn't characterize the visits as social. Evidently, until yesterday's visit, the monk was content to come and stare at him through the bars, his eyes shining with a manic glare, his expression that of a madman.

Lupa told me that he would stand motionless for as long as an hour, mumbling one word over and over, like a mantra. The word was *"rache."*

"The German word for revenge?"

Lupa nodded. "Exactly."

"What could he mean by that?"

Lupa shrugged. "I don't know. The word played a small part in one of my father's cases, but I don't see what connection that could have with Rasputin."

I didn't either, and Rasputin's irrationality was a common enough feature of his personality that I didn't think the question bore much thought.

In any event, when the monk had come by Lupa's cell yesterday, the visit had been different. He told Lupa that Czar Nicholas was gong to Spala again. Though it was only to be a short visit to military headquarters, it removed the last obstacle to our execution.

"How is that?" I said, my stomach turning over at the news.

"Evidently Alexis, the czarevitch, has prevented our execution to this date by interceding daily with his father. He developed a real attachment to you, it seems, and has been doing all he can to keep us alive."

"But why, then, doesn't the Czar simply free us?"

Lupa stamped on the cold ground to keep warm. His hands folded under his arms, his ruddy cheeks puffed out, he saw the guards approaching us and spoke with a grim urgency. "Rasputin says the Czarina will not allow that. She wants the execution carried out. Evidently the monk does, too. And with Nicholas gone, he gloats that there will be nothing to prevent it. And she seems willing to risk the wrath of both her husband and child over it."

"But why?"

"Obviously, she thinks—she's been convinced—that we're guilty and a danger to the Czar's reign."

The guard came and separated us. As he was leading Lupa away, I couldn't resist calling after him. "And when is the Czar going off to Spala?"

"Today," he said.

That was yesterday.

It is to be tomorrow.

An orthodox priest called at my cell an hour ago. Bearded, thin as a stick, smelling of horse and incense, he was no comfort. We spoke for a moment or two, and he offered to hear my confession. I refused, and not simply because he might have been a government spy hoping for a last-minute admission of my guilt. I have nothing to confess now—perhaps this writing has served that purpose. I am at peace, with myself and with the war-weary world.

After the trial, it took some time for me to reach any kind of peace with Lupa. He had involved me in this affair, and his deceptions to me had hurt me deeply and, more to the point, had helped lead us both to this pass from which there appears to be no hope for escape.

But the cause for which we have fought is greater than my personal concerns. I never for a moment doubted his sincerity, and if his methods were not those I would have adopted, still they had served him well enough in the past that his confidence in them seemed justified. There was always a guiding strategy behind his duplicity, and I have come to believe that the stakes justified the risks he took—even the risk of my own life.

Echoing Kapov, who said that if it would shorten the war by a day he would kill a hundred Minskys, I feel that if our attempt to save the Eastern Front gives France just one more day in which to emerge from this fray victorious, it will have been worth it a hundred times, a thousand times.

And what of Elena?

Of course it's clear that Lupa, hard pressed to come to some solution—any solution—was wrong about her. I am at a loss to explain his insistence that she was a cold-blooded killer, especially when he could supply no compelling motive for her to act. I can only hope that the shadow of suspicion he thrust her under will not harm her with the court. She has had a hard enough time without having to live down false accusations.

If there were only a way to prosecute Sukhomlinov, but that is a futile wish. His alliance with Dubniev would be enough to guarantee his safety even if he weren't such a sycophant to Rasputin and Alexandra. I am surprised that Lupa never came to accuse, or really even suspect, him—a sprightly offense against our accuser might have turned the tables at our trials.

And now, in spite of all, the Czar continues to fight. His mild manner must hide an iron will, or perhaps his talks with Alyosha have stiffened his spine. If that is the case, and my own influence had the slightest effect upon it, I must then count my mission a success of sorts.

My hands are shaking. These small justifications are cold

comfort as I watch the brittle strip of silver sunlight cross my cell for the last time. Tomorrow at this hour...

They've brought in someone to take my cell, an old, skinny, hawk-faced peasant, shuffling and muttering in Russian. The guard informs the man that I am French, and he goes into some sort of fit, snarling at me, retreating to the farthest corner of the cell. It is all great sport to the guard.

"Anyone but a frog," the boy—for the guard is a young bully—said. "That's what he requested. Hates you Frenchies."

He laughed again, kicking at the man on the floor of the cell. "Don't worry, Giraud, he's just another old radical going to the wall. Though tonight you'll have to cast lots for the bed."

He kicked at the old man again and said to him in Russian. "Tomorrow you get the bed. Isn't that right, Giraud? Tomorrow your bed is the cold, cold ground."

His laughter rang through the wing. "'Course, he won't be here long either."

Now I scribble to keep from going mad. My cellmate sits cross-legged, scratching at the floor, alternately cursing at me with exceptional venom, then tiring and singing snatches of gypsy folksongs.

I've had my last meal—a half potato soaking in dirty vegetable broth. The moon is coming up. It is very cold. I am afraid. I don't want to die.

My mind is going. I imagine I hear the old man say my name in perfect French. And again...

PART THREE

20

[KREMLIN FILE NO. JG-0665-4840-4851; PSS ACCESS, CLASSIFIED. ENTRIES INTO A LEATHER NOTEBOOK EMBOSSED WITH THE NAME JOHN H. WATSON, M.D.]

I thought the risk was too great, even for Sherlock Holmes.

After all, no one had ever before successfully escaped from the Fortress Ss. Peter and Paul. Holmes and I had discussed the alternatives from Sussex Downs to the Astoria here in Petrograd, and finally, Holmes saw no other solution. As dangerous as it might be, he had no choice.

His brother, Mycroft, as head of Britain's secret service, had been following the exploits of Holmes' son, who is using the name Auguste Lupa,* and upon his arrest for subversion had alerted my friend. We wasted no time, although the voyage here by ship seemed interminable. Holmes paced the deck in all weathers, terrified that he was already too late, that his son had gone to his execution.

"I must think, Watson," he said to my remonstrances. "I must have plans within plans. There will, at best, be only a little time, and I must not waste a second."

---

* Throughout Watson's manuscript, Holmes and Watson refer to Lupa as "John." To avoid confusion, wherever it appears, "John" has been changed to "Auguste" or "Lupa."—The Editor.

By the time we were in Russian waters, he'd decided upon his disguise as the Norwegian violinist Sigerson that he'd used after his disappearance following his duel to the death with Professor Moriarty at Reichenbach Falls. Sigerson, he reasoned, could play a convincing radical, and could probably get himself arrested. I thought there were extremely long odds against his success, and told him so.

"You're probably right, my friend, but what other choice have we?"

And against that argument, I was mute.

After first determining that we were not too late, that Auguste was still alive, we made calls on people whom Holmes thought might be able to bring some influence to bear. None of them were heartening, and Holmes began laying the groundwork for his own arrest.

Each day, disguised as Sigerson, he would leave our hotel for some underground meeting or another. On the fourth day, Holmes rushed into my room, his eyes flashing. I could hardly recognize this dirty, rag-tag musician as my friend. With matted hair peeking out from a misshapen cap, a charcoal stubble, and ill-fitting, filthy worker's clothes, Sherlock Holmes could be no one's idea of a cultivated Englishman.

Ignoring my startled exclamation, he asked me if I could be ready to join him downstairs within minutes. Since I'd been reading and watching the snow fall for the better part of the afternoon, I assured him that that would be no problem.

Within a quarter of an hour, two perfectly proper British businessmen were sitting in the lobby of the Astoria in the early, though already dark, evening. Holmes, in his three-piece gray herringbone, his conservative cravat, cane, and bowler, looked particularly distinguished as he sipped his whisky and soda. It was an effective transformation.

On the street, hansoms and sleighs came and went, depositing hotel guests and visitors at the wide swinging doors. Suddenly Holmes raised the newspaper he'd been holding up to his face.

"Ah, Watson," he said, "I'd thought as much."

"What's that, Holmes?" I saw nothing beyond the usual pre-dinner crowd.

"There! Just coming through the doors now. The delivery man and the porter."

There was nothing provocative about two such people in a hotel lobby, and I mentioned that fact to Holmes. "And you might put the paper down, Holmes," I added with some asperity. "I prefer to see the face of the person I'm speaking to."

Chuckling good-naturedly, Holmes complied. "You're right, my friend. The disguise either works or it doesn't."

The delivery man, holding a package of some kind, looked lost indeed. Walking halfway across the lobby, he stopped almost directly in front of us and perused the room. Finally, he went over to the porter as though asking for directions, and the two of them split up and left the lobby by different exits.

"That was instructive," Holmes said. "They have found my trail—or rather, Sigerson's trail. I hope I didn't make it too easy on them." He sipped casually at his whisky. "Well, my friend, I rather fancy I shall be arrested tomorrow."

"Holmes!" I said, but he raised his hand.

"Please, Watson, it's all arranged. Are you ready for your part?"

I assured him I was, and tried one last time to argue that there might be a better way, but he stopped me again. "Time is very short," he said in a tone that, were it not Holmes speaking, I would describe as desperate. "There is no time to enlist middlemen anymore. There is a rumor that the Czar may be going off to Spala soon. That leaves Alexandra to handle domestic affairs, and it is said she will somehow contrive to have the sentences carried out."

"How can you know that?" I demanded.

Holmes lectured me patiently. "The people Sigerson is allied with have spies everywhere, and it appears that Auguste and his friend Giraud are of interest to them as well as the Government—they betrayed the cause." He sighed and finished his drink. "No, Watson, I must act, and now."

Accepting his judgment, I must have lapsed into a brown study. Holmes picked up the newspaper again. I think he had only been reading it a moment, though, when he again folded it and placed it on his lap.

"You're right, Watson," he said quietly. "There is a feeling here. I'd be wise not to ignore it."

"Yes, there's that sense of..." Then, realizing I hadn't said anything, I stopped. Even after years of friendship with Sherlock Holmes, I was always disconcerted by his ability to read my thoughts.

But it was natural to him. Perhaps he was even unaware that he did it. He continued seriously. "To take it a step further," he said, "there seems to be—or at least I feel, as you do—a spirit of Moriarty in the land."

"Exactly what I was thinking!" I exclaimed. "Really, Holmes, this is too much! How could you...?"

"Tut, tut, Watson, what could be simpler? I observe you looking at the guests entering from the freezing street, you fold your arms across your chest and shiver in sympathy. Then your eyes light upon the painting of Napoleon's retreat hanging on the wall across the room. You're thinking of another bitter winter, another war. Finally, you come to our situation here, you scan the lobby and unconsciously your hand goes to the revolver under your coat."

"But how does Moriarty fit in?" I asked. Though he had described the exact process by which I'd arrived at my vague feeling of unease, even I didn't understand why Holmes' old nemesis had entered my mind. After all, Professor Moriarty had died at Reichenbach Falls twenty-five years before.

"What could be simpler, Watson?" Holmes said. "Moriarty was the Napoleon of crime. The painting of the little corporal triggered that memory." But before I could marvel anew at his logic, he continued. "I feel the chill myself. There is something, as though clinging to the walls—a sense of evil here. It almost has the Professor's signature upon it."

"But that's impossible. Moriarty's dead."

"I know." Holmes stroked his chin and his black eyes hooded over. "Yet, I feel him here. It is strange."

"Had he ever gone to Russia?" I asked. "Perhaps his worldwide net extended even to here."

Holmes tapped the newspaper. "I know he traveled extensively as a young man, while he still professed to be a simple mathematician. Yes," he said, striking his knee again, "yes, I remember now! He did come here to study. He acknowledges Professor Rudianko of the University of Moscow in the preface to his treatise on the binomial theorem." Then he added reflectively, "But I really believed that was before he'd begun his career, his criminal career."

"Perhaps it was," I said.

"And yet we both feel his presence somehow. It is odd."

For a moment, Holmes stared out into nothingness, perhaps remembering some of his past encounters with the grand master of evil, the only man who had ever been a match for him, Professor James Moriarty. Then, shaking himself as though shrugging it off, he stood up. "Well, there's nothing for it now, Watson, and we've got work to do. Shall we go in to dinner?"

I was not to interfere in any way with his arrest. My job, he said, was to appear, armed, at the bridge between the prison and the Winter Palace every evening for the next week after which, if he hadn't appeared, I was to book passage back to England.

He told me that there was a reasonable chance of arrest, monkey trial, and summary execution, but if he could somehow avoid that fate and get into the prison, he reasoned that his best opportunity for escape would be just after dark.

He had discovered that the full contingent of guards was reduced by two-thirds at night. Further, since no one had before escaped from the prison, he expected an attitude of unwary complacency. I tried to point out that they might be complacent because no one had ever beaten them, but Holmes refused to entertain any negative thoughts. No, he said, this was an ideal opportunity. He was sure of it.

Shivering in the gusting wind, I stomped from foot to foot, hands thrust deep into my pockets, my revolver securely tucked into my belt. This was my third night at the Neva Bridge and it was dark as Moriarty's soul in the still-early evening. Across from me, the mass of the Winter Palace loomed blankly at the river's edge, the occasional yellowish light from a window serving only to make the surrounding darkness blacker.

The Neva itself provided a basso undertone as it forced its way beneath the pilings at the center of the bridge. At its banks, and well out into the stream, it was frozen over, but at its center, the black water rushed with a churning urgency.

The situation over the past two days of waiting had sapped my confidence, and though no one respected the talents of Sherlock Holmes more than myself, I continued to believe that this time he had pushed them beyond their limits. Still, with a heavy heart, I was obeying his orders. If he met with success, I expected some klaxon rousing the gendarmerie at the prison at the news of the escape. Then perhaps a headlong rush into the narrower streets of the capital, my revolver keeping our followers at a distance.

The silence, therefore, lulled me. I leaned back against the bridge. Foot traffic was light, with only an occasional lone walker hurrying to his or her destination. After the intense clear cold of the last two days, the air had become heavier, with increased wind. Another blizzard was coming.

Looking to my right, I saw three men—one in the uniform of a prison guard—turn onto the bridge. As they came abreast of me, the guard raised his cap and whispered. "Come along, Watson. Step lively, now."

"Holmes!"

"Say hello to Auguste, and I don't believe you've met Jules Giraud."

We moved quickly and in silence back into the cover of the city, keeping to the shadows. We returned by back streets to the Astoria. By then it was close to midnight, and if the night clerk noticed anything strange in the old prison guard with the ill-fitting uniform, the two bearded derelicts, and the portly Englishman in his bowler and overcoat, he showed no sign of it.

As soon as we had left the lobby and were in the relative safety and privacy of the hallway, I could wait no longer, and asked Holmes how he had managed it.

"It was quite absurdly simple," he declared. "Almost disappointing, really."

Giraud, obviously not used to my friend's sense of humor, spoke up. "Actually, it stopped just short of being disappointing."

It must be no small strain to know you will be facing a firing squad in a matter of hours, and the drawn faces of Auguste and Giraud bore eloquent witness to that agony—the spectre of their aborted appointment with death.

Auguste is so thin that for the first time in my memory he resembles his father more than his uncle Mycroft. Holmes himself, having also been through an arrest, a trial, and imprisonment, appeared none the worse for wear.

Holmes and I have adjoining suites, and when we closed the door behind us, he suggested that Lupa and Giraud bathe and shave in each of the bathrooms. I had never seen him so solicitous. His son's trauma had not been lost upon him.

When we were alone, he poured himself a whisky and went to the gasogene, then sat in one of the armchairs, pulled out and lit his pipe, and smiled at me.

"Well, Watson, the fortress is not impregnable, as you can see." He took a pull at his whisky and crossed his long legs.

"We were very fortunate. It could have gone another way quite easily. I think the reputation of the place played into our hands."

"How is that?"

"Overconfidence. No one is looking out for an escape. There is only one guard on each wing at night." He chuckled. "I fancy they'll increase that after tonight."

"But even so, Holmes," I protested, "surely it couldn't have been that simple?"

"Psychology, Watson. Dr. Freud's tool, and a useful one from time to time. I bullied the guard into thinking he was bullying me, and finessed him into putting me where he thought I'd be most unhappy—with a Frenchman.

"Then, after the meal, if you could call it that, I revealed myself to Giraud. Since he was to be executed the next morning, it was plausible that he might try to kill himself, and I began screaming to the guard that he'd done just that. He lay still on his bed, and I convinced the guard he must have poisoned himself.

"A moment later, the guard entered the cell alone. After all, we were two old men—one of us dead—and he was a young, strong Cossack bully."

Holmes chuckled again, remembering. "It was but a moment's work. When he leaned down over Giraud, a simple baritsu technique rendered him unconscious. After that, dressed in his uniform and armed with his gun, it was child's play to overcome the one guard in Auguste's wing." He smiled again beneath his hooded eyes. "And here we are."

Before I could comment, the door opened and a well-scrubbed Auguste entered the room.

"Well, Watson," Holmes said caustically, "I think the diet did my son no harm. But perhaps we should see if we can order some food?"

The kitchen was closed, but we were able to have someone deliver an enormous pot of tea, several loaves of black bread, butter, some herring, a bowl of apples, and a round of hard cheese. The breakfast would have fed eight men under normal circumstances, but by the time Holmes had finished his own ablutions one hour later, nary a crumb was left.

I knew that Auguste, at least, was well on his way to recovery as he finished his third apple. Deadpan, he looked at me witheringly. "Thank you for the food, Doctor." His eyes twinkled behind the frown, "but you might at least have ordered some beer."

Through the window the aurora borealis played against the night sky as the four of us sipped at the last of the tea. The conversation had faltered, and I was beginning to think it was time to get some sleep, when Sherlock Holmes addressed his son.

"You really ought to get it settled, you know."

"Of course."

It was as though they had been having a long talk. "Unless you think we should leave it and try to get out of Russia."

Auguste shook his head. "The job isn't done."

"Well, if that's the case, I must tell you that we won't get anywhere with both of you so at odds." Holmes looked at the Frenchman. "We might as well have it out, M. Giraud. What's troubling you?"

Before he could answer, Auguste spoke. "Elena Ripley."

In a few words, as his companion nodded in agreement, Auguste outlined the case as it had developed up to that point. "But," he concluded, "Jules corroborated her alibi at the trial. It's left me without an answer."

"The answer is Sukhomlinov," Giraud said firmly. Where before he had been coldly polite, which I had attributed to Gallic reserve, I saw now that Holmes had noticed the truth—there was enmity between these two men.

"No, Jules, the answer is Elena Ripley. Pohl's death proved that to me. Our general was with Dubniev planning my arrest when Pohl was killed."

"Isn't it possible he did shoot himself?"

"I like to think all things are possible, Jules, but in this case, I would say no. Miss Ripley eliminated him because you and I made her believe that he was a threat."

"But Elena was with me when Kapov was killed."

Auguste sighed. "I know, Jules. They are major stumbling blocks, and yet my theory is the only one that is plausible. We must get around them."

Giraud's patience was wearing thin. *"Merde!"*

Sherlock Holmes stepped into the breach. "Monsieur Giraud, when all other possibilities have been exhausted, whichever remains, no matter how remote, must be the solution."

"I'll agree to that, but Elena was with me."

"The entire night?"

Clearly the subject embarrassed him, but to his credit he spoke up. "She was in my room when I went to bed, and she woke me in the morning."

Auguste nearly dropped his teacup as he pounced. "Good Lord, Jules, she didn't sleep with you? Why didn't you tell me that earlier?"

The Frenchman replied drily. "I wanted to save it for the right moment." Then, more seriously. "No. I am certain she was with me the entire night. And besides, Auguste, if you remember, the whole thing only came out at the trial."

Auguste was silent for a moment. "Yes, of course I remember, but clarify something for me. Were you asleep or not? If you were, how could you know she stayed with you? If not, then my theory is no good, but you seem unclear about it yourself."

Giraud furrowed his patrician brow. "Twice I recall being awakened by her during the night. Or she said it was the middle of the night..." He paused, and Auguste let him wrestle with it. "But why would she have made a point of telling me the time on both occasions?"

"She did that?"

Giraud nodded. "And it was dark."

"Jules, as you well know, it doesn't get light here until

nearly nine. Is it possible, just possible, mind you, that she returned to your room in the early morning, say seven or eight, contrived to awake you and somehow implant in your mind that it was still the middle of the night? Is that possible?"

The Frenchman's discomfort was difficult to watch. And yet, even if Auguste's hypothesis were true, I couldn't blame Giraud for not thinking of it. It was nearly Byzantine in its complexity. If Elena Ripley had done as Auguste suggested, she was a formidable enemy indeed.

Finally Giraud conceded morosely that it could have happened. Auguste, though, was on the scent, and wasn't about to let it get away. "I don't mean to offend you by pressing this, Jules, but do you realize how essential that one fact is? Would you mind going over the events of that entire night?"

In the next twenty minutes, we learned quite a lot that was new, and most of it was potentially damning for Elena Ripley. Giraud told us that she had come to his apartment after a party at Rasputin's that had been attended by "most of the court," and Auguste drew the assumption that that could very well have included Ivan Kapov, which would have given the woman the opportunity to arrange to visit, perhaps seduce, and finally poison the young nobleman.

When Giraud told how Miss Ripley had appeared with drinks for them both at his chambers, Auguste seized that moment, pointing out that she could have done to Giraud what he surmised she did to Kapov. Where had the vodka originally come from? Giraud didn't know. How did she know it was there? Didn't Giraud admit that he passed out after the drinks, and wasn't it possible he had been drugged? We all saw the doubt begin to grow in Giraud's mind.

In all, it was a far cry from the night-long seduction Auguste had envisioned. And Giraud was apparently ready to admit the possibility that Miss Ripley might not be so innocent as she appeared.

"Remember, Jules," he said, "the woman is a trained actress. If you couple her skills with any insight at all into how you might be feeling—alone, disoriented, excited by the attentions of an attractive woman—you create a stage upon which she can excel."

"But I don't understand," Giraud began, then stopped. "You still don't have a motive."

"Yes, but a half hour ago we thought Miss Ripley had been with you the entire night. Now it's entirely plausible that she wasn't. She could easily have left you, gone back to Rasputin's, returned with Kapov to the Palace and killed him, and finally returned to your room to sleep on your sofa."

Sherlock Holmes had been listening in silence, his briar burning steadily. Finally, he leaned forward, elbows on his knees, and addressed his son. "I don't see that we have much choice except to assume your logic is sound. So we need a motive for the woman, Ripley. Are there any other untied knots?"

Giraud sat up as though he'd been stung. "Rasputin's revenge," he said.

"What is that?" Holmes asked, and Auguste explained the strange visits of the holy man to his prison cell.

"He actually used the word 'rache'?" Holmes asked. "That's very singular." But for the moment, he chose to file rather than pursue that fact. "Jules, how does Miss Ripley feel about Rasputin?"

Giraud, looking beaten and exhausted, raised his head. "She acts like she despises him, but I don't know. I don't know anything anymore."

My friend stood up and crossed over to his son's companion. Resting a hand on his shoulder, he spoke quietly. "Hold out for a little longer. This is better than waiting to be shot."

Those words, so simple and so true, seemed to galvanize the man. His back visibly straightened, his gaze hardened. "Much better," he agreed.

At that moment there was a knock on the door. As it was the middle of the night and no one was supposed to know of our presence, we were all suddenly very much on our guard.

I pulled out my revolver, although I wasn't sure what I was going to do with it if it was, for example, the police looking for fugitives.

As I started to go to the door, Sherlock Holmes handed me his pipe. The gesture spoke volumes. No one but myself was in the room.

I pushed the door open a crack. It was an agitated young man. As soon as he saw me, he muttered something in Russian, glanced again at the door number, bowed apologetically, and moved on down the hallway.

Back in the room, Auguste spoke. "If that was someone knocking at the wrong door, we are very fortunate. If anyone saw us come up here and informed the police..."

Holmes nodded. "Auguste is right. We're in danger here."

Giraud spoke up. "I know where we can go."

We might have been in danger at the Astoria, but the next hour was truly terrifying. Using the back entrance, we made our escape from the hotel and followed Giraud as he led us through the black streets back toward the river.

Coming out of the shadows, we stopped across a square from one of the sides of the Winter Palace. The streets we had traversed had been packed and sanded, but even so, there was no escaping the severity of such a winter as Petrograd was experiencing. Snow and ice covered the sidewalks and boulevards—some of the back streets were impassable.

Now we faced the massive bulk of the Winter Palace, guarded and seemingly as impregnable as the prison across the way. I couldn't stop myself from asking. "Now that we're here, how do we get inside?"

Giraud shrugged. "By the roof," he said, and started across the square. There was nothing to do but follow him, though as we came closer, the task loomed more and more formidable—the forbidding walls seemed to rise as high as the sky itself as we entered the building's shadow.

But Giraud was undaunted. He turned to Auguste and

whispered, "The view from the prison wasn't completely wasted." So saying, and keeping to the edge of the square, he brought us up to where the river crossed behind the Palace. There, a mountain of ice led nearly to the gables of the roof.

"They piled the barricades here," Giraud explained. "I watched from the prison as the snow drifted and accumulated. I think we ought to be able to climb it."

It was not easy, especially the harrowing last push out over the lip of the roof. The wind had picked up and howled with a particular vengeance, throwing grains of old snow and ice into our faces as we clawed our way to safety, if it could be called such when any slip meant a fall to the courtyard below, and certain death.

The night seemed to go on forever. By my watch, it was closing on four o'clock, but the sky hadn't changed since I'd originally left the Astoria just after dinner, my heart in my throat, to see if Holmes could pull off the escape from prison.

Now that we were on the roof, a new uncertainty confronted us. Now, away from the shelter of the building, the wind chilled us even through our greatcoats, and over the vast expanse that covered the Winter Palace, in the dim moonlight we saw only a meadow of snow, seemingly unbroken until at the roof's edge it fell to nothingness.

We had to move—more, we had to get inside—or we would freeze, but there was no indication of where to go. Giraud, holding on to both Holmes and Auguste, ventured to rise and try to recognize something, and it was almost his last action as the crust of ice broke under him, dropping an avalanche into the courtyard and nearly taking him with it.

I give him credit for bravery. Barely hesitating, he pressed on, motioning that we follow him. Slowly, often crawling, our small party inched its way over and through the snow on the roof which in some places had drifted to over a meter in depth.

For what seemed an hour—though it must have been

a quarter of that time—we pushed on. Then, suddenly, Giraud pointed to an impression in the snow ahead, and a moment later we all were standing in a cleared area, like a bunker, in the middle of the drifts.

"I knew it," Giraud gasped, out of breath. "I knew Alexis would clear this spot on the first clear day."

He went to the door and began knocking, pounding loudly. We were still at great risk, I felt, and I wasn't alone. Next to me, Holmes had drawn the pistol he'd taken from the prison guard. It was well for Giraud to believe in the young prince, but even if he was an ally, anyone else might come to the door in response to Giraud's racket. If that were the case, it would be wise to be prepared.

As the latch on the door sounded, Holmes and I squatted down under the line of the roof. Auguste stationed himself behind the door, to slam it back shut if the need arose. A crack of light appeared from within and I cocked my revolver.

A young boy's face appeared in the light.

"Alyosha!"

The face broke into a smile. "Monsieur Giraud, *comment allez vous?*"

"Alive, and living. And you?"

It seemed a strange moment for games, but no one else said a word. The boy became aware of the rest of us, and his eyes widened. "The other escapees?"

Giraud nodded. "So you've heard already. May I present Doctor Watson, Auguste Lupa, and Sherlock Holmes. The Czarevitch Alexis Nicholaevitch Romanov."

The boy pushed open the door. "Won't you come in?" he said. "You must be freezing."

Sitting by the samovar drinking cups of hot tea, it still took us nearly an hour to warm up once we'd come inside. Alexis ushered us into a small sitting suite, decorated with pictures of naval ships and aeroplanes. The furniture was of a kind often seen in guesthouses in England—the chair Holmes immediately picked was, in fact, a duplicate of the old one he used to favor at Baker Street.

In other circumstances, it would have been amusing to see Holmes, pipe in mouth, lounging in front of a small coal fire in his familiar chair. As a younger boy, his son, about whom I've never written because Holmes had forbidden it, often would sit at his father's knee, soaking up the techniques and method for which my friend is so justly famous, and in several instances outdoing the Master.

(Would that Sherlock Holmes would lift that stricture! Some of the cases in which Auguste assisted his father, such as the Adventure of the Tiger's Paw, or the curious affair of the glass blower's apprentice, were textbook studies of the art of deduction.*)

But here there was no discussion of the niceties of detective theory. Auguste, Giraud and Holmes were wrestling with a cunning murderer who had almost done them all in.

Reluctantly, Giraud had finally acknowledged some doubt as to the innocence of Elena Ripley though I sensed that it was only his respect for Auguste's powers that had taken him that far. Before he would truly be convinced, he would need, as indeed we all would, a motive.

The Czarevitch had been a silent witness to the continuing discussion about Elena Ripley. Slight, with an extremely sensitive face, he sat upright on the couch across from me, listening intently. He wore a purple robe with the royal lions crest above the breast pocket, beneath which peeked the legs of a pair of flannel pajamas. There was a brace of some

---

* Editor's note: Watson's manuscript—obviously not intended for publication—was included in the file among a group of papers and personal effects of Alexis Romanov. It is assumed that, in the crush of events that followed, Watson never had the chance to retrieve these notes from the apartment of the Czarevitch. When the boy was arrested and his rooms searched, the Bolsheviks who were creating File No. JG 0665 presumably included any relevant papers in it.

kind on his left foot, but it didn't appear to hamper him. For one so young, he already projected a regal bearing.

Auguste had just finished outlining the facts to his father when Alexis interrupted. "Excuse me, I gather you are talking about my sister's governess?"

Giraud, sitting next to the boy, turned to him. "Yes. Elena."

"She was here, you know, earlier this evening."

Holmes and Auguste shared a glance. "Miss Ripley was in these apartments tonight?"

Alexis nodded. "She brought me the news about your escape."

"Is she all right?" Giraud asked.

But Auguste was more forceful. "How did she hear about our escape?"

The boy straightened up at the interrogation. He would not be rushed, though I could see it wasn't a matter of protracting the theatre. He wore the mantle of future Czar, and wasn't about to be manipulated.

"Monsieur Giraud, she looked as though she'd been beaten up. There was a swelling in her jaw, an abrasion on her cheek, and one eye was beginning to blacken. She said she'd fallen while running here to warn us. She was very upset."

Holmes put in, "Upset as though she was worried about our safety?"

He thought a moment. "No, I would not say that. Perhaps worried about her own. She said you, Monsieur Giraud, might try to come and kidnap me, that you were extremely dangerous and I should be on my guard."

"Elena told you I was dangerous?"

Alexis nodded, and Giraud hung his head.

"Did she think you'd already seen us?" Auguste asked.

"I don't think so, but it's possible. Everyone knew I'd been trying to block your execution. I don't believe you are traitors."

"I assure you we are not," Auguste said, "and we are very

grateful. But how did she find out about the escape so soon? Was there a general alarm?"

The boy leaned forward. "Oh, there's no mystery there. Rasputin had his contacts keeping him aware of your situations. When Rasputin was informed, she was with him."

Giraud nearly leapt from the couch. "Rasputin?"

But Auguste interrupted. "Why was Rasputin informed? What's his interest in all of this?"

The Czarevitch shook his head. "I don't know."

"But why was Elena with Rasputin? She hates Rasputin." Giraud was in shock.

"Oh no, Monsieur Giraud. In fact, she has moved to his building." The corners of his mouth turned down with displeasure. "The women seem to have a weakness for him. My own mother has . . ." But he let that hang.

"Elena Ripley is living with Rasputin?" Auguste asked. "There is no doubt?"

"I have said it."

Sherlock Holmes took his pipe from his mouth. He'd been quietly taking in this entire exchange. "Your Highness," he said, "why was Rasputin informed about our escape? Do you have any idea?"

"No, sir, I'm sorry."

For a moment, all was silence. Then Giraud, almost in a whisper, asked. "Did Elena get her job as governess through Rasputin?"

Alexis Romanov nodded. "All of the tutors were recommended to my mother by him. Including you, if you remember. And M. Giraud?"

"Yes?"

"Do you remember asking me to intercede with Tatiana on behalf of Miss Ripley?"

Giraud nodded.

"Well, I never got the chance to tell you before you were arrested, but I talked to Tati about it and she said you must have been mistaken. She doesn't remember any fight with Miss Ripley."

"They've never had a fight?"

"No. At least not according to Tati."

"Jules ... ?" Auguste began.

"You're right, Auguste. You've been right all along, and I've been a fool."

But Holmes was like a dog on a scent and couldn't be bothered with irrelevancies. "Never mind that," he said, "Let's review what we have. For some reason, Rasputin seems to be deeply involved in all of this. He obviously had a great stake in seeing your executions carried out, and one of his lackeys informed him immediately when we escaped. He flew into a rage, perhaps beating Miss Ripley because she was nearest to hand, then sent her to see if she could locate us."

"That's how I see it," Auguste said.

"Further," Holmes continued, "I think we can assume that Rasputin directed Miss Ripley in the murders."

Again Auguste nodded in agreement.

"Isn't that rather a substantial jump, Holmes?" I ventured.

"Our problem all along with Elena has been motive," Auguste replied. "Now that it's established that she is involved with Rasputin, it's at the very least worth exploring the possibility that she's acting under his direction."

Giraud couldn't see it, either. "But why would Rasputin want to weaken the Czar? And that was the effect of the murders. Surely he has everything he could want. Sukhomlinov and Paleologue both think he's the most powerful man in Russia, and it all rests on his proximity to the crown. It makes no sense."

"Unless," Auguste said, "the Czar's reaction to the killings was incidental."

"What do you mean?"

Auguste stood up, pacing in the small room. "I mean, Jules, that early in our investigation we were forced to consider the possibility that the murders were not politically motivated at all, that there was a personal motive behind them. At the time, we thought it was jealousy."

"Yes?"

Sherlock Holmes leaned forward, his eyes sparkling under their hooded lids. "Revenge."

"Exactly," Auguste said. "Assuming he's not a madman—and I'm convinced he is not—why did he visit me in prison? Is there any other possible meaning to the word *'rache'?*"

"And why did he use that word?" Holmes asked.

"Yes," Auguste agreed. "As you said, it's very singular."

"It is more than that," Holmes retorted. "I can think of few single words in any language that are so closely linked to my own career."

"Your career?" Giraud asked. "I don't understand."

I spoke up. "In the very first of Holmes' adventures that I had published,* that word—*'rache,'* scrawled in blood on the wall at the site of a murder—was one of the principal clues Holmes discovered. That word itself was on the frontispiece of the first edition of the published book.

"Gregson and Lestrade thought the victim had started to write the name Rachel, but Holmes reasoned correctly that..."

"Thank you, Watson," Holmes said. "I think we see the connection. The point is that the word is closely affiliated with me."

"And almost more importantly," Auguste added, "only with you. Alone, it has little significance."

"But that's impossible!" Giraud exclaimed. "Rasputin doesn't know you."

Holmes lifted his brows, his eyes flashing black in their deep sockets. Something had excited him. But to Giraud, after that brief flash, he only smiled mildly. "Still, it is an interesting avenue for conjecture."

He leaned over and struck a match against his heel, bringing the flame up to his pipe. "It is worth considering that though I don't know Rasputin, he may know me."

* A Study in Scarlet

"There's another thing," Giraud said, finally warming to the idea. "Why has Rasputin been working so hard to see our sentences carried out? And why was he so enraged at our escape? You never met the man, did you, Auguste?"

"Only the night Alexandra let me borrow the egg."

Giraud scratched his chin pensively. "And later that night, I swear he was at his apartment celebrating something."

Auguste stopped pacing and sat down again, his lips pursing in thought. Giraud leaned back on the couch, looking to Alexis as though the boy might provide some answer.

Sherlock Holmes refired his pipe and sucked on it reflectively. "Let us assume," he began, "that revenge may have been the motive for the killings."

"But revenge for what?" Giraud asked.

Holmes waved away the objection. "Let's ignore that for now. We must use the clues we've been given, even if they don't mean anything yet. Rasputin used the word '*rache.*' That has to mean something." Holmes looked at his son. "When were you called here?"

"After the third murder."

"And who...?"

"Yes," Auguste said, "I see what you're getting at. Alexandra requested that I come..."

"And the idea may have been Rasputin's." I finished the thought.

"Capital, Watson! Capital!" Holmes exclaimed.

"But wait." Giraud, showing his fatigue, put up his hand. "All this is fine theorizing, but isn't it rather far-fetched? What you're saying is that, for some unknown reason, Rasputin began murdering the Czar's friends so that there would be a situation where he could convince Alexandra to summon Auguste. And once he was here he would be lured into a trap."

Holmes fixed Giraud with a cold stare. "The trap was very nearly sprung."

And at that truth, we were all silent.

Never before in my long experience with Sherlock Holmes had I seen such a test of his primary deductive theorem: When all possibilities have been exhausted, then whatever remains, however improbable, must be the truth. Here we were breathing in the rarefied ether of pure deduction, and father and son were in their element. It was as though Holmes read my thoughts. "Should this bear out, Watson, you might have to take me out of retirement another time. There is much that is instructive in this for the true student of deduction."

"I think first we should make sure we get out of this alive," Auguste responded. "And I think I know how to begin proving our theory..." He looked to the czarevitch, "if you will continue to help us, your Highness."

The boy looked at Giraud briefly, as though asking for permission. Then, his face aglow with anticipation, yet with the most solemn expression, he addressed Auguste. "I will do anything to help my country."

Auguste nodded. "Thank you. You are a brave young man." The son of Sherlock Holmes leaned back in his chair for a moment, closed his eyes, and pursed his lips in that distinctive way of his. "All right," he said, "then here is my plan."

After another hour, we retired to bed. Holmes and I stayed where we were off the boy's bedroom, while Giraud and Auguste made do on makeshift bedding in the prince's chamber. Holmes was gracious enough to insist that I take the settee, where I could stretch out somewhat, while he remained slouched in his chair, his pipe barely glowing, no doubt rethinking his son's plans.

Outside, the wind shrieked from time to time. Snow from a new storm flung itself against the window. I knew that it was morning, but there was no trace of the sun, or of any light. In fact, the darkness was so complete that I felt I had never before been so surrounded by night. My eyes burning, my mind weary, I turned my back on my friend and to the room.

But for some reason sleep wouldn't come. Wonder over the day's events, and excitement and apprehension over those to come, conspired to keep me from the arms of Morpheus.

Suddenly I heard the slight creak of the door to Alexis' room, followed immediately by Auguste's whispered voice. "Father?"

There was a pause, then the door creaked again. Perhaps Holmes had fallen to sleep and hadn't heard him. But then, finally, he spoke. "Yes, I'm here."

Auguste must have entered. "May I bother you?"

"It's no bother. I'm awake, come in." In spite of the blizzard, within the room, all at once it was quiet as death. I could hear Holmes suck on his pipe. "Is the plan . . . ?"

But his son stopped him. "I haven't come to discuss the plan." Another pause, and I heard a chair being pulled over the floor. "I came to ask you why you're here."

Holmes let out a heavy breath. "You're my son."

"I've always been your son. What makes this different?"

"What do you mean, different?"

"You are here, with me. That hasn't always been the case."

"You needed me. They might have killed you."

"I have needed you before."

Feeling like an intruder, I wanted to announce that I wasn't sleeping, that I was hearing it all, but I couldn't make myself move. As their silence continued, I lay with my eyes open, staring at the back of the couch. A match flared as Holmes restoked his pipe, stalling for time. It was a moment fraught with personal danger for both of them—two towering titans of reason struggling within the snares of emotion. The coal fire settled with a hushing sound in the grate, and still no one spoke. One of them sighed. One of the chairs creaked.

Finally, Sherlock Holmes whispered in a strained voice.

"When I saw you, when you were a boy, it was too hard. It reminded me too much of your mother. I became immobilized. I couldn't afford that too often."

"And so you abandoned me?"

"I didn't abandon you. I saw you as often as I could bear it. We had a few summers."

"Yes, we had that." There was a flat harshness to Auguste's voice. "We did have a few summers." Then his voice softened. "Did you hate my mother so much? Was she that bad?"

I heard the hollow suck of the pipe. Then, at last, "No. No, I didn't hate her so much. I'm afraid I loved her so much."

I don't know whether the idea had never occurred to Auguste, or whether he'd chosen to create his own rationale for his father's distance. As his best friend, I had some inkling of the pain Holmes had endured through losing the only woman he'd ever loved. Of course, he never dwelt upon it, never even referred to it except obliquely, but it was his constant companion after '94, and I knew for a fact it haunted him still.

Quite a long time passed. Neither of them said a word. I fancied I could almost hear the workings of Auguste's brain trying to assimilate this new knowledge, to somehow fit it into his understanding of what had made both he and his father the persons they had become.

Finally, the chair moved and Auguste rose. "Thank you for telling me that," he said. "I'm sorry to have bothered you."

After the door closed and his footsteps had receded, Holmes' match flared again. The wind battered the window. Eventually exhaustion overcame me and I slept.

21

15/12/17
Winter Palace

The Grand Duchess Anastasia
Tsarkoye Selo

Dear Aunt Annie:

I don't know who else I can turn to. My mother seems more and more under the power of Rasputin and my father has gone off to Spala. You and Uncle Nicky have always told me that I could come to you if I needed help, and that time has come.

All that I request here must remain strictly between us. The gravest issues of state—in fact, the very future of the Russia we know and love—may be at stake, and I must count on your most complete discretion.

I know that Uncle Nicky has always been the most popular general in the army. Even my father holds him in awe, and though other less loyal subjects have misinterpreted their relationship, I know that the bond between them remains strong and that both you and he remain loyal to the Czar.

I am in a position where I have to act, and I need to call on the loyalty and love that both you and Uncle Nicky have for the crown. Forgive me if I sound melodramatic and overly vague, but there have been developments over which I've had no control that justify what I'm doing.

Briefly, my request is that you use your and your husband's influence (but under no circumstances my name) to request several generals and citizens who remain here in St. Petersburg to gather tomorrow morning, the 16th, at 9:00 A.M. at the French Embassy. If it is within your power, please also try to assemble some of the ranking elite of the Duma, and others whom you think, collectively, might be able to effectively testify before my mother on a most urgent matter of state.

I recognize that your actions, if viewed in the wrong light, might be construed as a conspiracy—even one that I have arranged—but I must ask you to trust me. I assure you that I am acting in good faith, that I will personally guarantee your safety and that of those you invite, and that someone else whom you trust is another party to all of this.

Please, Aunty, I implore you. My father's reign is at stake! You must act quickly and decisively!

You may send the messenger back to me with your response if you feel you must decline. Otherwise, if I don't hear from you, I will assume you are in my camp.

Praying that God will smile upon your endeavors in this cause, I remain your loyal friend,

Alexis Nicholaevitch

[KREMLIN FILE NO. JG 0665–4059; PSS ACCESS, OPEN]

The Winter Palace
St. Petersburg
16/12/17

Elena Ripley
20, 63–64 Gorokhavaya Street
St. Petersburg

Dear Miss Ripley:

Just a short note to thank you for your warning last night. I remain unmolested and so far today there is no sign of the fugitives. I have taken the precaution, however, of keeping my room off limits to all staff, and I've even instructed Derevenko to stand guard at the entrance to my wing when I am within. Thus, I feel certain that I am safe from kidnapping, and I extend to you my gratitude for your loyalty and concern.

I wonder if I might ask you to call on me tomorrow morning before you report to my sisters for their tutoring. There is a matter of some urgency that I would like to discuss with you, and I've instructed Derevenko to admit you.

Please give my best to our Friend. I know we have had disagreements recently, but my mother has asked me to forgive and forget, and I have decided to obey her. When this immediate danger has passed and the fugitives are caught, I will once again join the family and our Friend for evening prayers.

Hoping to see you tomorrow, I am

Alexis Romanov

[KREMLIN FILE NO. JG 0665–4071; PSS ACCESS, OPEN]

Dear Maurice:

Please accept the authenticity of Alexis Romanov's letterhead as evidence that we are safe and working for the Allied cause. For obvious reasons, I will not sign this note.

Tomorrow morning I must ask you to be prepared for some very unorthodox events. Several generals, Grand Dukes, members of the Duma, and other citizens are being summoned by Grand Duchess Anastasia to your Embassy. Shortly after their arrival, we will join you with a kidnap victim.

You will be harboring three fugitives and will be an accessory to the kidnapping. If you wish to absent yourself, I would not blame you, but I think you should be in attendance. In the best of circumstances, there will be a role for you to play, although we cannot predict the exact course events will follow.

I must stress that the entire War could hinge upon our success tomorrow. The hopes of all of France ride on your shoulders.

22

[KREMLIN FILE NO. JG 0665–4075–4087; PSS ACCESS, CLASSIFIED]

Maurice has requested a formal report, and I am only too glad to supply it. After the past days' events, I am grateful for an afternoon in a warm room, a snifter of cognac by my side, a ream of foolscap and a quill with a sharp nib. Most of all, I am grateful to be alive.

Lupa and I stood behind the door in Alexis' bedroom as Elena was shown into the suite in which we'd passed the previous night. When I saw her through the crack in the door, and in spite of all we'd surmised about her since our escape, I nearly couldn't go through with it. Her face, even with the abrasions she'd suffered (at Rasputin's hand?) was more beautiful than ever, her body fuller, somehow more womanly than I had recalled.

My heart went out to her. Could she be a murderer? It was unthinkable! I don't know what strength—or weakness —kept me in my hiding place behind the door.

She greeted Alexis, and when he introduced her to Holmes, she backed up a step.

"Sherlock Holmes?" she repeated.

Holmes nodded. "You know me, Madam?"

"Of course I know of you. I'm British, after all." She turned, smiling. "And you must be Dr. Watson."

482

Watson stuttered out a hello. His reaction to Elena was similar to the one I'd had.

Alexis played his part wonderfully. Holmes was here, he explained, as an emissary of King George, with a mission very much like my own, related to the Eastern Front.

Holmes had arrived (Alexis said) only two days before, and had just missed seeing the Czar before he'd gone to Spala for a week. It made little sense to follow Nicholas there since he was only staying at headquarters for a few days before returning, so Holmes had chosen to pass his time reviewing the Lupa affair and the Palace murders.

Holmes smiled thinly. "After all, crime is a bit of a hobby of mine."

As Elena had figured so prominently in the investigation, he had prevailed on Alexis to be introduced to her so that he could get her impressions.

She shook her head. "It's so sad," she said. "All those people killed. And now, since the escape, I've been scared to death myself."

"Oh?" Holmes said. "I'd understood that you were on friendly terms with the Frenchman. Surely he's no danger to you."

"I don't know, Mr. Holmes. I think that's been somewhat overplayed. We spoke occasionally, that's all."

That wound cut deep. It was the first time I had caught her in a lie, and, if anything, Lupa had underestimated her skill as an actress.

Watson looked at his watch. "It's time, Holmes," he said.

Elena looked at them questioningly.

"Would you mind accompanying us?" he asked in his blandest tone. "We have an appointment with the French ambassador on this very topic. We can talk on the way over."

Watson kept his hand in his greatcoat pocket, ready to persuade her with a gun if necessary, but Elena accepted Holmes' explanation, and the three of them left Alexis' chambers, talking casually of London's wartime theater.

There was no danger in Holmes' appearance on the streets

of St. Petersburg since as the radical Sigerson he'd been an unwashed, stubble-cheeked musician. Lupa and I, however, would be recognizable to any number of people, and to be caught would mean death. I don't think either of us forgot for a moment that only the day before we were to be shot at dawn. That knowledge leant a great deal of piquancy to our actions.

Alexis was puffed up with pride when he came back to his bedroom. "How did I do?" he asked.

"Satisfactory," Lupa said.

At the slight frown, I added, "That's the highest praise he can give. I thought you were wonderful."

"Yes," Lupa concurred, a trace of a smile showing, "very satisfactory. But now we have to go."

On some pretense or another, Alexis had obtained uniforms of the Russian navy from Derevenko, and Lupa and I had them on over our suits. Lupa's weight loss would make him hard to identify, but I felt safer with an eye patch and bandage on my jaw. Lupa limped, leaning heavily on a cane. Alexis saw that the hallway was clear, and then joined us as we walked through it to the gate.

After that, we were on our own. In the event, we sensed the stares of passing townspeople on the streets, but in the new snowstorm, no one stopped us, and we pulled it off.

At the embassy, I revealed myself to the guard and a moment later I was shaking Paleologue's hand.

"Thank you for staying," I said. "Are the rest . . . ?"

He nodded, motioning for us to follow him quietly, maneuvering us into a back room. When the door closed behind us, he took the cigar from his mouth and sighed heavily. "I hope you are right," he said.

We changed from our disguises while he brought us up to date. "They are all in the salon—Grand Duchess Anastasia, Kerensky from the Duma, Prince Lvov, Felix Yussoupov, Grand Duke Dmitry Pavlovitch, Dr. Lazovert, Colonel Sukhotin, half a dozen others, to say nothing of Holmes, Watson, and Mademoiselle Ripley who, need I mention, is enraged."

"But she stayed?" I asked.

"Of course. She's maintaining that she's innocent."

"And my father is . . ."

"He began by reviewing your trial testimony for the assembly. They are all rather skeptical," he added. "What do all those people have in common?"

"Love of Mother Russia," Lupa said. "It should be enough."

"Let us hope so. If you're wrong . . ."

He didn't have to finish. We knew the consequences if we were wrong.

Holmes was conducting the actual interrogation, while Lupa, Paleologue and I sat on stiff chairs just behind the door to the salon, listening to it all. Lupa had spent the previous day coaching him while Dr. Watson had written some notes and I had been on hand to supply any missing information. I needn't have bothered. As Lupa went over the events that had transpired since our arrival in St. Petersburg, I was amazed anew at the power of his mind.

The breadth and clarity of the briefing he gave his father made my reports to him seem, in retrospect, muddled, disjointed, inexact, even confusing. He seemed to have forgotten absolutely nothing of any importance that had to do, however remotely, with his case.

Listening to him, the suspects and victims once again came alive in my mind—the General and Katrina Sukhomlinov, Boris Minsky, Kapov, Borstoi, Pohl. As he unwound the story, his argument that Rasputin was somehow behind it all became more and more compelling, until we were all convinced that Rasputin was the man who had, albeit indirectly, summoned Lupa to St. Petersburg.

But if Lupa's powers were impressive, those of Sherlock Holmes were no less so. Paleologue, Lupa and I sat at our stations behind the door marveling at the great detective's recitation of the facts.

At first, Elena held her own, her anger giving way to calm

denials. After all, she thought there was no new evidence, and she'd brazened her way through it all before.

But the cracks did begin to show.

"I understand," Holmes asked, "that your relationship with M. Giraud began when you had a fight with the Grand Duchess Tatiana?"

"No," Elena replied, "I've never had a fight with Her Highness."

"Never?" There was a pause, which Holmes pressed. "Wasn't there something about Tatiana's Cockney accent in a play by Shaw? Would I make up such a detail?"

"You've seen Jules," she said accusingly. "You know where he is." Evidently she addressed herself to the assembly. "This man is hiding condemned fugitives," she said.

"Perhaps, Miss Ripley, but that's not the point right now. The point is your alleged fight with Tatiana. If you never had it, as you say, and Monsieur Giraud never referred to it, how then do you assume I've spoken to Giraud because I know what the fight was about? It must have happened as I say."

"No!"

Holmes let the silence build.

"We may have had a slight disagreement that Jules misinterpreted, that's all."

"Ah, well if that's all," Holmes said sarcastically, "we can leave it."

The cracks widened.

"...and so your alibi for the night of Kapov's death is that you were where?"

"With Monsieur Giraud."

From behind the door, we heard the murmur of the guests. Though St. Petersburg society was nearly as decadent as that of Paris, lack of discretion could still be cause for scandal.

"With the same M. Giraud whom you barely knew to speak to?"

"No, you don't understand. He was..."

"At the trial, you said you were with him the entire night. Did you sleep with him?"

"No, of course not. He's old."

Stung though I was, I could still hear the irony dripping from Holmes' voice.

"Whereas Kapov was young."

"Ivan was . . ." and then she was quiet.

"Oh, you called him Ivan. And though Giraud was old, you stayed with him the whole night? Why were you there? What did you do there? Weren't you in his room until he passed out, drugged by you, at which time you went to Kapov's? Didn't you use Giraud for an alibi, and that's all."

"No, you're making all that up."

"Perhaps. But you were at the same party Kapov had attended at Rasputin's that night, were you not?"

"Yes, that's true, but earlier."

"Why had you gone there?"

"I needed help at the court. I was afraid . . ."

"You were afraid of what? Your falling out with Tatiana that you deny. You are falling back into the excuses you gave Giraud, Miss Ripley. You should keep your parts straight."

"You're trying to get me confused," she said. The pitch of her voice had gone up.

"It's not very confusing," Holmes said. "You went to Rasputin to tell him that Giraud and Lupa had decided Kapov was the Palace killer."

"No!"

"And Rasputin then determined that Kapov should die an apparent suicide."

"No! It's all lies."

One of the assembly spoke up. "It's not all lies. You were at Rasputin's late that night."

Holmes questioned the speaker. "And who are you, sir?"

In a cultured, rather fey voice, we heard the response. "I am Prince Felix Yussoupov."

"And you attended the party?"

"I did. And so did Miss Ripley. We spoke early on."

"I've admitted I was there," Elena said.

"But you denied that you came back later," Yussoupov insisted, "and you did. Much later, when only a few of us remained."

"Was Kapov still there?" Holmes asked.

"Yes, of course," the Prince replied. "This woman left with him."

There was a long pause, after which Holmes asked, "You're absolutely sure it was this woman? Why didn't you bring this up at the trial?"

"What trial? My good man, I don't get involved in trials. I am still not even sure what this is all about—Anastasia asked me to come and I'm here. But I am certain this woman went home with Ivan. Look at her—she is beautiful! I wanted to escort her home myself."

Next to me, Lupa nodded to Paleologue. *"C'est presque l'heure,"* he said. "It's almost time."

The Ambassador left us, going around to the front door to the salon.

"Thank you, your Highness. Of course there was no trial for Kapov's murder—it was declared a suicide. I apologize."

Holmes kept the pressure on. "And so, Miss Ripley, after Kapov was out of the way, when you heard about Pohl's new information the next morning, did you have time to go to Rasputin or . . . ?"

"Leave Gregory out of this," she said determinedly.

"I don't think I'll be able to," Holmes answered. "When did you fall under his power?"

"I'm not, as you put it, in his power. We love each other. I love him. I've always loved Gregory. I never pretended otherwise."

Evidently she had forgotten her audience. The Grand Duchess Anastasia spoke up from where she sat. "But dear, you know that's not true."

"It doesn't matter," Holmes said, "what's important is that when Giraud told you about Pohl . . ."

"Told me what? I never knew anything..."

But I, too, had my role to play, and Lupa nudged me onto the stage. "All right, Jules. Now."

I walked through the door into the salon. "I did, Elena. I told you about Pohl."

Her eyes widened in shock or fear. "Jules," she whispered, not sure whether to inject her voice with relief or dread. Psychologically, Lupa had predicted correctly. The roles were becoming mixed in her mind, and panic had begun to set in.

But she wasn't ready to give up yet. Her eyes darted from me to Holmes to the small crowd gathered in their chairs, while she evidently decided on her next line of defense, her next role. Then, like a witch out of Macbeth, she raised an arm at me and shrieked. "There's your man! He's the traitor! He's been condemned to death, for God's sake. Don't believe him. He's lying."

Lupa had orchestrated it well. Just at that moment, before I could respond or anyone else move, the door to the salon flew open and a shocked Maurice Paleologue burst in.

"I'm sorry to interrupt..."

"Yes, what is it?" Holmes was abrupt.

The Ambassador struggled to regain his breath. "It's Rasputin," he gasped, paused, let the silence gather for another long second. "The starets has been killed. Shot by anarchists in the street."

Chaos erupted among the guests. Everyone was immediately on their feet. "Killed?" "Rasputin dead?" "It can't be true." But Paleologue swore that it was.

If Rasputin were dead, it would affect the fortunes of everyone in the room. Of course, Rasputin was not dead. This was Lupa's last daring gamble, but none of the assembly knew it.

I never took my eyes from Elena. At Paleologue's announcement, her face went white, but as the questions flew in the room, her color returned, her panic increasing as though she were caged.

"No," she said in a numb whisper, "no, no, no." And then, as the fact sank in, her composure began to fall away—it was frightening, like wax melting in the heat. The beautiful face took on the look of a madwoman—deranged, lost, insane.

Suddenly, she bolted from her chair and Holmes shouted. "Watson, stop her!"

"No!" She screamed again and again as Watson's arms closed around her. Her fists pounded at his face and shoulders as Paleologue, too, went to help try and restrain her—and even the two of them could barely hold her as she kicked and flailed, screaming, crying and swearing violently in Russian and English. "Let me go! Let me go to him, you bastards!"

And then Lupa made his entrance, coming halfway across the room to where she struggled. "Yes, let her go," he said.

She turned and all the passion in her nature became fused into a blinding hatred for Lupa. "No!" she screamed, again, in fury. "No! You can't still be alive!"

She turned back to Watson then as if to run from the sight of Lupa. The doctor stood blocking her way, and suddenly the life seemed to go out of her. Her shoulders slumped, she began to swoon. Watson stepped forward and she leaned into him, putting her arms around him for support.

It was done so perfectly no one could have foreseen or prevented it. At one moment, she had nearly collapsed, depending on Watson to hold her up, her arms around his waist, and at the next, she had wrenched the revolver from his belt, no doubt having felt it there during their struggle a minute before.

In a trice, she had turned, cocked the gun, and was drawing a bead on Lupa, not two meters away.

I was still across the room, behind Lupa, and had no chance to stop her, but Watson, his reflexes perhaps sharper than his wits, but no less welcome for that, leapt from behind, knocking Elena's arm as the first shot broke one of the windows behind us.

The Ambassador, too, jumped forward and knocked the

hysterical woman to the floor as she tried to squeeze off another round. Watson, on his knees, now scrambled for control of the weapon. All three grabbed for it, rolling together as Lupa, Holmes and myself stood helplessly awaiting the outcome.

There was another shot, muffled, and then all struggling stopped.

"My God! Watson!" Holmes exclaimed.

The doctor rolled onto his side. Paleologue sat up. Elena lay face down, motionless, the gun under her.

Lupa went down to one knee, gently turning the woman over. A huge red stain was spreading under her left breast. Watson took off his coat and put it under her head as the rest of the people in the room gathered in a knot around her. Her eyes, those beautiful eyes, opened and, surprisingly, she smiled.

"Now I will be with him," she said.

Lupa leaned over her. "You did kill them all, didn't you?"

She nodded weakly, the small smile still playing at the corners of her mouth. "Of course. Just as you said."

"And it had nothing to do with the war or with Nicholas."

Her breathing came wet and heavy, but the confession seemed to please her in some way. "Gregory wanted you here so he could disgrace you," she stopped, taking a painful breath, "so he could kill you."

Lupa shook his head in disbelief, as though this were the stuff of all of his nightmares. "But why? Why did he want to kill me?"

Her voice had become all but inaudible. "Because the son of Sherlock Holmes had to die."

"I don't understand," Lupa said, "I don't see..."

She sighed wearily, looking now not at Lupa, but at his father, Sherlock Holmes, who hovered over them both. "To make you suffer as he has suffered." She forced another breath. "As you made him suffer," she said to Holmes.

"How did I make him suffer?" Holmes asked. "I never met the man."

She shook her head, coughing, and for a moment I believed she had gone and we would never know. But then she opened her eyes again, slowly bringing them back into focus. "He never had a father," she said. "You killed him at Reichenbach Falls." She sighed one last time. "His father was Professor Moriarty."

She closed her beautiful eyes. Dr. Watson felt her neck for a pulse, then took his jacket from beneath her head and unfolded it carefully over her face.

In the light of subsequent events, it is tempting to assign some measure of the blame (or credit) to Lupa, but on reflection, I don't think that would be fair.

It must be remembered that the group that had gathered at the Embassy was not without great influence. Kerensky and Purishkevich were leaders in the Duma, Prince Lvov controlled the moderate faction of the aristocracy, Prince Yussoupov at twenty-nine was heir to the largest fortune in Russia. Anastasia was the wife of the second most important man in the armed services.

It was a close thing, but Elena's confession swung the balance of sentiment in the room toward Lupa and myself. Rasputin might have been able to predict that his actions could eventually weaken Nicholas enough to bring down the government, but that had never been his main concern. He had wanted revenge for his father's death—that had been his driving force ever since the first murder had given him the idea. And Elena had been his agent.

But to most of the people in the room, Rasputin's motives were unimportant. What mattered was what he had done— abused his relationship with the Czarina. In doing so he had undermined not only the power of the Czar but his willingness to prosecute the war. Russian society, adrift without the leadership of its crown, was crumbling under the weight of icons, scandal and superstition.

Rasputin was hated or feared everywhere but in the mauve bedchamber. When it was revealed that he had also been behind the Palace murders, some men were moved to act. Did Lupa know they would? I don't believe it. Did his charade announcing the monk's assassination put the idea in someone else's mind? Again, not purposely.

Lupa's first action after revealing the deception about Rasputin's death to the group at the embassy was to send Yussoupov to fetch Dubniev—both to surrender ourselves to him, and to arrest Rasputin. He did not know, could not have foreseen, that Yussoupov would not obey him. In fact, we spent the rest of the day at the embassy, after Elena's body had been removed, awaiting the inspector's arrival, not without a great deal of trepidation.

(Paleologue promised diplomatic immunity for us all if Dubniev proved intractable, but the situation still made me uncomfortable. We were, after all, not accused of the murders, but of espionage. In truth, I counted more on Alexis to influence his mother than on Paleologue's assurances.)

Rasputin, it turned out, was never informed of Elena's death. He spent the afternoon drinking with gypsies, then had an early dinner with Anna Vyroubova, who had heard of some plot afoot and warned him not to go out. But when he got to his apartment, Yussoupov was there with some good Madeira and an invitation to a wonderful party.

I do not believe, and never will believe, that murder can be a legitimate alternative to law. But I must say in defense of the conspirators that they probably perceived that they had no recourse to law, since the law here in Russia is the crown, and the crown in this case would never have prosecuted Rasputin. By all accounts, Alexandra was so under the sway of Rasputin that she might well have concluded that everyone that had gathered in the embassy—Kerensky, Lvov, Anastasia, even Paleologue and all the rest—was involved in our conspiracy. Given that background, it may be understandable, though not excusable, that Yussoupov and his friends did what they did.

23

[KREMLIN FILE NO. JG 0665–5022–5033; PSS ACCESS, CLASSIFIED]

TO HER MAJESTY
ALEXANDRA FEDOROVNA
CZARINA

Report on the Death of
Gregory Efimovich Rasputin
December 16, 1916

The starets was met at his home sometime in the late evening of December 16 by Felix Yussoupov. The two left by Yussoupov's car and drove to the Moika Palace. Present at the Palace were the alleged conspirators—Yussoupov, the representative Purishkevich, Grand Duke Dmitry, Sukhotin, and Dr. Lazovert.

When Yussoupov and Rasputin arrived, the other conspirators began playing "Yankee Doodle" on a phonograph to simulate a party in the upper rooms. Rasputin evidently had been lured to the Palace because Yussoupov had promised to introduce him to his wife, Princess Irina. (The princess was then and is now in the Crimea, for health reasons, and does not appear to have played any part in the conspiracy.)

Leaving Rasputin with poisoned cakes downstairs, Yussoupov announced that he was going to get his wife. Upon his return, he found Rasputin happily consuming the cakes, each of which, according to Dr. Lazovert, contained enough poison to kill several men instantly.

In shock over Rasputin's apparent immunity to the poison, Yussoupov poured wine and watched Rasputin eat cakes for the better part of two hours, during which time he played gypsy songs on a guitar while waiting for the poison to take effect.

Finally, his wits shaken, he went upstairs and borrowed a Browning revolver from Grand Duke Dmitry. Returning to the cellar, he spoke for a few more minutes with Rasputin, then, urging him to pray for his soul, shot him in the back.

The others, hearing the shot, rushed downstairs, where Lazovert pronounced Rasputin dead. No sooner had he done so, however, when the monk rolled over, opened his eyes, and with a cry, foaming at the mouth, leapt upon his assailants.

He tore an epaulet from Yussoupov's jacket and nearly strangled him. Escaping, the Prince ran upstairs, while Rasputin raged behind him.

Somehow Purishkevich had by now come into possession of the revolver. He pursued Rasputin out into the courtyard, where the monk had run trying to get away. Purishkevich fired at least four times, hitting Rasputin twice—in the shoulder and the head.

The conspirators now gathered around the fallen starets. Still very much alive, he looked up at Yussoupov and said, "Felix, I will tell everything to the Empress," whereupon they fell upon him again with their boots, fists, and a rubber club of Yussoupov's.

They then wrapped the still body in a curtain bound with rope and Lazovert and Purishkevich took the bundle to the Neva, where they pushed it through a hole in the ice, while the other three conspirators killed a dog and left it to bleed on the snow where Rasputin had fallen, in case anyone should question the blood on the snow.

Rasputin's body was found yesterday. The autopsy revealed that, in spite of the poisoning (his body contained, as Lazovert said, enough cyanide to kill several men), the three bullet wounds, each potentially fatal, a concussion and several broken ribs, he had finally died by drowning.

After he was dropped into the freezing water, wrapped in his shroud and tied with rope, he managed to free one hand. Witnesses who knew the starets while he was alive and have viewed the body swear that the one raised hand is in the same attitude as that which he used to give benediction, and that therefore his last action before death, much as our Lord's, was offering a blessing and forgiveness to his killers.

December 21, 1916

24

[KREMLIN FILE NO. JG 0665–5095–5100; PSS ACCESS, OPEN]
JANUARY 2, 1917.

Sherlock Holmes looked up from his first bite of wood-cock. "Delicious, Auguste, absolutely delicious."

Lupa nodded solemnly, allowing only the slightest turn of his lips as he accepted his father's compliment. He could not so well control his eyes, however—they shone with plea-sure.

"Where did you get woodcock here in Petrograd?" Dr. Watson asked.

"Monsieur Muret has his connections," Lupa answered, nodding graciously at our host.

Muret took his cue. "Who would not have done so? It's a great honor to have an Auguste Lupa in one's restaurant." He paused, "And, of course, you other gentlemen."

In the background, a trio of gypsy guitarists played softly. Lupa had spent the afternoon in the Villa Rhode's kitchen preparing the excellent dinner we were enjoying. Holmes, Watson, Muret and I were sharing a couple of bottles of Cornas while Lupa chose to drink Muret's good dark beer.

It was our first evening out since we'd been pardoned, and the celebration was most welcome. After several days of Em-bassy cooking, we were doubly appreciative of Lupa's talent, and fell to the meal with a vengeance.

When we'd all but finished, Dr. Watson was the first to speak. "There's still one thing I don't quite understand."

Holmes, his own humor completely restored by the successful conclusion of the case, mopped up the last of his sauce and ate it on a bit of Lupa's fresh bread, leaned back into the booth's upholstery and patted his stomach happily. "And all's right with the world," he said.

"Really, Holmes, there's no need for sarcasm."

Holmes wore a mild look of surprise, which seemed feigned to me. "My dear fellow," he said, "I'm afraid that came out wrong. Please forgive me. What is it you don't understand?"

Muret refilled the good doctor's glass and he sipped, then continued in his blustery way. "All of Rasputin's motives are clear to me—the revenge and so forth—but I don't quite see how he convinced Miss Ripley to do his bidding. After all, she didn't need him. She had her own career. What could persuade her to do his terrible work? What could he give her to make it worth the risk?"

Lupa didn't give his father a chance to respond. "Love!" he blurted out, as though it were a curse word. "Love, the most powerful force in the world."

"Just so," Holmes agreed. "When the only goal is to please a lover, anything else, everything else, is secondary."

"Even murder?"

"Anything," Lupa said, "it doesn't matter what." He stopped to take a drink of his beer, "which is why the damned emotion ought to be avoided at all costs."

I had to speak up. My infatuation with Elena may have nearly killed us, and her love for Rasputin was surely turned to the wrong ends, but I wasn't willing to propose a loveless world as the solution. "To the contrary, Auguste. It may make us either fools or heroes, but surely it's worth it. A life without it is an empty life indeed."

I must have touched a nerve, for Lupa appeared about to say something, then bit it back. Sherlock Holmes, though, leapt into the breach. "Let's not forget that love can also lead

people to do the right thing." He looked directly at his son
and his hard eyes softened. "It is, after all, what brought
Watson and me here to Russia. In more ways than one, Auguste, it's why you're alive."

Lupa, obviously grappling with strong emotion, swallowed
hard, then looked down, finally reaching for his beer. For
me, the admission of love from father to son is the most
natural thing in the world, but clearly that hadn't been the
case between Holmes and Lupa.

A fanfare of strummed guitars accompanying an outbreak
of applause gave my friend a moment of respite. The lights
were turned down, and from the stage I heard the haunting
strains of Varya Panina as she began singing, almost whispering, a ballad to an insistent rhythm like that of a heart
beating. As I had been the other time I had seen her, I
was captivated by her artistry, her passion, even though I
couldn't understand the words.

While she sang, the restaurant was quietly rapt in its attention, and if ever I was grateful that the world was through
with the vulgarity and the evil of Gregory Rasputin, it was at
that moment. When the chanteuse finished, the room exploded again with applause. There were few dry eyes in the
house, and none at our table.

As the applause continued, Muret got up and went to the
stage. Seconds later, he escorted a smiling Varya Panina back
to our booth. Upon being introduced to Lupa and I, she
stopped. "But surely you two . . . that night the *tyemniy*—
Rasputin—was here . . ."

"That's right," Lupa said.

She smiled and her face, with such unattractive features,
became a thing of its own rare beauty. She reached out her
hand, first to me, then to Lupa. "I know now who you are."
She paused, "Thank you."

Lupa, most uncharacteristically, held to her hand. "Could
I ask you a question, madam?"

"Surely, anything."

"That last song—what was it about?"

She shrugged, then answered in her deep, rich voice. "The same as always—love. That is all my songs. Love. What else is there? That is life, eh?" Lupa nodded and let go of her hand, and she went back toward the stage.

He hung his head for a moment and I could see him pursing his lips in and out, out and in. Then, straightening up, he looked across the table at his father.

"I'm thinking of going to England from here. I was wondering if I might stay a while with you?" he asked. "If you're too busy, I'd understand, but..."

"No, not at all. Capital idea!" Watson exclaimed, bursting in before Holmes could respond. "Holmes, don't you agree?"

The great detective nodded. "Of course," he said. "I'd like that." He nodded again, and smiled. "I'd like that very much. Stay as long as you wish."

Lupa leaned back in the booth and looked from his father to Dr. Watson and back to his father again. The corners of his mouth turned up a centimeter in what was for him his broadest grin. Behind us, the guitarists began the introduction to another song. He lifted his half-full beer glass and raising it to his lips, drained it in one gulp. Putting the glass down gently, he wiped his lips with his napkin and sighed deeply.

"Satisfactory," he said. "Very satisfactory."

25

French Embassy
St. Petersburg
14 janvier, 1917

Tania Chessal-Giraud
Le Vendange
Valence, France

My dear Tania:

I pray you have received my telegram, and more, that it arrived before the letter I wrote you from jail. I am well, and free, and on my way home. Paleologue (our ambassador here) assures me delivery of this missive by diplomatic pouch, and even so I am having a clerk copy it and leaving the copy here so you will believe I have written you during this long absence.

It has been a grueling experience, but now as I prepare to leave, I am heartened by the success of the job I came here to do. Or by both of them—Lupa's and Foch's.

In Lupa's case, our young friend, with some help from me but mostly with the assistance of his father, the famous English detective Sherlock Holmes, solved the mystery of the Palace murders.

More importantly for me, the Czar has finally accepted the French offer—my offer!—of arms and money in exchange for a commitment to the Eastern Front at least through the summer.

This is the best possible news for France and for the Allied War effort, and I am very proud of my part in it.

I want to tell you everything but most of it will have to wait until I get home. You will guess, at least, that Lupa and I were completely pardoned before I would be allowed to see the Czar again. He is such a gentle and good man. He felt terrible about our imprisonment, and apologized profusely, but he really viewed the entire affair as outside of his control. It is a strange dichotomy in a man with absolute power.

His son, Alexis, is the hope of Russia's future, if it is to have one. I can say without any exaggeration that without him, none of our successes could have transpired. I even suspect he orchestrated our pardon, though he insists that his mother came to her decision on her own. Nevertheless, if all royalty through the ages could have combined his humor, grace, courage, intelligence, and force of will . . .

Well, I will never be a monarchist, but suffice it to say the world would have been spared many of its worst tragedies.

I'm afraid that it's becoming less certain every day that the boy will ever wear the crown his mother has worked so hard to preserve for him. My joy in coming home and my pride in my mission are both tempered by conditions here. They are bad. They were bad when I arrived in October, and they have only worsened.

L'Affaire Rasputin has driven another nail into the coffin of the Romanov reign. No one seems able to credit the fact that Alexandra, so intimate with Rasputin, didn't see him for what he was. It is generally believed that she knew about his atrocious behavior and tolerated it, although the truth may be that she really never saw it, or believed he did the things of which he was accused. In either event, the result is that respect for the crown is practically nonexistent.

Revolution is on everyone's lips and in everyone's mind. As a republican, this should delight me, but somehow one senses anarchy ahead, and violence—not a new and better order, but a chaotic upheaval resulting in who knows what. It is a frightening time, and I am glad to be getting out.

Sherlock Holmes and his colleague Dr. Watson left for England on the *Standart*, the Czar's personal flagship, two weeks ago, and Lupa accompanied them. They set off just in time. The port, choked with ice, closed for the Winter only four days ago.

After spending some time with his father in Sussex Downs in England, Lupa plans to go to New York City. As an American citizen, he says he will be supporting that country's growing War effort in some capacity, and when this tragedy concludes (let us pray with an Allied victory), he intends to strike out on his own as a consulting detective. I wish him luck, but told him in no uncertain terms that my own involvement in his affairs is at an end.

There was a rumor that Nicholas was going to decorate us for services to the crown, but nothing has come of that, probably because of Alexandra—she is still hurt and bitter over Rasputin, and I think the mere sight of Lupa or myself reminds her of her own gullibility. In compensation, however, the Czar was more than generous to us, presenting Lupa with a small velvet bag filled with a dozen or so diamonds. He also gave me something that I plan to give to you, so for the moment I will keep it to myself.

I would have preferred to have taken the *Standart* when it left, but there were many details of the agreement to be worked out between the Czar, Paleologue and myself, and I wanted to see it through. Tomorrow, though, I will board the train and travel south to the Crimea, then across the Black Sea to Istanbul, to Athens, around the boot to Marseilles, and finally to your side. It is a longer trip, but safer, and after what I have been through here, that more than compensates. With luck, I will be home to see the first buds on the vines.

Outside the room I am using for an office here at the Embassy, the snow continues to fall, as it has so steadily during this brutal winter. I look across the deserted street and wonder at the events that took place nearly a quarter of a century ago at a little-known waterfall in a corner of Switzerland.

Rasputin is dead and Lupa lives. Why, then, as I look out on the frozen city, do I feel that Rasputin has had his revenge after all? The events he set in motion by his hatred still curl in eddies of unrest through the current of Russian life.

Last night I dreamed I was with Alexis in the Winter Palace. A blizzard was raging, but somehow we knew that outside a fire was devouring the capital. As the smoke reached us, we made our way, choking, to Alexis' "secret place" on the roof. St. Petersburg lay in flames all around us, and over the din of panic and suffering coming up to us from below, we heard another noise, a half-human sound that turned my blood to ice.

"Monsieur Giraud," Alexis asked me. "Why is Grishka laughing? Can we make it stop?"

As the roof caved in, I woke up, but in the howl of the wind outside I could still hear Rasputin's triumphant cry. And I was left with Alexis' question—can we make it stop?

Forgive me. I let myself grow maudlin as the storm increased. I've taken a break and shared a cognac with Maurice Paleologue, and my attitude is better. Why be pessimistic when there is so much to be thankful for? The Czar is still in power, the Eastern Front is alive, Rasputin is no more, and I must believe that Alexis someday will rule a powerful, stable, modern Russia with a fair and even hand.

Perhaps after the War, we can come back and visit as his guests. He is a wonderful boy whom you would love.

For now, I must get back to packing, and post this letter. I cannot say how much I miss you and love you, and how I long to walk with you again on the soil of our beloved France.

Your husband,
Jules

EPILOGUE

Two months after Giraud left St. Petersburg, Nicholas abdicated the throne, and the Russian Revolution began. The Romanovs—Nicholas, Alexandra, Olga, Tatiana, Marie, Anastasia, and Alexis—were arrested. They remained confined at Tsarkoye Selo for a while, then were transferred to Siberia and other outposts while the rest of the civilized world ignored their plight and a series of Russian provisional governments struggled to bring order out of the chaos.

In October, 1917, the Bolsheviks came to power, forged a separate peace with Germany, and proclaimed the Union of Soviet Socialist Republics.

On July 16, 1918 (New Style), after fifteen months of captivity, Czar Nicholas Romanov and his entire family were executed by a Bolshevik death squad in the cellar of a country estate in Ekaterinburg, a small city on the Eastern slope of the Ural Mountains.

Even after the Czar's government fell, Giraud's mission continued to bear fruit. Heroic efforts by Russian troops on the Eastern Front, newly fortified with French ordnance but still ill–equipped, diverted enough German divisions to allow the Western Front to survive until fresh American troops arrived on the Continent and tipped the precarious balance of power finally to the Allies.